BUFFALO JUMP

BUFFALO JUMP

HOWARD SHRIER

VINTAGE CANADA

Vintage Canada and colophon are trademarks.

www.randomhouse.ca

Author's Note
This book is a work of fiction. The legality of Internet sales of Canadian
drugs to the United States was in a state of flux during the writing of this
book. For dramatic purposes, I have set the story at a time when such sales
are outlawed.

Library and Archives Canada Cataloguing in Publication

Shrier, Howard
    Buffalo jump / Howard Shrier.

ISBN 978-0-307-35606-2

    I. Title.
PS8637.H74B84 2008   C813'.6   C2008-900592-9

Cover Design: Jennifer Lum
Text Design: Jennifer Lum

Printed and bound in Canada

10 9 8 7 6 5 4 3 2 1

To my wife, the incomparable Harriet Wichin.

Falling out the window
Tripping on a wrinkle in the rug
Falling out of love, dear
It hurt much worse when you gave up

Just don't tell me which way I ought to run
Or what good I could do anyone
'Cause my heart, it was a gun
But it's unloaded now
So don't bother

Jeff Tweedy, "Gun"

"Save one life and you save the world."

The Talmud

CHAPTER 1

Toronto, Ontario: Monday, June 26

I woke well before my alarm was due to go off, my hair damp and my skin tacky with sweat that had already dried. Why did I bother setting one? A dream almost always woke me near dawn. This morning's was about Roni Galil again: Roni and me in a hot, dry place, waiting for something to come around the corner. Sensing it, hearing it, dreading it. Our weapons at port arms, straining to see through eyes stung by whipping dust and sand.

On this morning, for once, I woke before the dream climaxed. My lips were cracked and stuck to each other and my eyes dried out from having a fan pointed at them all night. I had a small air-conditioning unit sitting on the floor of my bedroom, its plug curled around it like a snake. I'd brought it with me after the breakup but it didn't fit the window in the new place and I didn't have money yet for a new one.

I got out of bed and opened the door that led to the concrete balcony and stepped out. Stretched my right arm until it ached—which didn't take long. I had an unobstructed 180-degree view of the west side of the city, from Lake Ontario at the south end to the forested ravines that line the Don Valley Parkway heading north. Not even July and we were three days into a lung-buckling heat wave, with a great humid mass hanging over the city like a tent. The sun was a weak lamp behind damp muslin, smog diffusing its pale light into a harsh glare.

The media had been warning the elderly and people with asthma to stay indoors. Being neither, I chanced a few breaths. The air smelled like it was wafting out of a grave.

My apartment was nothing special, the kind you see in any Toronto high-rise built in the sixties and seventies. The kind of place a guy lands in when he's been turfed, which I had been two months ago.

It had an L-shaped living room/dining room combo, galley kitchen, decent-sized bedroom, utilitarian bathroom. Parquet flooring throughout. But it was rent-controlled—very reasonable by Toronto standards—and in a great location: Broadview and Danforth, at the western boundary of Riverdale, just across the Don Valley from downtown.

The best thing about it, what sealed it for me the minute I walked in, was the view: floor-to-ceiling windows facing west, nothing between me and the city skyline. It was spectacular at night, when the gleaming towers of the financial district seemed to rise straight out of the darkness of the valley. Even in the morning, it could take your breath away—if the smog didn't take it first.

I went inside and put on a pot of dark roast, then spent twenty minutes rehabbing my right arm, using an old inner tube looped around a closet door knob. Stretching it back and forth to work the injured triceps. Taking it easy at first, then moving farther away to increase the tension. The muscles had been damaged when a bullet tore through them two months earlier. My surgeon said at the time I was lucky: the 9-millimetre slug had broken no bones, severed no blood vessels, damaged no nerves. His definition of luck, not mine.

My name is Jonah Geller and I'm a consultant with Beacon Security, a Toronto firm that offers everything from surveillance to missing person searches, pre-nups to employment checks.

Up until a few months ago, you could say I'd been something of a rising star there. More specifically, until the Ensign case. Or, as some of my less tactful colleagues took to calling it, the Tobacco Debacle.

The assignment had seemed simple enough—a routine undercover job as a security guard at the Ensign Tobacco Company of Belleville, Ontario, one of Canada's largest cigarette makers. Our plan called for me to insinuate myself into the graces of two bent security men planning to hijack a truckload of cigarettes with the help of mobsters practised in this deceptive art. Make sure I was behind the wheel of the truck when it was taken. Be there when the load was turned over to a nasty Calabrian crew boss named Marco Di Pietra. Stay out of the way when officers from the Ontario Provincial Police and the Task Force on Traditional Organized Crime swooped down and made the arrests. Smile and accept whatever accolades and promotions came my way.

But as we Jews have been saying for centuries, *Der mensch tracht un Gott lacht* . . . man plans and God laughs. Or as my grandmother would say when holding my grandfather in particularly sour regard: *Man proposes, and God disposes.*

Since the Tobacco Debacle, I had been firmly ensconced in the corporate doghouse. The official line was I was on desk duty until my arm fully healed. Hands up if you believe that one. The truth is I blew the case by making a mistake a raw beginner shouldn't have made. As a result, Di Pietra and his chief enforcer, a half-Italian, half-Irish hood named Dante Ryan, walked out of court after taking up less than ten minutes of the judge's time.

All because in a moment of weakness, I'd been torn between my relationship and the job, and in that moment the relationship won out.

At least that wouldn't be a problem again. Not only had the case derailed my career and left me with a gunshot wound, it also proved to be the last straw for my girlfriend—now ex-girlfriend—Camilla Lauder. The lovely Camilla seized the opportunity to dump me while I was still in my hospital bed, stoned (but not nearly enough) on Percocet.

And badly as things went for me, they went far worse for an OPP officer named Colin MacAdam. I doubt his doctor told him he was lucky.

I had a quick breakfast of cantaloupe, cereal and coffee. I felt troubled by the dream I'd had—fragments of it flashing in my mind, with no coherent narrative, just familiar sounds and images in an all-too-familiar place. Thudding hooves. The cries of angry men. The higher-pitched cries of children. Echoes of gunfire and boots on stone.

Christ. Why did I even try to remember? The dream never ended well. Especially not for Roni. Get a morning paper delivered, I told myself. That or read the back of the cereal box. Get out of that place in my head where dreams clung like the last webbed patches of morning fog.

By eight o'clock, I was dressed in light summer clothing—khakis, a white cotton shirt and sandals—and out the door, hoping to get into work early like a good dog. The elevator let me out in the parking garage where I kept my white Camry. According to *Car and Driver*, it's one of the most common cars on Canada's roads. Investigators in books and movies might drive hot red Ferraris, vintage Corvettes, metallic Porsches and other cars that in real life would get spotted three minutes into a tail. Good luck to them. Give me an unremarkable but reliable yawner any time.

I slipped the key in and turned it and was greeted by a grinding, coughing sound, like something you'd hear on an emphysema ward. I tried it again. Same result.

So much for reliable.

I had owned the car only six weeks. Until Camilla torpedoed me, we had co-owned a silver Accord. But she'd been making the payments on her credit card to collect travel points, so the car was hers until further disposition, as was the little semi we had bought on a quiet Riverdale street just south of where I lived now. Not only did the law favour her because of her gender—like Camilla needed any help—but my lawyer, supplied by my brother Daniel's firm, was more or less human. Hers was all wolverine. You couldn't fight him with motions; you needed a leghold trap and a 12-gauge.

I dug out my cell and called CAA. A recorded message said they were experiencing a high volume of calls, and wait time for service was averaging ninety minutes. It told me my call was important and cautioned me not to hang up as that would cost me my place in line. I hung up anyway and called Joe Avila, the guy who'd sold me the car.

Joe owned a body shop and used-car lot on Eastern Avenue. A year ago, his sixteen-year-old daughter ran away, fed up with her parents' strict Old World rules about dating, makeup, tattoos and jeans that exposed pubic hair and butt cracks. Joe came to Beacon, terrified that his sheltered Mariela would be chewed up and spat out by the world beyond Little Azores: beaten, raped, impregnated, infected or all of the above. I found her crashing in a squalid bachelor apartment on Parliament Street with three other girls. Parliament sounds dignified but tilts as low as any street in the east end. Mariela mustered some bravado and attitude in front of her friends, but over coffee she confided that the only thing scarier than her current situation was what her parents would do to her if she went back. I reassured her that all they wanted was for her to be safe. Eventually she relented and I drove her home. When I needed a car, I got the Camry from Joe at a "family price."

When Joe answered, I told him the family jewel wouldn't start.

"You try CAA?" he asked.

"Ninety minutes at least."

"Probably not the battery anyway," he said. "I put in a brand new reconditioned one when you bought it."

Brand new reconditioned. I would have told Joe it was an oxymoron but what if he misunderstood? The man can hoist a car without the benefit of hydraulics.

Joe told me he was stuck alone at the shop because his goddamn nephew still hadn't showed up. He wouldn't be able to get to my place any sooner than CAA. "Okay, Joe. I'll cab it downtown. Can you meet me here after work and have a look?"

He hesitated. "Oh, man, Jonah. So many cars overheat on days like this, I could work all night. I'd be passing up a big payday."

"How's Mariela doing? Still getting straight As in school?"

Joe sighed. "Okay, okay. I get the point. I'll be at your place around six."

By eight-thirty, I was standing on the west side of Broadview, trying to hail a southbound cab. There were plenty going my way but all had passengers. I spotted an empty northbound hack but he had nowhere to turn around and waved me off.

By eight-forty, my shirt was clinging to the small of my back and I was no closer to work. Showing up late could only dim the view Beacon held of me. I was beginning to weigh my carjacking options when a 504 streetcar rumbled into view. Its route went south along Riverdale Park before heading west over the valley toward downtown. It would take me within a block of the office.

The streetcar was packed. I dropped in my fare, then took a deep breath and tried to squeeze myself down the aisle. It was like trying to blitz an offensive line. Every other person was sporting a backpack big enough to hide a body in. Most also wore headphones that kept them from hearing words like "Excuse me." Pressed against bodies overly ripe in the heat, I fought to protect my right arm and keep my balance as the streetcar ground down Broadview. We went past the statue of Dr. Sun Yat-sen, where elderly Chinese in wide-brimmed straw hats were performing tai chi on the grassy eastern slope of Riverdale Park. I could only envy their ease of motion and the space they had to move in. At Gerrard, nearly half the passengers got off, heading to shops in Chinatown East, east-bound and west-bound streetcars, the library on the corner or the Don Jail rise behind it, its dark Gothic wing hidden from view by a newer brick extension.

When the aisle cleared, there was an empty seat next to a well-dressed man reading the *Report on Business*. I was about to sit down when I saw an elderly woman facing the other way, her thin hand clenched tightly around a chrome pole, blue veins over bony knuckles. Even in this weather, she wore a wool coat. I tapped her shoulder softly and indicated the seat. She smiled and was about to sit when the streetcar lurched away from the stop. As she clutched at the pole to keep her balance, a thin man in jeans and a sleeveless denim vest swung into the seat I had offered.

He was about my age, which is thirty-four, but craggy and hard-looking, his ropy arms marked with dozens of crude ink tattoos. He shook his lank brown hair out of his eyes and propped his left foot up on the back of the seat in front of him.

"That seat was for the lady," I said. He ignored me and shook the hair out of his eyes again.

"She needs it more than you," I said.

"That so?" He gave me what was supposed to be a withering glare. Shook the hair. "Happens I had a rough fuckin' night."

I briefly entertained the idea of shaking his hair for him. "Look—"

"Just fuck off, okay?" he spat. "Just leave me the fuck alone, ya fuckin' kike."

Kike? Had he really said *kike?*

The old lady clutched the pole even more tightly. The businessman in the window seat buried his nose deeper in his paper. A few straphangers stepped away from us.

I guess he had.

I'm not what you'd call an observant Jew. I eat matzoh on Passover but have been known to top it with ham and cheese. My favourite Chinese dish is shrimp in lobster sauce with minced pork, the non-kosher trifecta. Truth be told, I'm an atheist, though I once flirted briefly with agnosticism. But I am a Jew to my marrow and proud of it. I believe in the people, the culture, the community. I especially believe in the concept of *tikkun olam:* repairing the world, leaving it a better place than you found it. And at that moment, it was my belief that the streetcar would be a better place without this piece of shit on it.

"It's all right, dear," the old lady said to me. "I'm getting off at Jarvis."

"Doesn't matter," I told her. "This gentleman is going to get up now and give you the seat."

"The fuck I am," he said and stuck out the middle finger of his left hand.

In any fight, you take what they give. I grabbed his hand and forced it downward and held it there. "Aaah!" he said, and who could blame him? It's a fast, simple move that causes intense pain in the wrist, all but forcing a person upward to try to ease it. As he struggled up out of his seat I kept the pressure on, my left hand free to block a punch—like he could throw one with the pain he was in.

"Feel that?" I asked.

"Aaah!"

"I'll take that as a yes. Want more?" I pushed harder until he went up on his toes.

"Naaa!"

"We're going to walk to the exit," I said. "You going to make trouble?"

"Naa-uuh!"

We walked toward the rear doors, my arm tight under his left. Two men walking up the aisle arm in arm—hardly uncommon in Toronto. We could have been practising our wedding march.

"Next time a lady needs a seat, you're going to give it to her." He didn't answer so I pushed the wrist back farther.

"Ah! Ah!" he said through clenched teeth. "Yes."

"And the word *kike*, you're going to expunge it from your vocabulary."

"I'm what?"

"You're going to forget you knew it."

"Yeah. Yeah-uhh!"

The streetcar stopped at Queen Street. I marched my new friend down onto the first stair, which automatically opened the doors, and gave him a shove. He exited ungracefully and stood on the sidewalk, flexing his hand open and closed, shaking it like there was something stuck to it. There would be numbness and pain, but both would subside in minutes.

"Hey!" he whined. "I got no more carfare, ya prick."

I dug in my pocket and flipped him a toonie and assorted small change.

"I'm still short a quarter," he said.

"I take no quarter," I said as the doors closed. "And I give none."

Jonah Geller. Repairing the world, one asshole at a time.

CHAPTER 2

C arol Dunn's smiling muscles were out of commission again. "Good morning, Jonah. So glad you could join us."

Carol had been Beacon's receptionist since it was founded by Graham McClintock after he retired from the Toronto Police Service. Somewhere near fifty, she presided over reception with total devotion to Clint, guarding his privacy and time as though both were more precious than air. She would take on a pack of pit bulls to protect him, and win. She hadn't spared me so much as a grin since the Ensign case. I had caused grief to Clint and the firm, after all. And here I was waltzing in ten minutes late, without a collared criminal or exonerated innocent to show for it.

"Car trouble," I said.

"Mm-hmm."

Carol could have buzzed me in but didn't. I dug out my ID card and swiped it through the magnetic reader fixed to the door jamb.

The Beacon office was open concept: in the centre area were four cube farms of four workstations each, each farm walled off by baffles for privacy and sound insulation. Around the perimeter were offices occupied by unit heads and senior consultants. Not long ago, I had seemed destined for one. Now I felt lucky they hadn't stuck me in a rain-soaked doghouse in the parking lot. Since returning from my four-week injury leave, I had been given nothing but supporting roles. I'd helped other consultants run background checks on prospective employees or spouses. I'd traced paper and money trails left by embezzlers, bail jumpers and deadbeat dads. I'd pored over transcripts of other people's interviews; reviewed videotapes to be used as evidence in other people's cases. I had done everything but lead a case of my own.

This was hurting my income in equal measure to my pride. The firm billed clients by the hour, and the more hours you logged, the better you did. Put in enough overtime on surveillance or undercover jobs, and you could earn a good living. At the moment, I was being offered neither.

I shared my cube farm with Jennifer Raudsepp, Andy Robb and François Paradis. Franny was fluently bilingual and spent a lot of time on the road, working cases in eastern and northern Ontario, which had the largest francophone populations in the province. This week, he was working in town, something to do with a nursing home. Andy was a wiry little guy, five-seven and 130 pounds, and terrific at undercover work. He could blend into any setting without drawing attention to himself. He didn't talk much but rarely missed a word other people said.

Then there was Jenn, a six-foot blonde who liked to tell people she was the shortest of four Estonian sisters. She was thirty but could pass for early twenties, with eyes as blue as a prairie sky and a smile that could make a man walk happily into a lamppost. She was also, to the chagrin of sighted straight men everywhere, openly gay. She lived with a lovely nurse practitioner named Sierra Lyons, and I got along better with both of them than I ever had with Camilla. As a trained investigator, I suppose that should have told me something.

When I first joined Beacon five years earlier, I had assumed most of the employees would be beefy ex-cops who'd put in their thirty years and wanted to top up their pensions. Clint quickly put that notion to rest.

"Cops might know how to conduct an investigation," he said, "but they've always had the badge to back them up. The authority to enter someone's home, search the place, compel them to answer questions. We don't have that luxury. People don't want to talk to us, they close the door and that's that. We have to be good talkers and better listeners. If the job is surveillance or security, give me an ex-cop. If it's money tracking, give me an ex-accountant or banker. But for undercover work or interviews, I'd hire an actor or a social worker before an old cop."

"You were a cop," I said.

"Yes, and after I hired myself I realized my mistake and vowed not to repeat it."

So we had people like Andy, who before joining Beacon had been a bartender, a hot walker at Woodbine Racetrack, a warehouse worker and a night watchman. People like Jenn, who had been a member of a women's sketch comedy troupe until she realized she'd always be looking up at the poverty line. And people like me, who'd had more false starts and accidental careers than I care to admit, including waiter, construction worker, ski guide and martial arts instructor. Among other things.

I was just settling into my chair when Andy and Jenn exited one of the meeting rooms. "Hi guys," I said. Andy said hi—a mouthful for him—and Jenn gave me the kind of smile that made me wish she were straight or that I were Sierra Lyons.

"How you doing?" she asked.

"Not too bad," I lied. "Where's Franny? Monday morning flu again?"

"Haven't heard a word."

I fired up my computer and logged on to our media monitoring software package. If Beacon Security had been mentioned anywhere in print or broadcast media, transcripts would be waiting for me. I had customized my profile so it would also deliver stories that mentioned certain competitors, the Ministry of Community Safety and Correctional Services, which oversees our profession, and other keywords.

What my career had come to: a glorified clerk.

It wasn't hard to predict the lead story in today's Toronto papers: the shooting death of Kylie Warren outside the Eaton Centre, at the city's busiest corner, in the middle of a sun-kissed Sunday afternoon. Kylie was the kind of young woman Toronto loves: athletic, blonde, an achiever from a good Leaside family with a bright future on Bay Street after completing both a law degree and the Canadian Securities Course.

Each paper had slightly differing accounts, depending on the witnesses they interviewed, but a rough consensus emerged: one group of four or five black teens walking south on Yonge came across another similar-sized group walking north. Words were spoken. Respect not paid. Shoves exchanged. Guns pulled. As one man fled across the street, another fired three shots at him. Two shots hit the wall of the restaurant Kylie was leaving. The third took most of her head off. The shooter had been identified as Dwight Junior Torrance, whose lengthy record included numerous assault, drug and weapons charges. He had been deported to his native Jamaica twice already, but kept slipping back into Canada, no doubt for the climate.

The widest coverage was in the city's only tabloid, the *Clarion*, since the shooting brought together three of its most urgent concerns: guns, good-looking girls and the ineffectiveness of the left-leaning latte-loving mayor and Toronto elite. "Year of the Gun!" the headline screamed. The coverage included a two-page spread in which every person shot to death in June—a record twenty-six—was memorialized. Almost every face was young and black. Some darker-skinned, some lighter. Some with shaved heads, some with dreads or braided rows. Apart from Kylie Warren, there was only one other white face: Kenneth Page, a fifty-two-year-old pharmacist with a glorious head of grey hair and ruddy complexion, shot to death in a car-jacking. Killed for nothing, like Kylie.

Until very recently, guns had been relatively rare in Toronto, whose citizens tended to kill each other with knives, beer bottles, fists, boots or any blunt object at hand. But guns were everywhere now, sweeping out of pockets, waistbands, glove compartments, backpacks and school lockers, bearing down on people like Kylie and Kenneth Page. Like me and Colin MacAdam.

I'd been on the other side of guns once—the shooting side—and hadn't liked it any better. I knew all too well what guns could do, to both the victim and the shooter. I told Clint when I took the job that I wouldn't accept any assignment that required me to carry a gun. He laughed and told me to relax, that Toronto wasn't L.A.

Of course, he probably wouldn't trust me with a stapler now, but that was fine with me.

It was lunchtime by the time I finished the media review, including all the weekend editions. I ordered in a roast beef sandwich from the deli on the corner and was just tucking into it when François Paradis made his entrance.

He was a big physical presence, Franny, with a grand black pompadour he vowed never to change and a booming voice that switched effortlessly back and forth between English and French, joking and cursing eloquently in both official languages. He was a few years older than me, kept fit at the gym and seemed to enjoy his life as much as anyone nearing forty without much to show for it. Which could be me if I didn't pick up my game soon.

"Good afternoon," I said.

"Like hell," he groaned.

"So what is it today? Flu? Asthma acting up?"

"Neither," he winked. "Her name is LaReine, *maudit Christ*, and she rode me all night like a bull. Big black girl, eh, has an ass like two melons. *Sacrament*, I never had it like that before. I'm afraid to take a leak, eh? My thing's so tired he can't lift his head to see the toilet. I'm afraid I'll piss all over my shoes."

"Not the Bruno Maglis."

"Any coffee going?" he said. "I need one bad, my friend."

"Might be some in the kitchen."

"Don't suppose you're heading that way."

"Don't suppose so."

"Listen," he said, leaning forward and dropping his voice. "Can you help me out with one thing?"

"Like?"

"The case I'm on, this nursing home thing. I met the client Friday and I was supposed to type up my notes but I had a date Friday after work—"

"With LaReine?"

He looked puzzled. "What? No, no, I met her just last night. Friday was this girl Micheline, friend of my ex-wife. I always wanted to plant her when I was married but I was trying to be a good husband back then. Stupid me, eh? So I ran into her at the track and I went for it, *tabernac*, and she was everything what I hoped for. Now I just have to make sure my ex finds out about it."

"Which ex?"

"Eh? Oh, Mireille, of course. Vicki doesn't give a crap anymore."

"So you ran into this girl at Woodbine?"

"Best luck I've had there in weeks. I even hit a four-hundred-and-twenty-dollar trifecta."

"But you said you had a date."

"When?"

"You said you couldn't type up your notes because you had a date. But your date was someone you ran into once you were already at the track."

Franny slumped in his chair and threw up his hands with a smile. "You got me," he said. "Caught me in my own lie. That is why you are a rising star—"

"Was. "

"Come on. See how you picked up my little fib?"

"Butter the other side later, Franny," I said. "You bugger off to the track and I have to type up your notes?"

"Clint said you were here to help if I needed it. And I do." He wheeled his chair closer. I could smell a musk of cologne, booze, coffee and, presumably, LaReine. He handed me a chrome microcassette recorder and said, "Double-spaced, please. Before end of business today is fine."

CHAPTER 3

Buffalo: the previous March

B arry Aiken entered his garage from the laundry room off the kitchen, so it wasn't until he opened the outside door that he felt the coldness of the rain and the bite of the wind. A raw, late winter day in Buffalo, still a few weeks shy of spring. Barry had to open the garage door by hand because the remote hadn't worked in weeks: the only loser on Lincoln Parkway getting his face wet opening the door to the outside world.

He heard the rumble of thunder in the distance, felt the dampness in his bones. Shivered and zipped his leather bomber as high as it would go. Barry hated driving to the west side but that's where Kevin was, and Kevin had the supply; Barry was all demand. He patted his jacket pocket, the inside one that buttoned shut, to make sure he had his wallet. He didn't like carrying this much cash, but what else was he going to do? Offer to write Kevin a cheque? Ask him if he took plastic? Right, then hang around until he stopped laughing.

Barry aimed his fob at the side of his Honda CR-V and heard it chirp as the lock disengaged. He got in and eased the seat back and adjusted the mirrors. Amy had been the last one to drive and he was much taller than she was, six-one to her five-five. He started the engine and put the gearshift in reverse, then put it back in park and turned off the engine. Got out of the car and retreated to a corner of the garage that was sheltered from the wind and the neighbour's view. He opened his silver-plated cigarette case—both the case and the bomber jacket had once been his dad's—and slipped out a thin joint.

Just half, he told himself, to take the edge off, get him to Kevin's and back. He needed to calm down. Needed *something* to calm him down. Until he saw Kevin, a joint would have to do. He lit up and inhaled deeply, holding it in his lungs, watching smoke spiral off the lit end. The neighbours would smell it if they were outside, but so what? It wouldn't be the first time. He exhaled and inhaled again, holding the smoke in until his lungs told him to cut that shit out and take in some air. He blew out a good-sized cloud and took one more hit, then butted the joint carefully against the cinder-block wall of the garage and put the remnant back in the case.

No more, he told himself. Not until you get home. Don't want to go past mellow into paranoid. Don't want to be all red-eyed if you get pulled over for some reason. Especially on the way back.

Thus fortified, Barry backed out of his driveway and drove down Lincoln Parkway, a wide boulevard with fine houses on large treed lots. That he lived in one of Buffalo's more affluent areas was due more to his father's efforts than to his own. His dad had left Barry the house when he passed away two years ago, and he and Amy had been more than happy to leave their frame semi near D'Youville College and live close to the Albright-Knox Gallery and the park system designed by Frederick Law Olmsted. Live as his dad had, in his dad's colonial-style brick house with the white portico in front, on a street where the neighbours were all professionals, just as his dad had been.

Asked what he did, Barry would say graphic designer. True enough but not in the sense it had once been. He had started out in fine arts, like everyone else in his sixties circle, and eventually had turned to Mac-based design to leverage his modest talent into a livable wage. He had been an in-house designer for more than twenty years, the last twelve at the Buffalo Municipal Housing Authority, churning out pamphlets, brochures, reports and newsletters until the latest round of cutbacks claimed him. Why keep a middle-aged man on staff with benefits when work could be farmed out to twenty-two-year-old techies straight out of college who knew all the latest design programs and would charge half the price, the bony-butted pimply little shits.

So now he was freelancing out of his home but work was hard to find. Maybe his lifestyle was catching up with him, or maybe he was just getting old, but he didn't feel as sharp as he once did. Things didn't click like they used to. He'd still be trying to master the latest page-making software when the company would release a new version. He couldn't put in sixteen-hour days like cyberpunks fuelled by junk food, caffeine and the inexhaustible energy of their youth. His income had tailed off dramatically. For now he had modest savings and a decent stock portfolio his dad had left him, but there wasn't enough to keep Barry and Amy going until their pensions kicked in. Thank God, thank God, thank God they had never had kids. Amy had wavered in her late thirties but Barry had held fast and hadn't he been right? Look at them now. How would they manage if they had teenagers? Amy wasn't faring any better than he was, financially or otherwise. Who needed a piano teacher with arthritis, barely able to play the notes her students stumbled through?

The worst thing about being laid off—worse than the drop in income or the blow to whatever self-esteem had accrued to him during a relatively unaccomplished life—had been the loss of his dental, health and prescription drug benefits. As a municipal employee, he'd had a good plan that covered Amy as well. Now they were shopping for a plan they could afford and having no luck at all.

Barry switched on his headlights and set the wipers to high as he drove toward Elmwood. Humps of snow were still visible on some lawns, so black with soot they looked like magma. Not even noon but almost dark, wind blowing the rain hard against the windshield. Remind me again why I live in Buffalo, Barry thought.

'Cause you got no fucking choice.

He had been born in Buffalo fifty-five years ago, the only child of a surgeon and a homemaker, his mom dying of breast cancer when he was fourteen. He had never lived anywhere else. Where could he and Amy go at their age? How would they find someone like Kevin in another town?

His dad had moved to Buffalo from Brooklyn after med school to take up residency at Roswell Park and had genuinely loved the town. Loved its history, its architecture, its smallness and slower pace. Well, you'd really love it now, Dad, Barry thought. It's smaller than ever, fewer than 300,000 people, maybe half the population of its heyday. When his mom and dad had arrived in 1949, Buffalo had been a Great Lakes port thriving on shipping, steelmaking and manufacturing. With those industries now in decline, and little to replace them, it was just another Rust Belt relic closing in on itself, best known for lake-effect storms that dumped snow three feet at a time and a football team that went 0-for-4 in Super Bowls.

Some Buffalo Bills player, he forgot who, once said after leaving for warmer climes: "Buffalo isn't the end of the world. But you can see it from there."

Barry could feel the tightness in his hip spreading up his back and under his right shoulder blade, the one that'd been going into spasm lately. God, getting old sucked. It wasn't just the hip, the leg, the back. Everything was starting to go. His eyesight: two new prescriptions in the last three years. His hearing, especially the right ear. Waking up mornings stiff all over, from his neck to his ankles.

Stiff everywhere but where it counted.

Barry had always pictured himself staying fit and virile into old age. He knew he still looked good enough. He had all his hair and wore it stylishly long. He thought he could pass for forty-five in the right light. He still had a couple of guitars around the house and could play passable rhythm if called upon. He wore hand-tooled cowboy boots and faded genuine Levis. No pre-washed designer crap; he had denim cred, goddammit. None of it changed the fact that he was closer to the end of his life than to the beginning. The vertical lines on his face were practically furrows. His jowls were beginning to sag. A wattle was forming under his chin. His feathered hair was greying. His body was betraying him at every opportunity, especially in the bedroom. Amy was still a gamer, up for pretty much anything, but lately even her most attentive ministrations had been for naught.

It could be worse, Barry told himself. You could be Larry Foti, who dropped dead of a heart attack before his fiftieth birthday. Or the guy who had worked next to him for six years at the housing authority, Marc Ormond. He had a cerebral hemmorhage in his sleep. His wife found him in the morning cold as ice, blood coming out of his ears and nose. People his age, his peers, his co-workers and old school chums, were dying of natural causes. Heart attacks, strokes and all kinds of cancer: the breast, the prostate, the blood, the brain, for God's sake.

He stopped at a red light. Through rain-blurred windows he could see the people on the sidewalks were mostly black or Hispanic. One kid with a bandana under a tilted ball cap pushed off the wall and ambled toward Barry's car.

Turn green, he implored the light. He felt like an idiot, carrying so much cash in his wallet. If he got mugged, that's the first thing they'd grab. A real pro would have thought of something better—like putting the money in a crumpled drive-thru bag under the seat. Sure, now I think of it, he berated himself. *Why when it's always too late?*

Barry had nothing against black people. He was just scared shitless of them. He believed it was a class thing more than a race thing. A black doctor wouldn't scare him. Or a black lawyer or actor or accountant. But the guys outside his car now were clearly not members of the professions, with their combative stares, baggy pants, untied runners, caps turned this way, that way, any way but straight. Barry was sure the one coming toward the car could see right through the car window, through the leather jacket and into his wallet stuffed with cash. *Turn fucking green*, he pleaded silently. Maybe he could outrun these guys if he had to. How fast could they run with their pants down around their thighs and their running shoes unlaced?

Who was he kidding? He could barely run anymore. An old lady in a walker could probably chase him down, and slap him silly too.

The light turned green and Barry lurched through the intersection fast enough to make his back end skid on the wet pavement.

Why did Kevin have to live on the west side? More to the point, why had he been made the new middleman? Everything had been fine the way it was before Kevin Masilek had been introduced as the new supplier. Prices had gone up, of course, to make up for this new layer of management, but not enough to warrant going elsewhere. The supply was safe and steady. Like it or not, this was the new regime, they'd been told. Barry figured, Why rock the boat when you can just keep sailing.

He started to weigh the pros and cons of smoking the other half of his joint.

Con: The car will stink, especially with the windows closed. Your eyes will turn redder. You could fuck up the transaction with Kevin. You could get so paranoid you'd turn around and go home to Amy empty-handed.

Pro: You know you want to.

The pro clearly outweighing the cons, he got the doob out of his silver case and lit up. He cracked the driver's side window just enough to let the smoke out. Everyone else's car windows were closed so who was going to smell it? Don't worry so much, he chided himself. Just inhale. Exhale. Inhale. Exhale. *Aaaah.*

Barry didn't want any toke burns in the upholstery so he powered down the window and chucked the roach even though it had a little mileage left. Then he turned onto the street where Kevin lived in a tall semi-detached frame house. He pulled up at the curb and parked, kept the wipers going as he glanced up and down the street, looking for potential assailants. There were none he could see. Maybe the rain was keeping everyone indoors. Feeling a rare moment of affection for Buffalo weather, he got out of the car and locked it. Dashed up the three concrete steps to Kevin's door and rang. Waited and rang again. Waited some more.

Shit. It was eleven-fifty and he had told Kevin he'd be by between eleven-thirty and noon. Hadn't he? He briefly regretted smoking the second half of his joint, confused now—had he somehow got the time wrong? The day?

No. Even in his buzzed state he remembered the call: he had clearly said today between eleven-thirty and noon. Barry rang again. Knocked. Fished a quarter out of his jeans and rapped it on a square glass pane in the centre of the wooden door. Still no answer. The nerves behind his sternum started to slither over each other like snakes. What if Kevin had forgotten? Christ, what if he'd been arrested? Where would that leave Barry and Amy?

Okay, he said to himself. Breathe. Breathe and think. Which he did until he remembered the cellphone clipped to his belt. He dialled Kevin's number and listened to it ring. Three times, four times, five, and then the voice mail kicked in. Barry disconnected without leaving a message. Maybe Kevin was having a shower, he told himself. Maybe he was on the can and unable to get to the phone. Barry pressed his ear to the glass pane in the door. He could hear music playing at the back of the house where the kitchen was, a raw bluesy sound that took him one second to recognize: the Allman Brothers Band, the classic 1971 concert at Fillmore East, before Duane died, before Berry Oakley died, before Gregg started dating celebrities and falling face-first into his pasta.

Barry smiled. Kevin was home after all. Just couldn't hear the bell over Duane's moaning slide guitar and the band's twin drum attack. He walked down the driveway to the rear of the house and went up the back stairs. He looked over at the adjoining yards and didn't see anyone—thank you, rain—and knocked loudly. Waited. Knocked again. Waited some more. Pressed his ear to the back door, hearing Berry lead the band into "Whipping Post." He thought he heard a door slam at the front of the house: could Kevin have gone to the front door just as he had come around back? Barry sighed and walked around the front again, hoping Kevin wasn't at this very moment going back. They could do this all day, he thought, like some kind of bedroom farce, only without the laughs. He was relieved to see the front door was open. Thank fucking God.

He stepped into the dark-panelled foyer.

"Kevin?" he called. "It's me, Barry. Hello?"

No answer.

Okay, so maybe he had gone out the back door to see who had been knocking. Barry walked down the hallway that led to the rear of the house, past the front parlour and dining room, the rooms all sparsely furnished. Whatever money Kevin was making was not being plowed into home decor.

"Kevin?" he called again. "Turn down the music, man. You got company."

Still nothing.

He looked down and noticed wet boot prints in the hall,

heading from the rear to the front. Barry's gut tightened. Turn around, he told himself. Follow those prints right out the door.

And go home with nothing? *Get a grip.*

He entered the kitchen and saw Kevin sitting in a round-back wooden chair: plump and paunchy, his head shaved to hide the fact he was going both bald and grey, wearing an old black T-shirt with the Rolling Stones logo on it, the red tongue lolling out of a wet-looking mouth.

Barry stood there a moment, not moving, not breathing, taking in the scene. Then he vomited on the floor, coffee and bits of breakfast muffin splashing off the linoleum and onto his hand-tooled boots.

Kevin was tied to the chair, his hands bound behind him with duct tape. His head was tilted back over the top of the chair and a knife, a boning knife it looked like, had been stuck through one of his eyes. It stood upright like a flag atop a mountain. His face was a bruised and battered mess; his mouth bloody behind a strip of duct tape. His forearms had ugly burns on them. Barry could see a blackened knife on the counter beside the toaster. Christ, the killer had heated the knife in the toaster and stuck it to him. Barry had no idea what to do. He had watched enough *Law & Order* to know this was a crime scene. He shouldn't touch a goddamn thing. But he already had: the front door, the back. He had called Kevin's number on his cell just moments before. He could practically hear the black lady lieutenant telling the grizzled old detective, "Check the phone logs. See who called the morning of the murder." Should he call 911 himself? Deflect suspicion? Not if it meant explaining to the cops why he was here, why his eyes were so bloodshot.

The only thing to do was get the hell out and home to Amy. She had a better head for things like this. For crises. He started to back out of the kitchen, wondering if he should mop up his vomit. Couldn't they test it for DNA?

Then Barry stopped and stared at the wall behind Kevin's tortured body, where a dozen or more cardboard cartons were stacked.

Holy shit, he thought.

He took the widest possible arc around Kevin's chair, careful not to step in any blood. He ripped a sheet of paper towel from a roll on the counter and wrapped it around his hand. Then he eased open the flap of the top carton.

"Holy shit!" he said out loud.

He knew he shouldn't touch the boxes, much less what was inside. Tampering with evidence was against the law.

Well, so was smoking a joint while driving in the rain.

In that moment, he made his decision: he was taking as much as the CR-V could hold. He hefted one carton, found it wasn't too heavy and walked it quickly to the front door. Then he reversed direction and brought it back to the kitchen. No point loading up in plain view. He left the house by the front door, closing it tight behind him, wiping the handle quickly with paper towel. Then he backed his CR-V down Kevin's drive. Popped the rear hatch and went back in through the kitchen door. It took less than five minutes to load the cartons into the car. His feet went out from under him once on the wet stairs, and he banged his tailbone hard on the bottom step, but he kept going, cursing and limping in equal measure. When the car was as full as it was going to get, he slammed the hatch, looked around, saw no one and went back into the kitchen. He used a long sheet of paper towel to wipe up his vomit, the smell of it almost making him spew again. Then he got the hell out.

He drove like a nun all the way home, obeying the speed limit, thankful he had smoked all the dope he had because otherwise he'd be blowing one now the size of the Sunday *Times*.

He could hear himself breathing loudly through his nose. Hear his own heartbeat. Hear the sound of each raindrop on his windshield and the sound of the wipers slapping side to side.

He heard car horns, diesel engines, the hiss of tires on wet pavement. And something else: something he almost didn't recognize because he hadn't heard it for so long: the sound of opportunity knocking.

He was so intent on that faraway sound, so happy to be hearing it again, that he didn't notice the forest-green SUV pull away from the curb and fall in line behind him.

CHAPTER 4

Toronto: Monday, June 26

Franny had the computer skills of an early hominid. He avoided typing notes or reports as often as possible, preferring to fill black pocket-sized notebooks in Palmer script, which the nuns at his school had drilled into him by dint of terror. I booted up his computer with the password he'd given me and groaned loudly when I saw the Windows desktop. Nothing had been saved to folders. There were no folders. His desktop could barely be seen for all the documents and applications scattered over its surface. Nor did his document names make any sense. They were cryptic abbreviations that might have been French, English or Esperanto for all I knew.

I created an electronic folder called "FP DOX" and dragged all Franny's scattered Word documents into it, save one: the standard intake Franny had filled out on his new client. Even he couldn't escape typing and filing one because it outlined the scope of the investigation the client wanted us to undertake and, more important, what he expected to pay.

The client was Errol Boyko, a single fifty-four-year-old civil servant who lived in North York. His mother had passed away recently in a nursing home called Meadowvale, owned and operated by the Vista Mar Care Group. Boyko wanted Beacon

Security to determine whether neglect, abuse or malpractice had contributed.

I created a new folder called Meadowvale and placed the intake form in it. Then I created a new Word document and pushed play on the tape recorder.

Errol Boyko: All her life, Mr. Paradis, my mother was a force of nature . . .

François Paradis: Franny's fine.

EB: Eh? Oh, sure. Franny. Mom was a big, robust, unstoppable, independent woman. When my dad passed away, she took over his hardware store and ran it better than he ever did. She didn't retire until she was seventy-five and when she turned eighty a few years ago, she was still living on her own, doing her own tax returns, taking pottery classes, hosting a book club and putting personal ads in the *Globe* for a companion. The last part I wasn't too crazy about but that was Mom.

FP: Sounds like quite a gal.

EB: Oh, she was. Until a year ago.

FP: What happened?

EB: A severe stroke. She'd had high blood pressure for years and it finally caught up with her. The stroke was devastating. She changed overnight. She couldn't read or write anymore, couldn't remember anyone's name. She started having anxiety attacks if you changed the channel or got up to leave the room or a cloud passed over the sun. Anything could set her off. Her doctor gave her medication to control the anxiety but she needed more care than we could provide.

FP: So you brought her to Meadowvale?

EB: It's not like I wanted to. I had to. My brother lives in Vancouver and has no interest in moving back. My sister's in Toronto but she's an alcoholic and God knows what else. She can barely take care of herself. I tried at first to keep Mom in her apartment with a caregiver. I was still hoping she would improve, you know? Regain some functioning. But it cost a fortune and she was getting no stimulation. The two of them sat in front of the TV all day. The woman was knitting sweaters she sold on the side and Mom was staring into space. Finally my brother and I decided a residential setting would be better for everyone.

FP: How did you choose Meadowvale?

EB: I called the Ministry of Health and Long-Term Care. They assigned me a case manager and she made the recommendation based on Mom's needs.

FP: Her name?

EB: Darlene Tunney.

FP: Did you check it out yourself?

EB: Absolutely. I did my homework. I went on a tour and I called a good friend of mine who had placed his father there a few years ago. He had nothing but good things to say about it. Mind you, that was before it was taken over by this Vista Mar group.

FP: When did your mother move in?

EB: Early in the new year.

FP: And when did she die?

EB: A month ago.

FP: We're very sorry for your loss.

EB: Thank you.

FP: You okay?

EB: Yes.

FP: Get you some water? Cup of coffee?

EB: A glass of water would be fine.

FP: As long as you don't mind it in a mug . . . here you go.

EB: Thanks.

FP: So what brought you here today, Errol? Why an investigation? The more specific you can be, the better.

EB: Are you close with your mother?

FP: Me?

EB: Yes.

FP: Well, we're a very big family, you know, I'm the second youngest of eight, so my mother always had her hands full, but we get along well. Iguess I try to call every Sunday.

EB: My mother and I were *very* close. Always. I was the baby of three and kind of her favourite. There was always trouble with my sister and my older brother is what you'd call aloof. It fell to me to look after her. I took on that responsibility, Franny. I took it very seriously. I gave it everything I had, everything, and I . . .

FP: There's some tissues behind you.

EB: Where? Oh, thanks. I'm sorry.

FP: Happens all the time. That's why we keep 'em there.

EB: Thanks. I guess what I'm saying is I need to know if they did anything to cause her death.

FP: What makes you think they did?

EB: At first, her doctor handled all her medication, in consultation with a neurologist, and things were fine. Mom didn't get any better but she was stable. Her blood pressure was under control. So were the anxiety attacks. Then the medical director at Meadowvale, Dr. Bader, persuaded us that he should take over her care. You know, being on the premises and everything. It made sense to me because—well, you know how it is trying to get a doctor to see you these days. Like trying to see the Pope. So I agreed.

FP: And things changed?

EB: Not at first. Or I should say not that I saw. I couldn't visit as often as I wanted. I'm an analyst at the Ministry of Finance and the months leading up to a budget—well, as bad as they normally are, they were even worse this year because of the size of the deficit we were projecting. So I only saw Mom on Sundays. She'd generally be okay—not too anxious, her colour good. I felt we had made the right decision. But a month or so before she died, I took a day off midweek to make up for all the overtime I'd been putting in and dropped by unannounced. It was like a bad movie. All the way down the hall toward her room, I could hear someone calling out, 'Help me, help me,' and I'm wondering, Who is this madwoman? Franny, it was my mother. She was hyperventilating, flushed, her eyes wild, half out of her mind. I called for a nurse and one came running, and the thing I remember is that she didn't seem concerned so much as scared.

FP: Scared of what?

EB: Of me. Of seeing me there. I asked what was going on and she wouldn't say a thing, just that she had to call Dr. Bader. A minute later Bader showed up with one of those little plastic cups with pills in it. Mom took them and eventually calmed down. He took her blood pressure and it was high as a damn bowling score, but he said it would come down soon. I demanded an explanation and he gave me some long, convoluted story about trying a promising new medication and needing to fine-tune the dosage. But the more I asked about it, the more evasive he got.

FP: Specifics, please.

EB: I asked to see Mom's file, because each medication is supposed to be logged, and he gave me a song and dance about how her records had been shipped by mistake to their archives and he'd have to fill out requisition forms to get them back. That made it two mistakes: one with the medication, one with the records.

FP: Okay. So mistakes were being made. Some of these places, you hear they're understaffed or—

EB: It wasn't just the mistakes, Franny. Mistakes I could live with. But like I said, I'm a budget analyst. All day long I look at income statements, balance sheets, expense reports, looking for the things that don't fit, that look inflated, that are just—out of proportion, I guess. And that's all I can say about it. The nurse's reaction seemed out of proportion. And so did Bader's. He was covering something up, I could feel it.

FP: Feelings aren't the best way—

EB: Then I *know*. I know something's going on. She wasn't getting her medication like she was supposed to.

FP: But why? What you hear about some places, they over-medicate to keep people, what's the word . . . manageable.

EB: I don't know why. Maybe they sell them to someone else.

FP: What kind of meds was she on, may I ask?

EB: Oh, God. All kinds. For her blood pressure, her anxiety, plus diuretics, anti-seizure meds . . .

FP: Not morphine or OxyContin or anything like that.

EB: No.

FP: All right, Errol. Did you confront Dr. Bader with your suspicions?

EB: [pause] I was afraid to. Afraid for Mom, I mean, not for myself. You hear stories about helpless old people being abused, and I thought if I made trouble they might take it out on Mom. I should have come to you then. Maybe if I had—

FP: Errol, let's stay with the things we can control here and now, okay? Did you consider moving her to another facility?

EB: It's not that easy. The good ones have long waiting lists. And what if nothing was wrong and I was just being overpro-tective? We'd move her for nothing, and people in her con-dition don't handle change well. After the stroke, every change in her routine was a huge setback.

FP: What did she die of, may I ask?

EB: Another stroke.

FP: This Dr. Bader signed the death certificate?

EB: Yes.

FP: So as I understand it, you want us to find out whether mistakes were made with her medications and whether they contributed to her death.

EB: That's right. My brother is fully behind this and very affluent. There won't be any problem with fees.

FB: Let's talk about that.

CHAPTER 5

Heading home on an eastbound streetcar, crossing back over the Don Valley, I saw the ornate silver inscription on the west side of the bridge glinting in the sun: "This river I step in is not the river I stand in." White plastic shopping bags floated on the surface of the Don River. Pop cans and milk jugs bobbed alongside them. Near the west bank a rusting shopping cart lay half-submerged. What you couldn't see—the chlorine and other spilled toxins—was even worse. A truer inscription would have been, "This river I step in will give me a wicked rash."

I arrived home feeling wilted. I thought about having a cold beer. I thought about calling my old friend Kenny Aber, to see if he wanted to pop by with a joint, which he was always good for. I finally decided against both and got my Rollerblades from the hall closet.

Getting down to the Don River bike path on skates was easy. All downhill, as it were. As long as my weight was centred over my blades, gravity did the rest, taking me down the gentle slope of Broadview Avenue. At the south end of Riverdale Park, just past Dr. Sun's statue, was a much steeper paved path that led down into the valley. I used my foot brake a little but mostly cut back and forth like a skier to control my speed until the path levelled out near a pedestrian footbridge that crossed the valley east to west. Halfway across the bridge was a metal staircase that led down to the bike path. I climbed down sideways, then started up the trail that followed the Don River north. It was less industrial than the southern trail and part of it was a defunct road, much wider than the bike path, that would give me a chance to sprint.

Normally after work this path was jammed with bikers, bladers, runners and dog walkers, but the heat was keeping people away. With no obstacles to dodge, I broke a good sweat by the time I reached the Chester Marsh, a wetland that had been painstakingly restored by volunteers and was now home to a bewildering variety of grasses, reeds and birds.

I crossed Pottery Road, a steep, curving access road that leads down from Riverdale to the Bayview Extension, taking care not to become a hood ornament as cars came rushing blindly down toward a level railway crossing. On my right was a small fenced-off gravel lot with a gap on the right side just wide enough to let bicycles and strollers pass through. There began a wide, even surface that ran parallel to the river. I picked up my pace, bent at the waist like a speed skater, feeling twinges in my right tricep each time my arm extended. Who knew gunshot wounds took so long to heal?

I went past two posts, about a hundred yards apart, on which hung bright orange lifesavers. The second one also had a long metal pole with a wide ring at one end. If someone fell into the river, you could fish them out with it. Or use it to clean out some of the trash. As I went past the embankment going up to the Parkway, I had the sound of traffic on my right and the river on my left, rushing sounds on both sides. Sweat stung the skin around my eyes but it felt good to get up a head of steam. I had been pretty sedentary since getting shot, partly because of the wound itself and partly because of the depression I'd felt looming around me ever since the Ensign case crashed and burned.

As soon as I got home, I showered and changed into shorts. While I waited for Joe Avila, I opened a chcap and cheerful Australian Cabernet, checked the cork for mould, then tossed it. I was about to pour myself a glass of wine when Joe called up from the lobby. "Down in a second," I told him.

Joe was just five-seven but looked like he'd been carved from the cliffs of his Portuguese village in the Dorro River valley. He had dark curly hair and olive skin. He wiped his right hand on the back of his coveralls and we shook. "Sorry I'm late, Jonah, but I got a call for a boost just as I was leaving. That's seventy bucks for five minutes' work and it was on the way here."

"Don't worry about it, Joe. Thanks for coming."

"I owe you for bringing Mariela home safe."

"You owe me for selling me a piece of shit car."

"Come on," he said, trying to look aggrieved. "There's nothing wrong with that car, not for the price you paid. You want to upgrade, I can put you in a two-year-old Camry or Accord for 10 per cent less than book."

"Just get this one running for now," I said.

I walked down to the garage door and opened it from the outside with a key. Joe drove his tow truck out of the circular drive and down into the garage and parked next to the Camry. Once I opened the hood, he slipped the hook of a caged lamp through an eyehole along the edge. He leaned in to have a look and I leaned in over his shoulder.

"You're in my light," he said.

"Sorry."

He checked the battery and pronounced it fine. I leaned in again.

"Jonah."

"Sorry."

"Why don't you go outside and have a smoke or something?"

"I quit."

"Then go outside and stick your thumb up your ass till I call you, okay? Otherwise we gonna be here all night."

It was so nicely put, what could I do but leave the man to his work?

I sat in the shade of a Norway maple on the lawn outside the building, stretching my hamstrings, listening to starlings chatter in the trees. I wondered what it would be like to move my mother into a nursing home. Not that we were anywhere near it. My mother was in her early sixties and needed assisted living like I needed another gunshot wound. After my father died, she became a real estate agent and now owned a thriving brokerage, Ruth Geller & Associates. Mom sat on half a dozen boards and committees that raised funds for the elderly, newly arrived Russian Jews, tree planting in the Negev desert, various hospital and medical research campaigns, her local Liberal member and either the Art Gallery of Ontario or the Royal Ontario Museum, I can never remember which. I wonder how she can.

Thirty minutes later, Joe drove the tow truck out of the garage. To my immense relief, my car was not hooked up to the back.

"Ignition coil was burned out," he told me. "Put in a new one and she started up fine."

"A new one or a brand new reconditioned one?" I asked.

Joe sighed. "Bad enough I had to come here in prime time. I also got to listen to your jokes?"

"Sorry, Joe. What do I owe you?"

"You know I don't like to take your money, Jonah, what you did for me and all, but I need a hundred bucks for the coil and I could use another hundred to make up for all the calls I missed."

Two hundred. Imagine if he *did* like to take my money. "Cheque okay?"

Joe looked at me like I'd suggested he pierce his nipples.

"There's an ATM at the corner," I said. "Drive me up."

I stopped at a deli on the way home to pick up some rare roast beef and sharp cheddar; nothing fancy but both would go well with the wine I had opened. It was nearly seven-thirty by the time I got home. I put the food containers down on the counter and got a wineglass down from the shelf.

And froze.

On the counter next to the bottle were three drops of wine that hadn't been there before. Three fat drops like blood on the white Formica. Then I heard a light footfall behind me and I knew whoever had broken in was still there, between me and the only way out. I closed my right hand around the corkscrew so the spiral end extended out between my middle and ring fingers. The little blade at the end, which I'd used to strip off the foil cap, was still open. It wasn't much as weapons go but an improvement over cartilage and bone. I took a deep breath and spun around and came face to face with a dark-haired, dark-eyed man.

Dante Ryan, Marco Di Pietra's feared enforcer and hired gun, was standing not ten feet from me, holding a glass of my wine.

He looked at the corkscrew in my hand and said, "You're not going to need that."

"What the fuck?" was the best response I could manage. My heart was hammering my chest like it wanted to crack it open from the inside.

"If I wanted you dead," he said casually, "we wouldn't be having this conversation. You'd have taken two in the head the minute you walked in and I'd be drinking alone."

I couldn't think of a damn thing to say to that.

"Pour yourself a glass," he said, nodding at the bottle of wine on the counter. "You and I need to talk."

CHAPTER 6

The last time I'd seen Dante Ryan was outside the University Avenue courthouse, right after Mr. Justice Hugh Kelly finished ripping a nervous young Crown attorney a new one for trying to indict Marco Di Pietra and his alleged associates on the flimsy evidence presented. Ryan, Marco and a sizable entourage were lighting up cigarettes when I exited. Marco had to put on a big show, of course, calling me Jewboy, pointing his thumb and forefinger at my head like a gun, cocking the thumb and making silencer noises in his cheeks. Ryan didn't say a word. He didn't have to. The look he gave me was enough.

Now he sat in my living room, legs crossed, sunglasses up in his hair, swirling wine in his glass, watching drops slide lazily down its side. His clothes were all black, as they'd been that day outside court: an expensive linen jacket, a silk crewneck top, pleated slacks, thin dress socks, soft leather loafers. A white scar ran up through his right eyebrow and a livid purple one snaked along the right side of his jaw. His hands had knots of scar tissue on some of the knuckles but the nails had been recently manicured. His eyes were dark but not as dark as you'd expect of a man who hurt or killed people for a living. They were not without humour.

"You got a piece of cheese to go with this?" he asked.

I managed to get the cheddar I had bought from the kitchen to the living room table, along with a cutting board, two knives, crackers and a bunch of red grapes.

Wine and cheese with Dante Ryan. What next? Champagne with Karla Homolka?

Ryan sipped his wine slowly. I held my glass so tightly I thought the stem might crack in my hand.

"Mind if I ask how you got in?"

"The building or the apartment?"

"Start with the building."

"You got a lot of old ladies here," he said.

"It's rent-controlled. Some of them have been here since it was built."

"They do their shopping at the Loblaws across the street, they come back loaded with bags or pulling their little carts. A young man in decent clothes comes over to hold the door for them, they don't ask questions."

"And the apartment?"

"Please. You want to keep people out, shell out for a decent lock, not the cheap shit that came with the place." He reached into the inside pocket of his jacket and pulled out a pack of cigarettes. "Smoke?"

At least it wasn't an Ensign brand. "No."

"Mind?"

I never let anyone smoke in my apartment but I figured a cigarette pack was the least deadly thing Dante Ryan could pull on me. I told him to go ahead and found an ashtray in the cupboard under the sink. It had been used precisely once since I'd moved in, when Kenny Aber came by with a joint of West Coast weed as his housewarming gift.

Ryan lit up with a slim gold lighter and exhaled. "I came to see you in a professional capacity," he said.

"Mine, I hope."

"Don't worry, I told you."

"It's hereditary."

"Whatever. You know who I am and who I work for. You know what I do. So before we go any further, let's agree that what gets said tonight never leaves this room. Whatever you decide. We clear?"

"Decide what?"

"Are we clear?"

"I'm not like a lawyer when it comes to confidentiality."

"I'm not talking rules and regs. If what I say to you gets back to the man I work for, his family or his crew, it will get me killed. I'm here because I got nowhere else to go. And because you owe me."

"Owe you how?"

He dragged on his cigarette and blew two perfect smoke rings, one through the other. "You cost my boss a ton of money on the tobacco job—at least a million—and he had to make a court appearance, which is down low on his list of favourite things."

"Then again, he walked because I fucked up. So maybe he owes me."

"You want to tell him that?"

Point taken.

"Anyway," Ryan said, "after the judge threw it out, we had a meeting to talk about what to do about you. Marco, as you know, is a hothead. He was all for having you killed. But there's an unwritten rule in our thing that you don't kill cops unless you have to. The heat is too intense. You're not a real cop, but your boss was and he could have called in favours. In the end, cooler heads prevailed, and that's the only reason you're still here."

"You were one of the cooler heads?"

Ryan smiled again. "I could say I was or wasn't and you'd never know the difference. So let's say I was and leave it at that." He butted his cigarette. I reached for my wine and drank a third of it down. Red wine is supposed to benefit the cardio-vascular system, at least over the long run. Short term, I just wanted my heart rate to decelerate into the low 200s, as I pre-pared to hear what this killer wanted from me.

It's not like I had no blood at all on my hands. But his were soaked to the elbows by comparison.

An Ontario Provincial Police intelligence officer named Chris Cook once told me that Dante Ryan was believed to be respon-sible for as many as a dozen gangland murders over the years, but had never been convicted of anything worse than assault.

"Guy's a walking arsenal," Cook said. "I'm told he usually carries at least two guns and he does nice work with a knife too."

Like he trimmed steaks for a living.

Cook was my OPP liaison on the Ensign investigation and laid the scene out for me the night before the bottom fell out.

Ryan had known Marco Di Pietra since childhood, Cook told me, but wasn't a made member of Marco's crew, and never could be, because his father wasn't Italian. "Not that his old man wasn't in the life, but he was Irish, one Sid Ryan, part of the West End Gang in Montreal. He spent time in Toronto and Hamilton in the late sixties, trying to work out a deal with the Calabrians on distribution rights for new drugs coming onto the scene. Only he knocked up a girl who's a cousin to a cousin of Vincente Di Pietra, better known as Vinnie Nickels. He wasn't boss then, still a capo under Johnny Papalia, but Sid still had to marry the girl or Vinnie would have killed him. You know these guys. They like to play the honor card when it suits them."

A month after his son was born, Sid's standing with the local mob apparently fell in a big way and he returned to Montreal. Legend had it he went back in two hockey bags.

The other interesting thing Cook told me was that an epic power struggle was shaping up within the Di Pietra family.

Vinnie Nickels had inherited the mantle of leadership when Johnny Papalia was ushered into retirement by a hitter who shot him twice in the head outside his place on Railway Street in Hamilton. But Vinnie Nickels, given the name because he had logged five murders by the time he was made, was himself in failing health now, advanced prostate cancer riddling his bones from the inside like an army of termites.

"On paper," Chris Cook said, "Vinnie's still in charge but from what one snitch told us, it's like King fucking Lear in Hamilton. Vinnie has three sons: Vittorio, the eldest, known as Vito, then Marco and Stefano. Vito and Marco are the real shit-heads. Known to police, as we say."

"And Stefano?"

"He's the straight man, as far as we know. Has an MBA and weighs a hundred and forty pounds soaking wet. Vinnie has him handling the legitimate investments, the real estate, the offshore accounts and all that. Wears a nice grey suit."

"So they're Regan and Goneril and he's playing Cordelia."

"If you say so. Anyway, Vinnie Nickels doesn't have long to live but he hasn't named a successor. He's playing it close to the vest and it's creating a lot of drama on the street."

"Who's the favourite?"

"Vito's oldest, so he expects to be. Anything less is a slap in the face. But he's a little dim. No one sees things thriving under him. Marco, on the other hand, is a mad motherfucker: no gift for long-term vision or diplomacy, but definitely has the skillset to run crews."

"So what's going to happen?" I asked. "Civil war?"

"Me, I'd like nothing better. Let the mutts take each other out. Marco looks like he's getting ready. He's out there muscling up, working his crew, building a war chest. He's call-ing in markers, kicking ass all over town, taking a piece of any-thing he can. If it comes down to him against Vito, he wants people on his side. And that's going to take cash, 'cause Marco doesn't have a winning personality. Guy's a Rottweiler, only not as cute."

"I need you to find someone," Dante Ryan said.

"You're hiring me?"

"Yeah. Except I'm not paying you."

"Then you're not hiring me."

"Okay, then. I'm *engaging* you. I'm *involving* you. I told you you owe me, and that's not a position you want to be in."

"What am I supposed to do? Find someone so you can kill him?"

"Believe it or not, I'm trying to help someone here. When you have all the information, you'll understand." He refilled his glass and held the bottle up in my direction. I nodded and he topped me up.

Ryan lit another cigarette and blew a stream of smoke toward the window. Mr. Considerate. "In the course of my duties," he began, "if and when I'm called upon to take someone out, it's usually because he's ripping Marco off or pissing on his turf or generally displeasing him in some other manner. Like that."

Just like that.

"But Marco also takes jobs on behalf of other people and subcontracts them to me. The tougher the job, the higher the price. Deals like this, I never know who put out the contract. Marco's the only one who knows and he doesn't tell. In theory, it's voluntary on my part. I mean, I work for Marco but I'm not formally in his crew. So I could say no to a job—in theory. But when Marco really wants something done, you do it. You don't want him thinking you're soft and you don't want to deny him the opportunity to earn. Especially these days."

Ryan took a manila envelope out of his jacket. He laid it on the coffee table but didn't open it. "Few days ago, Marco hands me this package and the biggest down payment I ever seen. He's giving me fifty grand for this job, which means he's charging a hundred at least, 'cause Marco never takes less than half of anything." Another drag on the cigarette, two more smoke rings floating toward the window. "I could use the money, Geller, I really could. But I don't have the stomach for this job. All the things I done in my life, all the guys I've done, I can't do this one. I swear to God I'd lose whatever bit of my soul I have left."

He took a photo out of the envelope and slid it across the coffee table to me. There were three people on the sidewalk in front of a large Tudor house: a big bear of a man with thinning dark hair, a pretty woman with brunette curls, and a small boy who looked to be four or five. The boy was on a multicoloured plastic tricycle with a long handle at the rear. The man stood behind the bike, handle in hand, ready to push, squinting in a way that made him look worried. The woman knelt by the boy, adjusting a helmet atop his brown curls. He was looking up at her adoringly.

"What did he do to get a contract put on him?" I asked, indicating the man.

"No idea," Dante Ryan said. "But it must have been bad because the guy who ordered the hit doesn't just want him dead." He pointed at the woman in the photo. "Her too," he said. Then his finger slid over to the boy looking up at his mother with that open look of love. "And him."

"The kid?"

"Yeah," Ryan said. "And he's supposed to go first. The kid, then the mother, then the guy."

"Then the father is the real target," I said. "What in God's name did he do?"

"What I need you to find out," Ryan said, "is who he did it to."

CHAPTER 7

The first bottle was empty and we were making headway on a Cabernet from Australia's Barossa Valley. The picture of the boy and his parents still lay in front of us on the coffee table.

The man's name was Jay Silver, Ryan told me, a pharmacist who owned a large outlet called Med-E-Mart on Laird Street just south of Eglinton. He lived in Forest Hill, where even the most humble abodes cost at least a million dollars. The wife's name was Laura; the boy was Lucas, aged five.

"Geller, I been in this life twenty years, which is like a hundred and forty in mob years. I got no illusions. I've done pretty much everything you can imagine and a few things you probably can't. But one thing I can say is anyone I ever had to take care of, they had it coming one way or another. They brought it on themselves. I've done Asian gangsters, Jamaican gangsters, Italians from other crews. I've done bikers, plenty of bikers, big hairy motherfuckers that look like they're one day out of the caves. I've done skimmers, snitches, deadbeats." He looked at me with a wicked grin. "Witnesses."

"Really? So if the Ensign case had gone to trial?"

"No way that piece-of-shit case was going anywhere."

"But if it had."

"You would never have testified, that much I can tell you. Nothing personal, of course."

"Of course. What about women?"

"Killing them? It's rare but not unheard of. A talkative mistress . . . a wife with an inheritance . . . a stubborn witness . . . I've never done it myself, which you can believe or not, but it happens. But on my father's grave, not once in all my years in the business have I ever harmed a child. It's never even come up. Sometimes you know deep down there's collateral damage when you off a guy who has kids. You know they're going to suffer and whatnot. But to actually target a kid," Ryan said, staring into the dark sediment at the bottom of his glass. "To put him in the sights. What kind of animal puts a contract on a kid?"

"What kind of animal takes one?"

He was up on his feet in a flash, vaulting the coffee table between us and throwing a fast right hand at my jaw. It missed as I tipped my chair backwards, hit the floor and rolled up in a defensive stance. His sunglasses clattered to the floor as he threw a left. I slapped it aside and used his forward momentum to push him up against the wall facefirst and pin him there.

"Marco, I meant!" I said. "Not you, Ryan! Marco!"

"Take your hands off me," he hissed.

"You going to try to hit me again?"

"I said take your hands off me or I'll kill you fucking dead."

I took my hands off him and stepped back quickly. I kept my hands up and stayed on the balls of my feet. If he reached for a weapon I would unload with everything I had. He didn't. He turned and glared hotly at me. Looking at his flushed face, I could see the man who beat people, broke their bones, killed them for his living. Then the rage seemed to go out of him as quickly as it had come. He pulled down the cuffs of his jacket and walked out the balcony door. I waited a moment, then followed. The sun was down now and the southern sky over the lake was a dark shade of indigo. But not as dark as the look I'd just seen on his face.

We stood together in silence. The towers of the financial district seemed to rise straight out of the blackness of the tree-lined valley, clustered together in a haze of light. To the north, the sky was a lighter shade of blue. The few stars I could see were bright, though not as bright as the backlit logos of the banks. The banks always win out in Toronto.

"Nice move there, Geller," he said. "I want to hit some-one, I don't usually miss."

"You had a few drinks."

"So did you."

I shrugged. "What's his name?" I asked.

"I told you. Lucas."

"Not him. Your son."

He didn't look at me. "Who says I have a son?"

"The way you tried to take my head off. This thing is per-sonal with you."

Ryan nodded. "His name is Carlo and he's almost the same age as Lucas. Turned four this winter. Sweet little guy. Must take after his mother." Behind the pride sounded a note of sor-row or loss. He lit a Player's and inhaled deeply.

"You see him much?"

Smoke drifted out of his nostrils as he stared out at the skyline. "What makes you think I don't live with him?"

I shrugged. "Reading people is what I'm supposed to be good at."

"Okay, Kreskin. His mother threw me out a few months ago. She's not supposed to know precisely what I do for a living but she knows. She knows. Maybe she can see it in my eyes. Smell it on me. I can only see Carlo at the house when she's there. And that's as much as you need to know about my fucking life."

When he finished his smoke, we went back inside. More Aussie Cab was poured.

"So what happens if I actually find out who took out this contract?"

"I change the motherfucker's mind. Get him to take the kid off the table."

"So he can wind up an orphan?"

"That's out of my hands."

"Nothing is ever out of our hands, Ryan."

"Spare me," he said.

"Why should the woman die? She didn't do anything either."

"I never said she did, but I have to provide a level of service."

I looked at her picture again, this slim dark-haired woman with a son who was five. I didn't want her to die. Too many people like her were dead already.

"Aim higher," I said.

"What I'm doing is dangerous enough already."

"There's an old Jewish saying," I said.

"Oh Christ."

"No, that's not it. It goes, 'Where there is no one else to be a man, be a man.'"

"What, like some gunfighter riding in to save the town? Some crazy samurai?"

"Those are my terms."

"You're dictating to me now?"

To move forward, sometimes, you have to appear to take a step back. "I'm asking you."

Ryan stood, swirled the wine in his glass, then drained it in one swallow. "Look, the truth is, in my heart, I agree with you. If the real beef is with Jay Silver, if this is something he brought on himself, he should pay. But all I can promise as regards the woman is I'll try. The main thing for me is to keep the kid out of it."

"What if the guy won't change his mind?"

Ryan smiled, but only just. "One time," he said, "a guy named JoJo Santini, a bit player in Hamilton, runs a few hookers and street-level dealers, he orders a hit on a friend of Marco's 'cause the guy's doing JoJo's wife. I go see JoJo, tell him this friend has Marco's protection and he has to call it off. He says, 'All due respect, Dante, I can't do that, else people are gonna laugh in my face.' I tell him, if you're giving me all due respect, shut the fuck up and do what I say. He starts hemming and hawing and in between a hem and a haw I grab him by the hair and stick a gun in his mouth. Not just any gun. A monster stainless-steel Classic Smith with an eight-and-three-eighths barrel. You cock the hammer on that thing, you give a man religion. Long story short, what do you think happened?"

"He changed his mind."

"And then his pants. There's nobody's mind I can't change, Geller. Nobody. So find him. Soon."

"How? If I can't tell anyone at work, I can't get any help. I'll be strictly on my own."

"Figure it out. It's not like you were my natural first choice. Normally we got all kinds of ways to find people— investigators, cops, bondsmen—I could find a guy in witness protection faster than you can find clean underwear. But on this thing you're my first, last and only choice. The only one I trust not to play it back to Marco."

"You trust me?"

"I fucking well have to."

"Why not just warn the Silvers?" I asked. "Tell them to get out of town."

"Because far as I know, the only people who know about this job are me, Marco and the guy who ordered it. If Silver takes off, Marco will know who tipped him. Look, this is a delicate time. Marco wants to be boss when Vinnie goes. He'll kill his own brother if he has to. I can't be seen moving against him in any way."

"What's my time frame?"

"None. The client wants it done like yesterday."

"And you come to me now?"

"I've never done anything like this in my life," he snapped. "Taken business outside the walls. If Marco knew I was here he'd kill me with a big fucking grin on his face."

He pulled a slim prepaid cellphone out of yet another jacket pocket. "You need me, push 1 on the speed dial. It's a brand new phone, never been used. All the same, for my peace of mind, don't mention names on the air: mine, yours, Marco's. If he gets wind, we're both compost."

"Don't worry. As much as I support the environment, I have no desire to be part of it."

"All right. Keep me posted. And thanks."

"Don't thank me, Ryan. It's the right thing to do."

"I meant for the wine and cheese. You did a nice little thing on short notice."

CHAPTER 8

Buffalo: the previous March

Ricky Messina was soaking his right hand in a big glass bowl filled with ice cubes. His left held a heavy glass tumbler filled with Johnnie Walker Black. He was leaning back in his leather recliner, curdled with frustration, waiting for the phone to ring. If it was a local call, it would be the sourpuss bitch downtown, telling him to expect a call from the man in Toronto. If it was the three-ring long-distance signal, it would be the man himself.

Ricky knew he was going to have to eat a certain amount of shit over what had happened and that was all right. Even if none of it had been his fault, he considered himself a professional and a solid management prospect. He accepted that with greater responsibilities came greater accountability. He'd bow and scrape enough to ensure continued employment and good health.

Everything had gone so smoothly at first. Ricky found out everything there was to find out from Kevin Masilek and was just starting to have fun when someone started ringing the bell. Ricky ignored it but the bell kept ringing. Then there was a phone call, then the front doorbell again, whoever it was not getting the message, not going away. Ricky abandoned the knife routine he'd pictured in his head and stuck Kevin straight through the eye, deep into the brain. He threaded a suppressor onto his High Standard Victor, wanting to whip open the front door and shoot the shit out of whoever had ruined his day, bullets hitting them like sharp, deadly punches. Then came a knock at the back door and Ricky almost jumped out of his coat. He said *fuck it* and stood by the front door with his ear pressed to the wood until he was satisfied no one was outside, opened it, looked around and slipped out. He eased the door shut and walked to his car as slowly as his adrenaline-charged core would allow. He pulled out of his parking spot quickly but quietly, doing nothing to attract the attention of other drivers. He was sure he hadn't been seen. He drove half a block, checking his rear-view all the way, then parked in the first available space and waited for someone to run screaming out of the house. Only no one had. So he'd gone around the block and parked again where he could watch the house. Follow anyone who came out.

The pain in Ricky's hand was radiating out of the meaty part below the pinky. The tendons of the pinky and ring finger couldn't be seen for the bluish swelling around them. One bad punch, that's all, after Kevin admitted how much money he'd skimmed. Kevin ducked and Ricky's right hand slammed the back of the chair the miserable fuck was tied to. That's when Ricky taped Kevin's mouth and stuck him the first time, using a boning knife from Kevin's own drawer, watching his eyes widen like some kind of scared pack animal. His mouth strained against the tape but it was past time for words. Past time for money. It was duct tape time. Knife time.

Poor Kevin was on Ricky's dance card.

Ricky had always liked knives. He had been killing with them since he was eight or nine, starting with frogs in a creek that ran between boulders on a wooded lot in Bethany, where he had grown up, east of Buffalo and north of Attica Correctional Facility. He'd throw his penknife at big bullfrogs, try to pin them to the dirt where they sat. He killed a mouse that got caught in a trap his dad had set in the mudroom, where you always heard them scurrying around in the walls. The mouse tried to fend Ricky off with its ridiculous little paws until he cut them off.

The first time he killed a cat, he didn't mean to. He was playing with it and it scratched him pretty badly. Okay, maybe he had been a little rough but that was no cause to rake him like that. He stuck the cat through the throat with a switchblade an older cousin had brought back from a trip to Mexico. Ricky loved the sound the blade made as it flicked out of the side. Later he learned that stilettos made better work tools because the blade comes straight out of the tip. Palm it, get up close to someone, and *snick*, there's a blade at their throat. Their groin. Their eye.

While he respected guns for their utility in work situations, and knew how to care for and use them, he didn't have the same feeling for them that he had for knives. Knives were quiet. They didn't send neighbours running to the phone. They were easy to get, easy to hide, and the penalties for carrying them were mild compared to guns. Knives didn't shatter windows or kill pedestrians if you missed. They didn't have serial numbers, require ammo or cost a grand on the street.

And he could play with a knife. He could cut a man plenty of times before he killed him, as long as he had a working gag. How could a gun compare to that? A gun put you off at a distance. A knife brought contact and intimacy. It invited you to dance.

He killed his first man at eighteen. After all the frogs, the mice, the cats, the friendly little mutt he'd come across in the Bethany woods, he had to do a person. He had to know what it felt like. He bought a grey lightweight raincoat at a thrift store, matched it with an old cap and runners, and set out looking for a vagrant or drifter no one would miss. He walked around under an elevated section of the New York State Thruway for hours, carrying a bottle of cheap sherry in a brown paper bag, waiting for full dark, watching, scouting, noting who hung in groups and who kept to themselves. What they were drinking, how much and how fast. Who was big and who was small. Who had cuts and bruises on their faces from losing past fights. Who had them on their hands from winning.

Near midnight he found his man: a loner, about sixty, shuffling slowly along in boots that had no laces, heavy duffle bags weighing down both shoulders. The sole of the right boot flapped as he walked. Ricky stayed well back of him, swigging from the bottle every now and then, spitting most of it back down the bottle neck. He wanted to look like he was drinking but didn't want to be drunk. Whatever happened, he wanted to remember every second.

Men gathered near pillars supporting the expressway, finding what shelter they could from the wind. Ricky saw shapes huddled under thin grey blankets that looked like they'd been stolen from shelters. Empty mickeys and bottles were strewn in the dirt, along with malt liquor cans and plastic rings from six-packs.

The old loner was a hundred yards ahead, kneeling against a fence that kept people off the Thruway, making up a little bed of discarded newspaper and cardboard. Then he sat and took a foam container out of a plastic bag and began shoving some kind of Italian food in his mouth with filthy fingers. Ricky gagged. This isn't even a man, he told himself. It's an animal, no different from the cats, the dog, even the brainless mouse he had dismembered. It eats like an animal. It smells like an animal. The closer Ricky got to this thing, the ranker its smell became, a mix of piss, puke, tomato sauce, more puke, tobacco and God knew what else.

Ricky let the paper bag slip down off his bottle as he walked past, and let his gait become more unsteady. If the guy was anything short of blind, he'd see a natural mark—a moon-faced kid looking drunk and vulnerable—with a nearly full bottle in his hand. If that didn't get someone's darker nature fired up, they plain didn't have one.

Ricky Messina's father was Sicilian but his mother was from the north and he had her colouring: dark blond hair and green eyes. His face was so round that kids used to call him Moon Face and Mooney before he gained some size and built it up hard in gymnasiums inside and outside prison. To this day people who didn't know Ricky might look at his open face and think him pleasant. That suited Ricky just fine.

As Ricky stumbled along the fence, trying to look drunk, like he was barely keeping his balance, he heard footsteps fall in behind him, heard the flapping of a leather sole against the ground. Ricky let go of the fence and reached in for his knife: not a stiletto back then, but a steel hunting knife bought second-hand at a surplus store. The bottle in one hand, the knife in the other, Ricky leaned back against the fence. He felt ready. He kept his eyes half closed as if passing out, but through lowered lids he watched the animal approach, hefting a chunk of concrete in one filthy hand. Ricky had learned patience killing animals; he waited until the bum raised the rock to bring down on Ricky's head and stepped deftly aside. The bum's hand came smacking down on a fence rail and he dropped the rock with a hoarse lupine cry.

Ricky spun the bum around, the bum older than he'd looked from a distance, closer to seventy than sixty. His beard was grey except around the mouth, where nicotine had stained it orange. One eye was covered by a filmy cataract. "Drink?" Ricky asked, and smashed the bottle across his face. The bum howled again, louder, but Ricky knew no one would care. Breaking glass means nothing but bad news to drunks.

Ricky then made his only mistake of the night: he stuck the man in the throat. Arterial blood sprayed Ricky from forehead to sternum. Blood in his face, in his eyes, God, on his lips and in his mouth, seething with the animal's vile germs. AIDS, Hep C, TB, they all flashed through Ricky's mind as he pulled the knife out of the man and shoved him to the ground. In thirteen years since that night, Ricky had never made that mistake again. If he needed to kill quickly, he did it from behind. If he had time, he knew where to put the knife so it neither sprayed nor killed too quickly.

When the phone rang, it was a long-distance signal: the man himself calling from Canada. Ricky let it ring once while he drained his Scotch; again while he prepared himself. Let the man vent, he told himself. Don't take any bait. There's too much keeping us together. He won't blow you out of the water.

He answered it right after the third ring and didn't speak again for three minutes.

Ricky had been listening to a terrific book-on-tape in the car lately: *The Manager Inside Me*. He thought it could really help a forward thinker like him define his goals more precisely and hack and slash his way toward them. While the man in Toronto was tearing strips off him every which way, Ricky stayed calm and detached. *The Manager Inside Me* had a chapter on that very subject, "Accepting Constructive Criticism."

The man fed Ricky more shit than he ordinarily cared to swallow, but nothing truly damaging was said, and keeping *The Manager Inside Me* in mind helped: the shit still tasted like shit, but it went down easier somehow. When the rant finally wound down, Ricky calmly responded point by point. First, a brief strategic assessment of their situation to show he'd weighed both the risks and opportunities. Then a review of their agreed-upon business objectives. Finally, his plan to break new ground where the earth had been scorched.

To Ricky's relief, the man agreed to everything. Yes, he warned Ricky that the time for mistakes was past but, before hanging up, complimented him on his strategic approach to damage control.

Man, Ricky loved that tape.

CHAPTER 9

Toronto: Tuesday, June 27

I know I'm in Israel but it looks like downtown Toronto. I'm with the Bar Kochba Infantry, patrolling the corner of Yonge and Dundas outside the Eaton Centre, where a busker in a sleeveless black denim vest drums on overturned food tubs and draws a funked-up head-bobbing crowd. I'm in desert cammies, cradling my Mikutzrar—a short-barrelled M-16 customized for urban combat—scanning the crowd for anyone whose clothing looks too bulky, too heavy for the heat.

Roni Galil, my sergeant, is next to me, asking for a smoke. I tell him I quit—he knows I quit, he listened to me whine about it long enough—then realize he means a joint, not a cigarette. I put my gun down on the sidewalk. I snap open a film case filled with a premixed batch of ground-up blond Lebanese hash and Marlboro tobacco that we always had good to go. I twist up a joint, but as I'm lighting it, a child in soccer shorts and tank top approaches. He has dark curly hair and looks just like his mother, which I somehow know even though she isn't there. While I tousle the boy's hair he picks up my M-16 and passes it back to someone in the crowd who passes it to someone else. When Roni takes the joint from me, I realize my weapon is gone. I have only my sidearm—not even the Sig Sauer they give to officers, just a standard 9-millimetre Beretta.

I want my M-gun back. I punch the boy hard in the face. His nose breaks and he gags as blood streams into his throat. I push my way through the crowd but everyone starts pushing back, kicking at my feet, trying to knock them out from under me. If I go down I'll never get up again, they'll fucking kick me to death. I plant my legs and clutch at their clothing, bunch it in my fists like a man trying to keep his head above water. I call for Roni but he's sharing the joint with people around him. He can't hear me. He's not even offering it to me, the shit. No one can hear me now, not above the screaming—my screaming and the screams of the mob and the boy with the broken nose.

The exact circumstances of my Israel dreams are never the same. Sometimes we're in a narrow alley and a torrent of water comes rushing at us, sucking us down in a vortex. Or a herd of camels thunders around a corner, egged on by small boys with sticks, nasty smelly animals with bony joints and deadly hooves that can split a man's head in two. In one dream, people in apartments overlooking the alley started throwing appliances at us, everything from fans and toasters to full-size ovens, fridges, washers and dryers. Whatever details might be different, it's always Roni Galil and me, trapped in a bad place with bad things happening all around.

It was 5:24 a.m. when I woke with the dream still in my mind. I knew I'd never get back to sleep and turned on the radio, looking for something, anything, to sweep away the image of the bloodied child. I caught a few West Coast baseball scores, then a news update. The heat wave was still the top story. Several related deaths had been reported, including a ninety-three-year-old woman whose power had been cut off for non-payment, leaving her without so much as a fan. Ontario Hydro spin doctors would have to take a break from defending their lucrative consulting contracts to deal with that one.

A smog alert had been issued for the area stretching from Windsor, in the southernmost reaches of the province, to North Bay, two hundred miles north of Toronto. Officials in North Bay liked to tout its clean air to tourists, billing the area as the Blue Sky Region and the city itself as "Just North Enough to be Perfect." Now their marketers would have to come up with a new slogan. Something like "North Bay: Not as Brown as Downtown."

My apartment didn't smell much better after all the cigarettes Dante Ryan had smoked last night. I opened both balcony doors and emptied and rinsed the ashtray he had filled. The evening had been so surreal I might have thought it a dream; a better dream than the one I had just had. But the photo of Lucas Silver and his parents still lay on my coffee table. The contract on their lives was all too real, if what Ryan told me had been true.

Was it? Could it be? Did he really care whether a five-year-old lived or died? Or was he using me in some way—to flush Silver out, or maybe set me up for Marco Di Pietra, who would never forget what I had cost him.

For the moment, I had to assume Ryan was telling the truth: that he wanted to save a life and needed my help to do it. I had things in this world to make up for, repairs to make, and I wasn't getting the opportunity to do it behind my desk at Beacon.

The first thing to do was stop thinking of myself as still being in recovery. So instead of doing a physio routine on my arm, I eased myself down to the floor to begin a salutation to the sun. I worked my body slowly and deliberately through the movements, feeling tightness in my back, shoulders and calves as muscles moved in ways they had missed for months. By the time I completed four salutations my right arm felt like a wolf had clamped its jaws around it. I was damp with sweat, much of it from the heat and humidity but at least some due to my own efforts.

I rolled up to a standing position and marked a place on the floor where two parquet tiles met. I planted my feet there and began working through the *sanchin kata*. *Katas* are designed to improve a martial artist's balance, fluidity and style, but they also provide a good cardio workout, even—perhaps especially—when done slowly and mindfully.

Sanchin is moderate in its degree of difficulty, with forty-seven moves in all, including eight attacks. Before my injury, I had done *sanchin* so often it felt ingrained. I could do it left to right or right to left, beginning to end or backwards. I had done it blindfolded but didn't think I'd be trying that any time today.

During my first go at it, I felt awkward, having to think about the moves rather than letting them flow through me. My goal was to begin and end at precisely the same spot, but I didn't feel rooted in it and even stumbled once in transition between defence and attack. I kept reminding myself to slow down, breathe more deeply, find the focus *sanchin* can bring.

My first karate teacher told me a *kata* was a fight against an imaginary opponent. Not that I needed imaginary opponents, with Marco Di Pietra back on the scene. I've since learned that *katas* can be far more than that. Like dance and other art forms, in the right hands they can express sentiments about life, justice and the self. Known in English as the Three Cycles Form, *sanchin* symbolizes three primary conflicts of life: birth, survival and death. Only when the life cycle has ended can it begin again. When I completed my first run-through, I rested a minute and sipped water, then started again. It went more smoothly as muscle memory began kicking in. But not until the third time did I finish where I'd begun, the marked parquet tile squarely between my feet.

By seven I was heading down Broadview in my revitalized Camry. The east-facing sides of the downtown towers reflected the rising sun as though they were aflame. Not the most comforting image in our post–9/11 world, but arresting nonetheless.

I wanted to get in to work early, whip through my media clips and forward anything pertinent to Clint and his department heads, then boot back out and try to get a look at Jay Silver and family in the flesh. I figured I could do all that and still be back at my cubicle by the time Franny reeled in.

Clint's black Pathfinder was in its reserved spot when I pulled into the Beacon lot ten minutes later. I had no idea what time he arrived in the morning. In five years I had never yet beaten him in to work. The smell of freshly brewed coffee filled the office when I swiped my way in. I was in the kitchenette pouring myself a mug when Clint appeared. He made a show of looking at his watch and feigning shock at my early arrival. The good humour seemed a little forced but I appreciated the effort.

"You're in early," he said.

"I'm helping Franny out on his nursing home thing."

"Good. I told him to call on you if he was overloaded."

"Oh, he was overloaded."

Clint smiled. He had known Franny a lot longer than I had, had no doubt witnessed many a late entrance. "Never mind, smart guy. How you doing otherwise?"

"Fine."

"You sure?

"Yeah."

"Bring your coffee to my office," he said. "I've been wanting to talk to you about something. Now's as good a time as any."

CHAPTER 10

first met Graham McClintock at the Dojo on Danforth, where I taught the evening adult class in intermediate *shotokan* karate. Most of the students were in their forties or fifties, from professional women concerned about the city's rising crime rates to film producers who wanted to look as buff as the younger actors and techies they hired. Clint was close to sixty then: an inch taller than my six feet, with broad shoulders, a narrow waist and thick, powerful legs. Photos of a younger Clint show him with flaming red hair but it was grey by then and cropped close to his skull. His eyes were a piercing blue that made Paul Newman's look flat.

From the beginning he stood out in both his degree of fitness and his aptitude for combat. He sparred with an intensity that intimidated other students, who tried hard to avoid being matched against him. If he sparred against me, he'd compete as if I were trying to make him my jailhouse bride. After class he'd hang around and ask questions about stances, weight shifts, feints and blocks. We developed a good rapport, Clint and I. My father had been dead more than ten years, and I enjoyed having him to both learn from and teach.

One night after class, he asked me to join him for a beer and a bite, his treat, so we cleaned up and went to Allen's, a Riverdale institution with more than 300 beers and many a fine whisky on hand. We washed hamburgers and sweet potato fries down with Dragon's Breath ale, then ordered shots of the Macallan.

When the drinks arrived, he said, "You've never asked what I do for a living. This town, it's usually the first thing people want to know about you. That and how much you paid for your house."

"It's not how I define people, so it's not how I get to know them."

"I'm not going to ask what you do, because I already know," he said. "But can I ask what you did before?"

There was no short answer. I wasn't like my brother Daniel; my academic past had been checkered at best. I was smart enough to know I wasn't stupid, but I had never been able to harness it in school. I was in my own world most of the time, mourning my father, insulating myself in a haze of hash smoke. When I was fifteen, sixteen, I used to sneak over to the adjacent apartment building to smoke dope with Kenny Aber, and from his bedroom window we could identify my family's unit by the one constant: my brother's silhouette against his blinds as he studied into the night. "Is that a cardboard cut-out or what?" Kenny would ask. "I swear he never moves."

No one ever said that about me. I was always moving, just not getting anywhere.

I told Clint a little about the things I had done after finishing Grade 12, starting with my years in Banff, on the eastern slope of the Rockies, where I tended bar and skied in the winter and worked construction in the summer. I also gave him a brief précis of my time in Israel, focusing on the beginning, not the end. Like many other young Jews dismayed by the materialism of their parents' generation, I had gone there searching for something purer and more demanding of myself. A collective dream I could be part of. While I gave only the briefest details of my army time, I did tell Clint how I had begun to study martial arts there, in the form of Krav Maga, a self-defence system designed by an Israeli army man. Roni Galil was my mentor. When I returned to Toronto, I abandoned Krav Maga for karate, needing at the time to leave all things Israeli behind.

"So is that it for you?" Clint asked me. "Martial arts instructor for life?"

"Why do I feel like you're interviewing me for a job?" I said.

He said, "Maybe it's time you asked what I do."

The walls of Clint's office were covered with photos of him with high-ranking cops and city officials, certificates of courses he had taken since leaving the Toronto force and framed newspaper articles about Beacon Security success stories. His large beechwood desk was covered with neat rows of current files. A laptop on his desk was networked to a large flat-screen monitor. He pointed to the visitor's chair in his office. I sat.

"How's the arm?" he asked.

"It's fine."

"A hundred per cent?"

"Maybe ninety."

"Let's see." He moved a row of files aside, rolled up his right shirtsleeve and planted his elbow on his side of the desk.

"You're kidding."

"Nope," he said. "Show me what you got."

I rolled up my sleeve and placed my elbow opposite his. We gripped hands and locked eyes.

"Go," he said.

There was no use trying to pin him. Being left-handed put me at a disadvantage to begin with; nor was my right arm quite the ninety per cent I'd claimed. I forgot about trying to take him down and focused instead on resistance, hoping he would tire. But when we had been stalemated at ninety degrees for thirty seconds or so, my triceps started to quiver. He put more into it; so did I. Clint's face grew a shade redder but I ascribed that to his Celtic roots, not any challenge I posed.

Carol Dunn picked that moment to walk in with a sheaf of messages and a stack of documents that looked like invoices. "Sir, I have Ted Sellers on the line about the number of surveillance hours we billed him and—"

We parted hands as quickly as clandestine lovers, but not quickly enough.

"Sorry," she said. "I didn't know Jonah was with you." *Obviously wasting your time,* her body language added.

"It was my idea," Clint said.

"Mm-hmm."

"An evaluation of sorts."

"I'm sure."

"Tell Ted I'll look at the file and get back to him. Anything I need to sign?"

"Two contracts, the letters you asked me for and we have invoices to pay."

He patted the desk and she laid down her file.

"Do you need anything else?" Carol asked sweetly. When Clint said no, she paused to throw me a look that was all stainless steel, then went back to her guard post. He asked her to close the door behind her.

"Okay," he said. "We have things to talk about."

"Like what?"

"Your health, mental and physical. Your outlook. How ready you feel to get back to—"

"Ready!"

"Not so fast, champ. Getting shot leaves scars, and I don't just mean the ones we see. I spent thirty years on the force and not every cop who got shot made it back to active duty."

"I am ready to go back to work. Real work, not typing Franny's notes or covering his big ass."

He said, "Jonah, you're one of the best hires I ever made.

You're smart, you're creative and you have good instincts. You can handle yourself physically and you genuinely give a damn about people. You were doing great work here until the Ensign case. We all know how badly that ended, and you went through a breakup on top of it."

"It would have happened sooner or later. And dumping me while I was in recovery was the best thing Camilla could have done. It got me straight past denial into anger."

"Have you talked to anyone?"

"Professionally, you mean?"

"The firm pays for it. Marital problems, trauma counselling. Depression."

"The only thing depressing me is being stuck at my desk. I made a mistake and I haven't been given a chance to make good."

"There are some things you *can't* make good."

I looked down at my shoes. They weren't doing much of interest but I kept on looking at them.

"People make mistakes all the time," he said gently. "In most cases, my policy is 'No harm, no foul.' Learn from it and move on. But serious harm was done this time. The bad guys walked. You got hurt. And Colin MacAdam will never work again. Not as a cop anyway."

I took a deep breath to quell the jumpy feeling in my gut. "I went to see him, you know."

"When?"

"The May long weekend. I drove up to the rehab centre and spent the afternoon with him."

"How's he doing?"

"I guess the correct phrase is he's doing as well as expected. He handles the chair pretty well. His detachment held a fundraiser and he'll get a motorized one when he leaves rehab."

"Did you talk about what happened that day?"

"No," I said. "We stuck to the things guys talk about when they don't know each other well. The weather. The Blue Jays' chances in the East this year, which was a somewhat short conversation. Who'd win the finals in the NHL and NBA. Free-agent signings we'd like to see. All the big issues of the day."

"But nothing about getting shot."

"No."

"Do you think he blames you?" Clint asked.

I could picture MacAdam wheeling himself along a walkway in the garden of the Trenton Convalescent Hospital and Rehabilitation Centre, his pale freckled arms moving it at a clip that was hard for me to match.

"He never said. We had our awkward moments, but there was no animosity. I think what we went through bound us together more than it set us apart."

"What about you?"

"What about me?"

"How do *you* feel about what happened that day? Do you blame yourself?"

"Come on, Clint. I know I screwed up."

"That's not what I asked."

"You my shrink all of a sudden?"

"Answer the damn question."

"I feel like shit, okay?" My voice rose. "I cost MacAdam his livelihood and the use of his legs and for the rest of his life he's gonna have to piss and shit in a goddamn bag. Does that answer your question, Doc?"

"Yes it does," he said in a softer tone. "Yes it does."

It was quiet in the office for a moment, except for the sound of my breathing. Good thing the door was closed: if Carol Dunn heard me talking to the boss like that, she'd bust in swinging a fire axe.

Clint said, "I needed to know."

"Know what?"

"Whether you accept responsibility for what you did. What you learned from it. What you'll do next time lives are on the line."

"Believe me, Clint, I never intended to get shot and I definitely intend to avoid it in the future."

He smiled at me. "I might have something for you later in the week. Nothing major, just a fraud case to get you back in the saddle. In the meantime, give Franny whatever he needs on the nursing home."

"I'll be standing by when he gets in," I said. Which I hoped wouldn't be for another hour at least.

CHAPTER 11

There was nothing significant enough in the morning papers to warrant circulation so I was back in my car by a quarter to eight, hoping Jay Silver and family weren't early risers. Traffic heading north from the downtown core was light and by eight I was parked outside the Silvers' home on Richview Avenue, which ran parallel to Bathurst where it crossed the Glencedar Ravine. Richview wasn't quite the heart of Forest Hill, with its mansions and gated lots, but the homes were large, verging on stately, mostly in neo-traditional styles. The cars parked along the street or on front-yard pads were late-model SUVs and minivans or high-end sedans.

The street was coming to life at this hour: people in business dress heading to work; joggers out for a run before the real heat started; kids going to camps or day care now that school was out; gardeners using nose-hair scissors to trim the hedges just so.

I called the office of Mitchell Weintraub, a cousin on my mother's side who is a real estate agent. I could have called my mother for the same information, but with Jewish mothers, there are no short phone calls.

"Hey, cuz," I said when he answered. "I wasn't sure you'd be in this early."

"With the market this hot? I'd sleep here if Cheryl let me."

"How's she doing?"

"Really great. We can feel the baby moving inside her now."

"*Mazel tov*, Mitch."

"Thanks. I think the excitement of becoming a dad is finally starting to overtake the total panic."

"That's great."

"Listen," he said, "I'm sorry I didn't call when you were in the hospital. We had just had the first ultrasound and we were in baby-brain world."

"You can make it up to me now."

"How?"

"Check out a house on Richview Avenue and tell me when it last sold and for how much."

"Richview?" he said. "Business going that well?"

"It's not for me, dopey." I gave him Silver's address.

"Two minutes," he said.

The hold system on his phone kicked over to a radio station playing some soul diva swooping through "Have a Little Faith in Me," adding trills around every other note and draining the song of all the power of John Hiatt's original.

When Mitch came back on the line, he told me Jay and Laura Silver had bought the house just over a year ago for $1.15 million.

"Any record of them selling another property at the time?"

"Two more minutes."

Which meant two more minutes of faux-soul: Michael Bolton's version of "When a Man Loves a Woman." More like "When a Man Rips a Kidney."

"Okay," Mitch said. "They sold a semi on Hillsdale at the same time, listed it at $649,000, got multiple offers, sold it for $689,000."

And bought a new house worth almost half a million more. *Where did you get the money, Jay?*

"Okay, Mitch. Thanks. Give my love to Cheryl."

"We going to see you Sunday? You can give it to her yourself."

"What's Sunday?"

"Hello! The Rally for Israel at Earl Bales Park. You're not going?"

Just what I needed. A stick to whack the hornet's nest this morning's dream had already stirred up. "I don't know, Mitch. I have plans."

"What plans? It's two hours of your time. Come on, Jonah, Israel doesn't have a friend in the world these days."

"I'll try."

"In case you need incentive, Cheryl has a very nice friend coming with us—very nice. Just in case love for *ha-aretz* isn't enough."

Love for *ha-aretz*, for the land of Israel. It had never been enough.

Shortly after eight-fifteen, Jay Silver walked out of his house to the midnight-blue Lexus in his driveway. He wore a brown tweed jacket that looked too heavy for the heat. He put his briefcase on the rear left seat, then pulled off the jacket and hung it on a hook inside the door. His shirt showed damp spots under both arms. He put his hands on his hips and stood staring at his front door. He shifted his weight from one foot to the other, folded his arms across his chest, then put his hands back on his hips.

"Are you coming or what!" he called.

"Just a minute," a woman replied.

He paced back and forth, looking at the house, at his watch, at the house. "What's taking so long!"

Laura Silver appeared in the doorway. She was what my mother would have called a Jewish Beauty, right before passing me her phone number: dark curls tumbling past her shoulders, a heart-shaped face with wide green eyes and a full mouth, her body slender but not starved. She said. "I'm just putting sun-screen on Lucas and we'll be out."

"Putting on sunscreen takes this long?"

"You know how he squirms."

"Who's in charge?" Silver said. "You or him?"

"Don't start, Jay." She was keeping her voice level and even, non-threatening, like you would with a dog whose tem-per you weren't sure of.

"Who's starting? I'm just asking, are you in charge or is he? If you didn't indulge him so goddamn much—"

"Jay!" There was steel in her voice now. "What is it with you these days? We are *not* late. We are in good time. Please don't make a big deal out of it. I'd rather take one extra minute to get Lucas ready than upset him and have to deal with that for the rest of the day."

"You're spoiling him, can't you see that? You're letting him know that if he fusses about something he'll get his way."

"Like you're doing now?"

That shut him up. Had I not been schooled in the art of unobtrusive surveillance, I would have stood up through my sunroof and cheered. But Silver wasn't through. He walked briskly up the driveway and into the house. His voice was too muffled to make out words, but his tone was impossible to miss. A moment later, he came striding out, pulling Lucas by the hand. The boy seemed small for five. He wore a Blue Jays cap and a T-shirt with a drawing of Winnie the Pooh and Piglet, holding hands and walking into a sunset. "Best friends," it said. With his shorts and sandals, he looked for all the world like a little sabra, a native Israeli. Even at a distance I could see the boy's lip trembling as he tried to fight back tears. Silver yanked the rear door open and hoisted Lucas into a car seat, then buck-led him in as the boy's face crumpled.

Jay Silver looked like he was going to slam the car door shut on his own son, but then the anger seemed to go out of him and he just stood with his hand on the door frame, his head down. Laura Silver came down the walk with Lucas's backpack, glared at Silver until he moved aside, then leaned into the car to calm her son. When order had been restored, she looked at her husband, her anger fading to concern. She spoke too softly for me to hear but Silver nodded. She patted his big upper arm, closed the side door and walked around to the driver's side. He got in the passenger side. They backed out and, with me following, Laura took Bathurst north to Eglinton, then headed east on Eglinton. She handled herself reasonably well for a Torontonian. Didn't run a single red light, mount any curbs, crash through a transit shelter or give anyone the finger.

The Med-E-Mart was one of half a dozen big-box retail stores in a power centre on Laird south of Eglinton. There was also a supermarket, a sporting goods store, an office supplies emporium, a hardware giant and a government liquor store. Jay got out at the curb in front of his store and leaned in to say something to Lucas, then held out his palm for a low five. He didn't get one. After a long moment, he withdrew his hand and straightened with a look on his face that struggled between contrition and anger.

As his wife pulled away from the curb, I watched Jay Silver put on his heavy brown jacket, perhaps to cover the sweat stains on his shirt, and trudge into his place of business.

CHAPTER 12

Beacon's business-services database showed that Jay Silver was the sole owner of Med-E-Mart. No partners to want him dead. It didn't seem he had ever gone bankrupt or stiffed anyone. What could he have done to deserve the horrible death someone intended for him, this civilian in a clean white smock? Given someone the wrong medication? Diluted it, like the one who'd been caught in Kansas? Could someone have died because of a mistake he'd made?

"Hey, Jonah, quit breathing so goddamn loud." I turned to see Franny cruising in at ten to ten, looking worse than he had the day before. "I got twenty guys in my head with jackhammers going. You got something for a headache?"

Yesterday's shirt had a few new wrinkles and a brownish stain just under the collar. His pompadour was at less than its majestic best. I said, "Sorry. Ask Jenn when she gets back."

"My notes typed yet?"

"Been home yet?"

Franny winked. "What's home, eh, but the place I lay my head? *Chalice*, I'd rather be where I can lay LaReine. That woman could crush coal between her thighs and turn out diamonds."

"That would account for your headache."

"Very funny. Listen, do me a favour."

I handed Franny the transcript of his interview with Errol Boyko. "Another one, you mean."

"Don't worry, when you start getting cases again I'm gonna be there for you, you'll see."

"What now?"

He scribbled a note on a scratch pad, tore it off and handed it to me. "This is the lady from the ministry who recommended Meadowvale to Boyko."

"Darlene Tunney."

"Yeah, like the fighter. Ask her if they've been in trouble before."

"I thought you were looking into that part."

"I was going to, only I have a breakfast meeting."

"Looking like that?"

"It's with LaReine, she won't care."

"Franny, you just got in."

"Exactly my point. Who's had time for breakfast?"

Darlene Tunney answered her phone in a thin, nasal voice that carried that air of unfounded authority favoured by provincial bureaucrats.

"Ms. Tunney, this is Jonah Geller from Beacon Security. I'm looking for information about a nursing home in Ontario."

"Have you tried our website? It has everything you need to help you choose the right home for your loved one."

"I'm not looking to place anyone."

"No?"

"We've been asked to look into the death of a resident at a nursing home called Meadowvale."

"We?"

"Yes. Beacon Security."

"By whom?"

"That's confidential."

"So are our files, I'm afraid."

"But you're familiar with Meadowvale?"

"I know the place."

"Our client suspects a resident was mistreated in some way."

"How?"

"Possibly deprived of her medication."

"Intentionally?"

"Yes."

"That's an extraordinary allegation. Has he filed a complaint?"

"Not that I'm aware of."

"Well, I thank you for bringing this to my attention, Mister . . ."

"Geller. Jonah Geller."

"And the name of your firm again?"

"Beacon Security."

"Well, thank you again and I will forward a note immediately to our investigations unit."

"Can you copy me on that?"

"I'm sorry?"

"Copy me on the memo. For our files."

"I'm sorry, we don't share that type of communications externally."

"Can you at least tell me if any similar complaints about Meadowvale have been filed."

"No."

"No you can't tell me, or no there haven't been any?"

"No, I can't tell you about any complaint unless it has been formally resolved."

"So have any been resolved regarding Meadowvale in the past?"

"No. I was just looking at their file and I would have noted any infractions or substantiated complaints."

"Why?"

"Why would I have noted them?"

"Why were you looking at the file?"

"Mr. Geller, this is an office of the government of Ontario, not some shoeshine stand where detectives pick up tips. If your client is prepared to file a complaint, we will look into it."

"You said you were going to look into it anyway."

"And I will. Good after—"

"A woman died," I cut in.

"An elderly woman," Tunney said. "In a nursing home. It happens every day. And when it does, the people who placed them there feel guilty. They look for someone to blame. Between you and me, I think your client is wasting your time."

"It's his time. He paid for it."

"Well, it's my time too, and we're very busy here," she said. "Everyone's taking summer holidays and we're severely understaffed."

"Could you at least tell me why you recommend Meadowvale to clients?"

She sighed impatiently. "Meadowvale is one of many facilities I recommend, depending on the client's needs. Now either file a complaint or don't. Until then I have nothing else to say."

Her voice was replaced by a dialtone. For warmth and humanity, it had her beat by a mile.

CHAPTER 13

The mission statement of the Vista Mar Care Group was heavy on saccharine but vague on specifics. Vista Mar had thirteen facilities across Ontario, according to its Internet home page. There were photos of each, along with links to testimonials from satisfied families. Meadowvale was by far the largest of the Vista Mar homes and the most recently acquired.

Along the home page's top banner were two icons: "About Us" and "Contact Us." I tried "About Us" first. I found the bio of the president and chief executive officer, one Steven Stone, aged thirty-two. He had earned a B. Comm. at York University, then took his MBA at the Richard Ivey School of Business at the University of Western Ontario. He founded Vista Mar a year after graduating.

Two years younger than me and the CEO of a sprawling corporation, while my current claim to corporate fame was being sole proprietor of an ass in a sling.

Also listed was the company's medical director, Paul Bader. Since earning his medical degree at McMaster University in Hamilton, he had worked at a number of geriatric facilities. Quite a number, in fact, given the year he had completed his studies. He had moved around a lot before joining Vista Mar.

When I clicked "Contact Us," an electronic business card popped up on screen: Alice Stockwell, director of administration and corporate secretary. I dialled her number and listened to it ring several times, hoping it would go to voice mail so I could hang up and pass the baton back to Franny. It was time for him to pull his head out of his ass and do his own work so I could turn my attention back to Jay Silver.

But on the fourth ring a woman answered in a cool, professional tone. "Alice Stockwell here."

"Good morning," I said. "My name is Jonah Geller and I'm an investigator with Beacon Security. I'd like to ask you a few questions about a case we're working on."

"Just a moment." I was put on hold for about a minute before she returned. I wondered if she had had to ask permission to talk to me, or perhaps had set up a recording. She said, "All right, Mr. Geller. What's this about?"

"We were engaged by someone who placed a family member in a Vista Mar nursing home. The family member died and the client has concerns."

"What kind of concerns?"

"It would fall in the area of malpractice."

"Well, I hope your client can prove it in court."

"No one is talking about court—"

"Because Meadowvale has an outstanding record of patient care. There has never been a finding of negligence or malpractice as long as I've worked here."

"I never said it was at Meadowvale. I said one of your homes."

"Oh," she said. "Well, Meadowvale is the largest and our corporate offices are housed here so—"

"How long?"

"What?"

"You said 'as long as I've worked here.' How long?"

"Three years. But—"

"Did you know Steven before that?"

"Steven? What are you—"

"Stone. Steven Stone. He started it four years ago, you joined soon after . . ."

"Mr. Geller, your questions are all over the map and I—"

"Why is that a problem?"

"Will you stop, please! Just stop."

I stopped. I was dying to hear what she'd say when she collected herself.

"It's normal for people to feel that way," she said.

"What way?"

"Guilty. When their loved ones die. We see it every day. They need someone other than themselves to blame and they choose us. Between you and me, I think your client is wasting your time." Singing from the same hymnbook as Darlene Tunney, almost to the word. I wondered if they had rehearsed.

Stockwell told me to submit any further queries by email and hung up. I left Franny a note about my conversations with Tunney and Stockwell. I suggested he get one of Beacon's forensic auditors to dig into the corporate structure of Vista Mar Care Group. And that was that. Let him pick up the thread when he got back from breakfast, or trying to tickle LaReine's cervix with his eyelashes, or whatever he was doing besides dumping his work on me.

If Jay Silver had ever been in trouble professionally, there was no record of it on the Registered Pharmacists' Association of Ontario website. An archive of news releases going back to the year 2000 included an alarming number of recalls of drugs found to be unsafe or counterfeit. A handful dealt with Internet sales to the United States and actions taken against Ontario pharmacists who had violated new rules against them.

There was no mention anywhere of Jay Silver. If he had ever given someone the wrong drug, adulterated drugs, copped them for his own use or showed up to work naked, it hadn't been in the new millennium.

Elsewhere on the RPAO site was a staff directory. I scrolled through it and called the office of Winston Chan, director of investigations. "I'm not sure there's much I can tell you," he said. "Our confidentiality regulations are very strict." But he did agree to see me at ten the next morning.

The phone rang seconds after we ended the call and I wondered if Chan had changed his mind. But it was Franny. "Thanks for the message," he said. "Now I only got one more favour to ask."

"Aw, fuck, Franny."

"Last one, I swear. Go out to this Meadowvale place and look it over."

"You're kidding. It's way the hell and gone out Kingston Road."

"Well, I'm in the west end now so you're closer."

"I have things to do."

"What? The newspapers? You didn't clip them already? Clint said you were available to help."

He had me. I couldn't say anything about the Silvers or even hint I had something going on outside of work. "Helping you is one thing. Doing all your work is another."

"You think I wouldn't do it for you?"

"It's never come up."

"Listen, Jonah, you want me to tell Clint what a great help you been, or that you bitch every time I ask?"

I sighed into the phone and hung up. Sighing wouldn't change anything but it didn't hurt either. I was pondering the best route to Meadowvale when Jenn flopped at her desk and dropped her knapsack at her feet. She was glistening with sweat. Her cheeks were bright red and strands of her hair were pasted to her neck.

"Where've you been?" I asked.

"Outside," she panted. "Since five this morning. No A/C. Just heat. Humidity. Smog. Misery."

"What were you doing?"

"Kelly Pride called in sick."

"Again? She's threatening Franny's record."

"Girl gives pride a bad name. She usually saves it for Fridays," Jenn said. "But she's too smart to work outside on a day like this."

"Where does that leave you?" I teased.

She fixed me with a glare.

"Sorry. What's the assignment?"

"You know that place out by Cherry Beach where they tore down the old refinery?"

"Where the new sports complex is being built?"

"Yup. Construction doesn't start until August," she said. "Meanwhile, someone has been dumping barrels of PCBs and other toxic waste there. We're trying to catch whoever's doing it so the owner can sue their ass and recover the cost of cleaning it up. I've been hidden in a little blind in the brush that overlooks the site, baking, sneezing and donating blood to mosquitoes." She pulled a bottle of spring water from her knapsack and drained it. "At least I'm not doing the night shift," she said. "Bugs'll be ten times worse."

"Why don't you go down to the gym and grab a shower."

"Oh, I'm sorry, am I offending you?"

"Only if you still smell like that when I take you to lunch."

"Ooh, lunch," she crooned. "My other favourite L-word."

"Well, a fast lunch, anyway, and then a drive."

"Where to?"

"Deepest darkest Scarborough."

"What's there?"

"A place called Meadowvale."

"Sounds cool and shady."

"How shady is the question," I said.

CHAPTER 14

S o who are we?" Jenn asked.
"Allan and Linda Gold. Good friends of my parents. My
brother's godparents, actually."

We were stuck on Kingston Road in the eastern beaches,
as a kid with a scruffy blond chin beard tried to back a beer
truck into the narrow alley beside a pub.

"Okay, Al," Jenn said. "Whose parent are we committing?"

"It's not a mental institution," I said. "We're *placing* my
mother there."

"And where do we Golds hail from?"

"Same as in real life. I'm from Toronto, you're from
Feedbag, Ontario."

"That's Fordham, city boy. Will they want to know what
we do?"

"They'll want to know we have money."

"And do we?"

"A family fortune."

"I like it," Jenn said. "How much?"

"As long as we're fantasizing, let's go big. Five hundred
thousand, left to us by dear old dad when he passed." As
opposed to the zip, zilch and bupkes my dad had left us.

"How long have we been married?"

I looked at Jenn in her yellow floral-print sundress that showed her tanned arms and legs to enormous advantage.

"Three years," I suggested. "Three rapturous sex-crazed years."

"In your dreams."

Indeed.

"So what are we looking for?"

I filled her in on what I had learned so far. "Let's see if they pressure us to accept Bader as Mom's doctor. And where they keep their records."

Ten minutes later, we parked in front of a ranch-style building of fieldstone and stucco with large windows and well-kept grounds. There was neither a meadow nor a vale in sight, but as nursing homes went, it was less bleak than I had imagined. It could have been a golf course clubhouse.

"Linda, darling?"

"Yes, Al?"

"Just to avoid any slips, let's not use names in there."

"Terms of endearment only?"

"Yup. Call me honey, sweetheart, dear. God of Thunder."

"Dickhead okay?"

"Regrettably, I've been called that more than God of Thunder in my time."

We crossed the parking lot toward the main entrance where a man who had just exited was lighting a cigarette. This guy was short but solidly built, with a round face a grandmother would want to pinch. His cigarette had the distinctive smell of American tobacco.

Jenn said, "Oh, dickhead dear?"

"Yes, honeypants?"

"The door?"

I held it open for her and we walked into the lobby. It was airy and inviting, with a terrazzo floor and fieldstone walls and light pouring in through floor-to-ceiling windows on three sides. A fountain burbled water into a small pool on the left side; on the right was a security desk where a burly man in a navy blazer watched a bank of monitors showing closed-circuit feeds. His name tag identified him as John. I signed us in as Mr. & Mrs. Allan Gold. The cameras, from what I could see, covered all entrances to the building, as well as a number of corridors and common areas.

When we asked John about a tour of the facility, he pointed at a slim, handsome woman of fifty or so across the lobby. She wore a cream silk jacket and skirt, and her blonde hair was pulled back into a chignon. "Ms. Stockwell is the administrator here. She'll just be a moment."

Alice Stockwell was engaged in a serious conversation with an earnest young man in a gorgeously tailored lightweight grey suit. I wondered if he was here to place a parent, or already had one in residence. Either way, he seemed displeased, lecturing Stockwell urgently through tight lips. Maybe he was another dissatisfied client like Errol Boyko, who feared something was amiss with his parent's care. But Stockwell must have allayed his concerns because they finally shook hands and he headed out the glass doors.

She came clicking over the tile floor toward us, hand extended, and we introduced ourselves without any flubs.

"Did you have an appointment, Mr. Gold?"

I shook my head apologetically. "Ms. Tunney did say we should call ahead but I've had so much on my mind since Mom's stroke . . ."

"Darlene Tunney referred you?"

"Oh, yes."

"She had great things to say," Jenn added. "You should be proud."

"Then I don't see any problem," Stockwell said, all sympathy but for the one quick look she flashed Jenn: taller,

younger, blonder than she. Like one Siamese fighting fish finding another in the same aquarium.

"Before I show you the facility, tell me about your mother.
You mentioned a stroke. Would you say the effects are mainly
physical or cognitive as well?"

I had decided to make "Mom" sound as incapacitated, and
therefore vulnerable, as possible. "Both."

"Oh, I am sorry," Stockwell said.

"She can't remember things from one minute to the
next," I said with a downcast look. "I'm afraid if she's left alone
she'll turn on the stove and forget about it, or take her medication more than once—or not at all." Jenn put her hand on my
shoulder and patted it for support.

"And she's on so many medications," I added. "Even before
the stroke she was dealing with diabetes and high blood pressure.
I take it the staff here is well trained in dispensing medication?"

She smiled coolly. "As good as you'd find in any hospital."

Given the state of health care in Ontario these days that was
hardly a ringing endorsement, but I smiled back as if reassured.

"Let's start our tour at the front desk, with our state-of-
the-art security system," Stockwell said. Big John took his cue
and stared intently at his bank of monitors. "We watch every
exit and entrance around the clock to ensure no one wanders.
That's very important for clients like your mother, Mr. Gold. If
they leave the home—which does happen at less vigilant
facilities—they die of exposure, hypothermia, dehydration.
They get hit by cars. It's terrible. And it simply will not happen
at Meadowvale, will it, John?"

"Not on my watch, ma'am."

The script was corny but I gave them points for tight
execution.

Stockwell led us across the lobby toward three glass doors,
our steps echoing off the stone walls. "Through the door on
the left is a locked ward where clients with cognitive deficits

reside. In addition to the cameras, all the doors in that wing are alarmed for extra security. Straight ahead through the middle door are the common areas: the dining room, day room, games room, clinic, dispensary and so on."

"Dispensary?" I asked.

"An on-site pharmacy where medications are kept and distributed. And on the right is where people who are still functioning and ambulatory reside. They don't need the same level of care and monitoring as someone like your mother would. Why don't we visit the common areas first," Stockwell suggested. "Lunch is over but you can see the sort of activities and interaction that take place on a typical day."

We went through the door into a hallway that led to a large sunny room whose windows faced out onto the grounds. There were forty or fifty residents in the room, along with a dozen or so attendants, all black or Filipina. "There is at least one registered nurse on duty at all times," Stockwell said, "along with nurse's aides and caregivers."

About half of the residents in the room were involved in some kind of activity: playing cards, backgammon, chess or checkers, chatting in groups or watching television in a semicircle of wheelchairs and club chairs. The others were lost in their own worlds: nodding off, staring into space, moving wet lips silently as if in prayer, picking invisible things off their skin and clothes, their frail bodies bent at near impossible angles in wheelchairs and hospital beds.

"If you look at the schedule on the wall there, you'll see we have interesting and uplifting activities virtually every day," Stockwell went on. "This afternoon, for example, we have a singalong with the choir director from a local church and you wouldn't believe how she gets them singing. We have art classes, movies, bingo. Always something going on."

I looked at one birdlike old girl twisted in a wheelchair. Her fine white hair floated up off her mottled scalp and was held by static to the headrest of her wheelchair. Her cloudy gaze wasn't focused on anything I could see.

Not everyone had something going on.

Stockwell moved us through the dining room, where she sang the praises of the staff dietitian and low-sodium, low-everything-else menu, then took us along a hallway that led to the residential wards.

"What's through there?" I asked as we passed a pebbled glass door marked Private.

"The staff offices and lounge."

Stockwell used a pass card to open the door to the locked ward. Most of the residents were in the dining room or day room, so she let us peer into rooms whose doors were open. There were both private and semi-private rooms, all with washrooms equipped with safety bars, non-slip surfaces and cords that could be yanked to summon help. Each room had different furniture, some of it quite old.

"Residents can bring their own furniture if it fits," Stockwell explained. "They're often comforted by familiar things. It can be the difference between feeling like they're in an institution or at home."

"That's good to know," I said. "Mom is very attached to her things."

"As Ms. Tunney probably explained, the government sets the basic accommodation rate on July 1 of every year," Stockwell said. "That's this coming Saturday, of course, and the rates will undoubtedly be going up, but since you came in today I'll guarantee you this year's rates even if you sign next week."

"That's very kind."

"The basic rate would put your mother into a semi-private room. Many families prefer to upgrade their parents to private—it's more restful that way. There is of course a premium for that but we can go over the fee schedule at the end of your visit."

"That shouldn't be a problem. Dad left Mom well cared for when he passed." Our financial status thus assured, I cut closer to the chase. "Would Mom's physician have privileges here?"

"Yes, if need be. But we are fortunate to have an extremely dedicated and capable medical director, Dr. Paul Bader, who works out of this very facility. Very well known in his field. Most families find it more convenient to have him supervise their loved one's care because he can keep better track of their condition and respond more quickly to any emergency."

There it was. The first push toward Bader.

"How long has he been with you?" I asked Stockwell.

"About two years."

"He moves around a lot."

"I'm sorry?" Her gaze sharpened a little.

"I looked at his biography on your website and he seems to have worked in a lot of different places. Should we be concerned?"

"On the contrary. I think it's a credit to his abilities that so many institutions have wanted him on staff," she said.

"Is he here today? Can we meet him?"

"I'll have to check his office."

"Please do."

Stockwell looked us both over, worked up a passable smile and walked to a nursing station at the far end of the corridor to make the call.

"Whatever they're up to, she's in on it," Jenn said.

"Right up to her chignon. Listen, when we meet Bader, let's see if we can find where they keep the medication records. If the opportunity arises, say you need the washroom and scope it out."

"Looking for what?"

"How much they keep on hand, for one thing. And how secure it is."

"Let's see if Blondie lets me off the leash."

Heels clicked loudly as Alice Stockwell came back. "You're in luck. Dr. Bader is in his office. He'll see you now."

We exited the ward and headed back to the common area, where Stockwell carded us through the door that led to the staff offices. Bader stood waiting outside his office: short and pear-shaped, with brown eyes, a full beard and curly brown hair. The effect was that of a warm and fuzzy bear, the kind who might break out in a Russian circus dance.

Introductions were made and we were invited to sit opposite Bader's cluttered desk, while Stockwell stood in back of us like a proctor overseeing an exam. Cabinets and shelves on the wall behind Bader were stacked with industry samples of medications.

"Alice tells me you have concerns about medical care at our facilities."

"Not concerns as much as questions," I said. "There are so many things we're working through right now. Mom's legal affairs, her investments, closing up her apartment . . . we're just a little overwhelmed." Jenn put her reassuring hand on my shoulder again. It was something I could get used to.

"Rest assured we'll do everything we can to make this part easier," the fuzzy doctor said. He was so sincere I wanted to climb over his desk for a hug. "Our standards of care meet or exceed those laid out by the province. We have policies in place to prevent patients from going missing, from experiencing extreme hot or cold temperatures, from choking, from being abused by other patients or staff. We train all staff in CPR and first aid, including the security guards. We have nurses available around the clock and I am on call when not actually on the premises."

"That's good to know."

"What about medications?" Jenn asked. "My mother-in-law takes quite a few and she can't keep track anymore."

"Once again, everything is done according to strict government guidelines. And of course we're a proud member in good standing of the Residential Care Association." Bader showed us a four-page form with a lot of shaded boxes and multiple-choice questions. "We do a complete assessment of my own design when the client is admitted and I personally sign any orders for medications."

"What if Mom's doctor wants to review what she's taking, make sure nothing is contraindicated? Are there records you can fax him? Or that he can come and see?"

Bader looked past me—at Stockwell, I assumed—then established eye contact again. "Absolutely. The records are available if we need them."

"Here on site?"

"Yes. Though as Alice may have mentioned, I'd be happy to serve as your mother's physician. If that made things easier for you."

"But you don't know Mom's history like her doctor does."

"It's her current reality that matters, not her history. I would see her virtually every day. I could monitor her condition and adjust her medications with greater subtlety and precision than someone who sees her twice a year."

"I guess that makes sense." I looked at Jenn. "Doesn't it, hon?"

"It does. It really does."

"Though I'd reserve the right to keep Mom's doctor involved if the change seemed overwhelming. If she needed . . . I don't know, continuity?"

"I suppose so."

"Terrific," I said. "I feel much better."

Jenn swivelled in her chair to face Alice Stockwell. "Is there a bathroom nearby?"

Stockwell pointed to a door down the hall. "It's a staff room so I'll have to swipe you in."

"Thank you," Jenn said, and the two of them left.

"About your mother's stroke," Dr. Bader said, his pen poised over the assessment form. "Was it diagnosed as ischemic or hemorrhagic?"

A little warning bell tinkled in the back of my mind. I hadn't done a lick of research on strokes, which I normally would have done in prepping a story. But it wasn't my case and Franny had given me no time. "You know," I said, "we don't have to do this part now. We've taken enough of your time. Linda and I should get back downtown. I'll get the details from her physician and call you."

"Why don't you give me his number. I can call him directly."

"I don't have it on me."

Bader's phone burred softly. He picked it up and spun around in his studded leather chair. He listened briefly, spoke even more briefly and hung up. He pushed off with his feet and spun slowly back to me. "Where was your mother admitted after her stroke?"

"Beth Israel."

"What day, please?"

He had me and he knew it. "It was night."

"All right then. What night?"

"It's all a blur. Listen, thanks again," I said. "I'm just going to wait for Linda in the hall."

When I got to the doorway, it was filled by Big John from the front desk. He clamped his hand hard around my left arm. I looked down the hall where Jenn had gone and saw no one.

"Sir?" John said. "Why don't you come with me back to the lobby."

"Where's my wife?"

"Ms. Stockwell will bring her along when she's done in the little girls' room."

Getting tossed out of the place didn't worry me as long as they tossed Jenn too, so I went along. But as we entered the lobby area, I saw two men getting out of an SUV outside the main entrance. One was the round-faced melonhead who'd been smoking outside when we arrived. The other was a tall concave guy in a mournful black suit. The Melonhead walked briskly toward the main entrance while the Suit took a paved walkway toward the rear. This did not bode well for me or Jenn. Time to loosen Big John's grip. I kicked back with my heel and caught him sharply on the knee. He gasped and let go of my arm. I drove my elbow back into his nose and felt cartilage give. I turned, grabbed his hair, pulled his head down and hit him again in the same spot with my knee. He dropped to the floor, moaning, gurgling and spitting blood.

The Melonhead was steps from the front door. I ran behind John's desk and scanned the monitors. Most showed empty entrances and exit doors. The day room. The dining room. Corridors in the residential area. The corridor outside Bader's office. A rear exit. There! Alice Stockwell was trying to push Jenn out the door from the inside; the Suit was trying to pull her out. Jenn was braced in the doorway, kicking any part of him that came close.

I grabbed the swipe card off John's belt as the Melonhead strode into the lobby. His eyes took in John's legs lying across the floor. I bolted out from behind the console and swiped myself back into the hall that led to Bader' office, pulling it shut behind me. I ran down the hall, hoping I was going the right way, looking left and right for a weapon of some kind. Around a corner I saw a woman in a pale blue uniform loading metal bedpans from a closet onto a wheeled cart. I grabbed one of the bedpans as I ran past her.

Jonah Geller: armed and ridiculous.

As I neared the end of the corridor, I could hear shoes scuffing against a tile floor. I peered around the corner to my left. Stockwell and the Suit had made no progress getting Jenn outside. The three of them were grappling in the hall.

Stockwell's chignon was coming apart and the Suit had a fresh welt on the bridge of his nose. When the Suit heard me coming, he squared himself to face me and reached into his jacket. Stockwell, suddenly without her tag-team partner, bolted out the open door onto the lawn with Jenn in hot pursuit. I whipped the bedpan at the Suit like a discus as he yanked a small automatic from his waistband. It caught him flush on the crown, where any cut bleeds like an oil find. Blood squirted straight up in the air and down into his eyes. I moved in and twisted the pistol out of his hand, then drove my knee into his solar plexus. He gasped and fell over in a fetal position. I ejected the magazine and pocketed it, ejected the round that was in the chamber and pocketed that too, wiped the pistol with my shirttail and dropped it in a wastebasket across the hall.

Out on the lawn was a sight to see. Jenn had Stockwell face down on the ground, rubbing her face in the sod. The cream silk suit was taking on a grassy hue. Stockwell was trying to push herself up off the ground but I didn't like her chances, not against my Estonian wonder girl.

No matter how much dirt Stockwell deserved to eat, it was time to go. The Suit and Big John were out of it but the Melonhead was still on the grounds somewhere. I pulled Jenn off Stockwell and we ran to the parking lot. We got into the car and peeled out just as the Melonhead came barrelling out of a side entrance, setting off an insistent alarm. I couldn't tell whether there was a gun in his hand but I assumed there was and shouted to Jenn to keep her head down.

We got out of there without a single shot being fired.

CHAPTER 15

A fter dropping Jenn at the office, I drove home to shower and change out of my bloody clothes. Then I headed out to the Med-E-Mart to see Jay Silver in his work habitat. I took Broadview north until it became O'Connor, then crossed the Don Valley on the Leaside Bridge. I had the windows down and Uncle Tupelo blasting through its live version of "We've Been Had" when my cellphone rang. I looked at the caller ID, lowered the sound, raised the windows and mustered my chipperest voice. "Hi, Ma."

"Everything okay, dear?"

"Sure. Why?"

"I haven't heard from you in a while."

"We spoke last week."

"Are we down to once a week now?"

"Come on, Ma. The last three times I called, you weren't home." A call to a Jewish mother must count whether she is there to answer or not. Elsewhere madness lies.

"When were these alleged calls?" she asked. "Give me days and times, mister. Let's see how your story stands up."

"Tuesday suppertime. Friday around seven. Sunday afternoon."

"Tuesday, I was at the museum," she said. "They had a

members-only preview of the new Chinese ceramics exhibit. It hasn't even gone to New York yet—we got it first. Friday was Shabbas dinner with the Golds. It's one meal I hate to eat alone, and both you and Daniel were busy. Maybe this week you'll come to me."

"We'll see."

"Which means you won't. And Sunday . . . Sunday I had a board meeting at *shul*," she said. "Did I tell you I was re-elected president of the sisterhood?"

"Of course you did. I congratulated you effusively, as I recall."

"All right," she said. "So your story checks out. Doesn't mean you can't call more often but at least you tried. So how are you, dear? How's your arm?"

"It's fine, Ma. A hundred per cent."

"I'm so glad."

"You don't sound glad."

"Well, it's just that if it's healed, you'll be going back out in the field, no?"

"Yes."

"And the last time you were in this field of yours, you got shot."

"Ma . . ."

"I saw you in that hospital bed, Jonah, and my heart was in pieces. It took so long for Daddy and me to conceive Daniel, we never thought we'd have another baby. When you came along, it was like a miracle. That's why we made your middle name Nathaniel."

Gift from God, it meant. Some gift. She was probably checking the returns policy as we spoke.

"All the women at the office, at *shul*, at the golf club, at openings, their sons either treat gunshot wounds or at least defend the ones who do the shooting."

"Can we not veer into career advice?"

"Who's veering? But you were such a clever child, every bit as smart as your brother, and from where I sit you're still struggling."

"So change seats. Pretend we're in a restaurant and they sat you near the kitchen."

"You probably don't remember but we had you tested in Grade 3 and your IQ was exceptional."

I didn't remember the test but had no trouble recalling the thousands of times she had brought it up since.

"Your teachers always said, 'Jonah is so bright, he just doesn't apply himself.'"

"Well, I'm applying myself now."

"To what? Really, dear, to what?"

"I like what I'm doing and I'm making a living."

"Darling, a one-bedroom apartment and a used car is not a living. You have to admit, I never pushed you to choose a traditional profession. I gave you plenty of latitude, especially after Daddy died. True?"

"True."

"I told you if you wanted to try the arts or something like that I would back you as long as . . . ?"

"As long as I worked my butt off. Which I am doing, by the way."

"I just want you to be happy, Jonah. Happy and safe."

"Don't worry. It's a very simple case."

"No gangsters?"

"No gangsters." Not that I was going to tell her about.

"So are we on for Shabbas?"

Hmm. Shabbas. Friday night. What would I be doing that night? Throwing myself in front of a bullet meant for Lucas Silver?

"Can I let you know?"

"Yes. I'll see if Daniel is free. And it wouldn't hurt you to call him either. When's the last time you spoke?"

"Not that long ago." Or not long enough, depending on where you sat.

"Call me when you get home so I know you're safe."

"Just today or every day?"

"Some boys call their mothers every day."

"There's a name for them."

"Smartass," she said.

"No, that's not it."

I thought we were done but she said, "One more thing."

What? A Jewish Beauty's phone number?

"Are you coming to the Rally for Israel?"

First Mitchell, now my mother.

"You really should make the effort. Connect with the community a little. See some old friends. Things are terrible in Israel, today, and not so good for Jews in plenty of other places. We have to show solidarity."

"I did my part for Israel, Ma."

"That was a long time ago, dear."

Not long enough.

I find it funny sometimes that our parents named us Daniel and Jonah, two men who are so sorely tested in the Old Testament. Maybe they were preparing us in a way for the trials that attend life as a Jew in a non-Jewish world. When we were kids, Daniel once told me, "If Mom and Dad had had another son, they would have named him Job."

The Bible says Jonah was ordered by God to go to Nineveh and tell the sinners there to repent or face His destruction. Because the people of Nineveh were enemies of the Hebrews, Jonah didn't see why they should be saved. Instead of heeding God's word, he boarded a ship bound in the opposite direction. Displeased by Jonah's disobedience, God whipped up a deadly storm that would not abate until the terrified crew cast Jonah into the sea. Jonah was swallowed by a monstrous whale and spent three days in its belly before he was spat back onto land with another chance to complete his mission. In the end Jonah learns that everyone—enemy or not—is entitled to salvation.

All the Bible says about Jonah's background prior to his contact with God is that he was "the son of Amittai." That's it. Four words. Nothing about his mother, siblings, what he did before God's call or whether he was any good at it.

The Book of Daniel, on the other hand, devotes six full chapters to his many gifts: how prodigiously learned and skilled he is in the arts and sciences, how unblemished in beauty and character. Living in forced exile, Daniel advises Babylonian kings with discretion and wisdom, masterfully interpreting their visions and dreams. Promoted above princes and satraps, he is cast into the lions' den, ostensibly for refusing to abandon his God, but in reality because he has stirred such jealousy among his rivals.

Six fucking chapters.

He gets more buildup than he could possibly live up to, then not only lives up to it but exceeds it by a mile. The more I think about it, the more I root for the lions.

So there you have us.

Daniel: gifted to a fault, rising effortlessly to the pinnacle of his profession and beyond.

Jonah: obscure, obstinate, punished for not doing what was expected of him.

My mother wants us to be closer. "You only have one brother," she tells me once a month. "Blood is thicker than water."

But we could hardly be more different. Daniel is always sure of himself: intelligent, yes, but imperious too. If Daniel ever made a mistake in his life, you wouldn't hear it from him. I knew only too well that I was capable of mistakes.

Just ask Colin MacAdam.

CHAPTER 16

There were no parking spots to be had in front of the Med-E-Mart, so I drove around back to the overflow lot and found a spot facing the loading dock behind Silver's store. I got my Zeiss field glasses out of the glove compartment. The loading dock was a deep concrete alcove with a steel door that could be rolled down after hours. The other three walls were cinder block. There were shipping tables along two of them, as well as stacks of empty wooden pallets and bales of corrugated cartons. Set into the back wall were double doors that led into the rear of the store.

An unmarked cube van was backed up against the dock with its rear doors open. One man was walking out of the van, wheeling an empty hand truck in front of him. A second, much bigger man was walking in, his hand truck piled high with four cartons, one hand holding the top case steady. I wondered why a pharmacy would be making deliveries by the case instead of receiving them. I put the field glasses on the men doing the loading. One was wiry, dark-haired, in his mid-forties, wearing a light grey suit. Not your average driver or shipping clerk. The other was big enough to show up on a topographical map, sweating through a powder-blue track suit. He looked six and a half feet tall and weighed some three hundred pounds, none of it soft, with a shaved head that grew straight out of his shoulders. He had gold hoops through both earlobes. Put him in a vest and pantaloons and he could pass for a guard outside an Arabian palace. The one where they kept the virgins.

Just as the two men had finished loading, the shipping doors swung outward and Jay Silver came out looking even more worried than he had this morning. He went up to the wiry man in the suit and spoke to him urgently, gesturing at the contents of the truck. The wiry man cut him off within seconds, sticking his index finger in Silver's face and giving him a talking-to. I couldn't hear a word but I could tell it was no pep talk. Jay Silver was supposedly sole owner of the company. No partners. But here he was on his own property and this runt was treating him like a fat kid in a schoolyard.

When he was done talking, the runt shoved Jay Silver toward the doors and followed him into the store. The big man waddled behind them. I slipped out of the Camry and moved quickly to the cube van. There were no markings on it; nothing visible through the driver's window to indicate who owned it or where it might be going. I slipped up a narrow side staircase onto the loading dock and looked in the rear of the truck, where I saw stacks with cartons labelled with the names of major pharmaceutical companies. Pfizer, Searle, Eli Lilly, Meissner-Hoffman, Merck Frosst.

The doors behind me banged open. I turned to see the runt and the big man.

"Can I ask what you're doing?" said the runt.

I said, "Sure."

We waited a beat until he realized I wasn't going to say anything more. I could tell I found it funnier than he did.

"I couldn't find parking in front," I finally admitted. "So I parked back here and I was just trying to find a way into the store."

"Why?" the runt asked. "You need painkillers?"

"No."

"Or maybe you do but you don't know it yet." He held out his hand. "Let's see ID."

"You going to show me yours?"

"Come on, smart guy. Hand it over or Claudio will extract it."

The big man smiled. His mouth was huge, made for swallowing things whole, but his teeth were small and unevenly spaced. His lower lip stuck out much farther than the upper. It gave his face an oddly sensual look, though I couldn't picture myself telling him that.

I made no move to present ID, so the runt gave Claudio the nod and he came toward me, moving like truly big men do, his arms swinging out away from his sides. He looked like he could pull a redwood out of the ground and pick his teeth with it. He was between me and the stairs that led down off the loading dock, and the truck was parked too close to the other side to allow passage. My best option was to fend him off and get into the store, where a crowd of witnesses might deter an all-out assault.

I feinted to my right, which got Claudio going that way, then crossed him up with a quick shift left. The lithe Steve Nash against the lumbering Shaq. I reached the double doors easily—just as Jay Silver pushed them open from inside. The left-hand door slammed my shoulder and knocked me down. Claudio took the opportunity to grab my bicep with a hand that closed entirely around it.

"What's going on?" Jay Silver asked.

"Never mind," the runt told him. "Get back inside."

"Who is he?" Jay asked.

"I said, never mind."

I decided a little confusion was in order. I held out my free hand toward him like we were old friends. "Jay Silver!" I said. "How the hell are you?"

"Huh?" He stared at me like he was wondering where we had met.

"You know him?" the runt asked Silver.

Silver didn't respond. Only his eyes moved, narrowing as if he were willing himself to understand how I fit into the mess he was in. The runt poked him in the chest. "I asked, do you know this guy?"

Jay Silver shrugged. "No."

"Then beat it."

"What are you going to do to him?"

"I told you, get inside. Mind your store. Make sure no one steals a lipstick."

Silver straightened himself out of his natural slouch. He was actually a pretty big man: nowhere near Claudio's size but towering over the runt and outweighing him by a good sixty pounds. "Now listen, Frank—"

"Shut up!"

Frank. Frank who?

"Don't make things worse than they already are."

"Shut the fuck up!" Frank hissed. "Get your fat ass inside before I kick it."

"This is my store," Silver said firmly. "My place of business. I don't care what's happened till —"

Frank slapped him hard across the face, then backhanded him harder the other way. Silver looked stunned, both cheeks glaring red. For a moment I thought he might go after him. Claudio must have thought so too because he let go of me and moved in on Silver but Frank motioned to him to stay back.

"Don't ever talk back to me," Frank said. "And don't ever, ever speak my name." He stuck his finger in Silver's face as he had before. "You got that, bitch?"

Silver swallowed hard like a child trying not to cry in front of his friends.

"Now get out of here and let the men take care of business."

Silver gave me a look that was shameful and apologetic at once. Frank snorted impatiently and grabbed Silver by the upper arm. "Fuck this guy up and get rid of him," he told Claudio, then marched Silver through the shipping doors into the Med-E-Mart.

I scanned the area around us, looking for room to move, identifying obstacles: two concrete pillars, the stacked pallets and baled cartons. Claudio had the obvious advantage in strength—and in scaring the living shit out of his opponent— but guys his size rarely have speed or stamina. If he wasn't a trained fighter, chances are he'd be gassed after thirty to sixty seconds of combat. It was time to get my well-trained ass moving. Get this big schlub wilting in the heat.

I started dancing, leading him to my left, then back to the right. He put his hands up in a boxer's stance and moved his feet pretty well for a beast his size. Maybe he had some training after all.

I snapped a few kicks at his knees, keeping my centre low, ready to lunge back if I had to. I made him move, kept him honest with the attacks I'd practised that morning. *Sanchin*, but with speed, torque and bad intent. Claudio wasn't used to being attacked and he definitely wasn't built for speed. Inside of a minute, sweat was pouring down his cheeks, his breath was coming hard, and his arms were slowing as they blocked my attacks.

"Stand still and take it," he said, almost panting. "You make me work, I'll fuck you up worse."

"No you won't," I said, a little more cocky than I actually felt. "You might be big, *Clod*, but size is all you got." Rather than continue the discussion, he threw a right my way. I blocked it, at considerable expense to my forearm, and kicked his left knee hard, then snapped his head back twice with short punches. He backed off, breathing hard, until he was leaning against one of the dock's cinder-block walls.

"Give it up," I said. "It's too hot for this."

He shook his big head, then reached over and picked up a box cutter off the floor. He thumbed the blade out and held it out in front of him. I grabbed a roll of packing tape off a shipping table behind me and flipped it in a high, slow arc from my right hand to my left, like a juggler. When I flipped it back, his eyes followed it. I flipped it a third time, back to my left, which few people expect to be your throwing hand. As soon as I caught it, I winged it at him from the hip like I was skipping a stone. It was still rising when it hit him in the mouth, drawing blood, a good deal of which he spat out on the dock. I moved in on him and faked a move to my right. When the box cutter moved that way, I kicked his arm with the arch of my foot and sent the box cutter skittering along the floor. Left with nothing but his three-hundred-plus pounds and too much testosterone, he charged at me with arms flailing. I waited until he was almost on me, then stepped quickly out of his way and kicked him in the small of the back, sending him crashing into a pile of empty pallets. When he turned to face me again, his eyes were hooded and there was more blood in his mouth to spit.

"I'm going to have to end this now," I told Claudio. "I'm way too hot."

"You haven't hurt me," he panted.

"I haven't tried."

No matter how big a man is, he can't strengthen his eyelids. Claudio could be three hundred pounds of muscle; his eyelid was one fold of skin like everyone else's. So I faked another kick at his knees and when he dropped his hands I jabbed two stiff fingers into his right eye. He yelped and clutched it with both hands, blinking furiously as sweat ran into the eye. I punched him hard and fast in the windpipe—another area you can't develop. He gasped and tried to draw in breath like a man about to blow up a balloon.

I should have stopped there but I didn't. I don't like guys who hurt other guys for profit. I kicked him hard in the ribs with the ball of my left foot, and heard a cracking sound. So pleasing was it, I pivoted and kicked him in the same place on the other side. He fell to his knees, not knowing which part of himself to hold first.

I leaned down, twisted one of his big meaty ears and said into it, "Don't threaten to fuck people up. It's anti-social."

Frank banged out through the shipping doors just then. I don't think the tableau in front of him was quite what he expected to see: Claudio in tears and me looking distinctly unfucked up.

"I think he needs eye drops," I said.

Frank turned quickly back into the store without a word. Maybe the eye drops were on sale.

CHAPTER 17

D anforth Avenue, known simply as the Danforth, is
Riverdale's main drag, a continuation of Bloor Street
that begins on the east side of the Don Valley. Thirty
years ago, Riverdale was a relatively quiet neighbourhood centred on Greektown and its many inexpensive restaurants,
cheese shops and grocers and the odd dingy bar like the Black
Swan. Then people started getting crowded out of downtown
neighbourhoods like the Annex by high rents and discovered
Riverdale homes were similar in style and size, the streets just
as leafy, and it was only three subway stops from the geographic
centre of town at Yonge and Bloor. Today rents and mortgages
in Riverdale are as high as in the Annex and other central
neighbourhoods. Small family restaurants have been replaced
by huge, high-end eateries that cost a million or more to reno-
vate, not including the cost of greasing the right city councillor.

The Danforth would normally have been jammed at this
time, people strolling everywhere, stopping to talk to friends
seated at crowded restaurant patios. This evening's withering
heat had most people dining inside, leaving the patios exclu-
sively to diehard smokers. A few young men were cruising in
muscle cars, but there was precious little to whistle at on the
sidewalks, unless you were drawn to the sunburned panhandler

outside the liquor store or the two Native men dozing on the steps of the Baptist church. The only busy place was the ice cream shop in Carrot Common, where families gathered on benches in a shaded courtyard, licking cones and ducking wasps drawn by the smell of sweets.

A few doors down from the ice cream place was my favourite restaurant, Silk Thai, owned by a middle-aged couple named Constance and Peter. I'd been a regular there since I started teaching at the dojo. The place had half a dozen tables and did a thriving takeout business too. Constance greeted me warmly from behind the counter. "Jonah! Haven't seen you in so long a time."

It hadn't seemed long to me, but the truth was I hadn't been going out much since getting shot. I asked, "What's my best bet tonight?"

"You ask Peter, he tell you satay chicken with peanut. You ask me, I tell you basil beef."

"Basil beef it is, with house special noodles."

"To stay? Table for you ready five minutes. Air conditioning is good, eh? Brand new. Peter get last one at Canadian Tire."

The air conditioning was fine but all the tables were filled with couples and families. If I was going to eat alone, it might as well be at home.

I had just finished supper when someone knocked on my door. I had the feeling it might be Dante Ryan but it was Ed Johnston, a retired teacher who lived on my floor. Ed was the unofficial mayor of the building, always trying to organize the residents against the property managers on matters related to rent, parking, repairs and recycling. He was slightly built, with a grey ponytail trailing out of a fishing cap. A large camera bag was slung over his shoulder and a tripod rested against the wall next to my door.

"Do me a favour?" he said.

"Sure, Ed."

"I want to get this sunset on film and I was wondering if you could walk down with me and help me set up. This heat has me breathing too hard."

I turned and looked out my windows. I'd been so caught up in thoughts of the Silvers, I hadn't even noticed the huge orange ball hovering in a northwest sky streaked with pink and purple bands. "Wow."

"Wow is right," Ed said.

I hoisted his camera bag onto my shoulder and picked up his tripod. "That's the spirit," Ed grinned, showing snaggly teeth that overlapped at the front of his mouth like demurely crossed legs. "If I get a good shot, there's a print in it for you."

We rode the elevator down to ground level, crossed Broadview Avenue and walked along the eastern slope of Riverdale Park. People sat along the grassy verge on blankets or lawn chairs, waiting for the sun to begin its dramatic descent. Down the slope near the north end was the main ball diamond, where a co-ed softball game was going on, men and women alike chasing listlessly after balls in the heat.

We walked about two hundred yards south until Ed said, "Here is good." I set the bag down and let the beauty of the sunset catch and hold me. The sun seemed big as a grapefruit moon in the polluted sky.

Ed coughed a few times and voided something into the grass. "Damn smog kills your lungs," he said. "But it brings out the best in a sunset."

"Doesn't make it too hazy?"

"Not with Kodachrome, my friend. The way the reds and oranges and pinks diffuse will absolutely blow you away."

As I watched the sun move north and west, a black-clad figure came into my peripheral vision. Dante Ryan was walking down Broadview toward us. He and I made eye contact and he indicated with a sweep of his head that I should join him. I waited until he was down near Dr. Sun's statue, then told Ed

I was going to stretch my legs a little. Ed was glued to his viewfinder and grunted something like "yup." I followed Ryan down the same path I had bladed down yesterday, past great weeping willows whose fronds hung limply in the heavy air. Ryan walked all the way to the west end of the park where a fence separated it from a brushy slope that led down to the Don Valley Parkway. Dozens of picnic tables had been stacked in large piles for Saturday's Canada Day festivities. I found him behind a stack that shielded us from the view of anyone on the park slope or the ball field. Pear-shaped swarms of bugs hovered in the humid air around us.

"How'd you know I was here?" I asked.

"I was on my way to see you when you and the photographer came out." He lit a cigarette and exhaled heavily, as if blowing out more tension than smoke.

"You okay?" I asked.

"Not exactly."

"What happened?"

"Fucking Marco happened. Made me come in and see him today."

"Why?"

"Why. So he could fucking check up on me, like I'm some new recruit. Made me go over every dollar coming in. Every fucking dime. The more money he needs, the more he thinks everyone's holding out on him. Then he starts up my ass about the Silver contract. Where am I at with it? What's taking so long? The client is calling. He wants it done." He stopped to draw on his cigarette. "But the good thing about Marco? The madder he gets, the dumber he gets. He talks more than he listens."

"And?"

"He let something slip."

"What?"

"I think the hit originated in Buffalo."

"Go on."

"Marco's chewing me out about the call he got from the client. He's doing his aggrieved thing, saying, 'Do I need this? Do I need heat from over the river 'cause you have to scout your location?' In our business, 'over the river' means one place and that's Buffalo. Home of the Bills, the Sabres and what's left of the Magaddinos."

"As in Stefano Magaddino?"

"The late, great Don. Since he passed on, I tell you, things have gone downhill there."

"Why?"

"A, none of your business, B, it's too long a story, and C, it's none of your business." He tried to blow a smoke ring but it came apart in the currents created by the rushing stream of cars racing one another up the Parkway. "So what about you? Find anything on Silver?"

"He's definitely up to something, starting with the company he keeps," I said, and told Ryan what happened on the loading dock.

"This Claudio can only be one guy," Ryan said. "Claudio Ricci. Not many guys look like him. They ever stop making track suits, he'd have to walk around naked. You bounced him around like you say you did, I tip my hat to you."

"He connected to anyone in particular?"

"He's in the life, but he's not attached to any one crew."

"A Buffalo connection?"

"Nah. Strictly local talent."

"And Frank?"

"I know at least three Franks who match that description, right down to the cheap suit. There's Frankie Tools, Frank the Tank . . . ." Ryan was about to rhyme off a third name when his expression changed. I had seen anger in his eyes the night before. I had seen contempt and humour and sadness. Now there was fear. Dante Ryan had just seen something behind me that scared the shit out of him.

I looked over my shoulder and saw two men walking along the fence toward us, both wearing dark glasses. I knew one of them on sight: wiry, with long black hair in ring curls that reached past his shoulders. I was about to ask Ryan what the fuck Marco Di Pietra was doing in Riverdale Park when Ryan's right fist crashed into my jaw and knocked me to the ground.

The bastard had set me up after all. All the talk about saving a child, saving his soul, the line he couldn't cross—all bullshit. Dante Ryan had gift-wrapped and delivered me straight into the hands of a man who wished me nothing but an untimely death.

lay on my back, trying to think. Could I take Ryan out and outrun them to the bike path? Or get over the barbed-wire fence separating us from the Parkway without tearing myself up or rolling down the slope into oncoming traffic?

Then Ryan yelled, "You stay the fuck away from her, you got that?"

Her? Her who?

"Dipshit motherfucker!" He kicked me in the stomach, pulling it just enough that it looked more vicious than it felt. "You go near her again I'll fucking kill you!" He squared up over me and delivered a kick to my groin that would have crushed my testicles had he hit them. Instead the impact came just to their left, bless him, on the inside of my thigh. It was painful enough, but didn't extinguish the possibility of fatherhood. I curled into a fetal position and took one more kick in the midsection. His shoe hit my folded forearms, rather than my stomach; still, I was glad his choice in footwear ran to leather loafers, not steel-toed boots.

He stood over me, panting, jabbing the finger down at me. "Get the message, motherfucker?"

Was he selling me out to Marco, out of his mind or running another game entirely? I had no choice but to let it play out. I lay in a tight curl as Marco Di Pietra and the other man came up to Ryan. I tried to keep my face hidden, like when I was a kid, terrified of the witch in *The Wizard of Oz*, trying to fall asleep with a sheet over my head. *If I can't see her, she can't see me.*

"What the fuck is this?" Marco said.

"Hey, boss," Ryan said. "Hey, Phil. What's going on?"

"Hey," Phil said. His voice was low and raspy, a heavy smoker's bass. I'd caught only a glimpse of him before Ryan knocked me down: bigger than Marco by a few inches and a good many pounds, with thick dark hair slicked back from a widow's peak. Despite the heat, he wore a Detroit Tigers warm-up jacket, which likely meant he was concealing a weapon.

"You ask me what's going on?" Marco said. He spoke quickly like always, with a metallic edge to his voice. "That's what I came to ask you."

"You followed me."

"I had to. You didn't tell me where you were going."

"I thought we were done."

"I'll tell you when we're done," Marco said.

"Whatever you say."

"So what's this here?"

"What?"

"The pube at your feet."

"Just something I had to take care of."

"Something you didn't tell me about."

"It's personal," Ryan said. I hoped he looked more confident than he sounded. Or was he showing a little submission to Marco, the way a weaker dog shows its belly to an alpha male?

"There is no personal, Ryan," Marco said. "There's only business. And anything that is business, you share. Otherwise, you're holding back from me."

"Come on, boss. You think I hold back from you?"

"I go by what I feel, not what I think," Marco said. "And something didn't feel right tonight. Right, Phil?"

Phil said, "Right."

"I had this instinct, didn't I?"

"You did," Phil said.

"I said, What's with Dante? It's like he didn't want to be around me. He couldn't wait to leave. Isn't that what I said?"

"Word for word," Phil said.

"So I act on my instinct. We follow you down here and what do I find? You doing business you didn't tell me about. What did I say, Phil? People turn on you, I said."

"Right," Phil said. "I remember."

"I said, people turn on you for the least incentive. Wave anything at them—cash, pussy, a new gun, a ride—they'll sell you out on the spot. Right, Phil?"

"Verbatim," Phil said.

"So who do we have on the ground here?" Marco said.

Oh fuck. I thought. *Here it comes.*

"A little business on the side? Maybe something for my brother?"

Ryan said, "No, boss, it's got nothing to do with Vito. I haven't even seen him since his daughter's confirma—"

"Did I ask when you saw him last? Did I?"

"No."

"It would be strange if you haven't seen him, even if it's true, because I heard he's been trolling around everywhere, flaunting cash at people, trying to buy them over to his side."

"He hasn't tried it with me," Ryan said.

"Why? You're not people?"

"He knows better than to try."

"Oooh. He knows. How the fuck would you know what my brother knows? He's so stupid even he doesn't know what he knows."

"Well, he hasn't tried."

"What if he did?"

"I'd tell him to stick it."

"Sure you would, Dante. Sure you would. So if this douchebag on the ground here has nothing to do with Vito and nothing to do with me, then who the fuck you working for? Buffalo now?"

"It's strictly personal, boss."

"Is he fucking your wife?"

"Come on."

"Is he eating your wife's pussy?"

"Hey!"

"Hey what? If he isn't fucking your wife or eating her pussy then it isn't personal and don't say that to me again." Then Marco said to me, "Stand up."

I stayed where I was and groaned softly.

"Stand him up," Marco told Phil.

Phil pulled me to my feet. I kept my head down, clutching my stomach as if in great pain. Marco walked over and grabbed my chin and lifted it. He was wearing black pants and a tight-fitting black shirt with orange-and-black flames reaching up as if consuming his upper body. If only.

I hoped he wouldn't recognize me; he'd only seen me the one time outside the District Court. But he said "Son of a bitch" softly, and raised his sunglasses up onto his forehead. The asshole had actually added a few blond highlights to his long black curls. "If it isn't Mr. Undercover."

I've never seen the eyes of a shark six inches from my own, but they couldn't have been more lifeless than the ones that stared at me now.

"You know him?" Phil asked.

"Fucking right I know him. Jonah fucking Geller. Sawed-off Jewish prick who played me for a fool, got me paraded around in court. Cost me over a million cash."

I could smell his breath, feel his spit against my face. I could feel my own anger surging through my limbs. I had never wanted to hit anyone as much as I wanted to hit Marco Di

Pietra in that moment, lay him out for what he had ordered to be done to the Silver family. A lot of people probably felt that way about Marco, which is why he had men like Phil around him. Men like Dante Ryan.

"What'd he do?" Phil asked.

"A few months ago, we had a tobacco job that went bad. You were still in Millhaven."

"Oh, yeah," Phil grinned. "We heard about that one." He stopped grinning when Marco turned the shark eyes on him.

"Ten million cigarettes up for grabs," Marco said. "Half a million packs. I had guys lined up to buy them three bucks a pack, could sell them for five and still beat the retail price by a mile. Everyone makes money. I would've cleared a million-two, maybe more, till the undercover kike turned up."

Marco grabbed my ears and pulled my face even closer. "You know how bad I could use that money now?" he hissed. "You know how many friends a million bucks could buy?"

Marco let go of me and turned on Ryan. "You said this was a personal matter? What the fuck personal matter could you have with this mangiacake?"

"That means white bread," Phil told me.

"I know what it means," I said.

"I been seeing this broad," Ryan said. "You know, since me and Cara split up. The broad calls today, says the same car's been outside her place all the time, following her around. I have a guy run the plate and Geller's name comes up. The husband hired him 'cause he thinks she's fooling around on him."

"Which she is!" Phil said.

"Yeah, thanks, Philly. So I call Geller, pretend I got information for him, sucker him to the park here to give him a message. A taste of what he'll get if he don't leave her alone."

"Yeah?" said Marco. "When we were walking over here, you were looking pretty chummy. Having this heart to heart."

"You know me," Ryan said. "I don't have to raise my voice. I was trying to keep it low-key with so many people around."

Just then a great shout went up from the southern diamond and a softball bounced into view. A game must have started there after we came down the path. An outfielder came loping after the ball with long strides, actually giving it a little effort. He stopped when he saw the four of us—one man with a bleeding mouth surrounded by three obvious thugs—and let the ball roll to the fence.

"You okay?" he called.

"Mind your own business, asshole," Marco told him. The right fielder was tall, in shape, maybe thirty with a mane of blond hair and a thick red-blond beard. God bless this province's Scottish roots. This guy wasn't walking away. He waved at some of the other fielders to come join him.

"This is no good, boss," Ryan said. "There's people everywhere. A guy up the hill with a camera, for Chrissakes."

"So why did you meet him here?" Marco asked.

"Who knew they'd play ball in this heat?" Ryan said. "Now he's got the message, let's go."

"Yeah?" Marco turned to me. "The message get through?"

"Sure," I said.

"I wanted to send you a message, you cocksucking Jew." He shaped his hand into a gun and snapped his thumb down against his index finger like a hammer. The extended finger jabbed the bridge of my nose, his nail breaking the skin. "Like that," he said, jabbing me again. "But I got outvoted. The old goats from my father's time, pussyfooting around like you were a real cop. Only they're not here now, are they? It's just me and you and I know you're not a cop. What do you say, Undercover Guy? How about I send a message right between your eyes?"

"Don't do it," Ryan said under his breath.

Marco turned away to look at Ryan. His profile was like a hatchet ready to split wood. "What did you say to me?"

"There's too many—"

"You said, 'Don't do it.' Like you were giving me orders. You're not even Italian, you Irish fuck, where do you get off?"

"I'm trying to keep you out of jail," Ryan said, nodding toward the softball players looking our way. More were walking toward us from the infield, carrying aluminum bats. Bench strength. You gotta love it in your team.

"It's a long slow climb back up to the street," Ryan said. "Take us ten minutes going uphill."

"Take me fifteen," Phil said.

"We do anything here," Ryan said, "someone's on a cellphone to the cops. By the time we get to our cars, the tac squad is waiting and the geezer with the camera has it on film."

Marco looked up the hillside to where a group of sunset watchers had gathered. They were all staring at us, some of them pointing. Ed was at the centre, hunched over the camera. *Stay there*, I pleaded silently. *Don't show Marco your face.* But he stood up, the damn fool. I hoped Marco had lousy eyesight to match his lifeless eyes.

"Someone could be calling right now," Ryan said. "We got unregistered weapons here."

"I got one, boss," Phil said. "Don't make me go back inside so soon."

"He's not worth it," Ryan said. "Like you said, he's a douchebag, a pube. He's nothing."

"A million he cost me."

"He'll cost you more if we don't go."

Marco sighed unhappily. "Okay, Dante, okay. You made your point."

"Just looking out for you, boss."

"I appreciate that," Marco said, with all the warmth of a jackal. He squared up to face me. "You got lucky this time, Geller. Won't happen again." He turned as if to walk away, then spun back and threw a wild right hook at my jaw. The punk couldn't help thinking he had a freebie coming, but his telegraphed punch was easy to slip. I backed away in a fighting stance. I had let Dante Ryan work me over, for both our sakes, but Marco would have to earn anything he got.

I backed quickly toward the open field where more people would see what was happening. Marco charged toward me, leaving Ryan and Phil in the shelter of the picnic tables. He squared up and threw a short left. I blocked it hard with my forearm. He threw a right and I banged it aside harder.

"What's the matter?" I asked. "You can only hit guys who are being held down?"

"You want I should hold him?" Phil asked.

"Stay right there! I don't need help." Marco rushed at me with his head down and tried to knock me over, dead easy to sidestep and trip. He went sprawling onto his knees and elbows.

"*Minchia!*" Marco yelled.

Phil translated again. "Prick or pussy, depends what part of Italy you're from."

"Fight like a man," Marco panted, his hands on his knees.

"And put you at a disadvantage?"

He rushed at me and tried to kick me in the balls. I swept his kicking leg up and away with my forearm and he fell hard to the ground, landing on his back.

I wanted to go after him, beat him worse than I had Claudio. But if I went too far the guns might come out, and with these guys, who knew where too far was?

Marco got up slowly and gave me the dead eyes. "That's it," he said. "I don't care how many people are around." He reached into his back pocket and came out with a black object that looked like a pen until he moved his thumb and a six-inch blade shot out the end. Then it looked a lot like a stiletto. He came at me, feinting with the blade, trying to get me to plant my feet. I kept my eyes on his knife hand. Marco lunged forward and swept the knife toward my chest. I backed far enough away to dodge the blade easily, but stepped in a rut and stumbled. He swept the knife at me again, slashing the front of my shirt but breaking no skin.

"Hey!" came a shout behind us.

I regained my feet and darted right, risking a quick glance. The cavalry had arrived in the form of half a dozen ballplayers.

"Come on," Ryan urged Marco. "We're drawing a fucking crowd here."

"All right, Jewboy," Marco said to me. Sweat was dripping off the end of his nose. "You get a free pass for now. But I'm not through with you, got it? You're dead meat, man. Dead kosher meat." He laughed and Phil chimed in a moment later. Ryan forced a grin. I clenched my fists.

"No one talks to me like you did," Marco said.

"More people should."

"Shut up, Geller!" Dante Ryan said. "Just shut it!" Was he still playing a part here or genuinely concerned that I was going too far? "And stay away from that woman's house, understand? You go near her again, I'll kill you myself."

"Get in line," I said.

"Come on," Marco said. "It's too fucking hot down here." He retracted the blade and put the knife away.

"You all right?" the big blond called.

I told him I was and thanked him. He and a few others looked like they wanted to take the bats to Marco, but I waved them off. Who knew what Phil might do if someone took a swing at his boss?

"Look out!" someone shouted. I turned just in time to see Marco rushing at me from the right, the knife blade back out, the knife hand driving toward my side. I tried to move out of the way but the blade tore my shirt and sliced through the skin between my right hip and my ribs. Warm blood started running down my side.

Marco thrust the knife again, this time straight at my heart.

Fuck him. Fuck his gunman too. I caught his hand in my right, locked his arm straight and drove my left palm hard into his elbow. There was a cracking sound like a twig snapping. The knife fell to the ground, followed closely by Marco, who screamed and rolled onto his back, clutching his arm. I ran toward the clutch of ballplayers, looking back over my shoulder. Phil was kneeling at Marco's side as he writhed and moaned in the grass. Ryan was staring at the ground like he wished it would swallow him.

I realized then it wasn't a ballplayer who had yelled the warning. It had been Ryan. And once the pain subsided, Marco Di Pietra would realize it too.

CHAPTER 19

N ot long after midnight, I eased myself out of a cab and walked gingerly into the lobby of my building. I had sixteen stitches in my side but was feeling no pain. I was happy as a clam, in fact, or at least as happy as a clam who has taken two Percocets and has plenty more in his shell.

All things considered, my brush with death—and I speak here not of being slashed by a psychopath but of dealing with the Canadian medical system—went as well as could be expected. The bearded ballplayer drove me to Beth Israel on the condition that I not bleed on the seat of his Taurus. "It's a burgundy interior," he said, "but not the same shade." Ed had wanted to come too but I told him to do himself a favour and go back to his apartment and not let anyone see him with me.

"I got pictures of them, the bastards," Ed said. "What should I do with them?"

"Nothing, Ed. Don't even develop the film till we talk."

The ballplayer, whose name was Mark, gave me a spare T-shirt from his duffle bag to press against the wound while he drove. When we pulled up to Emerg, I thanked him and his friends for not looking away from trouble.

"I'd recognize the guy," he said. "If it came down to a lineup."

"No, you wouldn't," I said. "Not if you're smart enough to play centre field. Feel no obligation to provide descriptions to the police, either. None of you. Let it fade. And thanks again."

On entering the ER, I was required to scour my hands with antiseptic lotion. Personally, I thought the blood leaking out of me posed more of a health hazard than my hands, but as my mother never tires of reminding me, I never went to medical school. Once sanitized, I presented myself, along with my health card, to a nurse behind a counter piled high with files.

She was a tall black woman with regal features and close-cropped hair dyed a ginger blonde. At the sight of my bloody side, she might have raised one eyebrow slightly.

"Take a seat," she said.

"Are you sure?" I asked. "They're not exactly burgundy."

"I didn't say take one home. Just take one."

I sat down and started flipping through two-year-old magazines, keeping the T-shirt tight to my side with my elbow. Thankfully, the waiting room was not as full as it would have been during flu season, when anyone with a sniffle heads straight to the nearest ER, instead of taking to their bed and watching daytime TV like normal people. Still, I worked my way through half a dozen magazines before my name was called. A second nurse with twinkling blue eyes and a mop of red curls led me to a curtained-off examination area. She gloved her hands and placed a thick gauze pad on a bed with pale yellow sheets, gripped my hand and eased me down onto my back so the pad was under the wound. She wiped away the blood that had dried on my skin and peered at the slash. I could feel fresh rivulets of blood run down my side like raindrops down a window. "Mm-hmm," she said.

The dreaded *Mm-hmm*.

She told me the surgical resident on call would be in shortly and left. It didn't seem short to me. The pain in my side was growing more intense, as was my fear of Marco Di Pietra. Whatever hate he'd had on for me before was nothing compared to what would be building inside him now. He was one sick man, and he had the men and money to move against me in ways I couldn't hope to defend.

Some time later—measured in throbs per second—a gloved and gowned doctor pushed aside the curtain. His photo ID said he was Dr. Klein. His mother probably didn't worry when he didn't answer his phone.

Klein wiped the gash clean of blood, then spread it apart with his fingers. I gasped loudly. "The laceration appears superficial," he said. "You're lucky your assailant slashed you instead of stabbing you."

"I wasn't assailed," I said. "I mean, assaulted. I fell on a wineglass."

His look was withering in its skepticism. "You got this from a wineglass? I suppose it bounced up and cut you front to back with a slashing motion?"

"Wow. It's like you were there when it happened."

"Mr. Geller—"

"David Wells told the same story when he was pitching for the Padres and everyone believed him."

"No, they didn't," Klein said. "They just couldn't prove otherwise."

"Precisely."

"All right, Mr. Geller. If you want to insult someone's intelligence, do it on your own time. You'll need some blood work and imaging. Then I'll see you in the operating theatre."

"You can't stitch it here?"

"We don't do glass cuts in ER," he said with a thin smile.

An orderly wheeled my gurney down a hallway and left me staring at the ceiling. I was trying hard not to remember the last time I'd been there: the aftermath of the Ensign case. I focused instead on a damp stain on the ceiling, trying to decide whether it looked more like Africa or a broken heart. Another orderly returned to wheel me into an imaging centre where a technician did an ultrasound test on my abdomen and ribs. I felt like a purchase being scanned at a checkout. About twenty minutes later, the first orderly wheeled me into an operating theatre where Dr. Klein waited with a surgical nurse.

"Your good fortune continues, Mr. Geller," he said. "The knife—"

"Wineglass," I insisted.

"The knife cut no deeper than the subcutaneous tissue. There's no damage to the muscle or abdomen. No organ pathology. Spleen and liver intact. We can patch you up here without putting you under."

Jonah Geller: unlucky in love, but freakishly lucky when shot or stabbed.

The nurse turned me onto my side, sterilized the area around the wound and draped it off. She wheeled over a tray on which rested scalpels, retractors and suturing equipment. Klein irrigated the wound, then picked a retractor from the tray and used it to spread the gash even farther than he had in the ER. I tried not to gasp and failed miserably. "No debris or contamina-tion," Klein said. "He must have washed the wineglass first."

He asked the nurse for five cc's of one per cent xylocaine. Given the pain I was in, it didn't sound nearly enough. He injected some of the contents under the skin just above the wound, then did the same just below it. While we waited for the local to take effect, Dr. Klein told me that new legislation required him to report stab wounds to police.

"No, it doesn't," I said. "That legislation hasn't been pro-claimed. Hasn't even passed third reading."

"You a lawyer?"

"From your mouth to God's ear. Anyway, you said your-self I wasn't stabbed. I was slashed."

"You're going to split hairs on this?"

"Two Jews arguing, Doctor, we could be here all night. Don't you have other patients?"

He admitted that he did. Then picked up a scalpel.

"Aren't I already cut enough?"

"Not nearly enough," he said.

"Don't worry," the nurse said. "The doctor just has to extend the laceration on either side to ensure a tight closure."

"If I didn't want him to worry, I would have said so myself," Klein muttered. For the next few minutes he sewed quietly. I knew the routine: catgut to close the deeper layers of the wound, silk to close the skin. When he was done, he wrote a prescription for my old friend Percocet and told me to take it easy for a few days. "No heavy lifting. No running. Come back if there's any sign of infection, such as redness, swelling or extreme pain. And you might want to pick up a stool softener. Most people experience constipation from Percocet. It's up to you to decide which is worse, that or the pain. Also, please remember that Percocet is a narcotic and that you may feel giddy—or in your case, giddier—after taking it. You might want to avoid driving."

"I'll be careful."

"And Mr. Geller?"

"Yes?"

"Stay away from stemware for a while."

I got off the elevator at 18 and walked slowly toward my apartment. I listened at my door and heard nothing. Checked the lock and jamb for signs of forced entry. Also nothing. I unlocked the door and pushed it open, then stood back against the outside wall and waited. I reached in and flipped on the light switch, then withdrew my hand and waited some more. If someone was in there lying in wait, maybe they'd get bored to death.

When I felt too tired to stand in the hall anymore, I stepped inside. There was no one in the living room or dining room. No one in the galley kitchen. I went in there and got my big chopping knife and made my way through the rest of the apartment. There was no one in my bedroom, bathroom or closets. No one on the balcony.

I was alone. As usual.

I went back to the front door and was locking the deadbolt when the phone rang. I almost stabbed myself with the knife at the sound; that would have been fun to explain to Dr. Klein. I set down the knife on the coffee table and answered my phone. Dial tone. Somewhere else a phone kept ringing—the cell Dante Ryan had given me. I found it on a chair in the bedroom where I'd left it while showering.

"Jonah Geller's armed guard speaking. How may I direct your call?"

"It's me," Ryan said. "How'd you make out?"

I gave him the stitch count. "It would have been worse if you hadn't warned me."

"Yeah," he said. "Well. I got caught up in the moment."

"I'm trying to say thank you," I said.

"I'm the one who should thank you," he said.

"For what?"

"You made him cry," Ryan said. "He cried all the way home. Whatever else happens, I saw the man cry. The man. Big fucking baby, more like it."

"His elbow dislocated?"

"Fractured in two places. One of them the funny-sounding one."

"The humerus."

"Yeah. The other one I forget. Doctor said he was lucky he didn't need traction."

"He's in a cast?"

"From his wrist to above the elbow. Looks like a fucking salesman, wants to shake hands with everyone."

"I guess I've moved up on his shit list."

"You *are* his shit list."

"He's lucky that's all I did to him. Tell me something. If Phil hadn't been there—"

"No names, I said"

"Okay. If it had been me and the big baby one on one, what would you have done?"

"Given you a standing ovation."

"Seriously, would you have stopped me?"

"From what, killing him? Can you do that with your kung fu shit?"

"I practise karate, not kung fu, but yes, I could have killed him. You'd be surprised how easy it is."

"No," Ryan drawled. "I don't think I would." I heard him suck in air and guessed he'd just lit up. "I got to get away from these people. They're poisoning me. I got to spend more time with my kid. I miss him so much—Christ, I even miss my wife. I want to do things normal people do. Take my boy fishing. To a ball game. Run a hose in the sun so he can see how rainbows are made. But my wife won't even let him leave the house with me. All this talk of war between the brothers, she's afraid someone will take a crack at me when I'm with our son. Or maybe I'll corrupt him just by being with him, like something'll leach out of me straight into him. All the kids his age, they play with water guns and shit? First time he picked one up, I swear, my wife turned white and ragged on me for fucking hours, how he's going to end up like me."

"She should talk to my mother," I said. "Ever since I got shot, she freaks if I don't answer the phone on the first ring. Nice Jewish boys aren't supposed to get shot, unless maybe they own a jewellery store."

"I'm a little curious about that myself," Ryan said. "I mean, I'm not generalizing or anything, but growing up in Hamilton, every Jew I ever knew, besides the few that got into our thing, they became doctors or lawyers or dentists or went into the family business. Scrap metal, shit like that."

"Did my mother put you up to this?"

"Come on. How'd you get to be a PI?"

"It's way too long a story," I told him. "The Percocet is kicking in."

"And I'm in the Aerosuites Hotel with nothing to do but listen to the elevators."

"All right. Let's just say school never clicked for me. I could follow what the teachers said on any given day, but I could never put it together like my brother."

"What's he do?"

"He's a lawyer, like a good Jew is supposed to be. Very successful. Very responsible. Rarely gets shot on the job. The apple of his mother's eye."

"Not your father's?"

"He died when I was a kid."

Dante Ryan said nothing. I remembered how his father, Sid Ryan, had been killed by the Hamilton mob when Dante was an infant. I was debating whether to ask him about this when a rather large yawn escaped my lips.

"All right," Ryan said, "I can take a hint. Anyway, given what happened tonight, I'd be careful if I was you. Get a professional in and change the piece-of-shit lock on your door. Check your car before you start it. Watch your back."

"I can barely watch my side," I said. "What about your boss? He figure out yet who warned me on the field?"

"Oh yeah. I told him I was warning him, not you. That a ballplayer was getting too close with a bat."

"Phil say otherwise?"

"Phil never says more than he has to. Frankly, I don't know what the fuck he saw."

"He Marco's regular bodyguard?"

"One in a series."

"Are you one of them?"

"Me? No. I don't guard bodies, I generate them."

"All right. I'm saying good night now. With the cavalry on speed-dial."

"More likely you'll need the bomb squad," he said.

CHAPTER 20

Buffalo: the previous March

Rich Leckie sagged down onto a bench beside Marty Oliver, raising his T-shirt off his belly to wipe the sweat pouring off his bald head. His stomach was white and soft, rolling out over the band of his shorts.

"It's official," he gasped. "I'm dying."

"You're not dying," Marty said.

"You're right. I'm dead already."

"That might explain your game tonight."

"Thanks, pal."

"Come on, I'm kidding. You're just out of shape."

"It's only a matter of time now."

"It's only a matter of time for us all, Tallulah. There's nothing wrong with you a little more exercise and a better diet wouldn't cure."

"Thank you and fuck you," Rich panted.

Rich and Marty played racquetball every Thursday evening, seven to eight, at the Delaware Avenue Y, a short walk from Marty's downtown office. But racquetball with Marty was the only exercise Rich got. Marty played racquetball with at least four other guys at the Y, played basketball Sundays in a fifty-plus league, and used the stairclimber and elliptical cross-trainer, sweating it out next to the buff women, chatting up any that didn't wear iPods.

They had known each other for nearly forty years—though both would probably reel at the thought—meeting in high school and staying friends through college, marriages, children and careers. Well, Marty's career anyway. Rich wasn't sure the dogged yet unfulfilling path he had pursued since earning his journalism degree could properly be called a career. Rich and Marty had discovered rock music together in the early sixties, when the potent Buffalo scene was presided over by legendary DJs like Tom James and George Brand, a generation of mesmerized teens following them like rats after plugged-in pipers. Rich and Marty formed their own group in high school—Contraband—with Marty on guitar and vocals and Rich on keyboards, trying to work his long-ignored classical piano training into some sort of blues-based attack. They discovered drugs together, beginning with pot, for which a lifelong affinity would develop, as well as acid, the latter experiment ending abruptly, and almost fatally, when the boys discovered that tripping on blotter was fundamentally incompatible with swimming in the Buffalo River. They had gone on road trips to Manhattan together, spiralling through the Adirondacks in the dark with Dylan's new electric sound blasting out the speakers and thick smoke trailing out the window. They had tried dealing dope briefly. Extremely briefly, it turned out, as the first toes they stepped on belonged to big, hairy-assed motherfuckers who could rip out their throats with one hand. And those were just the girlfriends.

Asked who his best friend was, Rich would say Marty without hesitation. But he wasn't sure Marty would say the same. He knew Marty had a lot more friends than he did, a lot more going on in his life, and felt sometimes that Marty looked at him more as a sidekick than an equal. He had to admit Marty was the more accomplished of the two: he hadn't worked any harder than Rich had in school, but did well enough to get into law school. Back then, Marty's intention (at least his stated intention) was to practise storefront law, help the underprivileged stick it to the man. Now billboards and bus-stop ads hawked his firm's personal injury services. Helping people stick it to the man's insurance company was more like it.

Rich took pride in the fact that he earned his living by writing, even if most of the work was corporate and catalogue copy, and the odd ghost-writing job for local luminaries who thought their lives worth documenting. He did well enough to keep his first and only wife, Leora, and daughter Leigh-Anne in a detached brick house south of East Ferry, but had never kept pace financially with Marty. Rich drove a sensible car that got good mileage, an Acura he'd found in the *News*, three years old with barely thirty thousand miles on the clock. The Leckies took car trips to visit family and the occasional all-inclusive at a beach resort, thanks mainly to his father-in-law, who was determined that his daughter and granddaughter should have a decent vacation whether or not Rich could provide one.

Marty had a sprawling home east of the Delaware Park golf course, where he lived with his three kids from the first marriage and a foxy second wife half his age. Marty had three imports just for himself (a sleek Jag sedan, a two-seater Benz convertible and an Accord he used strictly for lousy driving conditions or parking in dicey parts of town). The fox had a top-of-the-line minivan for ferrying the kids and a Miata for her downtime. Marty was always leaving for or coming back from some killer holiday. Now that he was managing partner, he let the young associates put in the hours, or made them do it if letting them didn't do the trick. Just a few weeks earlier, Marty had flown the fox out to San Diego to watch the Buick Invitational, Tiger Woods's favourite tournament. A few weeks before that it had been a two-week cruise in the Caribbean, with a nanny to run after the kids while he rubbed sunscreen into the fox's haunches, all while Buffalo was digging out of four-foot lake-effect drifts.

Both men would turn fifty-five this year but only Rich looked it. He had lost his hair early and what little there was left around the ears was grey and coarse. He was five-seven and thirty pounds overweight (forty if you believed Leora). The extra weight made his face look pouchy and he couldn't wear jeans anymore without looking like a tourist or a narc.

Marty, on the other hand, probably didn't weigh ten pounds more than he had in high school, right around six feet and one-eighty stripped. He'd be shiny with sweat after a game but not drenched like Rich, who looked like a mouldy gourd left out in the rain. Marty's arms and legs were toned and his pecs hadn't turned into tits. And if he had ever lost one lustrous hair from his head, two had probably grown in its place.

"I need fluids," Rich said.

Marty handed him a water bottle.

"There beer in that?"

"No."

"I can wait."

There was a knock on the glass door to their court and they looked out to see a young couple holding racquets. They wore expensive-looking outfits with matching headbands and wristbands. Marty looked at his watch, saw their time was up and waved the couple in. He and Rich collected their gear and headed to the showers.

They stood under their showerheads a long while, Rich rolling his shoulders forward and back under the hot water to loosen his muscles. Marty, damn him, had to tend to his hair like it was school picture day, washing it, rinsing it, rubbing in conditioner that smelled like coconut, rinsing it again.

When they were done they sat on a narrow pine bench in front of their lockers. Rich laid a clubhouse towel under his feet while he dressed—God knew what crawled around the carpets in this place—and used another to dry himself.

"So where to?" Marty asked.

"I was thinking the Drift."

"Really?"

"Why really?"

"Nah, it's just—well, they don't have much of a single malt list."

Christ. Marty could be a jerk sometimes. Worrying about single malts while Rich had to count his beers to keep expenses down. "Olmsted's has a better whisky selection," he admitted. "But their food's not worth the price."

"And the Drift's is? They deep-fry everything. Even the menus, I think. Aren't you watching your cholesterol?"

"I get it checked every year."

"And?"

"And it's always high."

"Your doctor put you on anything?"

"No."

"Why not? Murray Lightman's cholesterol was through the roof last year. He takes Contrex now and eats whatever he wants."

"Can we just get a beer, please? Believe me, I need beer more than Contrex."

"Joke all you want, but go see your doctor. Or mine, if you want. I'll get you in to see him."

"Marty, please. Drop it already!"

"Okay, okay. Fine. Sue me for caring."

The irony was, Rich's doctor had written a goddamn prescription. He just hadn't filled it, not at six bucks a pill every day for the rest of his life.

"What the hell," Marty said. "Let's make it the Drift. You did pretty well there last time, I recall."

"Oh, please."

"She liked you, Rich. What was her name?"

"Holly."

"Holly, right. Great name. Great gal. I still don't understand why you never called her. She was bright, she was cute. She practically made you take her number."

"I'm married, okay? Isn't that reason enough?"

"It hasn't always been."

"Trudy, you mean."

"Yes, Trudy. And wasn't there a proofreader you were after for a while?"

"Yes. I made a complete fool of myself and never even got to first base. Please, Marty. All I'm after right now is a burger and a beer."

"Why?"

"Because I'm hungry and I'm thirsty and not necessarily in that order."

"I mean why settle for so little?"

"So little what!"

"Remember what you told me at the cottage on Labour Day?"

"About what?"

"You and Leora."

"What about us?"

"You don't remember this?"

"Vaguely."

"Christ. Well, you told me—ah, jeez—you told me you stopped having sex like a year ago. 'She's frozen me out,' you said."

"I said that?"

"Your exact words."

"I was exaggerating," Rich said. "I was drunk."

He had been drunk, so much so that he'd wound up puking in the bushes outside Marty's cottage in the Finger Lakes, getting eaten alive by mosquitoes as he hunched over, helplessly retching. But he hadn't been exaggerating. His sex life with Leora was over and he couldn't care less, with all her dislikes and inhibitions, her rules and regulations, her no man's land and no-fly zones. He had liked the girl at the Drift. The woman. Holly. In her early forties, nice-looking, with a warmth and ease to her that suggested she'd be Leora's polar opposite in bed. But he couldn't chance it. The embarrassment and awkwardness were too much for him. Even if she said the right things, told him it was okay, *let's just cuddle and see what happens*, he'd lie there rigid, not knowing what to say, wanting to try again but dreading being exposed. Viagra would help but each baby blue pill was just another luxury he couldn't afford. Christ, his arteries were choking on their own plaque because he couldn't afford the Contrex.

"What's the matter?" Marty asked. "You look down. More than down. Depressed. You know, no one has to live with depression anymore. There are pills now that have virtually no side effects."

"Of course there are," Rich said. "There's a pill for everything. One for depression and one to lower my cholesterol. One to give me enough of a hard-on that I can try to pick up a woman without worrying she's going to laugh me out of bed. One pill to make you larger and one to make you small, remember? There's a pill for fucking everything, Marty, but my problem is I can't afford them. Just my luck, right? The only baby boomer in town who isn't sitting around pondering which of his residences to retire to."

"Nobody lives like that."

"You do."

"Practically nobody. And you've done fine for yourself. You have a nice house, a car—"

"And you have what, three of each?"

"Forget me for a minute. Compared to most of the world's population, you lead a charmed life."

"Great. Next to some guy in a rice paddy in Bangladesh, I'm a stunning success. It's only among the guys I grew up with and went to school with that I suffer by comparison."

"You chose an honourable path and stuck to it. You wanted to be a writer and that's what you are. I respect you for that. We all do."

"Yeah? I don't remember ever staggering drunk through campus saying one day I'd write the Great American Annual Report."

"Forget it. Let's go to the Drift and throw down a few. Make a move on a girl. Get laid. It'll do your self-respect a world of good."

"Didn't you hear what I said before? Things aren't working. And I really can't afford the cure."

"Maybe you can," Marty said with a smile.

"What are you talking about?"

"You remember Barry Aiken?"

"Sure. He was at college with us. Tall guy with long hair . . . he was an artist of some kind."

"That's him. He's a designer now."

"Married a really cute girl who played piano."

"Amy Farber."

"I always liked her. Didn't he wind up moving back to his dad's house?"

"That's right."

"On Lincoln Parkway?"

"Good memory. So Barry has a situation I think you'll find intriguing."

"What kind of situation?"

"I got the weirdest call from him just before I left work. Suppose you could get prescriptions at less than half the price? Maybe a third."

"What are you talking about?"

"Barry's holding."

"Holding? Christ, I haven't heard that expression in a million years. What are you saying, he has prescription drugs to sell? How did he—"

"I didn't ask, Richie. A lawyer never asks unless he already knows the answer."

"I wouldn't need a prescription?"

"Just cash."

"Well, that's a problem right there."

Marty leaned in a little. "Not if you do me a favour."

"What favour?"

"As a lawyer," Marty said, "there are boundaries I can't cross. Situations I can't be found in."

"I don't like where this is going. You want me to do something illegal because you're afraid to get caught."

"No one's getting caught, Nelliebelle. It's just that *if* something went wrong, no matter how unlikely, the consequences for my career could be fatal."

"But not for mine because I don't have one."

"I didn't say that. But as a lawyer I have to at least project a facade of integrity."

"What would I have to do?"

"Go to Barry's and pick up a package. Stop at my house. Go home. That's it," Marty said.

"Let me think about it."

"Sure," Marty said. He looked up for the waitress and caught her eye immediately, something Rich had never mastered.

It wasn't until after Holly came in and ordered a drink and gave Rich some eye contact and a wave that he leaned across the table and told Marty he would do it.

"Yeah?" Marty said. "You remember which house on Lincoln Parkway, or you need me to write it down?"

CHAPTER 21

Toronto: Wednesday, June 28

The pain in my side woke me before any bad dreams could. I was up before six, drinking coffee and waiting for a fresh round of Percocet to take effect. I checked the wound for signs of infection. None so far. Good to know Marco kept a clean blade. If my luck held, he'd scrub every bullet before he and his boys loaded their guns.

At six-thirty I opened my front door and looked up and down the hall. No werewolves, vampires or gunmen. I reminded myself to call a locksmith and get something sturdy installed, then took the stairs down to 16 and summoned an elevator from there.

The underground parking garage was cool and quiet at that hour. I walked softly toward the spot where my car was parked and waited a moment behind a bright yellow concrete pillar. Still quiet. I moved out to my car and looked at the hood. There were handprints on the dusty front end that showed the hood had been lifted and my heart started to pick up speed. Then I remembered Joe Avila had worked on it the other night; the prints were probably his. I unlocked the car and released the hood. I wasn't sure what to look for. Stray wires? Sticks marked TNT? A round black bomb bearing the trusted Acme label? Nothing seemed out of place. I eased the hood closed, then knelt down and peered under the chassis. A sharp pain shot through my side and I drew breath through clenched teeth. I got up slowly and leaned on the driver's door, trying to control the pain through measured breathing. Four in. Four out. Four in. Four out.

When the pain subsided I drove to a diner on the corner of Broadview and Danforth, where the breakfast special was three eggs, a ham steak (sorry, Ma), a whack of home fries, toast and all the coffee my kidneys could float. There weren't many other customers: just a taxi driver whose cab was parked at a stand outside, and a Goth couple who looked like they were ending their night rather than beginning their day. I dawdled over a second cup of coffee, reading a *Clarion* the cab driver left behind. The Blue Jays had lost in Kansas City—*Kansas City!*—when one of their serial arsonists trotted in from the bullpen, blew a couple of sharp bubbles with his gum, then laid a fat pitch in over the plate that was last seen heading over the fountain in centre field.

After breakfast, I drove back to my building and parked on the street, where it would be harder for marauding mobsters to sabotage my car. I rode up to 17, climbed one flight of stairs and listened at the hall doorway. A quick peek through the window showed no one in the corridor. I slipped into the hall and knocked on Ed Johnston's door. Ed was an early riser. His unit faced east and he often said he never missed a sunrise. But he didn't answer the first knock or the second. My first thought was that he was still sleeping; the second that Marco had sent someone to get the film from Ed's camera. I knocked louder. A moment later, I heard steps coming to the door and was relieved when Ed opened the door. He was dressed and had a mug of coffee in his hand.

"Jonah! You all right? Glad to see you up and around. You scared the hell out of me last night."

"I'm fine."

"You sure? That bastard cut you something awful."

"It looked worse than it was. A few stitches is all." I felt vulnerable standing out in the hallway, as if any moment the elevator doors would slide open and men with guns would barge out. "Can I come in?"

"Of course, of course. Get you a coffee?"

"One more can't hurt." If Percocet was going to constipate me, coffee might prove a valuable ally.

He handed me a mug and led me out to his balcony. The eastern view wasn't as dramatic as mine: no valley, no downtown skyline, just miles and miles of houses and trees, punctuated by the odd high-rise. But the early sun bathed it all in a golden light, the promise of another day. Another chance to get things right.

"Who were those guys?" Ed asked.

"The less you know, Ed, the better. Trust me. You don't want to get involved."

"They don't scare me."

"They should. They scare the shit out of me."

"Are you in trouble, Jonah?"

"No, just picking some up by association."

"Anything I can do?"

"There is, Mr. Mayor."

"Shoot."

"Is there somewhere you can develop that film yourself? Where you're the only one who sees it?"

"Sure. I belong to an Artscape co-op on King Street. I use a darkroom there in exchange for volunteering."

"Okay. Develop it today and make one set of prints. But don't show them to anyone. I mean *anyone*."

"Got it."

"When you're done, put the negs and the prints in an envelope with this address on it." I wrote the name and address of my brother's law firm. "Mark it to his attention:

urgent, personal and confidential. If anything happens to me, I want you to send it to him."

"If anything happens—"

"It's just a precaution. More than likely, I'll come by your place for them tonight."

"More than—Jesus, kid, what did you get yourself into?"

"You wouldn't believe it if I told you, Ed, and I'm not going to."

"Who the hell is after you?"

I said, "Do this for me and you'll be giving me all the help I need."

If only that were true.

I checked under the hood of my car again, then crouched to check under the chassis, getting the same shooting pain in my side for my trouble. There didn't seem to be a bomb and as it turned out, there didn't have to be, because as soon as I headed south on Broadview toward the office, a dark green SUV fell into line behind me. Didn't mean it was following me. Didn't mean it wasn't. I started making a series of turns no one with an actual destination would make. East, then north, then east again, then south, then west back to Broadview. The SUV followed.

I waited for a break in traffic and went north again, past the Broadview subway and streetcar terminus. Trying to lose the more powerful SUV on a straight road was a mug's game, but the Camry would handle quick turns better. I stayed in the left lane as we approached Mortimer so he'd think I was taking Pottery Road down to the Bayview Extension. But as we approached the intersection I checked my side mirrors, saw no one coming up inside, then yanked the wheel to the right and gunned it east on Mortimer. The SUV made the turn too, though not as nimbly, and was half a block behind when I took the first left. I drove through East York as quickly as I dared, taking every turn I could, trying to put a full block between us.

At Sammon Avenue, I rolled through the stop sign and turned right—getting a horn blast and extended middle finger from a woman in a LeSabre who had the right of way. With her between me and the SUV, I floored the Camry, imploring its six cylinders to give it their all. As I approached Pape, the traffic light turned yellow. Then red. I hit my horn and blew through the light, swerving to avoid a van starting through the intersection. Another horn, another finger; another day in the life of Toronto drivers.

When the LeSabre stopped behind me at the light, the SUV had to do the same. I took my first left, then another, doubling back west just as the SUV would be starting to roll east. I took another quick left the wrong way down a curving one-way street and shot down a long mutual drive that led to a garage at the rear of a house in the curve of the crescent. I turned off the engine and sat there breathing hard, my side throbbing from tension, from wrenching the steering wheel side to side. I stared straight ahead at the garage door. Whoever had painted it hadn't used the right primer. Paint was coming away in curling strips like birchbark.

Then a shadow appeared at my window. Someone knocked on the glass and my gut clenched like a fist. I was belted in, trapped, and in pain. I pictured a pair of thugs standing outside with guns drawn, ready to fire as soon as I rolled my window down. But there was no bulk looming there. Another knock: the sharp rap of a knuckle rather than the pounding of a fist. I powered down the window. A thin sparrow of a woman stood there, wearing a broad-brimmed hat tied around her chin with a flowery kerchief. She wore the kind of wraparound sunglasses older people wear to keep out the glare. She was at least seventy. *Okay, Geller,* I thought, *you can take her.*

"What the hell are you doing?" she demanded. "This is private property, not some parking lot."

"I'm sorry," I said. "I was—"

"You came the *wrong* way down a one-way street at high speed. There are children on this street, you know. Elderly people," she said, clearly not counting herself among them. "The way you people drive, you treat the whole city like your personal racetrack. Killing drivers, pedestrians, bystanders, cyclists, anyone in your way."

"I was being chased," I said.

"By who? The police?"

"More of a road rage thing."

"The way you drive, you probably deserved it." She held up a gardening trowel in one thin hand. "Now get off my property before I strip your paint job down to the metal."

I shifted into reverse. I wasn't so sure I could take her after all.

CHAPTER 22

"What happened to you?" Clint asked me. I flinched and spilled coffee on my hands and the counter in the office kitchenette. I hadn't heard him come up behind me and I was jumpy: if the guys in the SUV knew where I lived, they also had to know where I worked.

Clint was looking at the fat lip Ryan had given me during last night's little sideshow.

"It's nothing," I said. "I was accosted."

"Accosted."

"Mugged."

"By who? Mike Tyson?"

"Just a guy."

"Since when does just a guy get the better of Jonah Geller?"

"He had a friend."

"So there were two guys."

"Yes. I didn't see the other one at first. He came up behind me."

Clint sighed. "When did it become so easy to lie to me?"

"Clint, it's nothing, okay? Nothing to do with work. Let it go. Please."

He poured coffee into his mug and added a splash of skim milk to it. "If this is your way of showing me you're ready for a case, you might want to rethink your approach." He walked out of the kitchenette before I could respond. It was just as well. I had nothing to say but more lies.

Andy Robb was alone in our cube farm, researching the sports memorabilia market in preparation for an undercover job at a firm that was reportedly flooding Toronto with fake sports jerseys, photos and other artifacts.

"Check this out," Andy said. "Remember Mickey Truman?"

I looked up from MediaTron, where I'd been reading follow-ups on the Kylie Warren shooting. "Sure," I said. "Played first base for the Blue Jays way back when. Good bat, no glove, as I recall. Moved like an elm tree out there. Should have been a DH."

"He was killed in a car crash last March, down near Dunedin."

"I remember. During spring training, wasn't it?"

"Yeah. They brought him back as a hitting instructor."

"What about him?"

"His rookie card, in mint condition, was going for less than five bucks before he died. Now it's up over twelve. Two hundred and forty per cent increase, just because he got himself killed. Funny how someone can be worth more dead than alive."

No it wasn't, I thought. Not in the least.

Founded largely by Scots, Toronto was once the most homogeneous of cities. A century ago, diversity meant you took your Presbyterianism through the mellowing filter of Andrew Melville instead of straight up from John Knox himself. Today, Toronto is reportedly the most multicultural city in the world, with the greatest number of countries represented among its immigrants and more than a hundred and thirty languages and dialects spoken. Driving west on Bloor near the University of Toronto, looking for a parking spot, I saw people in every skin tone you could imagine, from blue-black to coffee with double cream to the palest bleached rose. In the hot weather, many were stripped down to T-shirts and tank tops, showing off colourful tattoos and other body art.

Toronto had been so conservative once, so buttoned-down and Victorian. Now the old girl had not only thrown off her crinolines, she'd gone and had her labia pierced.

I finally scored a parking spot west of Spadina and walked back past stores that catered to every aspect of campus, bohemian and eco-vegan life: a copy shop, two sushi joints, a tattoo and piercing parlor, a bookstore catering to spiritual seekers, a cycle repair shop and a store that sold only products made from hemp—except, of course, the combustibles.

The Registered Association of Ontario Pharmacists was in a Georgian mansion on Huron north of Bloor, in a block of mansions that housed medical and therapy practices, embassies, private clubs, galleries and the one true bane of the Annex: fraternity houses. The entrance to the college was framed by a large stone portico with four columns. Tall leaded windows were set in fieldstone bays. Winston Chan greeted me on the ground floor and walked me up a flight of carpeted stairs to his office.

Chan was a heavy man in his forties, with a black brushcut and rosy patches on both cheeks that made him look merry. His office was lined with shelves that contained books, thick binders and stacks of paper. He sat behind his desk and clasped his hands behind his neck; I took the club chair facing him.

"Like I told you on the phone, there are strict limits to what I can tell you," Chan said.

"I know so little, anything is bound to help."

He turned his computer monitor out of my line of vision and tapped in a password. "Here we go. You said his name is Silver, eh?"

"Yes. First name Jay."

"Strange. I don't have anyone by that name in our registry," Chan frowned. "There's a Samuel Jason Silver. Could that be the same?"

"Is he the only Silver you have?"

"Yup. His registered location is the Med-E-Mart on Laird Boulevard in Leaside."

"He's the one."

"I'll be honest with you, Mr. Geller, I've just told you pretty much everything I can about him."

"You're kidding."

"Unless he's been disciplined by the Association in response to an investigation."

"Can we check?"

"I'm doing it as we speak," said Chan, the bright blue of his monitor reflected in his wire-rim glasses. "Hmm," he said after a moment. "Nope, nothing here. Looks like he's kept his nose clean, as far as we're concerned."

"How tight a rein do you keep on your members?"

"Not as tight as I'd like. There are thousands of pharmacies in the province. We can't inspect them more than once every three years or so, and even then we mainly look at their prescriptions for signs of irregularities. Our mission is to protect public safety; we don't concern ourselves with business practices or anything like that. Now what's this about? Has Mr. Silver done something I should be aware of?"

"I don't know. Between you and me, a threat has been made against him and I've been asked to look into it."

"But not by him."

"No."

"Otherwise you'd be asking him these questions, not me."

"Right."

"Then on whose behalf are you investigating?"

"A member of the family." I left out the part about it being a notorious crime family. "Can I ask a hypothetical question?"

"You can always ask," he said.

"Why would a pharmacist ship goods out of his store instead of taking them in?"

"What kind of goods?"

"Sealed cartons from the manufacturer—enough to fill a cube van."

Chan mulled that one over. "Well, there are circumstances that would allow for it. Some pharmacies have wholesale licences that permit them to ship quantities of drugs to other pharmacies—if they comply with federal legislation, of course."

"Do most of the drugs they ship go to the U.S.?"

"They used to. It was the primary market because of the price differences."

"How big a difference?"

"Depended on the drug, of course, but on brand-name drugs still under patent, it was easily three times the Canadian price. And in U.S. dollars to boot."

"But Canada has banned sales to the States."

"We had to," Chan said. "The U.S. administration wanted to protect the American pharmaceutical industry. And Canadians were afraid all our drugs would be sold to the States and there'd be nothing left for us."

"Could a pharmacist still make money shipping drugs to the States?"

"Only if he skirted the law."

"Anything else he could be doing with those cases?"

"As I said, pharmacies will buy products for other pharmacies, for a markup, of course. He could also be supplying a larger facility, such as a hospital or clinic."

"A nursing home?" I asked.

"Sure."

"Who conducted Silver's last inspection?"

Chan consulted his computer screen. "Sumita Desai. A little over six months ago. Want me to ask her about it?"

"Please."

Chan picked up his phone and dialled a four-number extension. "Sumita? Winston here. Could you pop in for a minute? Hmm. Okay, then, quickly: early this year, you inspected a place called Med-E-Mart on Laird. Ring a bell? Okay. I have a gentleman here in my office who'd like to ask you about it, so I'm going to put you on speakerphone. No, it's okay, he's a licensed investigator . . . Sumita, I said it's okay. Don't be such a worrywart. He's got my curiosity going." Chan pressed the appropriate button and I heard "Yes, but—"

"Sumita, say hello to Jonah Geller."

"Oh. Good afternoon, sir," she said. *Good ahf-tuh-noon, suh*, in a deep voice with a lovely accent that blended Indian and British tones.

I said hello, then asked, "When you inspected Mr. Silver's pharmacy, Ms. Desai, was there any indication that he had more product on the premises than he should?"

"Not at all, *suh*. Everything seemed quite in order to these eyes."

"Was he cooperative?"

"As far as I recall. Put it this way: he didn't stand out as being uncooperative. I would likely have noted something at the time."

"His prescriptions were all legitimate?"

"Absolutely. As Mr. Chan probably told you, any prescriptions not written by an Ontario physician would have triggered the alarm, raised the red flag if you will. Well, maybe not both but certainly one." The quip came with a deep rich laugh that made me want to go to the nearest bar and order something creamy and tropical.

"So he passed the inspection?"

"With flying colours. My report at the time indicates he ran a good business. Everything above board."

Chan looked over to me to see if I had any more questions. I shook my head. "Thanks then, Sumita," Chan said, and
hung up.

I wondered how Silver could have passed an inspection
so recently yet still managed to upgrade from Bayview to
Forest Hill.

"There might be another way to go at this," Chan said
thoughtfully. "The pharmaceutical companies tend to get suspicious if unusual quantities are being ordered. You might
check with them to see if any have concerns about Mr. Silver."

"I'll do that. Just for argument's sake, what would a cube
van full of prescription drugs be worth?"

"Depends entirely on the drugs and where they're going
to be sold," he replied. "At one time, the hottest product would
have been something like OxyContin, better known as Percocet
or Percodan, which is widely prescribed for pain control."

Tell me about it.

"Heroin addicts who can't get the real thing find it a reasonable substitute," Chan said. "Hillbilly heroin, I believe they
call it. But smuggling it wouldn't be profitable anymore because
the patent expired in the U.S. and their generic versions are
cheaper than ours. No, the real money now would be in medications with mass market appeal that are still under patent.
Brand-name drugs for high cholesterol, high blood pressure,
diabetes—all these things that affect the older crowd—
especially as the baby boomers get up there in years. The market would be staggering."

He reached for a calculator and began punching in numbers. "Take something like Contrex, which is a popular cholesterol drug. Retails for about $1.65 a pill here. Each carton would
contain a hundred and forty-four vials of one hundred each.
That's about $24,000 per carton. If there are a dozen cartons per
skid, each skid is close to $300,000. You said a cube van?"

"Yes."

"Probably holds eight skids . . . Wow. You're looking at a value of $2.5 million before it crosses the border. If you sold them in the States for three times the price in American dollars? You'd be looking at a profit of $6 million or more per van. Oh, and wait!" he said. "If the Canadian patent had expired and a generic version were available, but it was still under patent in the States, it could sell for up to ten times the price!" He sat up then and looked at me intently. "You think Jay Silver is involved in something like that?"

It had to be something like that. Why else would a big schmuck of a pharmacist with a nice wife and son get pushed around his place of business by a hood in a shiny suit?

"Have there been any similar cases that ended in disciplinary action?" I asked Chan. "Pharmacists who abused their wholesale licences?"

Chan looked at his monitor while clicking away with his mouse. "There was one recently," he said. "Bit of a sad case."

"I don't suppose you can give me his name," I said.

"Normally, no," said Chan. "But in this case I don't see how it could hurt because he was killed last month."

As soon as he said the name Kenneth Page, I remembered the ruddy, white-haired man whose photo had appeared in the *Clarion:* the pharmacist shot to death in his driveway during a carjacking.

Make that *supposed* carjacking.

I shaded my eyes with my hand as I walked back along Bloor toward my car, wishing I'd brought a ball cap. The heat and glare were withering. At Bloor and Spadina, I stepped back into the shade to wait for the light to change. A young woman with spiked black hair, combat pants and a white tank top stood with a sign around her neck that said "Karma: 25 cents." It didn't say whether the karma would be good or bad, but that's its nature anyway. You get what's coming to you.

Years ago, Peter Ustinov famously called Toronto "New York run by the Swiss," a tribute to its diversity, its cultural and financial clout, its safety and cleanliness. In those days, American film crews had to daub their own graffiti and spread their own garbage to make Toronto look gritty enough to substitute for an American city. Now we had more garbage blowing in the wind than they did, and every mailbox, doorway and light pole on Bloor was tagged with graffiti. This one intersection had panhandlers on all four corners. Northeast: the karma girl. Northwest: an Ojibwa man with a bandana around his forehead and a misshapen nose that had been broken many times, weaving on bowed legs directly into the paths of pedestrians with his palm up. Southwest: a grimy, grizzled old man on an overturned milk crate, shaking a coffee cup, a few coins jingling at the bottom. Southeast: a lean man slumped in a wheelchair, the stump of his left leg held straight out by a metal support. The homeless were everywhere now, holding out their coffee cups, their ball caps, their trembling hands. In the richest city in the country, where bankers, brokers and lawyers gathered in impregnable towers, men and women picked cigarette butts off the streets and foraged in garbage cans for something edible, their clothes black from sleeping on grates and in thickets. They held up hand-lettered signs asking for spare change. They spun stories: *Just trying to scrape up bus fare home, brother.* They muttered into their chests or barked or yipped or swore or mumbled with thick, woolly tongues.

People had always come to Toronto to seek their fortunes: from towns up north where industries die out; from Down East where the fishery has been exploited beyond renewal; from reserves that offer Natives little besides unemployment and abuse. Someone should tell them this isn't Toronto the Good anymore, that it's a city feeding on itself like a man on a hunger strike, devouring runaways, the mentally ill, the luckless, the reckless, anyone who can't move fast enough to get out of its way.

Someone else was going to have to repair this part of the world. I had my hands full with the Silver family.

When the light changed, I fished a quarter out of my pocket, then another, and dropped both coins in the hat at the feet of the karma girl.

"Make mine a double," I said.

CHAPTER 23

No homicide detective likes outside interference. They are not given to providing confidential information to private individuals. They do not like being second-guessed by amateurs, and when it comes to murder, that's what most of us are. In five years at Beacon, the closest I'd come to investigating a homicide was the week I spent working for a wealthy Rosedale woman who was sure her husband's apparent suicide had been staged to cover up his murder. Fine. If that was what she believed—had to believe—she could afford to indulge it. My first three days convinced me there was no evidence to support her contention or refute the official finding of suicide. Four more days with my client—who had all the charm of a magpie—not only convinced me that her husband had in fact killed himself but that I would likely have done the same had I woken up married to her.

Nonetheless, after leaving Winston Chan's office, I presented myself at the Toronto Police Service Homicide Squad, housed in police headquarters at 40 College Street, and asked to speak to the lead investigator into Kenneth Page's death. I was told to find Detective Sergeant Hollinger.

Hollinger—first name Katherine—was in her mid-thirties, with glossy black hair and hazel eyes, the hair pulled back, though not severely, and held in place by a clip inlaid with mother-of-pearl. She wore a navy suit over a white blouse and no jewellery apart from pearl studs in her ears. Her partner was Detective Gregg McDonough, built like a defensive back and dressed in a grey suit, white shirt and pale pink tie. He was about forty, with thick red hair finger-combed high off his forehead and a red chin beard salted with streaks of white.

"You have information about the Kenneth Page murder?" Hollinger asked.

"More like questions."

"Whoa," McDonough butted in. "You with the media?"

"No, I'm a private investigator." I held out my photo ID but McDonough ignored it.

"A rent-a-cop," he rasped, in a voice that probably had been coarsened by years of yelling at people in bars, arenas and interrogation rooms. "A cupcake."

Hollinger took my ID and looked it over. "Why does Beacon Security have questions about this case?"

I hoped none of this got back to Clint, since he'd have no idea what I was doing here. "Is it still being looked at as a car-jacking?"

"We're kind of busy, creampuff," McDonough said. "Or maybe you haven't heard a girl named Kylie Warren got killed."

"I heard."

"And yet you're still here."

"What's your interest in Mr. Page?" Hollinger asked. Her voice was a pleasant alto, far easier on the ears than McDonough's aggressive bark. She smelled better too. "Do you represent his family? We've been in contact with them and they haven't expressed any concerns with the investigation."

"Which has yielded?"

"You don't get to ask questions yet."

"Come on, Kath," McDonough said. "If we need a useless appendage hanging around wasting our time, I'll call someone in from Corporate Services."

Hollinger rolled her eyes and handed back my ID. "Come on," she said to me. "You can buy me a coffee downstairs."

Upon closer examination, I realized that Katherine Hollinger's eyes were not hazel. They were a golden honey colour and looking into them was painless. We were sitting in the lobby of 40 College drinking coffees I'd bought at a Starbucks concession. She was inspecting the marks left on my face last night by Dante Ryan. "What happened to you?"

"Bumped into a door handle."

"With knuckles on it?"

"A German design."

She levelled her eyes at me. Pretty much levelled me too. "Why are you asking about Kenneth Page?"

I sifted through a combination of lies, omissions and half-truths, looking for the most plausible to present, then said to hell with it and started with the truth, or some of it. "We're investigating a nursing home on behalf of a client," I said. "He thinks they were shorting his mother on medication before she died. I've been doing a little research into prescription medicines and I came across the name Kenneth Page in connection with illegal exports to the U.S."

"You've been to the pharmacists' association?"

"Right before I came here. Are you still treating his death as a carjacking?"

"Have you got something better?"

"The papers said his car was found at the airport the night he was killed. Who kills a guy for his car only to dump it an hour later? I know public transit has deteriorated but that's extreme."

"It's possible the killer didn't plan to use force and panicked."

"How many times was Page shot?" I asked.

"Twice."

"In the head?"

"Yes."

"Front or back?"

"Back."

"Contact wounds?"

"Not quite."

"But close."

"Yes."

"No one heard the shots?"

"No."

"Any signs of a struggle? Defensive wounds? Skin under the nails?"

"No."

"So the killer was calm enough to shoot Page twice in the head from close range, possibly with a silenced weapon, but he panicked when he got what he came for?"

"People," she said. "What are you going to do?"

"Is it safe to assume you're exploring other avenues of investigation and the carjacking angle is all you're showing to the public?"

"Is any assumption safe?" she asked.

CHAPTER 24

got back to the office shortly before noon. Fucking Franny hadn't rolled in yet. I felt like a Finn in one of those wife-carrying contests, with Monsieur Paradis playing the role of the two-hundred-pound bride. I tried to turn down the slow boil building in me and put in a call to Mark Palmer, manager of stock operations at Meissner-Hoffmann Pharmaceutical, one of Canada's largest drug manufacturers. Winston Chan had suggested him as a possible contact. Meissner-Hoffmann's office was in an industrial park north of the city in Vaughan, so I phoned rather than subject my aching side to the rigours of driving an hour in each direction.

The way Palmer guarded info at first, you'd have thought the company made weapons-grade plutonium. "How do I know you are who you say you are?"

"Didn't Winston Chan tell you I'd be calling?"

"He told me Jonah Geller would call but how do I know that's you?"

I suggested he look up Beacon Security and call me through the listed switchboard number and he calmed down. I told him what I was looking for without mentioning Jay Silver's name.

"We make it very difficult for a pharmacist to get more than his fair share of goods," Palmer said. "Our protocols are very tight. Every process is audited. The raw materials are weighed at the start of a shift and signed by two managers, and we have to have precise reconciliation at the end of the day. What goes in in powder form must come out in pill form. And yes, we weigh anything that spills or is damaged and we reconcile that too. No one is taking anything extra out of here. If you want to come for a tour of the plant, you'll see, it's all in a separate area."

"I don't understand. Separate from what?"

Palmer laughed into the phone. He had a sharp nasal voice and I pictured someone tall, thin, middle-aged, grey. "Sorry if I wasn't clear. I meant the opiates. Narcotics. The codeine-based products. Isn't that what this rogue pharmacist of yours is up to?"

Rogue pharmacist. Didn't quite have the same chilling ring as rogue cop or elephant.

"No. I think it's your everyday prescription medications, the ones that are still under patent." I rhymed off some examples Winston Chan had mentioned.

"Oh," Palmer said. "That's different. The narcotics are really what we watch. The benzodiazepines—sedatives and such—are kept in a caged-off area, but they're not as closely guarded as the opiates. And the medications that have no mind-altering effects, they're kept on open shelves like in any warehouse. In other words, not watched closely at all."

"So what about something like Serentex?" According to Meissner-Hoffmann's website, this was the company's biggest seller, an antidepressant with few side effects that still had four years to run on its patent.

"It could go out the front door without too much scrutiny, especially if the pharmacist has a wholesale licence."

"Which he does. And he used to have an Internet business so big orders aren't new for him. It's not like anyone would see a sudden spike."

"He could stockpile a fair bit before anyone got too wound up about it," Palmer told me.

An hour on the Internet brought Kenneth Page into sharper focus. According to the *Clarion* article, which I fished out of our recycling bin, he had owned a large independent store called the Drug Pharm in Etobicoke. I logged onto its website, the centrepiece of which was a tribute to the slain owner, "whose tragic death will not impede the Drug Pharm staff from fulfilling his mission." The site billed the store as "one of Ontario's leading retail and wholesale suppliers of health care products."

So Page, like Jay Silver, had held a wholesale licence. According to his bio, Page had graduated from the University of Toronto School of Pharmacy in 1980 and begun his career as a junior pharmacist with a national chain, eventually working his way up to franchise owner/operator. Five years ago, he sold the franchise and went back to school. Armed with an MBA from the University of Western Ontario, he founded the Drug Pharm "destination store" on Lakeshore Road at Islington. The destination store turned out to be the only store. The rest of the business was online. You could order pretty much any medication for pickup or delivery, as long as your prescription was written by a physician in Ontario.

Drilling deeper, I learned that Jay Silver had also gone to U of T Pharmacy, but had graduated six years after Page. Their paths would not likely have crossed there. But they could have known each other professionally. Both owned large independent stores; they could have met at functions or trade shows. I did another Internet search using both their names.

Several hits came up immediately. The highest probability rating went to the electronic newsletter of the Independent Pharmacists of Ontario, called—I kid you not—*IPOthesis*. The March 2005 issue featured a story on independent operators using "clicks and mortar"—a combination of retail stores and the Internet—to grow sales at a faster rate than companies that focused on one or the other. Both Jay Silver and Kenneth Page were cited as successful examples.

I returned to the list of hits. The ninth item on the first page of ten was a link to an article written by Kenneth Page when he'd been an MBA student at Western. Published in the business school quarterly, it showed how retailers could drive down operating costs through supply chain improvements that reduced inventory in warehouses and got products straight onto store shelves with minimum handling. "Stores that grow their Internet business will have particular need for just-in-time delivery and door-to-floor replenishment," Page wrote.

The same publication carried an article written by Jay Silver one year later. It focused on growing revenues through improved forecasting and replenishment models. I flipped back to the website of Silver's Med-E-Mart and checked his credentials. He had earned his MBA exactly one year after Ken Page.

Now I was sure they knew each other. Two MBA grads whose terms had overlapped. Both independent operators with large stores. No chains to keep an eye on them. No head office to answer to. Both with an interest in Internet sales, especially to the States before the legislation changed.

One dead and the other's family threatened with extinction.

Ryan thought someone in Buffalo had ordered the hit. From what Winston Chan had told me, the profit motive in smuggling prescription drugs over the river was huge. If Silver and Page had been involved, then people on the Buffalo side might be trying to muscle in. But on whom? Whoever was running the Toronto end, it clearly wasn't Jay Silver, not the way he got slapped around by Frank. Nor did Frank or Claudio strike me as masterminds, criminal or otherwise. If I knew who they answered to, it might lead to their masters in Buffalo. But how to find this out without exposing Ryan?

I was asking myself this question for the tenth or eleventh time when Clint came out of his office and asked everyone to gather round. His face was grim, closed up like a fist, and I wondered if the company was going under or being taken over by a competitor. Then a worse thought occurred to me: Clint was sick, something awful like cancer or a brain tumour.

It was worse.

"Guys," he said, clearing his throat. "I . . . I don't really know how to tell you this. It's never happened in all the years I've . . . that we've . . . Christ, I'm just going to say it. We lost one of our own today. Franny Paradis is dead."

A buzz went up around the room. Clint raised one hand for quiet and got it. Jenn, standing next to me, reached for my hand.

"He was murdered, guys. Shot in his car. Apparently it happened late last night or early this morning on Commissioners Street. I just spoke with detectives from Homicide. They're still processing the scene and they'll be talking to family members first, but they'll be here tomorrow morning to interview me and anyone else who knew Franny well. Jonah, Jenn, Andy—you were his roommates, as it were, so they'll want to talk to you first. They'll also want to look at his computer and his files. Until then, no one touches either, is that clear?"

People nodded or muttered their assent. Most looked numb, staring at walls, windows, objects, floors.

"Any help you can give them, people, anything at all, be as forthcoming as possible," Clint went on. "Maybe his murder is connected to his work here, maybe it isn't. But anything we can do to help the police, we do. All right. If you're not working on anything urgent right now, why don't you call it a day. Go have a drink or go be with your families. Rest up. But tomorrow, people, you come in here ready to do anything, and I mean anything, the detectives ask of us. We'll do our best to stay out of their way but that doesn't mean we stay on the sidelines. We'll share information with them but any leads they don't pick up, any trails they don't follow, we'll be all over it. I'll work up a plan tonight and hand out assignments tomorrow."

Clint turned back to his office. I realized that sometime in the last minute I had let go of Jenn's hand and started rubbing my upper arm. Right where I'd been shot.

Buffalo: the previous March

Amy Farber sat at the round oak table in her kitchen, removing vials of pills from their cartons. Her left hand was giving her more trouble than the right, the twisted knuckles looking like bird claws gripping a roost. It was a good thing she didn't have to open any vials. These days, childproof caps were pretty much Amy-proof too.

She always listened to classical music when she worked in the kitchen. Tonight it was Vladimir Horowitz playing a remarkable sonata Scarlatti wrote after moving from Rome to Madrid in mid-career. Amy herself couldn't play Scarlatti anymore: the rapid notes, hand crossings and leaps were beyond anything her stiff hands could manage. But Horowitz could— could he ever—evoking the vibrant sights and sounds of eighteenth-century Spain just as Scarlatti had experienced them when he arrived.

Above the music she could hear Barry and Rich Leckie laughing in the den at the front of the house. Barry had probably taken Rich outside for a toke while Amy was filling orders for him and Marty Oliver, this after Barry had promised no one would come until tomorrow.

Dear God, what had he gotten them into?

He had stumbled in the side door that afternoon after

going to see Kevin, his hands shaking, bursting into tears as soon as the door closed behind him. She couldn't get a word out of him no matter what she asked. He flopped on the couch in the living room without even taking off his boots, still in his dad's old bomber jacket, crying until the sleeve was wet with tears and snot. She soothed, she patted, she murmured. When the crying finally stopped she handed him a box of tissues. He blew noisily into several sheets, then got up and washed his face in the sink. He went back out the door to the garage without saying a word. When he came back in ten minutes later, she could smell pot on his jacket and in his hair. He was carrying a cardboard carton. He handed it to her—surprisingly light for its size—and asked her to take it to the kitchen, the first words he had spoken since getting home.

There were seven cartons in all. Once they were piled in the kitchen, he took Amy's hand and walked her to the table, where they each took a chair. He was still wearing his jacket. He told her that he had gone to Kevin's and that Kevin had not been there. It looked like he had cleared out but these cartons had been left in his kitchen.

"I just took what I could fit in the car," he said. "Things we need and maybe some of our friends would want."

They opened the cartons. Each held hundreds of vials containing hundreds of pills. There were a few drugs she'd never heard of, for fighting various forms of cancer or the rejection of transplanted organs. But most were familiar medications to lower cholesterol, grow hair, raise erections, fight depression, soothe anxiety, induce sleep, induce wakefulness, regulate insulin, treat infections and—*yes!!*—reduce pain and inflammation due to arthritis.

"Why would Kevin leave all this sitting there?"

"Honey, he wasn't there for me to ask."

"Then why did you come in crying like a baby?"

"Ames, I didn't—"

"Look at your sleeve, Barry. You were blowing snot bubbles."

"I didn't sleep well last night. I'm overtired."

"Bullshit, Barry. You toked yourself into a stupor last night, like you always do, and fell asleep during the movie."

"It had subtitles in five fucking languages, honey. The lead character was a violin, for Christ's sake."

"What happened at Kevin's? Tell me or get rid of it. I mean it, Barry. I'll trash every last pill, I swear."

"Trust me, Amy. It's better if I don't."

"Oh, my God. What did you do?"

"Don't get paranoid."

"Then tell me what happened instead of making me imagine the worst."

He looked at her like a little boy lost in an airport. Tears welled in his eyes and his chin trembled. "It *was* the worst, Amy. The worst thing I've ever seen in my life." He pitched himself forward, folding his long body across the table, his face buried in his arms, and began to cry again. She came around the table and tried to soothe him. She could feel his tears running down her bare arm and her own heart beating against his back. After a while he pushed himself up into a sitting position and blew his nose again. She watched this man of hers, her husband, take in deep breaths and blow them out, his cheeks puffed up like a trumpeter. He shrugged out of the leather bomber and let it slide to the floor beside him. The overhead light brought out the cross-hatched lines in the pouches forming under his eyes. She could see the old man he would one day be, taking after his father in looks if not character.

Barry took another deep breath and told her everything that had happened from the time he arrived at Kevin's to the time he entered their house in tears.

When he was done, Amy said, "Jesus, Barry, what if we get caught?"

"By who?"

"What do you mean who, the police! Who else would there be?"

"Whoever killed Kevin."

"You didn't think about that when you took the stuff?"

"I don't know. At the time, I guess I figured it's not exactly heroin. It's not even pot. And you never had a problem doing that. Remember third year? We'd buy a lid of Acapulco Gold off Jackie Rispoli and parcel it into grams. Get what we needed free."

"What I needed, maybe. There was never enough for you."

"We can get rid of this stuff quickly and quietly, just among friends. And it's not like I'm going to smoke the profits like I used to. I'm not going to run out to the garage for a hit of Lipitor."

"You would if you had nothing else. And third year was different, Barr. We were kids, we had nothing to lose."

"Do we have that much now?"

She couldn't say they did.

"No one saw me," Barry said. "I was in and out in a few minutes. It was pouring rain the whole time. Everyone was inside."

"I want it out of here in two days tops."

"Agreed."

"And we don't leave one trace of evidence it was ever here."

"Except for massive piles of cash," he grinned, throwing his arms around her.

"This is a one-time thing, Barry Aiken. Understand?"

"Of course it is, babe. Even if I wanted to do it again, I wouldn't know where to get more."Amy booted up the computer and looked up every drug in their possession on MedlinePlus.gov, noting what it was for and who among their circle might need it. Then she spent half an hour surfing websites of major pharmacy chains to find the average current retail price of each product, which ranged from five dollars a pill for the more familiar ones to more than thirty for cancer and anti-rejection drugs. They had more than a hundred thousand pills. Even if they sold them for a fraction of what they were worth, she could buy all the painkillers and anti-inflammatories she'd ever need. They could enroll in a VIP health plan with every benefit imaginable. They could travel somewhere warm, escape the Buffalo winters that made her joints ache and swell. She could free her mind from the worries that had shrouded her since Barry was laid off.

"Five bucks a pill minimum, fifteen for the expensive stuff," Barry argued.

"Three dollars," she said. "And the cancer and transplant drugs are free to anyone who needs them. I won't make a penny off them."

"But Ames—"

"The higher the prices, the longer it'll take to unload, and the more people we'll have coming through here. I want this kept to the New Fifty group and friends we can trust to keep their mouths shut."

Barry agreed and went off to start making phone calls, starting with Marty Oliver.

"Why him?" Amy asked.

"He's the closest thing I have to a lawyer."

Listening to Rich and Barry giggling in the front room now, Amy wondered, not for the first time, whether Barry's lifestyle was finally catching up with him. All the dope he had smoked, the acid and mushrooms he had tripped on. Was he finally coming unhinged? Taking a chance like this: was it a sign that his moorings were slipping, easing him out from shore into water whose colour warned of hidden depths?

Amy had fallen hard for Barry the first time she saw him on campus. He was studying fine arts; she was majoring in piano, unaware that her own immune system would one day turn on her so badly she'd barely be able to play Chopsticks, let alone Chopin. Barry had black hair straight down his back like a Native American in those days. He was lean; he could wear those skinny black stovepipe jeans without looking ridiculous, unlike Rich, whose pear-shaped body demanded something more forgiving even in his youth. Barry had enjoyed considerable acclaim as a student, winning a faculty award for works inspired by Frank Stella's minimalism, discrete blocks of bold colours separated by thin lines Barry scraped across the canvas with his thumbnail. Then he'd gone post-modernist, influenced by Andy Warhol and his celebrity portraits, only Barry didn't know any real celebrities, so his work lacked the connection between subject and style that Warhol exploited. Then it was on to Robert Rauschenberg's emerging pop-art sensibility, Barry screening archival images onto canvas in jarring contexts, trying to confront society, as he then explained it, with society's own face. And that was Barry, Amy eventually realized. Talented enough to soak up influences and talk the talk, but always riffing on someone else's style rather than developing one of his own. He went only as far as his modest talent and even more modest work ethic could take him, and that had not been very far at all.

Amy, on the other hand, had made the most of her musical gifts, always working as hard as, if not harder than, other musicians she met in schools or competitions. It wasn't until her last year that she could see other students pulling away from the pack and realized a concert career was not to be.

Neither Barry nor Amy wound up at the forefront of an artistic revolution, as they'd once hoped, Buffalo being several hundred miles northwest of said forefront in New York. But both found work that made good use of their skills, Barry in graphic design, Amy as a piano teacher and rehearsal accompanist for musical theatre, ballet and dance companies. They liked their jobs and lived well. They had great friends, most of whom they'd known since college. But what had it all amounted to,

Amy sometimes wondered. What impression had they made on the world? They had never had children: supposedly a mutual decision but it was Barry who had never been ready, Barry who always ended the discussion, Barry who wouldn't have unprotected sex with her unless the time was safe.

So unlike his father. Amy had adored Norman Aiken; she found in him a warmth and unconditional love she had never felt with her own parents. He loved classical music and was as knowledgeable about it as she was. He had a baby grand in the living room and often asked her to play—something Barry would never do unless it was old Beatles songs or faux-classical crap by pretentious old buggers like Keith Emerson or Rick Wakeman. When Norman died and left them the house, Barry had wanted to sell it and bank the profits. Amy insisted otherwise. She was ready for a real life, a real house. Her arthritis was already evident and she wanted out of their semi on Franklin Street, with its thin walls and warped doors that let in the frigid air of winter. If they were going to live the rest of their lives together without children, she wanted a home that felt warm and safe and solid.

She heard more laughter from the den and then a swell of music, the opening chords of "Let It Be" ringing like a church bell.

"Barry?" she called. "All done."

Footsteps clumped down the hall and Barry and Rich joined her in the kitchen. She handed Rich two plastic shopping bags. "This one is yours," she said. "And this is for Marty. Twenty-four hundred all together."

"A steal at twice the price!" Rich's eyes looked bloodshot and his tongue was sticking to his mouth. Barry had obviously rolled the good stuff, the indoor weed he bought from a thin black guy named Crawford, who lived on Hampshire down by Grant.

Rich pulled a thick wad of bills out of his pocket and began thumbing hundreds and twenties into a pile. When he was done, Amy recounted it, despite the rolling of Barry's eyes, and put it into a box of Tide she had emptied out.

They were going to need more boxes.

"Before you go, Richard, there's something I must show you in the den," Barry said.

Amy sighed. She knew what that meant: *Let's roll another joint.* It was always time to roll another one. Goddamn Barry sometimes. Goddamn him and his appetites and impulsiveness. Goddamn the rut he'd gotten himself stuck in sometime between the Summer of Love and Woodstock. Guys his age still running out to smoke behind the garage, acting like eternal adolescents even as their bodies began to crumple and fail. The heroes of 9/11, the ones who brought down the plane in Pennsylvania: *"Let's roll"* had been their rallying cry. It was Barry's too, the cry of a big gangly kid who once told her he smoked too much dope because he had never been breast-fed.

The doorbell rang. Amy didn't hear Barry move to open it, even though he was at the front of the house.

"Barr?" she called. He didn't answer. Of course he didn't. He wouldn't want to put off rolling his joint.

"Jesus," Amy sighed, and left the kitchen. At the front door, she looked out the glass panel. A delivery man stood there holding an insulated vinyl pizza-warmer.

"Barry?" she called. "Did you order a pizza?"

No answer. The music in the den was louder now. Some shrill rock classic: Nazareth or AC/DC.

"Barry?"

Of course he had ordered a pizza. That's what arrested adolescents do when they get the munchies after a toke behind Mother's back.

She opened the door to a pleasant-looking young man with Cupid's-bow lips and a face as round as the moon.

CHAPTER 26

Toronto: Thursday, June 29

No morning that starts off with Percocet and a stool softener bodes well for the rest of the day. But I needed both and in equal measure.

The mood at the office was sombre when I arrived. Clint's office door was closed; shadows visible through a pebbled glass panel suggested he was meeting with at least two people. Throughout the workspace, colleagues were clustered in groups of three and four, asking one another about the investigation, funeral services, Franny's family, which of his ex-wives would make the biggest scene, Vicki or Mireille.

Jenn and Andy were in our cube patch drinking coffee. I got a subdued welcome. Andy barely looked up and whatever he said was unintelligible. Jenn smiled weakly and nodded at a third coffee on my desk. "I brought that for you just in case."

I thanked her and took off the lid. Wisps of steam rose briefly into the air before disappearing. I stared at Franny's desk, at his dark computer monitor. He hated the thing. I could picture him sitting there, cursing the computer, the keyboard, the mouse, the software and the entire nerd universe that made them possible.

At nine on the dot, Clint emerged from his office. Behind him were Detective Sergeant Katherine Hollinger and the knuckle-dragging redhead, McDonough. He smirked when he saw me. Hollinger smiled. I smiled back, only it came out more like a goofy grin. I reminded myself I was on Percocet and to mind my manners.

Clint called for everyone's attention and got it fast. "People, I'd like to introduce Detective Sergeant Hollinger and Detective McDonough. They're leading the investigation into Franny's death. I've asked them to give you an update, then we'll talk about how you can help. Sergeant?"

Hollinger stepped forward with a black notebook in hand. "I can't give out certain details, for reasons you people understand better than most, but here's what we know. The deceased was found in his car on Commissioners Street, behind a warehouse owned by the Erie Storage Company. Based on evidence gathered at the scene, that is where the murder took place. Not a dump site, in other words. The deceased—"

"Franny," someone called out behind me. "Please." It was Darrel Mitchell, an older investigator, long divorced and one of Franny's drinking buddies.

"I'm sorry," Hollinger said. "Franny had multiple gunshot wounds in the head, face and neck from a smaller-calibre weapon, probably a .22 with a sound suppressor, which is why it attracted no attention until this morning. Preliminary time of death is between midnight and two a.m. Obviously we need to know what the deceased—what Franny was doing at the warehouse. Was he meeting someone? Was it in regard to a case? We're tracing the owner of the warehouse, obviously, but it's a numbered company and we haven't yet tracked down an actual person. We're canvassing the area, speaking to watchmen who were on duty last night. Asking for video footage from neighbouring companies with security cameras. We hope to pin down the exact time Franny drove down Commissioners, and see who preceded or followed.

"We're going to speak to everyone here who knew him. We're counting on you to provide us with leads. There might be questions you don't like. Did he gamble, was he a doper, was he seeing someone's wife? But you know we need to ask them and you need to answer. We'll look into his ongoing cases and any enemies he might have made in the past."

"Start with his ex-wives," Darrel said, and got a good laugh, easing some of the tension in the room.

"We'll be using the conference room for interviews," Clint said. "Stay at your workstations, please, until we call you. If you need to leave for any reason, let someone know where you're going and keep your cell or pager on. No exceptions. Jonah?"

I looked up.

"We'll start with you."

The four of us sat at a rectangular cherry wood conference table, McDonough and Clint at the heads, Hollinger and I across from each other. She wore an olive-coloured pantsuit today, with a white blouse underneath. Her hair was bunched at the back of her neck and held there by some combination of leather and chopsticks. No jewellery again, save for her ear studs. Definitely no wedding ring or tan line showing she had worn one any time recently.

Not that I had the urge to observe McDonough that closely.

Whoa, boy, I told myself. The Percocet has clouded your judgment and lowered your inhibitions—a deadly combination in the male of our species. I told myself I was in the presence of a woman who not only might prove immune to my charms but was armed and trained in the use of deadly force. Then I hoped I had told myself this silently.

"If it isn't the cupcake," McDonough said.

"You know each other?" Clint asked.

"We met yesterday," I said.

"Regarding?"

"A case we're working," McDonough said. "Your man was asking about a victim named Kenneth Page."

"Why?" Clint asked. "I thought you were helping Franny with his nursing home inquiry."

"Just a long shot I was checking out for him," I said. "Nothing came of it."

"Big surprise," McDonough said. "So, come on, cupcake, show us your highly tuned powers of observation. Crack the case open. Drop it in my lap like they do on TV."

"All right," Clint said. "There's no need for that."

"Sure," McDonough said with a mirthless smile.

Hollinger said, "Tell us about the case you were helping the victim with."

I told them what I knew about Meadowvale and the Vista Mar Care Group, starting with the Boyko interview and ending with a much abridged version of the melee that took place at the end of our visit.

"Let me get this straight," McDonough said. "These scuzzballs are stealing pills from old ladies so they can turn around and sell them elsewhere?"

"I can't prove it, but that's what I think. Jenn will agree."

"Don't worry. We'll talk to her next."

"What part of the case was Franny working?" Hollinger asked.

Man, how to answer that one? As far as I knew he hadn't done a damn thing other than entertain LaReine.

"Jonah?"

It was Clint who had called my name. "What part was Franny handling?" he asked.

"He was . . . um, looking at the big picture while I was checking facts on the ground."

"What the fuck does that mean?" McDonough barked.

"That he doesn't want to answer the question," Hollinger said.

"Out with it, cupcake," McDonough said.

Clint said, "Anything you know, Jonah, anything at all."

"Okay. He met a woman on Sunday named LaReine. Don't ask me where. The only thing he told me was she's black and built. It seems they hit it off and we didn't see much of him after that."

"You have her contact information?" Hollinger asked.

"Check his cellphone. Her number should be one of his recent calls."

"So anything we need to know about his case we have to get from you?" McDonough said.

"Guess so."

He said, "Terrific," yet I doubted his sincerity.

"Why would he have gone to that warehouse?" Hollinger asked.

"No idea."

"Would he have known it from a previous case?"

"Not that I'm aware of."

"What exactly *are* you aware of?" McDonough asked.

"From what you told us earlier," Hollinger said, "you were doing all the work on this case while Mr. Paradis was seeing a new girlfriend."

"That's right."

"You might have to explain what a girlfriend is," said McDonough.

Hollinger made eye contact with me. I'm pretty sure her eyes rolled a little. "Gregg?" she said sweetly. "Mind getting us some coffee?"

McDonough glared at her. He was either seriously ticked or they were running an above-average good cop/bad cop routine.

I said to him, "Just a dollop of milk for me. No sugar."

His face turned red like a match head about to ignite. Definitely ticked.

"I'll show you where it is," Clint said, leading him out and closing the door.

"So," Hollinger said. "You were doing Franny's work while he was romping around. Were you annoyed?"

"Of course."

"How annoyed, Mr. Geller?"

"Please. Call me Jonah."

"Are those his knuckle marks on your face, Jonah?"

You have to love a question like that, especially when delivered with a fetching smile. "No, these are not Franny's knuckles."

"Whose then?"

"An unrelated dispute. A misunderstanding that got out of hand."

"And into your face."

I shrugged.

"Your side too? Take one in the ribs?"

"Why?"

"The way you've been moving in your chair. You're hurting there."

"I hadn't noticed you noticing."

"You never will. What started you looking into Kenneth Page? What led from the nursing home to him?"

"I told you, it was a long shot that didn't pan out."

"Let's hear it anyway. And don't hold anything back."

I batted my eyelashes and said, "Would I hold anything back from you?" *Oh, God, Geller, you Percocet-addled puppy, shut up. And stay shut.*

"Come on," she said. "Meadowvale. Page. What's the connection?"

"Places like Meadowvale get their drugs from somewhere. Often a pharmacy with a wholesale licence."

"Which Page had?"

"Yes. He could get large quantities from manufacturers without questions, and the doctor who runs the home, Bader, could write phony scripts until his hand cramped up."

"And sell them to whom?"

"The most lucrative market seems to be the States."

"And who's taking receipt there?"

"No idea," I said. "Not yet."

I never did get a coffee out of McDonough. He returned with one for Hollinger and one for himself. Clint had gone back to his office to take a call from Franny's mother, Dorothée, in Ottawa. I went over everything again with McDonough in the room. He perked up at the thought that Franny might have punched me out, but Hollinger reminded him that Franny's autopsy showed no bruising or other marks on his hands to suggest he had recently hit anyone.

Which she had known when she asked me about it. Katherine Hollinger was a girl who liked to have fun. Definitely not your average homicide sarge.

After I got back to my desk, Jenn was called in. Andy stayed focused on his research. He didn't like to talk at the best of times, and this was anything but. I went to the men's room, where I ensconced myself in a stall to check my wound. I untucked my shirt and held it up with my chin. The adhesive strips holding the gauze dressing in place came away easily but the pad itself stuck to the gash. I winced and sucked air and pulled until it came free. The wound itself looked good: red around the edges but no pus or other sign of infection; the gash itself warm and tender but not hot. I put the dressing back— Dr. Klein had warned me against changing it myself—and washed down two more Percocet and another stool softener. The stalemate between them was continuing apace. There'd be a reckoning at some point. Like an economy heading toward recession, maybe the best I could hope for was a soft landing.

Hollinger was waiting at my desk when I got back.

"Tuck your shirt in," she said. "We're going out."

CHAPTER 27

Franny had lived in a high-rise on Carlton just east of the old Maple Leaf Gardens, where the Leafs played for sixty-odd years—some very odd—before moving to the Air Canada Centre, where corporate revenues could flow more freely. I had never been inside his place. Any time people from the office got together for drinks after work, it was usually at a bar on King or Front.

Outside his apartment door, Katherine Hollinger handed me a pair of disposable surgical gloves. "Put these on."

"I'm not contagious," I said.

"Or infectious," she shot back. "You know the rule. No touching."

"I know."

"Not even with the gloves."

"I get it. No touching. I'll pretend we're in high school." *Oy.* Was it just the Percocet that made me so giddy around her?

"You see anything at all, let me know."

"Of course."

"More convincingly, please."

"Of *course.*" I snapped on the gloves.

"Much better." She opened the deadbolt with a single brass key and in we went.

Franny's one-bedroom apartment was about the same size as mine, but his windows faced south onto a blighted stretch of Carlton frequented by low-rent hookers wobbling on too-high heels and in too-tight skirts. I much preferred my view of the city skyline and the Don Valley. The Track, as this part of town was known, had a darkness all its own.

Franny's living room/dining room combo was effectively divided into three functional spaces: a eating area, living room and office.

The eating area consisted of a round table and two chairs, over which a chandelier hung. It didn't look like he'd dined there recently. The table was covered in newspapers from the weekend, the Sunday *Clarion* on top.

The living room had a black leather sofa and recliner facing an entertainment centre with a large flat-screen TV and stereo system. Next to the recliner was a small table on which rested a number of remotes and on the floor beneath that a pizza box. That's where he probably ate his last meal. Books and CDs filled smaller shelves in the entertainment unit, along with DVDs of action films featuring muscled-up Hollywood hunks and whippet-thin fighters out of Thailand and Hong Kong.

The office was built into a corner of the living room, its centrepiece an old-fashioned rolltop desk with dozens of pigeonholes that should have been stuffed with notes, bills, statements, parking tickets, takeout menus and other detritus of metropolitan life. They were empty.

I asked, "Where is it?"

"What?"

"It. Everything. His mail, bank records, phone bills."

"We took it all downtown," Hollinger said. "Gregg and I will sort through it there."

"Does he move his lips when he reads?"

"Easy, you. He's my partner."

"But you're the brains."

"Someone has to be."

The artwork was all generic: prints of a waterfall pouring over moss-covered rocks, a hooked marlin breaking through aqua waters, red-tailed hawks wheeling over a green forest canopy, all in the same chrome-and-glass frames. They could have come from any hotel chain.

I turned to Hollinger. "Did you find a notebook on him?"

"I don't have the complete inventory."

"He wasn't much for computers."

"So we've gathered."

"He usually had a black notebook in his jacket pocket."

"Thanks. If we find it, I'll let you know."

The kitchen was a small galley like mine. A few basic pots and pans in the cupboards. A dish set that had to have come from Ikea. One drawer had cutlery and a few utensils, the other a thick sheaf of takeout menus. It wasn't hard to guess which got used more.

The bathroom had the basic items a man needed to keep himself shaved, showered and reasonably well groomed, plus a few more. Grecian Formula: who knew? A tube of K-Y jelly and a box of 12 condoms, about half of which remained. A few prescription medicines, including one for arthritis pain.

The bedroom had room for a queen bed, a dresser and night table and little else. The closet had the usual mix of inexpensive suits and casual clothes, along with a collapsible ironing board and shoeshine kit. Of course he'd have those, the old-fashioned lug. A freshly pressed shirt, a shine and his pompadour in place, and he'd be ready for action in no time.

So who would murder him? There was nothing to indicate he was living beyond his means. If anything, the apartment was distressingly plain. And too much like my own. Same little kitchen and bathroom, same parquet floors, same fixtures and windows. Same little place built for one.

Was this my future? Nights alone eating in front of the TV, an array of remotes at my side? Would the ghosts that followed me home from Israel ever stop rattling their dusty bones long enough to let me settle down, fall in love again, do more than simply keep my head above Toronto's ever-rising tide?

I turned to Hollinger. "Can I ask you something?"

"You just did."

"Do people call you Kathy?"

"Not since they issued us Glocks."

"Kate?"

"Friends and family only."

"So it's Katherine then?"

"No, it's Hollinger. Detective Sergeant Hollinger if you want to be formal."

"Okay, Hollinger. Why'd you bring me here? You've carted out everything that matters."

"How do we know what matters?"

"How would I? I've never been here before and I didn't really know him outside work."

She pursed her lips and looked down and shifted her weight from foot to foot. When she had made up her mind about whatever she had been pondering, she said, "Sit."

We sat on the leather couch.

She snapped off the gloves and indicated I could do the same.

"I hate these things," she said. "Even the powdered ones make my hands clammy."

"So why were we wearing them? If you've removed all his documents, surely you've processed the place."

She held my gaze with hers, held it more gently than any cop in my experience ever had, and asked, "Who wants you dead?"

"Excuse me?"

"I thought I spoke clearly. Who wants you dead?"

"I'm not following."

"Then you're not trying. Your colleague, Ms. Raudsepp, provided an interesting piece of information this morning. Something you couldn't have known."

"Why?"

"Because it happened after you left the office Tuesday."

"What happened?"

"According to her, Mr. Paradis came in sometime after three o'clock. He was there until at least seven. Just after six this call came in."

Hollinger pulled a small chrome tape player from her briefcase. "All incoming calls to Beacon Security are recorded, correct?"

"Of course," I said.

"Then have a listen," she said, and pressed play.

Franny: Hello?

Male voice: You the detective looking into a nursing home called Meadowvale?

Franny: That's me. Who's calling, please?

Male: I have information.

Franny: What kind of infor—

Male: The helpful kind. As long as you can pay, say, five hundred cash. That a problem?

Franny: It depends on the information, of course. It's the client who pays.

Male: You bring the cash, I'll bring what I know. Then you decide if it's worth it.

Franny: I don't think so.

Male: Okay, three hundred. What I know about this place, your client can sue the shirts off their backs.

Franny: Who are you?

Male: I used to work there, okay? See what I'm saying? I know all kinds of shit about it but I got to keep a low profile. I don't want them to know it was me who told you. Tell you what, man, we'll start with a hundred, okay? Like a down payment. You like what I got, we'll talk terms.

Franny: Why don't you come by the office now?

Male: I told you why. Look, there's a warehouse on Commissioners just west of the recycling plant. Erie Storage. Park behind there at twelve-thirty tonight with a hundred cash and I'll tell you enough to show you I'm your man.

Franny: I don't think so.

Male: You think I'm going to all this trouble to rob you of a hundred bucks? I could mug an old lady for more.

Franny: I'm not worried.

Male: Then be there. You'll solve your case hands down.

And then the line went dead. The caller had suckered Franny cleanly, lowering his price until it was no obstacle, then making his information sound so tantalizing—*the ex-employee who knows what really went on*—that Franny had followed it blindly to his death.

"Jonah," Hollinger said.

"Yes, Kate?"

Her smile all the way gone now. "The call came in on your line. Your buddy François answered it for you. Maybe he wanted to pay you back for everything you'd been doing for him. So let me ask again: who wants you dead?"

I said, "The voice on the tape sounded American. 'You'll *salve* your case hands down.' Like from Chi-*cah*-go."

"Or Buffalo," she said. "They've got that Midwestern *ah* sound too. Does that ring any bells?"

"No."

"I'm surprised you're not being more forthcoming. Aren't you still recovering from your last gunshot wound?"

I looked at her with new-found appreciation. "You checked me out."

"It's what I do," she said. "So how's the arm?"

"Much better, thank you. And you'll have to take my word for it. I'm not up for arm wrestling."

She gave me a quizzical look.

"Never mind," I said. "Long story."

"The gang you were investigating on that job, the Di Pietras. Heard from them lately?"

"No," I lied.

She said, "Maybe they reached out to touch you."

CHAPTER 28

When we got back to Beacon's office, Hollinger went back to interviewing employees in the conference room; I stayed down at street level. I knew I should get back upstairs—Clint had made clear that we were all supposed to be on hand—but the thought that I had been the intended victim had my head buzzing like a hive of bees with anger issues. I called Dante Ryan instead and told him what had happened.

"All right," he said. "That's enough. Be outside your office in half an hour."

"To do what?"

"I'll tell you when I get there."

"I can't leave the office now. My boss'll shit a brick."

"Let him," Ryan said. "You got other things to think about. Besides, you're no use to him dead, right?"

"No."

"Or to me, so get ready to take a ride."

"Don't take this the wrong way, Ryan, but when guys like you say let's take a ride, guys like me usually wind up dead."

"There a right way to take that?" he asked.

Ryan's car was a three-year-old grey Volvo Cross Country wagon, with a child's car seat strapped in the right rear position and shades on the rear windows that featured Looney Tunes characters: Bugs, Daffy, Elmer Fudd and Yosemite Sam. Elmer and Sam were both armed to the teeth, Elmer with a shotgun and Sam with a brace of pistols.

"You're kidding," I said as I got in.

"Not what you were expecting?" he asked.

"An SUV, maybe, or a Town Car. A Hummer. Definitely not the Dadmobile."

"That's the point," Ryan said. "I drove a car like this even before we had Carlo. You know why? People see what they think they see. Someone sees this tub leaving a scene, they think I'm another witness, a passerby. Not the . . ." He stopped short of whatever he was going to call himself.

He adjusted his rear-view and side mirrors; he must have reset them while he was waiting for me, to give him a clear view of anyone approaching his car.

"How's the DVP at this hour?"

I shrugged. The Don Valley Parkway is also known—for good reason and entirely without affection—as the Don Valley Parking Lot. The only northbound highway on the east side of the city, it's always jammed, and conditions only get worse in the summer when the city crams a year's worth of repairs into a few short months. "It should be bearable. It usually doesn't clog up seriously for another hour."

Ryan took the elevated Gardiner Expressway west to the northbound DVP. I liked the way he handled a car: aware of everything going on around him, cool and economical behind the wheel. Maybe it was a product of a life spent watching his back, but he seemed to anticipate what other drivers would do—handy in a city where few drivers have skill or judgment. Seconds later, as if to prove my point, a motorcyclist roared up on our right, bent flat over the front of his bike, going at least twenty miles an hour faster than anyone else. He swept through our lane a foot from our front bumper, then did the same to the car in front of us, cutting sharply back to the inside lane.

"You believe this lunatic?" Ryan said.

"He'll make a good organ donor."

"You know what depresses me? We could find out who ordered the hit, change his mind, save the kid's life, settle things with Marco and still get killed by a moron on a bike."

"If that's all that depresses you, it's the first sign you're not Jewish."

"Don't worry," Ryan said. "I got plenty else on my mind."

"Such as?"

"Such as Marco ordering a hit on you, but with someone other than me. It could mean he didn't believe our little act in the park."

"You certainly did your part to sell it," I said.

"No joke, Geller. Marco's not the sharpest knife in the drawer but he has his instincts, and if they tell him I've thrown in with you, we're both in extremely deep shit."

"It wasn't Marco who ordered the hit."

Ryan actually took his eyes off the road at that, giving me a sideways look that was mostly bewilderment, salted with a dash of scorn. "What do you mean?"

"Think about the timing. Marco didn't get to the park Tuesday night until well after nine o'clock. The phone call Franny answered came in two hours before that."

"Jesus, Geller, how many people you got after you?"

I told Ryan how Jenn and I had infiltrated Meadowvale, ending with our escape from the two hoods who had tried to corral us. I described the Melonhead and the Suit. Ryan didn't say anything but his grip on the wheel tightened. I could see blood draining out of his knuckles.

I said, "What?"

"The guy with the round face."

"What about him?"

"There's a guy out of Buffalo looks like that. I mean, if I was asked to describe him, I'd have used the same words you did."

"He have a name?"

"Oh, yeah," Ryan snorted.

"Suddenly this is funny?"

"His name is Ricky Messina. He's loosely connected to the Magaddinos."

"And what does he do exactly?"

"Ricky is in my line of work."

"Great. He any good?"

"He's not in my league, if that's any comfort."

"Not much."

"I met him once at a funeral I had to attend for appearance's sake, and he's all punk. You know what I heard? He gave himself a nickname instead of waiting for a made guy to give him one. He's taken to calling himself the Clip. Ricky the Clip, 'cause he clips people. Sounds more like a barber in a one-stool shop, you ask me."

"What the hell was a hit man from Buffalo doing at a nursing home in Ontario?"

"Either he's looking for a place to put his dear old mother," Ryan said, "or that place is dirtier than you think."

Fifteen minutes and as many near-collisions later, Ryan exited onto Highway 7 and drove west. After a long stretch of car dealerships, body shops and fast food outlets, he pulled into a small strip plaza and parked.

"Wait here," he said. He popped the trunk latch, then got out and went to the back of the car. When he came back he was carrying the kind of large metal case photographers use for cameras and lenses. In the middle of the plaza, between a beauty salon and a butcher shop, was a storefront whose windows were covered with newsprint. Taped to the door was a For Rent sign with no phone number on it. Ryan knocked. A moment later, a thin man in a white shirt and dark slacks opened it. He and Ryan embraced briefly, clapping each other on the back.

Ryan pulled some money out of his pocket and handed a bill to the man and nodded his head toward an Italian restaurant that anchored the west end of the plaza. The man walked over to the restaurant and gave Ryan a wave before entering. When Ryan beckoned me, I got out of the car slowly, my side sore from the ride. Once we were both inside, Ryan locked the door and said, "We got maybe half an hour."

The place was set up like a café, with red vinyl chairs and wood veneer tables. A tall fridge with glass doors was well stocked with beer and wine, and behind a counter at the far end was an espresso machine and a shelf that held bottles of single malt and blended Scotch, grappa, vodka, gin, cognac and rum.

"Social club?" I asked.

"More like a conference centre." Ryan opened a door at the back and led me down a steep staircase into a basement with a cement floor and heavy curtains over all the walls.

"Jesus Christ," I said.

There were guns everywhere. Dozens of them. Pistols on tables, rifles leaning against walls, shotguns in locked cabinets. Boxes of ammunition labelled by calibre.

Ryan set his case down on a table and flipped it open. Six handguns were set in thick grey foam. "This is my Glock 20," he said, pointing to an automatic. "Hits like a Magnum *and* holds twenty rounds. Next to it is its baby brother, the Glock 29. Smaller and easier to conceal. Only carries ten rounds but if you need more than that you're in the wrong business. Now this," he said, pointing to a huge nickel-plated revolver, "this is the Smith & Wesson Classic I took to see JoJo Santini. How'd you like to chew on that barrel? Eight and three-eighths inches of stainless steel. The little one with the long barrel is a .22 Colt."

"They think that's the kind that killed Franny."

"He was shot close?"

I nodded. "Head and neck."

"That's all a .22 is good for is close-ups. Otherwise, you're better off throwing it at a guy than shooting him with it. Now this—this is the one: a Beretta 9-mil, the Cougar model. This is good. This is *nice*. Not too heavy, not too long a barrel—a little under four inches—packs ten rounds and there's hardly any recoil. Not too accurate from a distance, but if you need it at all, it'll be up close."

"If I—me? You brought me here to get *me* a gun?"

"They tried to kill you twice already. You want to keep going up against them unarmed?"

"I'm not licensed to carry a gun."

"Neither is Ricky the Clip, for Chrissakes. Neither is Marco or Phil or me for that matter. We don't have licences but we all got guns."

"If I get caught with an illegal weapon, I'd lose my investigator's licence."

"Get caught without one, you'll lose a lot more. Suppose Ricky shows up at your door. What are you going to do, demand to see his licence?"

"I can't take it. I won't." My stomach was twisting and my breath seemed harder to find. It wasn't the penalties I was thinking about, or my licence. It was the feeling of hot desert air filling my lungs, of sand stinging my eyes.

He held the Cougar out to me, butt first. "If you walk out of here without the gun," he said, "keep walking. Make your own way back to town."

"Why? Why is it so important that I carry a gun? You care that much about me?"

"Pal, I care about *me*. If we're in this together, you might wind up having to watch my back and I don't want you there empty-handed. You might be good with your fists but you can't throw a punch fifty feet. Someone's drawing down on me, you gonna stand around yelling *Haiee-ya!*, maybe break a plank with your head? Uh-uh. Not how I work. You're going to take the gun, you're going to fire the gun until you know what the fuck you're doing, and then you are going to take the gun home so you can stay alive until this is over and keep me alive if it comes to it." He pointed to the far end of the basement where life-sized silhouettes of men were taped to the walls.

"A practice range?" I asked.

Ryan went to the nearest wall and pulled away the curtain to reveal what looked like sheets of egg cartons. "It's pretty soundproof." One of the silhouettes had a black and white photo where the face would be. "Recognize him?"

I did. It was Stewart McClelland, chair of TFTOC, the Task Force on Traditional Organized Crime. "We call it Tough Talk," Ryan said, "because that's all they fuckin' do." He racked the slide on the Beretta, pushed off the safety and pumped three shots where the heart would have been. The three holes he made were close together; any one of them would have been a kill shot.

He handed me the gun again. This time I took it. "Aim for the chest," he said.

I closed my hand on it and felt the weight. About the same as the one I'd once carried, one and three-quarter pounds. It had been so long since I had held one. So many years ago. So many dreams.

"Don't stand stiff-legged," he said. "It's okay to crouch a little like you're in a batting cage. You lefty or righty?"

"Lefty."

"Don't pull the trigger, just squeeze it. And don't forget to breathe. It's not healthy."

I remembered Roni Galil saying the same thing to me. With his heavy Israeli accent it came out "breeze." *Breeze, Yonah, before you shooting. Don't forget to breeze.*

I remembered lying in bed Tuesday night, feeling pain where Marco had cut me, feeling alone and vulnerable and wishing I had a gun. Now I did and I felt worse.

I took a breath and settled into the modified Weaver stance Roni had taught me. Left hand holding the gun, left arm extended, right hand cupped around the left, right elbow tucked against my body. Right leg forward, right knee bent, weight evenly placed. Centred. Rock solid. Back on the bike.

I pictured Marco up there instead of Stewart McClelland. Marco standing over Lucas Silver with that stiletto of his, pulling Lucas's head back by the hair to expose his throat all soft, all white. I pictured the mother screaming and Marco smiling, the knife going toward the boy's jugular and me the only one who could stop him. I exhaled and fired at the centre mass of the silhouette in front of me. And kept firing until the clip was empty.

CHAPTER 29

Buffalo: the previous March

"How much do I owe you?" said the woman at the door.

"Lady, you have no idea," said Ricky Messina, his face breaking into a wide grin. "No idea at all."

He put his hand in the vinyl warmer and brought out his High Standard Victor. An absolute beauty, five and a half inches of blue steel with gold-plate detailing. She didn't seem to care for it much, but that was fine by Ricky. Her scared eyes and open mouth just added to her allure, which was considerable, even though she was on the old side for Ricky, letting her hair go grey.

"Who else is in the house?" he asked.

She glanced around wildly, a pulse beating visibly in her throat. He laid the barrel of the gun against where it beat. "Tell me how many," he said. "Or you'll be one less."

"Two," she said quickly.

"Men?"

"Yes," she said.

"They have guns?"

"I—I don't—"

"Strictly yes or no," Ricky said.

"No."

"Where are they?"

"The den. Right there." She indicated a closed door with a nod of her head.

"Knock."

She swallowed as if trying to wet her throat enough to speak.

"Knock, I said. Now."

She rapped on the door with the heel of her hand. "Barry?" she called.

"Just a sec," a man answered.

Ricky heard footsteps on the hardwood floor, two sets, and a high-pitched giggle. When the door opened, he saw two men in their fifties: a Mutt 'n' Jeff act, one of them tall and thin with longish grey hair, the other shorter, rounder, balder. Both froze when they saw the gun pointed at Amy.

"Let's adjourn to the living room, shall we?" Ricky said.

Neither one moved.

He pushed the gun into the soft tissue of her throat, making her gag. When he pulled it away, the suppressor at the end had left a circular imprint. "Fucking adjourn, I said."

"Okay, okay," the tall one said, his hands up—though he hadn't been told to put them up. The pear-shaped one followed him out of the den.

"Either one of you assholes her husband?" Ricky asked.

The tall one took long enough to say, "Me."

"I don't know," Ricky said to the woman. "Couldn't a cute girl like you have done better?"

This was working out beautifully. He could have found himself up against real heavies like he had at other times, gun-nut bikers or connected shitheads with ambition. But here were two softies, grey old farts looking like they'd die of fright before he had a chance to kill anyone.

In the living room, he made them sit together on the couch, bunched together like they were in the back seat of a small car. He stayed standing, the gun held casually in their direction without pointing at anyone in particular.

"Look, man," the tall one said.

"Don't call me man, man," Ricky said. "My name is Ricky. And you are?"

No one on the couch answered.

He pointed the Victor squarely at the tall man. "Did you not hear me ask your name?"

"Barry," said the tall man.

"Barry what?"

"Aiken."

"And you?" he asked the woman.

"Amy Farber."

"You didn't take his name?" Ricky asked.

"No."

"Just as well. You might not be married much longer. What about you, pudge?"

"Richard Leckie," the chub said, looking down at the ground.

"Another Richard!" Ricky exclaimed. "You don't by any chance go by Ricky, do you?"

"No," he stammered. "Rich, mostly."

"That's good, Rich," Ricky said. "You might have just saved your own life, 'cause there's only room for one Ricky and that would be me."

"Um . . . Ricky?" Barry said. "We have some cash in the house. And a laptop and a digital camera and an iPod, the four-gig nano."

"You think I'm here to rob you?" Ricky said.

"I guess—"

"You calling me a thief?"

"No!"

"Good. Because that would really insult me, coming from a friend and partner."

Barry gaped at him. "I don't get it."

"Sure you do, Barr. You took something that belongs to me and that makes you my partner. Right?"

Something that sounded an awful lot like denial started coming out of Barry's mouth so Ricky stepped forward and kicked Rich Leckie hard on the kneecap. Rich toppled to the floor, clutching his knee, his eyes screwed tightly shut. Amy came off the couch but Ricky put his free hand between her breasts and shoved her back into a sitting position, then aimed his pistol at Rich's head.

"I'm guessing Rich is a friend of yours and you don't want his brains all over the rug, am I right?"

Barry shook his head, too frightened to speak. The woman, to her credit, at least cried, "No," and then in a tight, choking voice said, "Please."

It didn't take long for Ricky to get the story. Barry babbled it out like a child caught stealing by his dad. He hadn't known who the goods belonged to. He hadn't meant any harm. He'd acted on impulse. He'd give it all back, every last pill.

"That's all right," Ricky said. "You can keep it." Which provoked a stunned "Wha?" from Barry.

Ricky said, "You keep it, you sell it, you give the money to me."

Barry nodded his head vigorously, saying, Of course, of course.

Then Ricky said, "Same with the next batch. And the next."

"What do you mean?" Amy said. "What next batch?"

"You work for me now," Ricky said. "You're my new distributors."

"How can we do that?" Barry said. "We're not drug dealers."

"You are now," Ricky grinned.

"But—"

Ricky kicked Rich Leckie's other knee, drawing a howl of pain, and told Barry to shut the fuck up. "You took the goods from Kevin's house with the intention of selling them, right?"

Barry nodded.

"So obviously you had customers in mind."

"Just friends."

"Well, your friends are my friends now," Ricky said. "And together we're going to get happy. Any questions?"

"No," Barry mumbled.

Then he told Rich to stand up. Rich tried but fell back onto the carpet.

"Pick him up," Ricky told Barry. Barry knelt down and put his arms under Rich and stood him up. Then Ricky waved Barry back to the couch with his gun.

"How you feeling, Rich?" Ricky asked, using his nice voice, his wouldn't-hurt-a-fly voice.

"Okay," Rich gasped.

"I hope you understand that was nothing personal there," Ricky said. "Business sometimes requires out-of-the-box thinking, if you know what I mean."

Rich said nothing.

"Do you?" Ricky asked.

"Do I . . ."

"Know what I mean about out-of-the-box thinking."

Rich nodded.

"Good," said Ricky, then slammed the butt of his gun against Rich's nose. The breaking cartilage sounded like pretzels snapping. Rich's hands flew to his face but blood flowed freely from inside his nose, as well as a cut the gun butt had opened on the bridge.

"Oops," Ricky said. "Guess you'll have to get that rug cleaned after all."

"What was that for?" Amy demanded. "He didn't do anything to you."

Ricky asked her if she had ever read a book called *The Manager Inside Me* or heard it on tape.

"No."

"There's a very strong chapter about cultivating your

employee culture. That's what that was for. You work for me now and you need to know what that means. You listening?"

"Yes," she whispered.

"And you?" he asked Barry.

Barry nodded, his eyes bloodshot through half-open lids.

"The rules are simple," Ricky went on. "You do what I tell you, when I tell you, and everything's fine. You account for every penny and every pill. In return, you get your medications free. Understand?"

"Yes," Amy said. Barry just nodded.

"But if you steal from me, you die. You tell anyone about me, you die. You question anything I tell you, you die. And not quickly. I'll skin you both alive and roll you in salt. That clear?"

They both nodded.

"Then it's settled," Ricky said with a smile, as if he'd just concluded a minor transaction with a friend or neighbour. *Sure, you can borrow my lawn mower, friend. Just have it back by Sunday.*

Then he turned to Rich. "But what about you?" he said. "What do I do with you?"

Rich looked like he was going to lose control of his body functions right there on the rug. "I swear," Rich said. "I won't say a word."

"You swear? What's that to me? I don't know you. How do I know you're a man of your word?"

"I am," Rich gasped, at the same time that Amy said, "He is."

Ricky laid the gun barrel against Rich's broken nose. Rich closed his eyes and tried to stop the trembling of his chin.

"Maybe if we were friends," Ricky said. "Maybe then I'd know. How about that? Want to be friends with Ricky?"

"Oh, God," Rich said. He began to cry.

"What?" Ricky said. "Rich and Ricky, Ricky and Rich. What could be cuter than that?"

CHAPTER 30

Toronto: Thursday, June 29

We were heading back to town on the DVP, the traffic only marginally lighter than it had been going north.

"Admit it," Ryan said. "You're dying to tell me."

"Tell you what?"

"Where you learned to shoot like that. One minute you're the all-Canadian virgin scared shitless of a gun, the next you're drilling the target like the Rawhide Kid."

My shots had been every bit as well placed as his, all bunched within a fist-sized area near the heart. "I was in the army," I said.

"Get out," he said. "I thought the army was strictly for jugheads who flunk out of shop."

"I didn't say the Canadian army."

"American?"

"IDF."

"What?"

"Israel Defense Forces."

Ryan whistled. "Ah."

"Ah what?"

"They got a rep, don't they? Being tough. Take-no-shit types. So what, you volunteered?"

"Yes."

"Why there?"

"It's a long story."

"So give me the condensed version."

I closed my eyes for a moment, wondering how much I could tell him. Wondering why I felt like I could tell him things I had never told my own brother.

"I was living in Banff," I began, "teaching skiing in the winter and working construction in the summer. I was seeing a Jewish girl from Winnipeg. She wanted to go to Israel for the summer and work on a kibbutz."

"A what?"

"A collective farm. Kind of a Marxist model the early Zionists brought from the old country."

"Jewish Commies? Talk about two strikes against you."

"I went with her but things between us didn't work out. She left. I stayed."

"Let me guess. You met another woman."

"No, I met *the* woman. Dalia Schaeffer."

"Israeli?"

"Nope. You believe in coincidence?"

"No. I have no use for it."

"She was from Toronto. Grew up maybe ten blocks from me in Bathurst Manor. We even went to the same elementary school, except she was two years behind me and who pays attention to younger kids at that age. So we meet in Israel. She has this wild hair—jet black, piles of it, totally untamed—and the most amazing blue eyes. First time I look in them I'm gone. I am pinned to the mat. And her mouth, Ryan, you couldn't be in the same room as it and not want to kiss it. And stay kissing it."

"Jesus, you had it bad."

"No, I had it good. I had it so good. This was the woman I was going to be with for the rest of my life. Make babies with. Curly-headed babies."

"Like Pacino in *Godfather I*," he said. "He meets Apollonia and everyone says he's been hit by lightning."

"That's exactly what it was like. I was so dazed, so in love. Like never before. And never since."

"What happened?" Ryan asked.

"Israel happened."

Our kibbutz was called Har Milah. It was in the far north of Israel, on a finger of land that jutted up like a peninsula, surrounded by occupied southern Lebanon on one side and Syria on the other. We grew oranges, olives and avocadoes. Pressed our own olive oil. Grew grapes for a neighbouring kibbutz that made wine: surprisingly rich Chardonnay, grassy Sauvignon Blanc and a deep, spicy Shiraz that could have come from Australia.

The sabras, the native-born kibbutzniks, were cool to outsiders; they knew most of us weren't there for the long haul. But if you worked hard enough and stayed long enough you could gain a certain measure of acceptance. After a while they stopped calling me *G'veret*—Hebrew for Missus—and settled on Yoni, short for my Hebrew name, Yonah. It was tough work, up at four in the morning to get a full day in before the heat became too oppressive.

"One morning," I told Ryan, "I'm gathering up fallen oranges in our grove when a fat one drops on my head. I look up in the tree and there's Dalia with the sun behind her, this wild hair in silhouette. She says sorry to me. *Sleecha.* Okay. I go to pick up the orange and she says to a friend in Hebrew that 'the new American has a nice ass.' Little did she know Mama Geller had paid for years of Hebrew school. I look up and tell her I'm Canadian, not American, but that's okay because she has a nice ass too. She threw another orange at me, lost her balance and just about fell into my arms."

I stayed long past my planned departure date—almost two years longer. Dalia and I became inseparable. Stuck on a waiting list for a private room at the kibbutz—unmarrieds slept dorm-style—we made love every chance we had, sneaking into the orchards at night to find privacy, lying in fragrant grass amid the smell of citrus blossoms. I was so smitten I kept dreaming about eggs: eggs frying on the hood of my car, hard-boiled eggs spilling out of my pockets, a street busker juggling half a dozen. I would tell Dalia about these dreams and she'd laugh and say I wanted to make babies with her.

Then came the rockets.

Hezbollah fighters operating in southern Lebanon launched a barrage of Katyushas against civilian targets in northern Israel, in retaliation for an Israeli helicopter strike that killed six Lebanese civilians. More than six hundred Katyushas fell over three days, mostly in and around Kiryat Shmona. Hundreds of homes were burned or destroyed. Thousands more sustained some degree of damage. Schools and daycare centres were hit. So were factories and other industries. One housing development was hit eight separate times.

Two hundred thousand people were evacuated from Kiryat Shmona and the surrounding area. Dozens were injured, mostly by shrapnel and flying glass, and many more were treated for shock. They said it was a miracle only one person was killed.

The rockets that fell on Har Milah came on the second day of bombardment as people were setting out for work and for school. One rocket hit the shed where we packed avocados, sending thousands of dark green chunks into the air. I remember Zvi Dalphen, a skinny New Yorker, saying, "Guacamole, anyone?" and getting a good laugh.

Another one hit our chicken coop. Hundreds of birds blew into a fountain of red and white flesh, blood and feathers. No one had anything funny to say about that.

Late that afternoon, a Katyusha hit an electricity pole on the road outside our quarters. It blew chunks of concrete the size of bowling balls in every direction, smashing windows, breaking through walls, damaging furniture. One piece of concrete tore into Dalia's right leg, just above the knee, as she stood just outside the door, trying to get a signal on her cellphone so she could tell our families in Toronto we were fine.

She started to bleed. And bleed. They told us afterwards her femoral artery had been severed. Even if we had had phone service, even if we had had electricity, even if the roads had not been blocked by damaged cars, even if most of the people who could have helped had not already been evacuated, she never would have made it to a transfusion site. She would have bled out no matter what.

We should have left, but Dalia had not wanted to leave the animals, the chickens, the crops. They were our livelihood.

So only one person died during the bombardment. Some fucking miracle.

About five weeks later, I reported to the IDF recruitment centre in Jerusalem and volunteered for the army as part of a program called Mahal, under which non-Israeli Jews could sign up for a fourteen-month tour as long as they had not yet turned twenty-four. I made it by just a few months and began training for the Bar Kochba Infantry.

And that's as much as I told Ryan on the drive back.

The rest is between me and my dreams.

CHAPTER 31

When Ryan dropped me at the office, I made straight for the parking lot and stowed the gun and ammunition in the trunk of my car, inside a storage tub that held jumper cables, candles, matches, a blanket and other necessities of life on Canadian roads.

The office was a hive of activity, with most of the worker bees beating a path to and from Clint's office, accepting or reporting on assignments relating to Franny's murder. Just as Darrel Mitchell came out with a thick sheaf of pink file folders under one arm, one of two other investigators standing outside the door went in immediately; the other moved closer to the doorway to keep his spot.

Clint paged me at my desk about ten minutes later. Unlike the other bees, I was asked to shut the door to his office and sit.

"So," he said. "Sergeant Hollinger thinks it's you they wanted, not Franny."

"That's what she thinks."

"And you? The truth this time: have the Di Pietras made contact with you?"

"No. Why would they? The Ensign case is over and they've left me alone so far."

"The bruise on your face, Jonah."

"I'm telling you, Marco Di Pietra did not leave these marks on my face."

"And I'm telling you this is not the time to go off-grid on me. You've been a team player from day one. And I need a team now like I never have before, not even when I was a cop."

"Clint—"

"At least all the cops under me acted like professionals. They never left unannounced or showed up looking like a john who got rolled." The look on his face started moving past disappointment, headed toward disgust. "All right," he said without making eye contact. "If you're through leaving me in the lurch for today, get busy on this." He handed me five bright yellow folders thick with documents. "These are Franny's cases for the last year. Cross-reference any and every location he mentions, no matter what the circumstances, and note what company owns it. See if you can find any link at all to the crime scene."

"I'm on it," I said.

"I'll be working late," he said. "In case a sudden urge to tell the truth comes over you."

Heading home that evening, I was reasonably certain no one followed. There were plenty of dark SUVs on the road, but none seemed to contain gunmen of any size or shape. The greatest threat they posed was the drifting attention spans of drivers trying to juggle cellphones, cigarettes, lattes, CDs, makeup, road maps and, every once in a while, a function actually related to staying in one lane.

I parked in my garage and sat with the windows down, my mind numbed by arcane details of real estate transactions. I knew a lot more about how companies could make money by flipping properties but was no closer to knowing why the Erie Storage warehouse had been chosen as the place to kill Franny—or me, as it were.

I listened for the scrape of a sole on concrete, the intake of breath through an oft-broken nose. Nothing. I knew I should take the Beretta upstairs—load it, rack it, keep it handy—but I wasn't ready to admit it to my home. The garage seemed empty, but there were alcoves and doorways on the way to the elevators, places a gunman could hide with a pistol held down along his leg. The curse of Jewish imagination, where enemies lurk behind every pillar and post. I left the gun in the trunk, waited until a van was exiting the garage, and walked out beside it, looking around as I made my way up and around to the front lobby. There was an ambulance pulling out of the circular drive: not an unusual sight in a heat wave, with so many older tenants afflicted by heart trouble and other ailments.

I was walking down the hall to my apartment when I saw Ed Johnston's door was open. I could hear a man's voice and it wasn't Ed. I slowed down and stayed close to the wall. I stopped outside his door and listened. Heard the man's voice again. One of Marco's men? The voice was neither angry nor threatening. Then I heard a woman's voice, soft and low, and knew Ed was okay. He just had company.

Then I heard the woman begin to cry. I reached the threshold and looked in. Two men and a woman: Ed's daughter, Elizabeth, whom I recognized from photos in the apartment, and two men in sport jackets. There was blood on the parquet floor and bloody footprints leading out the door. The prints hadn't shown up in the dirty grey hallway carpet. The men looked like plainclothes cops.

"Can I help you?" one of them asked me. He was heavy-set, with the mournful face of a basset hound.

"I'm a neighbour," I said quietly. An ugly thought hit me then: it had been Ed in the ambulance leaving the building. "What happened? Is your father okay?" I asked Elizabeth. She was older than me with dry blonde hair cut in an unflattering bob and pale blue eyes that were red-rimmed from crying. She looked like she wanted to say something but couldn't.

"Someone beat him up," the basset said.

"How bad?" I asked.

"To a pulp." Ed's daughter sobbed as she heard this. "Sorry," the cop muttered. "He has head injuries, possibly a fractured skull. Broken fingers. Broken ribs. Broken jaw."

The daughter fished a tissue out of her purse.

"Can we get your name, sir?" the cop asked.

"Geller," I said. "Jonah Geller."

Elizabeth stopped wiping her eyes and looked at me coldly. "You're the investigator."

"Yes."

"Dad talks about you all the time," she said sourly. "He said you made life around here more exciting. So what was this? Some excitement you brought home with you."

"What kind of investigator are you?" the basset asked.

"The licensed kind."

"Got it on you?"

I got my ID out of my wallet and handed it to him.

"Beacon Security, eh? That's Graham McClintock's outfit, isn't it?"

"Yes."

"They're legit," he told his partner, who looked East Indian but not Sikh: no turban or beard. "Clint was on the job thirty years, all of them good. You know who would want to hurt Mr. Johnston?" he asked me.

"No."

"The only thing they stole was his camera. Plenty of other stuff around. A laptop right there on the dining room table. His wallet, his watch. Even the tripod, I'm told, is worth money. But one camera's all they took. Know why that would be?"

Sooner or later, someone would tell him about the fight in the park and how Ed had taken photos of it. His hound dog ears would pick up my name soon after that. Between the ballplayers, sunset watchers and other onlookers, there had been dozens of witnesses. More than enough would know me, if not by name, as that guy who lives in that building—Ed's building.

For now, I said nothing. Giving up Marco's name wouldn't help Ed. The goons who beat him wouldn't have left anything behind to incriminate the bastard.

I was also starting to hatch a plan of my own to deal with Marco Di Pietra and the police would have no part to play.

CHAPTER 32

In a film canister in one of my kitchen cupboards was a tight bud of British Columbia's finest pot, curled around its own stem like a serpent around a caduceus. Kenny Aber had left it the last time he'd visited, his way of trying to excavate me from my down mood. "When the going gets tough," Kenny said, "the tough get ripped." I toyed with the idea of rolling a little joint but abandoned it quickly. I needed a clear head to decide what to do about Marco—at least as clear as I could be on Percocet.

I sat in front of the TV a while. The heat wave was still the top story, because Torontonians love nothing better than complaining about our weather, which is generally too hot or too cold; it's all too rarely just right. I watched footage of hardy swimmers cooling themselves in the foul waters of the eastern beaches; two men squabbling over the last upright fan in an appliance store; people crowded around a refrigerated truck in Kensington Market, relishing the cold air wafting out of it.

Then my mind stopped drifting. It stopped somewhere very specific. I switched off the TV and called Dante Ryan's cell. When he answered, I asked if he had plans for dinner.

"You haven't seen enough of me today?" I could hear loud cartoon voices in the background, and a boy's high-pitched voice saying, Daddy, look what SpongeBob's eyes just did.

"You're at home?" I asked.

"Yup. All this shit going down with the Silvers, I needed to get rid of the creeps I feel. Spend a little time with my kid. After I dropped you off I phoned Cara, asked if I could help put him to bed."

"I need to talk to you but not on the phone."

"You don't sound so good."

"A not-so-good thing happened."

"To you?"

"My neighbour. The photographer."

"Fuck," he sighed.

"We really need to talk," I said.

"Just a minute, honey."

"Don't honey me, you rogue."

"I was talking to my wife, wiseass. Hang on." He covered his mouthpiece and spoke to someone else, then came back on the line: "We're putting Carlo to bed in an hour. I'll come by after that on one condition."

"What?"

"There a decent pizzeria near your place?"

Ryan arrived with a Barolo—a 1999 Ornato, he said. "Didn't want to take another chance on the plonk you keep in that closet."

I had sworn off wine because of the Percocet but that was before a Barolo arrived. I swirled the garnet-coloured wine gently in the glass, inhaling its rich dark cherry aromas. It tasted even better than it smelled.

The pizza I'd ordered had hot Italian sausage, roasted red peppers, tomatoes, mushrooms and onions. "They call this combination Calabrese," I said. "What do you think?"

"First of all, I'm only half Calabrese, on my mother's side. Second, I've never been there. But from how my mother cooks, I'd say it's authentic enough." He dealt with a long string of cheese coming off his pizza and wiped his chin. "Where my mother was born was some rugged place, what I hear. The people too. No one you want to mess with. A lot like Sicilians. Calabria's right across the straits from Sicily and the one thing they had in common? The government up in Rome was always screwing them both. Screwing them or ignoring them. That's why the Mafia wound up running things in Sicily and the 'Ndrangheta in Calabria. Someone had to."

Ryan finished his first slice and washed it down with wine. "If my dad had come from there too, we wouldn't be having this discussion," he said. "I'd be a made man, a lifer, and that would be that."

"What discussion are we having?" I asked him.

"Hey, you asked me to dinner. Said you needed to talk. How about you tell me what the discussion is, then I'll tell you if we're having it."

"Here goes," I said. "I don't care so much that Marco tried to cut me in the park. That he sent goons chasing me around East York. But beating up an old man who couldn't defend himself . . . Ryan, they cracked his skull, his ribs, his jaw. At his age, he'll never be the same. If he lives through the night."

"So what do you want to do?" he asked.

"Go after him," I said.

His dark eyes seemed to warm from the inside. "Really."

"What else can I do? Hide the rest of my life? Hide all the people around me? Look over my shoulder because this freak has it in for me? No. I'm not going to stand around while I or people close to me get shot at or beaten or killed."

"You're going to kill Marco Di Pietra."

I took a deep breath and listened to the words echo inside me. They rang absolutely true. It made me feel like I had lost my moral compass. Like I'd dropped it under my heel and ground it back into sand.

"Yes," I said. "If it's me or him, it might as well be him."

"You're going to do this alone?"

"Not too many people I can ask for help."

He put his pizza down and wiped his hands on a paper towel. "Cara made something very clear to me tonight. The only way to get back with my family is to find another line of work. But my thing isn't something you just walk away from. The kind of exit program we have, you don't wanna know."

"No one leaves?"

"Made guys, never. They take an oath that their thing will always come first: before family, before the law, before their own lives. Some old guys are allowed to step down when they get sick—like Vinnie Nickels if he'd hurry the fuck up—as long as they're not under indictment or active investigation. You know they're not going to flip."

"But you're not made."

"No, I'm what they call an associate. Like I'm some fucking greeter at Wal-Mart. But even though I never took the oath, I might as well have. I know where bodies are buried. Literally. Any that weren't burned or dumped, I fucking buried."

"And if Marco was gone?"

"His brother Vito would take over for sure. I've only ever worked for Marco, no one else, so I might be able to work things out with Vito. I got no beefs with him. No loyalties to anyone else. No legal problems hanging over me. Nothing he'd have to worry about. Maybe he'd let me retire." He pulled out his cigarettes. "Mind?" he asked.

I had eaten enough for the moment. I went and got the ashtray.

"So are you throwing in with me?" I asked.

"Answer one question first. Where's the gun I gave you?"

"Um . . ."

"Don't tell me."

"Sorry. It's still in the trunk of the car."

"Man, what are you gonna do if someone shows up with a gun? Excuse yourself while you run down eighteen floors?"

"I forgot."

"You know your kung fu shit won't stop a bullet, right? You're not delusional on that point?"

"Not on that one, no."

"It's a hell of a piece, Geller. Costs like a grand on the street."

"I'll tuck it in my underwear tonight."

"Get serious. How are you going to kill a depraved fucker like Marco if you won't even handle a gun?"

Since I had no logical answer, I was relieved to hear someone knock three times on my door. Ryan had his Glock out before the third knock. He put his finger to his lips and pointed to the door. We both got up and moved toward it. He motioned me to the left side, where the handle was, and braced himself against the wall on the right, gun up beside him. I peered out through the peephole and saw no one.

"Who is it?" I called.

"Katherine Hollinger."

Oh, God. The good detective sergeant at my door. I was giddy enough around her with just Percocet in my system. Now there was half a bottle of Barolo in me too, not to mention the wild-card stool softeners. "Just a minute," I said.

Ryan looked at me inquisitively. I nodded at the balcony door. He put his gun away and padded quietly to the door and slipped outside. I opened the front door and there Hollinger was, in jeans and a T-shirt under a coral linen jacket. Her black hair was out of its clip and framed her face like a pair of loving hands.

"Hello, Jonah."

"Hi."

She looked at me as though expecting to be invited in, but I stayed parked in the threshold.

"Got a minute?" she asked.

"Sure."

"You going to ask me in?"

"Uh-uh."

She looked past me at the coffee table and saw the pizza, the wine, the two glasses. "Oh," she said. "Company?"

"You're good," I said.

"You still have no idea."

She was starting to acquire a tan. By midsummer there'd be dusky skin to go with her jet-black hair and lioness eyes. Eyes I couldn't stop looking at. I hadn't come up with the right colour yet, having pondered hazel, honey and caramel. I was determined to keep trying.

"What's up, Detective?" was the best I could say.

"That's Detective Sergeant to you. Just wondering if you'd given any more thought to who tried to kill you."

"I'm not convinced that's what happened."

"I am," she said.

I was feeling giddier as we spoke. It was either the Percocet and Barolo or the eyes. Whatever their true colour was, looking into them was still painless. "Kate," I said. "Katie. Were you worried about me?"

"Geller, please."

"I think you were, a little."

"I'm a police officer. It's my job to worry about persons who might be the target of a violent offence."

"Thank you," I said.

She said, "You're welcome. And on that note, I'll leave you to your date." She looked out at the balcony again. "I'm surprised."

"What?"

"That he's a smoker."

"Who?"

"Your . . . companion?"

"What makes you think it's a he?"

Hollinger nodded at the picture window behind me. Broken rings of smoke were drifting into the night. "I've seen a thousand women smoke in my life. I've never seen one blow smoke rings like that."

"You *are* good."

"I told you. Enjoy the rest of your evening, Geller."

"You too, Kate. Or can I call you Katie?"

"Not when I'm working," she said.

"Please tell me, *please*, you're not fucking her."

"Not that it's your business, but why not?"

"She's a cop, isn't she?"

"You could tell that from the balcony?"

His shrug was both immodest and condescending. "From across the street, I could. I got an extremely developed nose for the law."

"Well, just to make you feel better, she's not just a cop. She's a sergeant in Homicide."

"Jesus Christ," he said. "Or what is it you people say? *Oy?*"

"If I was sleeping with Katherine Hollinger," I said, "*oy* wouldn't even begin to cover it."

"So why else was she here at this hour? Last I heard, they were clamping down on overtime."

"She's worried about me," I said.

"You should consider wiping that idiot grin off your face."

"You grin like that when you talk about Carlo."

"As I should. He's so quick, so smart. He's at that age where they learn something new every second of every day. You should see him do a puzzle. I know he's done them before, but he finishes them so fast, his little brain whirring along, so proud 'cause Daddy's watching. I tell you, this kid . . . I was watching cartoons with him when you called, me on the couch and him lying on my chest. I could feel him breathe, smell his hair. He'd had his bath and he was all clean in his PJs, this sweet little package. And I couldn't help wondering, how do people get so fucked up? How does someone like Marco start out smelling like shampoo and toothpaste and turn into a rabid fucking wolf?"

Rabid. The perfect word for Marco. And you can't let rabid animals live among you. They have to be killed. Shot down as they cross the town line.

"So Cara would take you back if you could quit."

"She still loves me. I could tell today, the way we sat and talked. For the first time in a long time, we stopped talking at each other and both listened a bit. We actually communicated, like she was Oprah and I was fucking Dr. Phil."

I almost made a crack about him fucking Dr. Phil but decided to go on living instead. "What did you decide?"

"That I need to get out. Retire undefeated. Do whatever it takes to keep my little unit together. I never had that with my mother. I want Carlo to have it with us."

"Anything else you can do to make a living?"

"I don't know. Run a restaurant maybe. Hey, don't you smirk," he said. "My day job, you want to call it that, I run the restaurant in the plaza we went to today."

"Where you sent the guy?"

"It's mostly a paper arrangement. I need a legitimate-looking income on my tax return. A manager runs it day-to-day but I hang around. I pick up things. Tell you something else might surprise you."

"What's that?"

"I'm not a half-bad cook. My mother was fantastic and I learned a lot from her."

"Doesn't surprise me at all," I said.

"No?"

"Nope. The OPP warned me you were good with a knife."

"You're not as cute as you think, Geller."

"Katie Hollinger thinks I'm cute."

"Katie? Oh, Christ, the sergeant."

"She does, I can tell."

"Great. My partner wants to dick a homicide dick."

"We're partners?"

"On this particular venture."

"The killing of Marco Di Pietra."

"It's either that or wait to see if Vito tries," Ryan said.

"You think he will?"

"If Vinnie Nickels doesn't get off the fence soon and make a pronouncement, there's a war coming for sure. Vito associates me with Marco so he might decide I'm worth killing once it starts."

"Or before."

"True. If, on the other hand, we get rid of Marco, Vito would have less incentive to mess with me. He might let me go. He fucking *has* to." He tried and failed to keep his emotion out of his voice. "This life I made for myself . . . ever since this thing with the Silver boy . . . fuck, getting out is all I can think of. I can't keep waking up in a cruddy hotel, living out of my car. Not that I blame Cara for kicking me out. Who wants to live with me and my ghosts?"

I'd been asking myself the same thing since the day I flew home from Israel.

CHAPTER 33

Toronto: Friday, June 30

Roni and I walk through a narrow alley between cinder-block buildings. The sun is directly above us, blazing hot, making me squint so hard my head starts to hurt. There are more soldiers patrolling ahead of us and behind us, part of a sweep through the camp to clear it of militants before Passover, when their attacks usually surge.

There are no adults in the alley. None we can see. Just Palestinian children lined up against the walls on both sides, calling out to us first in Arabic, then Hebrew, asking for money, chocolate, cigarettes. Many have bandages around their heads, their hands, their ears. Some have a crutch or a stick to lean on.

"Chuparim," they cry, using the Hebrew word for good-ies or treats. "Tan lanu chuparim." Give us treats.

Roni has a cigarette going and one boy, bolder than the others, steps in his path and holds out his hand. "Come on," the boy says in perfect Hebrew. "One cigarette. A fair price to let a Jew devil pass."

Roni can't help but smile at him. The boy looks twelve or thirteen, not a whisker on his cheeks, a young Sal Mineo with full, soft lips and unspoiled skin. Roni cradles his M-16 in his arms and reaches into his pocket for his Royals. As he does, the largest of the beggar kids, a stocky kid about sixteen with his arm in a sling, jumps on Roni's back. He pulls a long thin blade out of the sling and stabs Roni in the neck. A second assailant, no more than eighteen, swings a stout walking stick at my head. I sidestep his lunge and club him to the ground with the stock of my gun. This is madness, they're nothing but kids. But there Roni is on the ground, blood streaming from his neck as he fights to keep control of his gun. Children swarm him, clawing at his rifle and his sidearm, tearing at his helmet, trying to pull it off, swinging sticks and crutches at his body. Half a dozen rush at me too. I try to call for help—other soldiers from our unit are no more than a hundred yards away—but saliva pools at the back of my throat and I have to keep swallowing. Words won't form. I kick at the children to back them off and raise my M-16, fire a burst of three. Hebrew voices crackle over my radio. Other patrols converge from both ends of the alley, their boots thudding on ancient stone. I yell at the children to get away from Roni. The boy who looks like Sal Mineo swings a crutch at my gun barrel, trying to knock it from my hands. I kick him in the stomach and send him crashing to the ground. Suddenly men come spilling out of adjacent doorways. Hard men, unshaven, holding knives, machetes and hatchets. They don't seem to care that I have an M-gun levelled at them. I shout "Halt" in Arabic. The young Mineo gets up and throws himself at me again, grabbing my gun barrel. I head-butt him with my helmet, shattering his nose, and he falls to the ground choking on blood. As the first assailant raises his hatchet I fire a three-shot burst into his midsection and he goes down. The others pause and I back away fast, breathing hard, my finger depressing the trigger halfway. I hear running footsteps behind me, and I turn to see four soldiers coming up fast behind me. As I turn back I see a man hack at Roni's body with a machete. Trying to sever his head. I don't even shout a warning. I point my Mikutzrar and pull the trigger. The first burst slams him against the wall of the alley; the second keeps him dancing herky-jerky. I hold the trigger and keep firing. I can't kill him any more than I already have but I can't stop. He falls to the ground and the last few bursts tear into the wall behind him, blasting chips of stone into the air. One child screams and clutches her face and blood pours out over her knuckles and down the backs of her hands. A woman runs out from a doorway and gathers up the child, wailing as loudly as the child herself. Roni Galil lies on the ground, a dark blood stain spreading over his shoulder and chest. His neck is cut completely open. His vest didn't protect him there. There's pink froth on his lips. I hear a voice, moaning and crying as if in terrible pain.

I can't tell if it's him or me.

"You okay?"

"Wha—?"

"Are you okay?" Dante Ryan asked. I blinked and focused on the image before me: Ryan with a tea towel draped over one shoulder, offering me a cup of coffee.

I sat up, got a sharp pain in my side for my trouble, and looked at my bedside clock: 5:54 a.m.

"I been up a while," he said. "Tidying a little."

"Knock yourself out."

Ryan left the coffee with me and went down the hall to the kitchen. I shuddered, trying to shake off the last vestiges of the dream. It was the closest I had ever come to reliving what really happened in that brutally hot alley, how we had almost been overwhelmed by children sent to fight us. Like Ryan, I felt the threat against the Silvers was dredging up feelings and images faster than I could tamp them back down: Roni's savage death; young Mineo with the broken nose; the girl hit by debris or a ricochet from my gun; Dalia's naked body glistening in a moonlit orchard after making love; Dalia's leg—bloody, dusty, bones exposed—nearly sheared off by a concrete missile.

I made it into the bathroom before the crying started. Grieving for Roni and Dalia. Raging at men who used children to fight their war without end. I ran water to drown out the sound as I leaned sobbing against the cool tile wall. Tears spilled down my face into the sink, where they mixed with water and swirled down the drain.

When the crying was done, I blew my nose and washed my face. If Ryan made one smart remark, he was going off the balcony, guns and all.

CHAPTER 34

B elieving one should never commit one's first premeditated murder without a nutritious breakfast, I took Ryan to the Family Restaurant. He had bacon and eggs and I had the same heart-stopping ham-and-eggs special I'd had the day before.

At a quarter to eight, I dropped him at the long-term parking lot at Pearson International Airport, then parked his Volvo in the short-term lot and waited. Eighteen minutes later he pulled up in a black late-model Altima. He got out and handed me a pair of thin leather driving gloves. "Don't touch anything in or on the car without these on," he said. "Case we have to ditch it unexpectedly."

He transferred his metal photographer's case from the trunk of the Volvo to the Altima, along with a brown canvas sports bag.

"A long gun," I said.

"Not just a long gun. A Remington 700 PSS. The weapon of choice of better police services everywhere. If it's good enough for an FBI sniper, it's good enough for me. Accurate, reliable, comes with a scope and takes a suppressor if you need one. Plus the recoil is manageable if you stay away from magnum rounds."

"And we need this because . . . ?"

"In your haste to rid yourself of Marco Di Pietra, and the burden he has become, you fail to consider one important factor."

"Yes, Professor?"

"Call it the carnage factor. Unless we can find Marco alone, we have to take out whoever we find him with, be it a bodyguard, a hooker or anyone else. How many people you prepared to kill?"

He was right. Shit. My focus had been on eliminating the threat Marco posed to me and everyone around me. I had to start seeing the bigger picture.

"You want to keep casualties to a minimum?" he asked.

"Of course."

"The closer we have to get, the messier it's going to be. The long gun gives us a chance, understand?"

God help me, I did.

We left the airport via a narrow road where a work crew was regrading a roadbed in the fierce heat, images of the men rippling above the hot asphalt like waves in a mirage.

"Where are we likely to find Marco?" I asked.

"He's no nine-to-fiver but he has a few regular stops."

"Where's his house?"

"The new part of Woodbridge. A big pile his father-in-law built him, all floodlit pink brick inside a ten-foot fence."

"I thought he lived in Hamilton."

"His father does, him and the other old-timers," Ryan said. "The guys who wanted to run Toronto without actually having to live in it. But our generation prefers Woodbridge or maybe Guelph if you want something more rural. Cara's—my house—is in Woodbridge, and I got to your place last night in under thirty minutes, Highway 7 to 404 and down the DVP. It's the best of both worlds. Close to downtown but the houses are new and you get space for your money. Anyway, hitting Marco in his house is out of the question. There's always people around, including his wife and kids and his mother-in-law, plus the usual armed entourage."

"Marco has children?"

"Unfortunately."

"And he could still have Lucas Silver killed? How many children?"

"Three with the wife, two boys and a girl. Couple more outside the friendly confines."

"Five kids. The bastard doesn't deserve a single one."

"Hey, for all I know he likes dogs too."

"Where else does he go?"

"There's places he eats, drinks, goes to get laid, watch people get beat up. Again, you're always going to have too many witnesses."

"So what's left?"

"One of his so-called businesses is a trucking company just off Highway 7, a few minutes from here."

"The one where the Ensign smokes were headed?"

"That's right. It's mostly for show—gives him a way to launder money coming in. But he keeps a few trucks on hand, half-tons and cube vans, to haul slot machines, cigarettes, booze, whatever. He runs a sports book out of the place and hosts high-stakes Hold'em tourneys. Sucks in fools who think they can play 'cause they've seen it on TV. It's as close as anything he has to an office. He turns up most days at some point or another. Let's start there and see what's what."

"Would he be there this early?"

"No, he's a night owl. But there's a guy, Tommy Vetere, kind of runs the place: answers the phones, takes bets, hands out gas money to the truck drivers, like that. He's usually there by nine. And he might know when Marco's coming."

"He would tell us?"

"He would tell me. Remember how nice I can ask?"

"What if he's not there?"

"We'll scout it out. See if there's some way to use the long gun. Can you shoot?"

"Me?"

"It's your gig, man. Also, I can distract Marco. Show myself. Chat him up. Lead him outside. You can't do any of that without him taking a body part as a souvenir."

I pictured Roni Galil standing over me as I lay on my belly, sighting down the barrel of an Israeli sniper rifle called a Tessler during training. "If you have to shoot someone, Yoni, I hope he's big like a house because that's all you going to hit. Should I get you a slingshot like our King David used against Goliath?" But that was early on in my training. By the end I had become a decent marksman.

"I can shoot," I told Ryan.

"There's a fence around the property. Bushes along most of the sides and trees at the back. Trucks parked here and there. Maybe we can set up a blind where you can take him out as he's getting out of his car. With his arm in that cast, moving like he is, he'll present a beautiful target, don't you think?"

"A stunner," I said.

A few minutes later, Ryan turned off Highway 7 onto Minden Road. He pointed to a red and white sign up on our right. "That's the place. Aspromonte Trucking. Little joke of Marco's."

"I don't get it."

"Aspromonte's in Calabria. In the old days, that's where the 'Ndrangheta hid kidnap victims while they waited for ransoms to be paid. They'd stash them in a cave if they were giving them back alive. Dump them in a crevice if they weren't."

Aspromonte Trucking sat on a wide, dusty asphalt lot. Its immediate neighbours were a retailer of farm implements and a lumber yard. The entire property was surrounded by an eight-foot cyclone fence topped by three strands of barbed wire; the only entrance visible from the road was a gate, front and centre, that hung halfway open. The building was one storey, about the size of a service station, half the frontage given over to a large garage door that was rolled down shut. There were two half-ton trucks parked to one side, with enough space for a third between them. A black Escalade was blocking the front door.

"Christ," Ryan said. "That's Marco's."

"He's here this early?"

"Or this late. Maybe they had a poker game last night."

"Would it still be going?"

"Not with no other cars here. But maybe we caught a break. If it went real late, he might have crashed here. There's a room at the back with a bed in it."

He drove a few hundred yards past the gate and turned into the lot of a company that made wooden shutters in a California style. There were only a few cars scattered in its lot and we parked as far as we could from the entrance, partially blocked from view by a cedar hedge.

"You think Phil and Tommy are with him?" I asked.

"Does it matter?"

I sat in the stolen Altima, my mouth feeling dry. I had not taken Percocet this morning, wanting to keep my head clear. My side ached but the real discomfort lay elsewhere. In the next few minutes, three men might die: Marco, Phil and this Tommy Vetere. And that was if we got lucky and neither one of us joined in. We were talking about men like pieces on a game board. I had signed onto this mission to practise *tikkun olam*, to repair a part of the world that badly needed it. Save an innocent life. And maybe we still would. Maybe we'd save the entire Silver family. But how many lives could pile up on the other end of the seesaw before it slammed down to the ground and sent our end lurching up?

"Tell me about Vetere," I said.

"What's to tell? He's been in Marco's crew for years. Before that with Vinnie Nickels. He's no altar boy, if that's what you're worried about. He's broken his share of bones. He's fired

his guns. He's never affronted me personally, so I have no feelings for him pro or con. But if he's in there with Marco and this
is our chance, then I say he has to go. It's the life he bought
into, just like me."

"Isn't there a way to make Marco come out alone?"

Ryan thought about it and said there was. I didn't like the
way he smiled when he said it.

"Go on," I said.

"I go in alone. I tell him I have something in the trunk for
him."

"And that would be?"

"You."

CHAPTER 35

I had to say this much for the Altima: it had a roomy trunk for its size and the owner kept it clean. Nothing in there but a Sunday golf bag with half a dozen clubs and a putter, and a set of jumper cables. The carpet was coarse and the overall smell was of grease and metal, but I couldn't complain.

Not that I didn't at first.

"Are you out of your fucking mind?" I'd yelled.

"Admit it," he said. "You don't trust me. After all we been through, the way I've put my ass on the line for you, you think I have another agenda."

"What do you want from me? I was raised to think the goyim have it in for Jews. So a guy like you tries to talk me into the trunk of a car—"

"Goddamn it," he barked. "I keep telling you, you dumb fuck, if I wanted to kill you, you'd be dead. How many opportunities do I need? Your apartment Monday night, I could've put two in your head right there and been done with your dumb ass. Drunk the whole bottle of wine by myself. Tuesday in the park, all I had to do was keep my trap shut and Marco would have stabbed you in the heart. But no, I stuck my neck out and warned you but this you somehow forget. Which brings us to Wednesday. Where were we Wednesday? Oh yes, a soundproof room full of fucking guns. I could have done it then. Or this morning, while you were having a bad dream, moaning like a broken-down whore, I could have popped you right in your bed with a pillow on your face and nobody would have heard a sound."

His voice was strained, his eyes dark, his fists curled tight. Then it came to me: he was hurt. Dante Ryan was genuinely hurt by what I'd said. He'd shoot me dead on the spot if I suggested as much but there it was. I slowed my breathing until my weight settled and my anxiety passed.

"Sorry," I said. We made eye contact and bumped fists, our hands encased in tight black leather.

We spent a few minutes making me look roughed up. Shirt untucked and smeared with dirt. Face too. Hair all over the place, like Lyle Lovett on a windy day. I got in the trunk with Ryan's metal gun case and the canvas bag that held the Remington rifle. I put my hands behind me and Ryan wound coarse yellow rope around them loosely, so it would give way with a good yank. We ran through it a few times to make sure.

"There's three ways this can play," he said. "One, I don't like the odds—say there's just too many guys inside for us to handle. I give Marco some bullshit story about setting up the Silver hit for tonight. You stay in the trunk and we drive away. Two, the odds seem in our favour. There's no more than one or two guys besides Marco. I get Marco to come out alone to see what's in the trunk. I open the trunk, you act dopey and scared, I pop him right there. You get out, he goes in, we go inside and take care of the others."

"They won't come running when you shoot Marco?"

"Not with the right tool." He opened his jacket. Sewn into the lining was a slim sheath from which the cross-hatched butt of a handgun showed. He turned so no one at the window-shutter place could see anything and eased out a slim long-barrelled gun with a silencer threaded into the barrel. "It's a subsonic .22," he said. "With the suppressor on it, all you'll hear is the dry-fire. You could cover the sound with a cough."

"Do we have to go inside? Can't we just drive away with him?"

"After I've shown myself? Haven't you been listening? Geller, we have to do what we have to do and not make mistakes. One shred of evidence links it back to us, we're both dead. Tits up in a field somewhere."

"Why would Vito care? We'd be doing him a favour."

"He'd still have to avenge Marco. For the family's honour, and to keep people from thinking he did it."

"What's the third scenario?"

"Marco wants to come see what's in the trunk but the others come too. In which case, I'll bring them out and open the trunk. You act scared."

"I won't be acting."

"I take you out of the trunk and walk you inside. Might have to kick you around again."

"You enjoy that part, admit it."

"Better me than Marco. As soon as we're in the door, you get the rope off your hands and pull the Beretta and we shoot the shit out of anything that moves."

"You're going to get into a gunfight with that popgun?"

"Relax," Dante Ryan said. He opened the other side of his jacket and there under his left arm was his Glock 20 in a breakaway shoulder rig. "If we go toe-to-toe with them, fuck the suppressor. I'm not going to care who hears what."

We tucked the Beretta Cougar in my pants at the small of my back, a load in the chamber, the safety off. I climbed into the trunk. As Ryan closed it I told him to watch for speed bumps and potholes. "You hit one with this gun where it is, the crack in my ass will have company."

The car pulled out of the lot, made two left turns and stopped again. The driver's door opened and closed and footsteps receded into the distance. I was in virtual darkness. The trunk was uncomfortably hot. No, hell was uncomfortably hot. The trunk was baking me like a chicken. No air conditioning. Precious little air of any kind. The coarse carpet stung my face and neck where sweat was running freely. I tried to take my mind off the discomfort by visualizing the moment I would rip my wrists free of the rope, pull the gun out of my pants and point it at whoever was closest to me.

I tried not to visualize much after that.

Then the door to the building creaked open and banged closed. Footsteps approached. I tried to determine whether there was one person or more. It sounded like one, which likely meant Ryan hadn't liked the odds and we were calling off our raid.

I thanked God silently—a knee-jerk reaction from my upbringing. Or maybe there are no atheists in car trunks.

When the trunk opened, light burst into the pitch-black space and blinded me for a moment. I squinted at the silhouette standing over me. There was no need to act scared as I was coming by it quite naturally. But there was definitely just the one man there, and as my eyes adjusted, I could tell it was Ryan. He held out a hand to help me out of the trunk.

"What?" I whispered.

"Scenario four," he said and started back toward the office, his black loafers kicking up swirls of dust.

CHAPTER 36

Tommy Vetere was an indistinct man with pockmarked skin and hair the colour of wet cardboard. He hadn't shaved in at least a few days and hadn't been that careful the last time he did. His short-sleeved white polo shirt rode up on his paunch, showing more hair and gut than most visitors would likely want to see. There were two bullet holes in his chest a few inches apart and another in the middle of his forehead, black stippling around it from unburned gunpowder that had blasted straight out of the gun barrel into his skin. Two shots knocking him off his feet and onto his back, the third to make it official. The pool of blood around him was tacky near the outside edges. He'd been dead for hours.

Phil didn't look any better. He was face down in the hallway that led from the main area to the back room, two bullet holes in his back and a certain kill shot where his neck met his spine.

We found Marco in the small room Ryan had mentioned. It was the size of a child's bedroom with a single bed, a side table, a beer fridge and a television set on a wooden crate. Marco lay on his back, his right arm and hand held in the shake position by the cast around his fractured elbow. There was a hole in his chest, where his heart would have been if he'd had one. Another in his head, the same *coup de grâce* Tommy had received, with visible tattooing around the wound. Marco had been asleep when he got it and I could see why. On the side table was an empty bottle of vodka, next to that a vial of Percocet. Same dose as mine. I tried to find it in my heart to feel sorry for Marco, shot down in his sleep without a chance to defend himself. After a few minutes I gave up and went to try it on Tommy and Phil.

Dante Ryan had a cigarette going. "For the smell," he said. "They won't mind if you don't." It was hot in the office and a nasty odour came from Tommy in particular, a combination of coppery blood and the contents of his bowels, which must have given way when he knew he would die.

At the centre of the room was a round table that could seat seven card players, covered with crusted Chinese food containers and plates, empty beer bottles and glasses, ashtrays, and bowls with chip and pretzel crumbs. There was a big-screen TV in one corner with a satellite receiver—handy for a bookie—and a couch and two recliners grouped around it. One corner of the room was set up as an actual workspace: desk, filing cabinets, three hooks in the wall on which sets of keys could be hung. One set was missing. There was also a large corkboard, where waybills, gas receipts and miscellaneous paperwork were thumbtacked.

"So Vito got to him first," I said.

"Looks like."

"You think he did the actual shooting?"

He shook his head. "Vito's not your man of action. He's a big mother, don't get me wrong, but big like Herman Munster. Or the guy who was Raymond's brother on TV, the cop with the sad eyes and the hanging jaw. A clumsy guy. Not much of an athlete or a fighter. You ask me, he hired it out."

"What will his father do?"

"What *can* he do? The man can't get out of bed. It's Buffalo that Vito has to worry about. If he was their choice for boss, he'll get a coronation. If not? Could be his funeral."

"Who do you think they'd back?"

"Depends if they wanted a hand grenade or a puppet. But it's decided now and maybe that's best. What do they say? Nature hates a vacuum?"

"Abhors it."

"Yeah, well, so does Buffalo."

"Hey," I said. "You think Vito brought in this Ricky the Clip for the job?"

"If this is his work," Ryan said, "he might be better than I thought."

We drove back to the airport to drop the Altima, then started a slow creep southward on the 427 in Ryan's Dadmobile.

"What now?" I asked.

"Wait for the news about Marco to get out."

"What about the contract on the Silvers? Does this give you leeway?"

"Short-term, sure. There's confusion. A void. No communication from the top. No one should expect me to carry out a hit I might not get paid for."

"And long-term?"

"When the client hears about Marco, he'll know he has a problem. He'll have to speak to someone else to confirm the job or try to get his money back."

"Did he pay it all up front?"

"Half," Ryan said.

"So this might force his hand. Flush him out."

"Just might."

We drove in silence. Ryan handled the car in his usual impeccable way, ignoring the many challenges and insults other drivers dealt.

"Want me to drop you at your office?"

"Not especially," I said.

"Home?"

In fine Jewish tradition, I answered his question with a question: "Is this over for you?"

Ryan glanced over at me, then back at the road ahead. "Is what over?"

"This—this case, I guess."

"A case? We're on a case? Holy fucking justice, Batman!"

"Call it what you want. You came to me because you were in a bad spot. Now Marco's dead, maybe it's over for you. Maybe you want to fade out somewhere and wait to see how the chips fall."

"And you don't?"

"I can't. I still don't know who killed Franny," I said. "Or who's running this racket. Nothing's over for me."

"So where to?"

"If you get in the left lane now, you can take Eglinton east."

"Where to exactly?"

"Jay Silver's Med-E-Mart."

"For what?"

"A friendly chat."

"I wouldn't mind if it got unfriendly," he said. "I'm all pumped up with no one to do."

I knew exactly what he meant. My feet were tapping restlessly, my thigh muscles jumping. My biceps felt as if I'd been working them hard, though I'd lifted nothing heavier than ham steak this morning. Like a pitcher who warms up but doesn't get into the game, I was juiced on adrenaline that had been building all morning, still taking in the fact that Marco no longer had to die at my hands.

We were taking an eastbound route I'd learned from veteran airport cabbies, making good time with few cars around to imperil us.

"Is the mob in Buffalo that much heavier than here?" I asked Ryan.

"Up until a few years ago, no question: they were the head office and we were the branch plant. Buffalo was a real power, mobwise, all the years Don Magaddino was in charge, and that's like fifty. You know about the Don?"

"I know his name. I was briefed on his organization when the Ensign sting was being planned."

"Don Stefano Magaddino was a member of the original national commission that laid out the structure of the organization and assigned territories to the major families. He was up there with Lucky Luciano, Joe Bonanno, Tommy Lucchese, all those guys. A cousin to Joe Bonanno, in fact. Not that it stopped them from occasionally trying to kidnap or kill each other."

"How'd he wind up in Buffalo?"

"There was trouble in New York and he had to leave. Took a look west and moved to Buffalo. It was a happening place then and he ended up running the town and everything around it, including southern Ontario. Took that over from Rocco Perri, if the name rings a bell."

"He the one at the bottom of Hamilton Harbour?"

"So the story goes. Everyone after that, including Johnny Papalia and Vinnie Nickels, answered to Magaddino. You want to talk smuggling? This pill business of yours is piddly compared to the booze that used to cross the river."

"Until Prohibition ended."

"Nothing ended. Just the commodities changed. Dope going this way, guns going that way. Cigarettes, as you well know, pinball machines, illegal aliens, whatever. When I was a kid, we made runs to Buffalo all the time. I always drove because I was the only one of my gang whose name didn't end in a vowel. Buffalo and back, a thousand times. At first, we'd just try to bull-shit our way across. Sometimes we'd order hockey tickets and dress like assholes and say we were going to watch the Leafs play the Sabres, like I'd cross the street to watch those bums. Once we were established, it got easier. We'd have a friendly border

guard on a certain shift and we just had to say Mr. Lewis sent us.
That was Vinnie Nickels' brother Luciano. Uncle Looch knew
every bent border guy, what shift he worked, how much you had
to pay. We'd get a lane number from Looch, load up our goods
and head out on a Buffalo jump."

"A which?"

"What we called these runs of ours. Come on, we were
kids. We had our own code words like everyone else. With us a
smuggling trip was a Buffalo jump."

"It means something else out west," I said.

"Out west where?"

"Alberta. It was a kill site for Indians."

"Hey, my kind of topic. What kind of kill site?"

"They harvested buffalo by running them over a cliff."

"No shit."

"This was before horses came to the New World. The
Plains Indians hunted on foot with spears."

"Not too productive."

"No. So they came up with a system for mass killing."

"The human spirit," Ryan said. "You just can't keep it
down."

"They'd fence off runways that led from the grazing area
to the cliffs. Then one would imitate a buffalo calf crying in dis-
tress. The lead buffalo would move toward the sound and the
herd, being a herd, would follow. Then a few guys with capes
and blankets would run up behind and start a stampede down
these fenced-off lanes. The leader couldn't see what was in front
of him until he roared off the cliff and dropped thirty feet onto
solid rock. The whole herd would come crashing down behind
him. Any that survived were finished with spears."

"And they called it Buffalo Jump?" Ryan asked.

"Head-Smashed-In Buffalo Jump, to be exact."

"Yeah?" Ryan laughed. "We had a few of those too in the
old days. Plenty of heads got smashed."

"But things in Buffalo have changed, you said."

"Since Don Magaddino passed, there's been a different class of people at the top. No sense of vision, barely a step above union leaders. Plus half of them are in jail now. Give credit where it's due, law enforcement has been pasting us lately. You got wiretap technology you never had. You got RICO legislation in the States. You got agencies cooperating instead of pissing up each other's pant legs. There's no more Teflon Dons anymore. Plenty of guys are doing serious time. You got more wise guys dying of natural causes in prison than on the street. When did that ever used to be?

"The funny thing is I've spent my whole life trying to prove I belong to this thing," he said. "To their thing. Lamenting the fact that my father was Irish. That I couldn't be made because of his name. That I had to remain an associate. Given the dirty work. The outsider's work. Now I look around and wonder why. Why do I want to belong to this? Why did I ever? Half of them don't have the brains God gave a sheepdog and the other half are just plain dumb. And for this so-called family I'm losing my real family, my wife and my boy, who give me more in ten minutes than Marco and his crew could in ten years. I've heard all their jokes. I've heard every war story. Do I need to hear again who they beat, who they shot, who they fucked and how much it cost?"

Ryan eased a cigarette out of his pack, lit it and opened his window a crack to draw out the smoke.

"I'm going to tell you something, Jonah Geller, on the understanding that if you repeat it to anyone, ever, I'll hunt you down and kill you like the dog you are."

"Some lead-in."

"I was watching *The Lion King* with Carlo yesterday. And there's a part when the king dies, right, and the little guy, Simba, thinks it was his fault. He's calling, 'Dad, Dad . . . ' He's apologizing, getting desperate, tearing up, and I suddenly picture the same scene with me and Carlo, him finding me dead somewhere. Tears start filling my eyes and going down my cheeks and I wipe them away and more keep coming. I haven't cried in thirty years. My stepfather used to beat me for sport and I never cried once. But here I am watching a fucking cartoon, for Chrissakes, and I'm blubbering like a schoolgirl who just got dumped."

He drew on his smoke and stared intently ahead.

I said, "If you need to cry some more, I won't judge you."

"Shut up."

"You can let that side out with me."

"Shut *up*."

"Your vulnerable side."

"You're this close, Geller."

I crooned, *"Put your head on my shoulder . . ."*

"This fucking close."

"Whisper in my ear . . ."

"I'm warning you. "

"Bay-bee . . ."

"I'm gonna throw you out the sunroof in one fucking second. "

"Okay, Ryan."

"Won't even slow down."

"I said okay."

"I never should have said a word to you. In my hour of sensitivity, you turn into a cheap-joke artist at my expense."

"It's the Jewish way," I said. "Laugh your way through the pain."

"I'm Catholic, I'm armed and I'm pissed at you," he snarled.

"So maybe we'll do it your way," I said.

CHAPTER 37

We were past Yonge Street and making good time when Jenn called my cell. "Where are you?"

"On the road."

"On your way in, I hope."

"Not directly."

"Are you nuts? Clint's already mad at you."

"I'll be in as soon as I can."

"Shouldn't keeping your job be a priority?"

"He's that pissed?"

"Have you ever seen his betrayed look?"

"Oh, God, not the one where he looks like a hound dog?"

"An abandoned hound that's been beaten with a stick."

"I'll call him," I said.

"It's your ass."

"I know. Listen, how busy are you?"

"Manageable."

"See what you can find on the Vista Mar group and Steven Stone. Check what year he got his MBA at Western. See if it overlapped with either Jay Silver or Kenneth Page, both spelled the way they sound. And if there's anything Stone has written in the business school quarterly, download it. I bet it has to do with supply chain improvements or using Internet sales to broaden commercial reach."

"Aren't you a biz-head all of a sudden," Jenn said. "Should we expect a suit and a buzz cut?"

"Not this quarter," I said.

Backed up to the loading dock at the Med-E-Mart was a half-ton truck. It was twice the capacity of the one I'd seen last time and the same size and model as the two I'd seen parked on the Aspromonte lot—with an empty space between them. I could see at least three men near the rear. We kept driving past a larger loading dock that serviced Silver's closest neighbour, an office supplies depot. We parked behind a trailer that had been uncoupled from its tractor and left on struts. I sidled up along it, knelt behind a tire bigger than I was, and looked at the dock through my field glasses.

There were four of them. Frank was directing two young men in slacks and nylon sport shirts as they loaded the truck. Claudio was holding himself stiffly with his elbows close to his sides. The eye I had jabbed was a puffed-up red and purple mess.

Not to be uncharitable, but I hoped he felt worse than he looked.

One of the young studs was pushing a mini-forklift loaded with a skid of cartons; the other was bringing cartons out of the store three at a time on a hand truck. The man with the forklift manoeuvred his load to the rear of the truck and used a control on the handle to raise it to eye level. The name Contrex was visible on every carton through a shroud of shrink wrap. He walked the load into the truck, was out of sight for half a minute and came out pulling the empty lift. I had driven trucks the size of this one in Banff. It could hold at least sixteen skids stacked in rows of four, two over two. And since the goods weren't breakable, dozens of single cartons could be piled on top of and around the skids.

Where was Jay Silver while all this was going on? Inside the store, powerless to stop it from being pillaged? Or somewhere else, unaware of the situation. Maybe unaware, period.

The next skid held cartons labelled CoRex—the name of Canada's largest manufacturer of generic drugs. As the man steered it toward the truck, his load slid suddenly forward. He probably wasn't used to handling a lift and hadn't pushed the forks all the way through to the end of the skid. He used a handbrake to stop the forklift but the load kept going, toppling forward to the concrete floor of the dock. "Fuck!" he yelled—I could lip-read it through the field glasses as well as hear it. The shrink wrap split along one side on impact and the cartons spilled out every which way along the dock. A few fell down to ground level. "Shit!" the man yelled.

The two men were going to have to slug the cases in by hand, and neither Frank nor Claudio looked ready to help. I jogged back to Ryan's car, hunched over like Groucho Marx.

"Drop me off around the front," I said. "I'm going inside. I need to see if Silver's there."

"And if he's not?"

"Then I want to see who's letting these guys clean him out."

"What if Frank or Claudio sees you?"

"Frank I can take in my sleep, and I think Claudio's had more than enough of me."

As soon as I entered the store, I could hear raised voices at the back counter where a dozen people were crowded around a pharmacist, waving slips of paper at him and barking questions. The man was holding up his hands as if to say *It's not my fault.*

"I'm sorry for the inconvenience," he said. "We're having an inspection and we have to freeze the inventory until it's complete."

"Why are they inspecting you?" an older man demanded. "What's wrong with the place?"

"Nothing, I assure you."

"I want to speak to the owner."

"I'm sorry," the pharmacist said. "He called in sick, of all days."

"What am *I* supposed to do?" asked a woman in her seventies, bent over a chrome walker. "I have to take my medicine the same time every day, that's what they told me. Like clockwork, they said."

"We've arranged for your prescriptions to be filled at Dotson's, right around the corner on Eglinton."

"Maybe Eglinton is right around the corner for you. You know how long it takes *me?*"

She flinched as the man with the hand truck banged in through the doors from the shipping area. He wheeled it over to a room to our right, was gone for a moment, then came back out with three more cases, followed by a tall dark-skinned woman with thick black hair in a braid that fell below her belt.

"That's the inspector," the pharmacist said. "If you have any questions, please speak to her. I've told you all I know."

The crowd surged toward the woman, who seemed momentarily startled.

"Why can't we get our prescriptions?" a man called out.

"I'm sorry, sir," she said. *Suh*, in a rich Brahmin accent. "But regulations specify that no products can be dispensed during an inspection."

I had spoken to her only once on Winston Chan's speakerphone, but I knew her voice instantly: Sumita Desai, enforcement officer for the Registered Pharmacists' Association of Ontario. No wonder nothing had come up in Silver's last inspection. She was in on it. No red flags went up? No shit.

"Why are they taking all this stuff away?" another man asked. "Is it being recalled?"

"Not at all," the inspector said. "We are conducting a routine inspection to ensure the safety of all medications and the continued good health of consumers like you. The sooner you allow us to complete it, the sooner business can get back to usual. Shouldn't be more than an hour or two."

There was some general grumbling but people started to disperse. "I'll take you to Dotson's," a middle-aged man told the lady in the walker. "My van seats seven if anyone else needs a ride."

Sumita Desai was heading back to the exit door when I moved into her path. Her hair was a dark glossy marvel, her eyes every bit as black. "Excuse me," I said. "Can I ask why you're inspecting these premises?"

"I'm sorry, *suh*. Our process is completely confidential."

"I had a prescription filled yesterday," I said. "How do I know it's safe?"

"Take it up with your pharmacist," she said.

"Have you spoken to Mr. Silver today? Informed him about the inspection?"

"He couldn't be reached," she said. "I am told he is ill." Her voice didn't sound warm and tropical anymore. It was clipped and precise and very, very cold.

CHAPTER 33

"They're saying he called in sick," I told Ryan.

"But you think it's worse than that."

"Ryan," I said.

"What?"

"You didn't—"

"Didn't what?"

"Take the initiative."

"Get the fuck out. If something happened to him, it wasn't me."

"The *emmes?*"

"The who?"

"The truth?"

"Look, Geller. I know I'm a low-life to you," he said. "You've made that perfectly clear."

"Oh, come on."

"But I didn't kill anyone today. Yet. Check my BlackBerry, you don't believe me. You'll see, nobody killed this week. No men, no women, no kids."

"Okay, okay. I believe you."

"Like I give a shit."

"Don't get your feelings hurt again."

"How about taking responsibility for your words?"

"This from a hit man?"

"Quit harping on that. Quit defining me only by what I do. What I've done. I'm more than one dimension but you don't see it. Despite everything I've told you, despite the other sides of me you've seen, you still don't consider me a whole person."

"Okay," I said. "When this is over we'll go into couples therapy. For now, we have to stall that truck for an hour."

"Why?"

"I'm going to Silver's house."

"What?"

"If something's happened to him, I need to know. And if nothing has, I'm going to make him tell me who we're up against."

"I told you we can't contact him."

"Not when Marco was alive, we couldn't, because he'd know it was you who told. That's not the case anymore."

Ryan pondered that for a moment. "You said an hour?"

"His place is fifteen minutes each way—if I pretend I'm in NASCAR. If he's there, another half an hour maybe to get the truth out of him."

He flipped me the keys to the Dadmobile. "Promise me one thing: if his house is a crime scene, you don't even stop. You're driving my car, don't forget."

"Agreed."

"So the challenge you present me, as I understand it, is to delay that truck for at least one hour without arousing suspicion."

"That's right."

"Not a problem."

"No?"

"It's a pharmacy," he said. "They got rubbing alcohol and whatnot on the shelves?"

"Sure."

"They got a sprinkler system?"

"One would think."

He took out his slim gold lighter, flipped open the top and rolled the flint wheel until a steady flame appeared. "Then I got everything else I need."

I sat in Ryan's Volvo watching Laura Silver through my field glasses as she pulled weeds from a bed of pink and white impatiens in front of her house. Lucas was on the same multicoloured tricycle I had seen in Ryan's surveillance photo, riding up and down the mutual drive between the Silvers' house and their neighbour's. Laura was wearing jeans and a light denim shirt, a worn straw hat perched atop her hair. Her work gloves were muddy, so whenever sweat began to run down her face, she wiped it away with her bare forearm.

She stopped to take a long drink from a bottle of spring water and then called Lucas over. "Come have a drink, honey."

He pedalled up the drive toward her, helmet askew atop his dark curls, bare tanned legs pumping as fast as they could, making *vroom vroom* sounds with his mouth and sounding at least as good as my Camry. When he reached Laura, he got off the tricycle and drank greedily from her bottle until water spilled down his chin and the front of his shirt.

I got out of the car and walked slowly, casually, toward the house. Lucas was squatting beside Laura as she pulled up a clump of spiny weeds, digging a trowel into the earth to make sure she got the roots.

"What are you doing?" I heard him ask.

"Getting rid of weeds."

"Why?"

"Because they won't let the flowers grow if I leave them there."

"They look cactusy."

"That's why Mama wears gloves, honey. So those little thorns won't prick me." Lucas picked a small trowel from a set of coloured plastic tools and began copying his mother's movements.

"Mrs. Silver?"

She twisted around, still on her haunches, a startled look on her face.

"Sorry," I said. "I didn't mean to surprise you."

She stood up and placed herself squarely between me and Lucas. She had sea-green eyes and smooth tanned skin and a light spray of freckles across her nose. "What is it?" she asked.

"Is your husband home?" Not the single smartest question, perhaps, to ask a woman standing alone with her child.

"Who's asking?"

"My name is Jonah Geller. I'm a private investigator." I held out my photo ID for her to look at. She glanced back at Lucas, then took off one glove and came close enough to reach for my card. After examining it, she handed it back and asked again what I wanted.

"Just something I need to discuss with Jay."

"Does he know you?"

"We met the other day."

"I'm afraid he's not feeling well."

"I know. They told me at the store."

"And you came anyway? What's so important that you'd disturb a sick man at home?"

"That's between me and your husband."

"I don't think so. Tell me what it's about or get off my property."

Her steady gaze told me two things: I wasn't going to get past her; and she might be the right person to talk to. Someone who might make Jay come clean better than I could, and without having to punch him in the mouth.

I plunged in. "In the course of a recent investigation, I came across information that suggested there was a threat against your family."

Any hint of pleasantness left her features. Her brows lowered and her mouth tightened into a thin line. "What kind of threat? To harm us? Is this some kind of . . . of blackmail?

"I'm trying to save your lives."

"From what?"

"It involves your husband," I said, which drew me an even darker look. "Anything more, I'll just have to repeat to him, so why don't the three of us sit down for a minute—or stand out here if we have to—and I'll tell you what I know."

She backed away from me, holding the trowel in front of her. Clumps of black soil dropped from it onto her deck shoes. "Lucas," she said. "Go ring the bell and ask Daddy to come out. And tell him to bring his phone—can you remember that?"

"Yes, Mama."

"What are you going to do?"

"Call Daddy."

"And?"

"Ask him to bring his phone."

"Good boy," she said. "Then you can watch a show if you want."

His little face lit up with delight. "Already?"

"Honey, you've been such a good helper, you can watch an episode of *Thomas*."

"Yay!" he cried and skipped up the walk to the door.

"Let me see your licence again," Laura Silver said, holding out her bare hand; the other still gripped the trowel. I handed her my ID and she looked at it intently, checking my face against the photo. When she gave it back, she said, "I've memorized your details, Mr. Geller, and I'm warning you: if this is some kind of sick attempt on your part to generate business, I will have your professional association *and* the police all over you."

"Laura," I said, "it's nothing like that."

She was startled by my use of her first name—which was why I had used it. "Well, what is it?"

I said the one thing I thought might get her past the idea that I was the one posing the threat. "*Tikkun olam.*"

"What?"

"Oh. I thought you'd know—"

"I know what it means. But what does repairing the world have to do with my family?"

Jay Silver chose that moment to make his entrance at the front door, a cellphone in one hand and a golf club in the other. He started fast down the walkway.

"Hon? What's going on?" he called. "Lucas said I should come out with my phone. Who is this guy? Is he bothering you?"

"I'm not sure," Laura said.

"Get away from my wife, you." He sounded sterner than he had on the loading dock of his store, when Frank had slapped him for talking back. I moved away from Laura and held my hands up in a surrender position, trying to appear non-threatening.

Silver was wearing a loose sweatshirt and baggy khakis and hadn't shaved. He might well have been ill. His eyes were red and puffy and his skin had a sallow cast to it. He shaded his eyes with his hands and looked me over.

"Wait a second. I know you," he said. "The loading dock. You knew my name."

"Lot of good it did me."

"I was afraid—I thought—"

"You thought Claudio got rid of me."

"He said he knew you, Jay," Laura said. "That you met at the store."

The simple fact that it was true seemed to throw Silver off.

"What is going on, Jay? Who's Claudio?"

"Please," I said. "Let's do this inside."

"Do what?" Silver demanded.

She walked over to him and spoke quietly, her hands clenched into fists. He leaned his head down so she didn't have to strain upward, an old habit between spouses with whispered secrets to share. Then his head snapped up at something she said and he glared at me hotly. I centred my weight and let my limbs go loose in case he took a run at me. He handed the phone to Laura and hefted the golf club in his hand. An iron, at least, not a wood; if he connected with my head he wouldn't be able to drive it more than thirty, forty yards tops.

"What's this bullshit about a threat to my family?"

"It's not bullshit and you know it."

"Get off my property," he said.

"Who told you to stay home today?" I asked.

"Nobody," he said. "I wasn't feeling well."

"Was it Frank?"

Laura's head was swivelling back and forth between us as if she were watching a tennis match. "Frank who?"

"Was it Steven Stone?"

He gripped the club more tightly, trying to maintain a fierce glare, but I could see it ebbing little by little.

"Put the club down, Jay. Let's talk while it can do you some good."

"You think I'm afraid of you?"

"No reason to be," I said. "I'm here to help."

"I don't need your help. Now get in your car and drive away before I cave your damn head in." He drew the club back and took a few steps toward me. He was way out of shape. Probably had never been in any shape to begin with. His weight was too far forward and he had the club too far behind him for a short swing. He should have been thinking baseball, not golf.

"Claudio couldn't handle me, Jay," I said. "You really think you can?"

He didn't answer. He charged like a demented bull and took a swing that would have taken a divot out of my skull had I stayed where I was. Instead I did what he least expected: I charged back at him. With his long, looping swing, I was able to get inside its arc, grab the shaft of the club and pull in the direction of his swing. The club stayed in my hand. A three wood. He tumbled over my hip and onto the grass. I snapped the club over my thigh, but only after confirming it was graphite, not steel; it was the club I wanted to break, not my leg. I tossed the two pieces under his car and went over to Silver. Laura was already huddled over him.

"Now can we talk?" I asked.

"Call the police," he groaned. "Tell them I was attacked."

Laura flipped open the phone he had given her.

"If you're going to call the cops," I said, "try Homicide. Ask for Detective Sergeant Hollinger."

Laura asked who at the same time that Jay asked why.

"They're investigating Kenneth Page's murder."

"Now I know you're full of it," he insisted. "Ken wasn't murdered. It was—"

"A carjacking? By a guy who didn't want the car? I don't think so. And neither do the police, by the way. It was a professional hit, Jay, just like the one that's been put out on you. And Laura. And Lucas."

Laura Silver looked absolutely stricken, as though she were about to collapse to the ground. But she didn't look nearly as bad as Jay. He knew what I was saying was true. She leaned over her husband and spoke in an urgent whisper. I couldn't hear a word she said. But Jay Silver did. And when she was done talking he got up and walked over to me slowly.

"What do you want to know?" he said.

"The Internet was the best thing that ever happened to my business," Silver said. We were sitting in my car with the engine off, a slight cross breeze blowing through the open windows. Laura had gone inside to stay with Lucas. Silver had promised to tell her everything when he got inside.

"Something like ten thousand people turn sixty every day in the U.S., and most take at least one medication a day. Their parents, if they're still alive, might need five or ten a day. Do you have any idea how hot that market is? They're starving for affordable medication. We couldn't fill prescriptions fast enough. The higher prices, the U.S. dollars, it made a huge difference to my business. When the law changed, I stood to lose that entire segment. Go back to counting margins in pennies, not dollars. Then I got a call from this fellow I'd gone to school with at Western."

"Steven Stone."

"Right. He asked if I wanted to keep the U.S. business going. I told him I couldn't order large enough quantities without drawing attention."

"Unless you had a chain of nursing homes as a client."

"Yes. Steven said the Vista Mar group would justify any quantities I ordered. So I agreed."

"As did Page."

"Yes. Steven said the more pharmacists were onside, the more money we'd make. Economies of scale and so on. He asked me to get some of the other independents together for a presentation. You should have seen it. Everything was so professionally done. He wowed us, Mr. Geller. I guess he emphasized the opportunity and minimized the risk."

"It's not minimal now."

"God, no."

I remembered something Winston Chan had told me. "Page was hit with an inspection, wasn't he? That's what got him killed."

Silver nodded. "He had a hearing coming up and he'd already been disciplined once by the college. A second suspension could have cost him his licence."

"So he wanted out."

"Demanded would be a better word. Ken had a temper. Thought he was pretty tough."

"He had no idea who he was up against."

"None of us did."

"You knew his death was no carjacking."

He nodded. "As soon as I saw the news. The timing was too coincidental. I told Stone I wanted out too, but he said forget it."

"He threatened you?"

"Not at all. He was as scared as I was."

"Of whom?"

"His partners. He told me they'd bought into the operation as silent partners, then took over. He said I should wait until the fuss over Ken died down. And I tried. I swear I tried. But I started waking up in the middle of the night with my throat closing in on itself. I could barely breathe. I was lashing out at Laura, at Lucas. Every time the phone rang, every time someone rang the doorbell, I jumped. I didn't want to go to work in the morning and I'm someone who loves to be around people. So I called Stone. I thanked him for his advice but I told him I was done and if anyone came near me or my family or my store I'd call the police and tell them about Ken. He told me I had to set up one more delivery."

"The one I interrupted."

"Yes. And that was the last I heard until this morning when Frank called. He said if I came into work today he'd burn the store to the ground."

"Stone never said who his partners were?"

"Only that they were brothers. I didn't know if he meant brothers as in family or as in . . . you know, black guys. And that's all I know. Now what about you? How serious is this threat?"

"Dead serious," I said. "The only reason you're still alive

is the man who got the contract couldn't stand the thought of killing your wife and son too."

"Oh, God," he said. "Oh, my God, what do I do? What the hell do I do?" He shut his eyes tightly but couldn't stop tears from snaking down his plump cheeks and dropping down onto his thighs. "My family is all I care about. I got into this to provide better for them, not get us killed. I'll go back to working in a shitty franchise if I have to. I don't know what I was thinking. It's just when the Internet business took off, for the first time in my life I had breathing room. We could move out of our starter home. We could consider private school for Lucas—and the way the government was driving the public system into the ground, that was no small priority. I've never committed a crime in my life, Mr. Geller. I've never even cheated on my taxes. How does someone like me wind up with a price on my head?"

He was the only one who could answer that.

"Listen to me, Jay," I said. He didn't respond. "Jay!"

He looked up, his eyes red and his cheeks glistening wet.

"Are you listening?"

"Yes."

"Get your wife and son and whatever you need for a few days and leave town. Now."

"But the store—"

"Forget the store. Your insurance will cover it. Be out of here in half an hour."

"But where . . ." He drifted off, unable to finish the question.

"Somewhere no one would think of looking for you. Not a cottage or a friend's place. Just drive at least an hour or two in any direction but south and check into a motel. Take plenty of cash so you don't have to use credit or debit. If there is anything you need to buy on credit—gas, whatever—do it before you leave the city."

"For how long?"

"Until I know if the contract's still on."

"Where are you going?"

"Back to your store. I'll follow the truck and see where it goes."

"Buffalo," he said. "I don't know where exactly, but that's where they all go."

I gave him my home, cell and office numbers and wrote down his cell. Silver held out a big hand. "I'm sorry I didn't help you," he said. "On the loading dock, I mean."

"It's okay."

"No," he said. "It's not."

As he got out of the car, I asked if he was going to tell Laura everything.

"No one tells anyone everything," he said.

CHAPTER 39

Three fire trucks were pulling out of the Med-E-Mart parking lot when I got back. Dozens of people crowded around the front entrance, peering through the plate glass windows, looking like they were waiting for the all-clear to re-enter. A number of them were smoking, including Dante Ryan.

"You missed quite the show," he said as he got in the car. "Complete and utter chaos."

"Just the way you like it."

"Oh, yeah. Alarms going off. Sprinklers sprinkling. Sirens blaring, fire trucks barrelling. Everybody running out of the store except Claudio, Frank and their boys, who were running in."

"Maybe arson is your future."

"No way," he said. "Look what the sprinklers did to my shoes."

As we spoke, one of Frank's men rolled a dolly stacked with damp cartons onto the loading dock, followed by Sumita Desai, whose waist-length hair was soaked through—as were her clothes.

"She's not half bad," Ryan said, "except for the miserable look on her face."

"When did they start loading again?"

"Just a few minutes ago."

I gave Ryan a synopsis of Silver's story: how he, Page and other independent pharmacists had been drawn—suckered?— by Steven Stone into the cross-border scheme.

"Makes sense," he said. "You can't scare the shit out of an organization. You can't make a head office wet its pants. But independent operators are different. They're the stragglers we cull from the herd. They always have the option of saying no. But will they say it to someone with a gun?"

"So the hit was ordered to keep Jay Silver from going to the police."

"It's more than that. Including the wife and kid makes it a message to the others."

"They're right to be worried about him," I said. "This is not the Rock of Gibraltar we're talking about here. He's falling apart."

"So what's next?" he asked.

"Silver says the truck's going to Buffalo. I want to follow. See who takes delivery." I looked at Ryan, trying to read something—anything—in his dark eyes. "You interested?"

"You asking for my help?"

"I just thought you might be curious."

"You asking for my help?" he repeated.

"Would it make a difference?"

"Jonah," he said. "Are you asking for my fucking help or not?"

"Yes," I said. "I'm asking for your help."

"There," he said. "Was that so hard?"

When the truck doors were finally closed and locked, Frank got behind the wheel. Claudio eased himself stiffly into the passenger seat. Compared to him, I was moving pretty well. I hadn't taken Percocet in more than twelve hours now and wasn't going to until this was over. We pulled out with Ryan back behind the wheel and followed them west on Eglinton to Bayview.

"How much you think the load is worth?" Ryan asked.

I remembered the calculations Winston Chan had done in his office. The truck had taken on sixteen skids of twelve cases each. One-sixty plus thirty-two . . . one hundred and ninety-two cases. Call it two hundred. Each case holding a hundred and forty-four bottles of a hundred pills each. Close to three million pills.

"At least ten million," I said. Then I remembered at least one skid had held generic drugs, and revised my estimate up to fifteen. "And it's all profit," I told Ryan, "because Silver paid for the inventory, not them."

"Them who is the question."

"All Stone told Silver was his silent partners were brothers."

Something tugged at the back of my mind—too far back to make any sense. I took out a notebook and pen and wrote Vista Mar, staring at the letters as though working an anagram or cryptic crossword, willing them to fall into place and make some kind of sense to me.

Vista Mar.

A view of the sea.

I thought of the stone crevices in Aspromonte where they dumped kidnap victims no one would ransom.

Steven Stone.

A set of keys had been missing from the pegboard in Tommy Vetere's office at Aspromonte Trucking. The two trucks parked on the lot had just enough space between them for a half-ton like the one we were following. Aspromonte was run by Marco and Marco had two brothers.

Vista Mar.

Run by brothers.

Vista Mar.

Vito Marco.

Vista Mar. Mar for Marco. And Vista, with minor tweaking, for Vito and Stefano, the third brother. The one with an MBA from the University of Western Ontario.

"Ryan," I said. "What does Di Pietra mean?"

"Fucking misery to most people."

"In Italian, please."

"Di is of and Pietra means stone. So Di Pietra is 'of stone.'"

I said, "Jesus Christ."

"Don't you mean *oy?*"

I told Ryan what I was thinking: that Stefano Di Pietra and Steven Stone were one and the same. That Vista Mar was owned by the Di Pietras. The nursing homes were theirs and so was the prescription drug smuggling operation. Stefano the legit-looking front man, Marco and Vito the muscle behind him.

"Makes sense," Ryan said. "Any time a product becomes contraband, our territorial imperative kicks in."

"So with Marco dead, that whole load belongs to Vito."

"Been a good day for him all around," Ryan said. "He eliminated his competition for boss and his war chest just got heavier by millions."

"Would Stefano go along with Vito killing their brother?" I asked.

"What's he gonna do, throw a loafer?"

The truck turned onto Lakeshore Boulevard, then rumbled up the first on-ramp to the elevated Gardiner, bound for Niagara, Fort Erie and the U.S.A.

Dante Ryan and I were off on a Buffalo jump. Minus the Head-Smashed-In part, I hoped.

CHAPTER 40

Buffalo: Friday, June 30

A scream was building inside Amy Farber and she wasn't sure she could keep it in much longer. She could feel it swarming her insides, trying to force its way up through her body and out her mouth. She pursed her lips tighter and breathed in through her nose. It was like fighting the urge to vomit. *It's okay*, she told herself. You get this way every time. It will be over soon enough. Keep busy, she told herself. Make yourself do something. Come on, girl, get up and go. At least get the table ready. *Now!*

She walked unsteadily to the dining room, staying close to the wall, keeping her hand on the wainscoting. She knew she shouldn't have taken a painkiller, an anti-inflammatory and a sedative all at once, but she also knew when the night was over and all the people had gone, Ricky Messina would come to get his money. She'd have to look him in the face, in the eyes—he would insist—and she'd relive everything that had happened the night he came to their door dressed like a pizza boy.

She pushed the table against the far wall so people would be able to serve themselves buffet-style. Hip-checked it home hard enough to rattle the plates on the wooden rail that ran around the dining room walls above eye level. She opened the bottom drawer of their pine hutch, a Mission-style knock-off they had found in East Aurora, and took out a clean linen table-cloth. Everything else was going to be plastic so the tablecloth might as well be nice. She had plenty of plastic wineglasses and juice cups left from last month's event. Barry would be back soon with the paper plates and the fruit platters. Had she asked him to stop at Premier Liquors? She couldn't remember. She just wished he'd get back. She didn't like being alone in the house anymore, no matter how many lights she turned on or what music she played. Even low-dose ambient New Age made her jump.

Amy pushed the dining room chairs against the wall to open up some space and unfolded four bridge chairs. At least thirty people would be coming between six and eleven, judging by orders received. That was her deal with Barry: every shipment that came in had to be sorted, sold and out of the house within forty-eight hours. She couldn't stand it any longer than that.

Amy wondered if Rich Leckie would come. No one was seeing much of him these days. Marty Oliver was picking up his goods for him and paying for them too, all the things Rich had needed before and some new ones too. She admitted to herself she didn't want Rich to come. She knew she'd take one look at him and burst into tears.

A door banged close by and she grabbed the dining room chair nearest her and held tightly onto its frame until she heard Barry shout, "I'm home."

He came clumping in with plastic shopping bags in both hands. "That's everything," he said. "Plates, forks, knives, spoons, cups, nap—"

"We didn't need cups."

"What?"

"You said you got cups. We didn't need cups. We still have cups left from last time."

"Okay, so what's the big deal?"

"We didn't need them. What's so hard to understand?"

"Honey, they don't go bad or anything. We always need cups."

"That's right, Barry. Always. For the rest of our goddamn lives, thanks to you."

"Me? Ah, Christ, what are you crying for?"

"I can't keep doing it, Barry. Every time I know he's coming here, I want to run. I want to get in the car and drive to a hotel where nobody knows me and lie in bed with the covers over my head until he goes away or dies. But he won't let me. He tells me I have to be there, so I am. He tells me I have to look into his eyes, so I do. He tells me . . . he . . . oh, Barry," she sobbed, "what did you do? What did you fucking do?" She sank to the ground slowly, wrapped in her own arms, her face tight to her shoulder and twisted in misery.

"Every time, Barry," she panted, "every time he comes for the money he makes me hand it to him and he holds onto my hand and won't let go. He rubs it between his fingers and he smiles at me like I'm supposed to like it or something, and I don't know if I can make it through without screaming, Barr, I swear I don't know if I can."

"Ssshhh, Amy, you'll make it through. Take a sedative, honey."

"I just did, you miserable shit."

"Amy, please."

"Well, who got us into this? Who else but you would be stupid enough or stoned enough to steal a shipment of drugs and not expect someone would come for it. For *us*, damn you."

"I know I fucked up, Amy."

"Then get us out of this."

"How?"

"I don't care. You got us in, get us out."

"What do you want me to do, go to the cops? Because apart from that I don't know what else to suggest."

"At least don't let him touch me, Barry . . . Barry? Look at me, goddamn you. Say you won't let him touch me, not this time. Not my hands."

"I . . ."

"You what?"

"I'll give him the money."

"He always says I have to."

"I'll do it tonight. I promise."

"Don't promise, Barry. Swear. Swear on your life."

"I do, Amy. I do. I will. I swear."

She looked up at her husband, so much taller than she was but half her size in heart. She wondered if Rich Leckie even crossed his mind anymore.

CHAPTER 41

The Queen Elizabeth Way: Friday, June 30

I f you could fly as the crow flies, you could get from Toronto
to Buffalo in no time. Thirty-some miles across Lake Ontario
and a short run south. Confined to land as we were, the truck
barely managing sixty miles an hour, we faced a drive of at least
two hours, not counting border delays. Along the curving shore
of Lake Ontario we went, passing through Mississauga and
Oakville and the Hamilton steelworks sprawled along the harbour, flame coming out of one stack and dark smoke out of
the others. Swarms of gulls wheeled through the infernal sky,
their bellies grey with soot. Wind buffeted the car as we
climbed the steep rise of the Burlington Skyway and left the
hellish landscape behind.

At least following a truck on a highway was relatively easy.
We could hang back a good number of cars and keep its tall
white box in sight.

When my cellphone rang, I checked the caller ID and
groaned.

"What?"

"My boss," I said and pressed Talk.

"Jonah!" Graham McClintock barked. "What the hell is
going on? You blew out of here yesterday with barely a word
and you skip out today of all days?"

"I'm onto something, Clint. To do with Franny."

"Not that you've seen fit to share with me. Or Homicide."

"I'm chasing it down now. By tomorrow I should know the whole story. Who killed Franny, everything."

"Forget tomorrow," Clint said. "Get down here now."

"I can't."

"Yes you can, if you want to keep your job."

"Clint, I–"

"You and I need to talk, Jonah. You get to my office now, look me in the goddamn eye and tell me what's going on!"

I had to buy time. I resorted to an old trick I've used on my mother when she gets into one of her "Why isn't Jonah a doctor/lawyer/husband/father/chief rabbi of Toronto" rants. I turned the radio on and moved the dial between stations, then turned up the volume so the interior of the car was filled with static. I held the phone close to one of the speakers and shouted, "What's that? I couldn't hear that last part."

"Get down here now!" he bellowed.

"Clint? Clint? Are you still there? You're breaking up."

"To the office!"

"Clint? Damn this phone! Clint? Can you hear me?"

"Yes, I can hear you perfectly."

"Clint?"

"You can't hear me?"

"Are you there?" I asked.

"Ah, fuck!" I heard him say.

I had to face it: there would be no happy ending to this. If I didn't get killed I'd almost certainly be fired. What then? Hook up with another firm? Strike out on my own? Work for—God forbid—my brother's law firm? I stared out the window at nothing in particular. The little devil on one shoulder suggested asking Dante Ryan for a cigarette. The angel on the other said, *Who'd blame you if you did?*

Some little angel.

While I had my phone out, I called Information and got the number for Beth Israel. I asked the receptionist for Ed Johnston's room but the call was transferred to a woman with a pronounced Caribbean accent who told me I'd reached the nursing station on his floor.

"Can you tell me how Mr. Johnston is doing?" I asked.

"Are you family?" she asked.

I should have said yes. Instead I said, "I'm his neighbour."

"You'll have to speak to a family member then. His daughter's in his room. Should I transfer you?"

I remembered how Elizabeth Johnston had glared at me, blaming me, this investigator who'd brought trouble to her father's door. "Could you just tell me if he's alive?" I asked. "Please. Let me rest easy."

"He's doin' well as could be expected, precious," she said. "Now do you want his daughter or not?"

I said I'd try again later, thanked her and hung up.

"He hanging in?" Ryan asked.

"From the way the nurse sounded, just barely, I guess."

For a while I watched wooly grey clouds the size of destroyers stack above each other over the middle of the lake. Then Dante Ryan said, "Want to hear something funny?"

"Please."

"Or maybe ironic is the right word."

"What?"

"First time we met, you were driving a truckload of contraband and I was riding shotgun behind. Now these goons are driving a truck half the size, worth five times the profit, and you and me are the ones riding behind."

"That's not funny or ironic. It's plain fucking weird."

"So I have two questions about that caper," he said.

"I don't know, Ryan."

"What?"

"I can't tell you company tales. When this thing is resolved, we go back to our respective sides of the fence."

"I told you plenty about my business. More than I ever told anyone outside the life, my wife included."

"True."

"So?"

"Tell me the two questions first."

"One: how you cracked our gang. And two: how you . . . how should I say it . . ."

"Blew the case?"

"Blew the living shit out of it, I was going to say."

"It's a long story."

"We're an hour from the border."

"It's not a bad story," I allowed.

"Then tell it, brother," Ryan said. "Let it unfold with the miles."

I let a minute tick by while I thought about where to begin. "All right. About a year ago, the federal finance minister pushed through a huge tax hike on cigarettes."

"Six bucks a carton," Ryan snorted. "I was pissed off and I don't even pay for mine."

"He said it would protect the youth of the nation by making smoking hard to afford."

"Bullshit. The youth of the nation just steal more out of their parents' wallets."

"Plus smokers of all ages instinctively started looking for ways around the tax. It's the Canadian way," I said. "Tax us if you can."

"And naturally your criminal element stepped in to provide courteous black-market service," Ryan grinned. "Christ, everyone and their mother got involved. Natives, bikers, Asians and of course your . . . ah, traditional organized crime types."

"Of course. The problem was that smokers didn't just want cheap cigarettes. They wanted cheap *Canadian* cigarettes."

"You blame them? You ever smoke an American brand?"

I nodded. "I used to be a smoker. I tried Camels once."

"And?"

"Didn't even taste like the best part of a camel."

"There you go."

"Anyway, getting the product into the U.S. was easy. The manufacturers ramped up production for the export market, supposedly because more Americans suddenly wanted to enjoy their products. Truckloads—convoys—were lined up at every land border crossing from the Thousand Islands bridge to the Windsor Tunnel. But packages destined for export have a seal that says they can't be sold in Canada. So they had to be smuggled back."

"Which is where the Akwesasne Reserve proved so convenient."

"It was practically designed for smuggling," I said. "Only one narrow stretch of the St. Lawrence River separates the Canadian and American sides at Cornwall. Every Mohawk with a boat was bringing cartons across the river."

"And wholesaling them to us."

"And buying bigger, faster boats with the profits. The OPP and RCMP together couldn't stop more than one in ten."

"Ten?" Ryan said. "That's what they told the media. They were lucky if it was one in twenty."

"The government finally had to roll back the tax because the only people profiting from it were you criminals."

"A sad day for us because cigarettes were an attractive product. Big markup, steady market, and they don't break if a truck rolls. But," he said, "there's always other commodities. Booze, guns, people, perfume, knock-offs, dope and now, as we know, basic drugstore crap."

"The tobacco companies would have gotten away with it too," I said.

"But?"

"An investigative journalist uncovered documents that left them with a lot of 'splainin' to do. To the RCMP in particular."

"That's what you get for writing shit down."

"An investigator told me one executive from Ensign Tobacco couldn't take a crap without leaving a paper trail."

"But Ensign turned out to be your client."

"And you know why."

"That stupid court order. Thirty million cigarettes, consigned to an incinerator. Going up in smoke for nothing."

"They were marked for export, with no export market to send them to. And the feds looked at it as a way to punish the companies and take the heat off the finance minister for the flip-flop."

"But all thirty million? No. We couldn't let it happen. Too much to resist. We knew our guys could sell them in less time than they took to burn."

"Which is why I was undercover," I said. "Ensign knew someone was after the load."

"How?"

"The guy who hired me was Vic Ryder, their director of security. He'd installed a magnetic card system throughout the plant. Anywhere employees went—offices, storage areas, the manufacturing line—they had to swipe their way in. Ryder could track who went where and when, make sure the guards were patrolling where they were supposed to and not napping in a warehouse. One day he saw two people entering the sealed area where the export cigarettes were being stored prior to incineration."

"McNulty and Tice," Ryan said.

"Yup." Gene McNulty was a shift supervisor in warehouse security; Christopher Tice a security guard.

"Ensign brought me in as a security guard and put me on the same shift as Tice. One day I followed him out when he went for a smoke and caught a whiff of weed. Guy was getting high at ten in the morning. I called a friend in Toronto and had him courier me an ounce of top-line B.C. bud. My boss shit a brick when I expensed it."

"*A friend with weed is a friend indeed,*" Ryan quoted.

"You bet. I got Tice high a few times. Took him out for drinks after work. Hinted I was hard up for cash. Told him I'd once held a Class A trucker's licence."

"Did you?"

"No. I'd driven plenty of trucks but nothing over Class D. Late one night, we'd had some beer, a joint, and Tice, as you know, was a pathetic, insecure shit who needed to impress people. Talk tough. He let a few things slip. Including the big name."

"Marco."

"None other. I passed it on to Ryder and my boss next morning and they called in the Task Force on Traditional Organized Crime."

"Tough Talk? How'd they come riding in?" he asked. "On white horses with their thumbs up their butts?"

"Hey, they were good at getting warrants," I said. "McNulty's home phone . . . Tice's . . . they listened in on calls to Marco."

"So you knew everything?" he said with a smile.

"Up yours, Ryan."

"What?"

"Don't give me that innocent look. Did we know everything . . . you know goddamn well we didn't. We only thought we did."

"You knew the plan," he teased.

"We knew three trucks were going to the incinerator but only two would unload. The third would go to Marco's."

"How'd you get on as his driver?"

"The OPP wanted eyewitness testimony all the way, but Tice was slated to guard the load. Driver's seat was my only way in. Only McNulty had already hired someone."

"The big guy with the glasses, Arthur Read. Him, Tice, McNulty, they all knew each other from Hamilton."

"Our plan was to have Read picked up just before the incineration regarding a supposed theft from the Ensign warehouse. They'd keep him long enough to force McNulty and Tice to find another driver."

"You."

"Me."

"But the Class A thing was bullshit."

"Ryder set me up at the Road Scholar Institute near Belleville. I crammed sixteen weeks of material into six hours at the wheel."

"That's it?"

"I told the instructor I didn't need to learn maintenance, freight handling, fuel economics, weight restrictions, first aid or the subtleties of the Motor Carrier Act. I just needed to know how to take a tractor-trailer on one haul and manoeuvre it backwards and forwards at a loading dock."

"Lucky he didn't think you were a terrorist. Like the guy who wanted to fly the plane but not land it."

"He might have but Ryder vouched for me. I learned how to handle a ten-gear transmission, use air brakes and get through an obstacle course. My ability to back up left a little to be desired, but I was only going to have to do it twice. Everything was golden until the weekend before the incineration."

"What happened?"

"What always happens?"

Ryan took his eyes off the road—a rare thing for him to do—and looked at me, an impish spark in his dark eyes. "What was her name?" he asked.

"Camilla Lauder. The lovely Camilla. I won't go into our relationship, which at that point was dying faster than a fruit fly. We hadn't been seeing each other much while I was undercover. I'd work in Belleville all week and go home weekends, usually to a frosty welcome. She didn't care anymore whether I was around. With one exception. Saturday the 22nd, we were invited to her boss's house for dinner."

"What'd she do?"

"Financial analyst at a brokerage firm."

"And you expected warm and fuzzy?"

"I'm not taking relationship advice from a guy living in the Aerosuites Hotel."

"Ow. Touché."

"Her boss lived out in Etobicoke. It was the first time he'd invited spouses and significant others and we had to be there six o'clock sharp for drinks. I told her no problem, because the incineration was scheduled for Monday. I would work a swing shift Friday and drive in first thing Saturday morning. Be home by noon at the latest. Be showered, shaved and on my best behaviour in time for dinner. It would have worked out perfectly, but you gaping assholes changed the date."

"We didn't, actually," Ryan said. "Monday was a smoke-screen. It was always going to be Saturday, 'cause the incinerator only had one shift, eight a.m. to noon, and it was never that busy after eleven-thirty. The Ensign trucks were supposed to roll in at five to twelve when there was no one around but the intake guy, and we had him bought and paid for."

"Our wiretaps didn't pick up the change until Friday night. Ryder called me at midnight. I should have called Camilla right then but she had chronic insomnia and if I woke her she'd never get back to sleep and blame me and be pissed off, as usual."

"Christ, did she sleep in a coffin?"

"Maybe she should have tried. So I didn't call. Read was arrested at dawn Saturday and by eight o'clock, Tice was bang-ing on my door, asking if I wanted to make a quick thousand to drive a truck to Woodbridge."

"A thousand? The cheap fuck. Him and Read were split-ting ten."

"I never collected anyway. By eleven o'clock, we were loaded up and on the road. We followed the other trucks to the incinerator. I managed to dock mine without maiming anyone. We had fifteen minutes to kill to make it look like we were unloading. Tice made a call on his cellphone—to you."

"I remember. We were pulled over on the highway just past the on-ramp, waiting to escort you to Marco's."

"Tice finished the call and went for a smoke," I said. "I took the plunge and called Camilla on his phone. Saturday mornings she usually went to Pilates, so I figured I'd get the voice mail and leave a quick message. I never dreamed she'd answer."

"How manly of you."

"You wouldn't say that if you knew her. Turns out she'd skipped Pilates because of a headache. She was in a pissy mood to begin with and when I told her I might be late, she flipped. Absolutely flipped. A longshoreman would blush at the names she called me. I was trying to calm her down when I saw Tice coming. So I hung up on her. Like throwing gas on the fire, right, but what could I do? Tice got in and told me to roll. When we were a half-mile from the 401 on-ramp, he called you with a heads-up. Being a lazy sonofabitch, he hit redial."

"Because *his* last call had been to me."

"Only now he gets Camilla. He's not expecting a woman, so he says, 'Who the fuck is this?' And she gives it right back: 'Who the fuck are you?' I could hear it right through his other ear. She must have seen the 613 area code on her caller ID, because she asks, 'Are you with Jonah?' He goes, 'Yeah.' And she blows me out of the water. Like a killer whale. Like a depth charge. She says, 'Are you undercover too? If you are, or even if you're not, tell Jonah if he's not home by five o'clock he can go fuck himself because he'll never fuck me again as long as he lives.'"

"Nice mouth."

"So Tice is on to me, right? He has to be. Just to make sure I ask him what the call was and he says, wrong number.

Then he starts dialling you. Five digits in, I hit him with the best straight right I can manage while driving this beast of a truck. Catch him in the jaw, his head bangs against the window, he's out. The tractor starts going one way and the trailer the other but I somehow get control and make it onto the 401."

"Blew right the fuck past us," Ryan said. "Much to our surprise. You were supposed to come along nice and slow, let us fall in behind."

"Now I'm barrelling down the 401 with no backup and no way to contact anyone, because the phone fell under Tice's seat. Then I see the Trenton exit, with the little sign saying there's an OPP detachment."

"So that's why you got off there."

"You remember that off-ramp?"

"The cloverleaf. You were going round on nine wheels, not eighteen," Ryan grinned. "We were freaking out, thinking you were gonna roll it over and we'd have to stuff ten million cigarettes into an Escalade."

"But I made the turn. Then the road finally straightened out, remember, and you guys came tearing up behind me trying to pass."

"With the back of the truck swinging like a hooker in pumps. Almost drove us off the goddamn road."

"Sorry. My six lessons didn't include evasive action. And that's when the OPP cruiser showed."

"We almost hit him head-on," Ryan said. "We swerved out to pass you and boom, there he was. We ducked back in just in time and then we could see him in the rear-view, braking, turning around, coming after us with the siren, the lights, the whole package."

"And you had to leave empty-handed."

"Hey, you don't know how much that hurt."

"Marco made it pretty clear the other night."

"Never mind. Get to the part about getting shot."

"You like that part? Okay. Now I have the cop behind me and it looks safe to pull over. Takes me a couple of football fields to slow the truck down but finally I stop and get out, start walking back to the cruiser with my hands in plain sight. The cop gets out with his holster unsnapped and his hand on his gun butt, asks me what the hell's going on."

"What was his name again?"

"Colin MacAdam. I tell him it was an attempted hijack and he should call for backup in case you guys come back. He's about to call it in when Tice swings open the passenger door with a gun in his hand and opens fire. MacAdam goes down. I'd forgotten about Tice. I should have remembered he wouldn't stay out that long—I'd only hit him with my fist, not my elbow—but in the heat of the moment, I just forgot."

"Did you know he had a gun?"

"No. They weren't standard issue for Ensign security. But I still should have been more aware."

"Strictly hindsight. So?"

"So MacAdam went down. I scrambled over there, tried to get his gun out of the holster. I almost had it out when Tice shot me in the arm. Then he came walking over with the gun in his hand and a shit-eating grin on his face. He was going to kill us both, the mangy prick. When he was two feet away he pointed the gun at my head. I closed my eyes, kicking myself for calling Camilla. She didn't care about me anymore. She only wanted me at the party so she wouldn't be the only one alone. For that one mistake, calling her on his phone, I was going to die, a cop was going to die, and all you fuckers were going to walk. When the gun went off, I didn't feel a thing. I figured it was the difference between the speeds of light and sound."

"Like when you see a batter hit the ball, then hear the crack of the bat."

"Right. I'm waiting for my head to blow apart. Bracing myself for darkness, stars, whatever you see in your last second alive. And nothing happened. I opened my eyes and Tice was down on the ground, spread-eagled on his back with a good-sized hole in his forehead. MacAdam had his gun out. Got it free while Tice was bearing down on me and shot him dead. And that was pretty much that."

"How'd he make out?" Ryan asked.

"MacAdam? Paraplegic. The bullet hit his armpit where his body armour couldn't stop it. Ripped his spinal cord on the way out. He'll be in a chair the rest of his life."

"That bothers you?"

I took a long look at the man beside me. "Of course it does. If you had been in my place, it wouldn't bother you?"

"No," Ryan said.

"Why the hell not?"

"You didn't shoot him," Ryan said.

"He wouldn't have got shot if—"

"If what? If you hadn't called your girlfriend? If you had hit Tice harder, knocked him out longer? If you'd known he had a gun? If MacAdam had slept in or caught a cold or had a flat or was on the night shift? Had his body armour on right? The man knew the risks when he took the job."

"I can't just—"

"It's behind you, Jonah. Walk away. That's what I do. And I keep walking."

"Well, I can't. Not if I want to stay human."

"Human, my hard hairy ass. What if someone comes bearing down on you with a piece? Or on me? You gonna have the jam to shoot your way out? Or you gonna be weighed down by all this *what if* shit? 'Gee, if I pull the trigger it might do this, it might do that, it might ricochet off Ricky the Clit's bowling ball head and hit some old lady on the sidewalk.'"

"So if you were in my place, you wouldn't feel guilty about MacAdam?"

"I didn't say that. Jews don't own the market on guilt. I'm

Catholic, man, I was guilty before I was born. Sure, I'd help the guy out if I was in a position to. Lay out for a nurse or a wheel-chair or whatnot. But I wouldn't carry it around my neck the rest of my life. Because staying human, as you put it, isn't my priority."

"What is?"

"Staying alive."

When my phone rang again, I was relieved to see it wasn't Clint calling back. Then not so relieved when I remembered that the 808 exchange in Toronto is reserved for its police service. I answered anyway.

"Hey, Geller," Katherine Hollinger said.

"Morning, sarge," I said. Ryan shot me a look. I shrugged.

"I thought maybe you'd like to have coffee."

"I would," I said. "Sometime next week?"

"I was thinking more like now. In my office."

"Is this a social coffee or a business coffee?"

"We'll discuss that over the coffee. Fifteen minutes?"

"Can't," I said. "I'm on the road."

"All roads lead back to Homicide," she said.

"Not this one."

"Why?"

"I'm taking a drive."

"Turn around."

"Okay, Kate," I said. "What's going on?"

"Ballistics, Jonah," she said.

She had my full attention.

"The gun that killed your friend Franny?"

"Yes?"

"Same one killed Kenneth Page. The very man you were asking about. So why don't you stop whatever you're doing and get down here. Coffee's on me this time."

"As soon as I get back."

"From where?"

I heard a loud, abrasive voice say "Gimme that phone," and then McDonough was on the line. "We're not asking, Geller," he snarled. "We're telling you to get your useless butt down here now."

"What do you need a useless butt for? Or should I say another one?"

"Come on, cupcake. Come put your bullshit story on the record."

"Lighten up, McDonough. We're on the same side."

"Same side? We're not even on the same field," he rasped. "You're a waterboy, Geller, a hanger-on. You couldn't make the real grade, so you grab on to coats like mine. Don't give me crap about being on my side. You're more like something stuck to my shoe."

"And yet you request the pleasure of my company."

"I'm not requesting shit. I'm telling you to get down here."

I sighed, then fiddled with the radio again and brought the static back up. "What's that, McDonough? I couldn't hear that last part."

"Get down here now!" I heard him bellow.

"Are you still there?" I called. "What's that you said? Damn this connection. I'm afraid we're breaking up."

The Niagara Peninsula lay ahead of us, a dark outline in the haze over the water. We were in wine country now, passing vineyards where bright strands of wire were intertwined with vines to keep them in neat rows. I told Ryan what Hollinger had said about the same gun killing Page and Franny.

"You know what I'd like to know?" he asked.

"What?"

"Where Ricky Messina was when they were getting killed."

"Why him?"

"Because people are dying and it isn't me killing them. And because there's a Buffalo connection."

"Maybe we'll get a chance to ask him."

"Fine with me," he said. "Once I get my guns out of the trunk."

We went through Grimsby, Beamsville and Jordan, bypassed Niagara-on-the-Lake, and headed southeast toward Fort Erie. Traffic thinned out once we were past the exit to the Niagara Parkway and the Falls, so Ryan stayed farther back from the truck than before. Away from the escarpment, the land was entirely flat. We drove past copses of poplars trembling in the warm wind.

I said, "You said something about your stepfather before."

"Yeah?"

"That he beat you. For sport, you said."

"So?"

"What was his problem?"

"His problem? I was his problem. Me, Dante Ryan, only son of Sid and the former Mrs. Ryan. My mother was still young and good-looking when she married Dominic. Everyone figured there'd be more kids, but nothing happened. Usually they blame the woman, call her barren, but my mother already had a baby so everyone knew the problem was him, not her. I was living proof he didn't have the goods. So every chance he got he made me pay. Christ, if I was breathing too loud I got smacked."

The highway narrowed from three lanes down to two. Ryan moved to the right and slowed slightly, letting a few more cars fall in between us and the truck but always keeping it in sight.

"I tried to kill him once," Ryan said. "I was maybe seventeen and he had given me a royal beating because he thought I was stealing cigarettes from him. Which I was but fuck him anyway. The next night I go out on a B and E with my friends and I find a gun in the house, in the guy's bedside table in one of those purple Crown Royal bags. A .38 snubbie. The next time Dom tried to lay a beating on me, I put the gun on him. Told him what a useless lazy ugly fucker he was and pulled the trigger. Nothing happened. The ammo was so old it wouldn't fire. Just my luck, I break into a house where the guy keeps a limp-dick gun in a bag. He really gave it to me that time, Dom, I mean with all the trimmings. I couldn't walk right for a month. That's when I started teaching myself about guns. Never bought or stole another cheapie. To this day I arm myself only with the best."

"Is he still with your mother?"

"Dom? Nope."

"Still alive?"

"Definite nope."

"What happened?"

"I left home soon as I could. Once I was established and could support my mother, she had no more use for him. I'm pretty sure he was beating her too. So she kicked the bum out."

"And?"

"He must have been overcome with grief. Maybe burdened with remorse over the way he treated her. Fuck, the way he treated me. Either way, a few weeks later, sadly, he took his own life."

"How?"

"Shot himself in the head."

"How many times?" I asked.

CHAPTER 42

Buffalo: Friday, June 30

R ich Leckie watched through a gap in the curtains as his wife and daughter left the house. He flinched when the front door slammed, even though he knew it meant someone going out, not coming in. He watched as they got into the car, watched Leora back out of the driveway onto the street, not paying attention as usual, forcing an eastbound driver to swerve around her back end, flashing a finger and blasting his horn.

And finally they were gone. He was alone, thank God. He was on his way back to bed when a dark thought crept into his mind: Leora hadn't locked up behind her. The new deadbolt hadn't turned. It made a distinctive click and he hadn't heard it. Panic rose up in him. He felt like rats were crawling over his bare feet. He could hardly swallow his own spit. He had to go down and lock up but what if it was too late?

What if Ricky was already in?

No. It couldn't be. Rich would have heard something. Footsteps. Old floorboards creaking. A high girlish laugh. The sound of a gun barrel slashing through the air. Of cartilage breaking.

He had to go downstairs now, before it was too late, and lock up. Stupid fat fucking Leora, putting him in a spot like this. Okay, she didn't know about Ricky—he told her he had gotten mugged that night—but she knew better than to leave the door unlocked. This was still Buffalo, and hardly the best part. He tried to breathe through the panic but the best he could manage were shallow gasps. He looked around for something he could use as a weapon, settling for an African fertility statue Leora had bought four years before Leigh-Anne was conceived. Eighteen inches high and made of acacia, as good a club as he would find. Clutching the statue in his right hand, holding onto the banister with his left, he moved silently down the stairs. Halfway down, his bathrobe fell open and he cursed but couldn't close it, afraid to let go of the banister or his club. As he neared the bottom of the stairs he paused—exposed, vulnerable, ridiculous with his shrivelled little turtle-head dick hanging there in a nest of grey hair—and listened with every ounce of concentration he could muster. He could hear the air conditioning unit humming away in the front room. The fridge rumbling in the kitchen. Water dripping—why couldn't Leigh-Anne ever close the faucet all the way? But no footsteps, no laughter. No sound of a round being chambered. And then he could see the front door, saw that the deadbolt handle was horizontal, not vertical—locked, thank God—and he took the last step down, missed it and landed jarringly hard on his left heel. His knee hyperextended and slid forward, sending him hard onto his back, fertility statue still in hand.

Then came tears. They leaked out of his eyes at first, then fell in hot wet streams, his body shaking like he was having a seizure. He let go of the statue and pressed his fists to his eyes and curled up on the floor and held himself tight, rocking back and forth until there were no tears left. When he felt strong enough to stand he made his way into the kitchen where he blew his nose, then ran cold water into his cupped hands and gently washed his face. He sat down heavily at the kitchen table, flexing his knee gently and rubbing his tailbone.

I've lived a good enough life, he thought. Kept more or less to the straight and narrow. Did most of the things expected of me, other than make the big bucks. So what in God's name did I ever do to deserve Ricky Messina?

He shuddered as the name entered his mind. The face, round and benevolent. He tried to banish Ricky from his mind but Ricky wouldn't go.

Ricky dressed like a delivery man, with a gun at Amy's head.

Ricky kicking him and breaking his nose.

Ricky shoving him into his car, driving him to Forest Lawn Cemetery.

Pulling off the road and yanking Rich out of the car, sending him stumbling into the darkness away from the lights along the road.

Ripping Rich's pants down and bending him over a freezing cold gravestone.

Hurting him so badly. Making him do such vile things before leaving him bleeding, shaking, gagging on the ground.

"We understand each other now, don't we?" Ricky had said. "You so much as call my name in your sleep, I'll bring you back here and bury you alive."

Rich knew he would never get the images out of his mind; he would never get the taste out of his mouth. What was the use in trying?

He thought about breakfast but had no appetite. He thought of getting dressed and going for a walk but it was too hot out. He wondered if he could make it to Barry and Amy's tonight, or if it was better just to let Marty handle it.

He thought of the Buffalo River and the time he and Marty had plunged in on acid.

He thought again about going back to bed and wondered how many pills he had left.

CHAPTER 43

Buffalo: Friday, June 30

Whessen the white truck passed the first highway sign for the Peace Bridge to Buffalo, it pulled over onto the shoulder and stopped, hazard lights flashing.

Ryan had to keep going—no way to stop without drawing attention—but he took his foot off the gas and coasted.

"What's he up to?" I asked.

Ryan looked at the dashboard clock. It read 3:50 p.m. He said, "Shift change, I bet."

"What?"

"He's waiting for a shift change at the border. Four o'clock, half the guys change over."

"He's got someone on the inside?"

"Let's find out."

Ryan had told me his crew often crossed the border by getting the name of a bent Customs officer from Vinnie's brother Luciano. Ryan got this Uncle Looch on the phone as we neared the crossing.

"Uncle?" he said. "It's me. Yeah, that me. How you doing? Good, good . . . Yeah, I know. We all feel terrible, but what can you do? He had good health all his life. As long as he's not in pain . . . Listen, Uncle? We got anyone on today at the bridge? Yeah, that one. Yeah? Comes on at four? Perfect. Okay. Give her my best too, Uncle. Thank you."

"Lane 9," he said to me. "Any bets that's where our truck goes too."

Security going into the U.S. was tighter than ever these days, whether you were flying, driving or taking the train. The lines stopped a good hundred yards from the crossing and inched forward from there.

"Open the glove," Ryan said. "Give me the folder there."

I handed him a green vinyl folder that had his registration and insurance papers.

It was four-fifteen when we pulled up to the booth in lane 9. As Ryan had predicted, the white truck was in the same lane, seven vehicles back.

The U.S. Customs officer leaned out of his booth, a heavy man of fifty or so, with exploded blood vessels in his nose and cheeks, watery eyes and a tremor in his hands. He looked like he'd sell his mother into slavery for a drink. "Citizenship?"

"Canadian," we said in unison.

"Where you heading today?"

"Buffalo," Ryan said.

"Purpose of your visit?"

"Pleasure," Ryan said.

It didn't feel that way to me.

The guard held out his hand. "Licence and registration, please." As Ryan passed the guard his folder, he said, "Regards for you from Mr. Lewis," he said. The guard's eyes brightened and his face moved ever so slightly in the direction of a smile. He kept Ryan's folder tightly closed as he withdrew into his booth. He knew the drill, knew there'd be five U.S. hundreds in there, tucked in by Ryan while we waited. Much stabbing of computer keys ensued in the booth. Then the guard leaned back out, beaming at least sixty watts brighter than he had been before, and welcomed us to the U.S. "Have yourself a nice day," he said.

I'd settle for surviving it.

We pulled away from the booth and into a parking area. Ryan raised the hood of the car and checked the oil while we waited for the white truck to clear Customs. Checked it a few times, then slowly topped it up.

"Would Looch say anything to Frank?" I asked.

"Like what?"

"Like 'Gee, you're the second call I've had today. First was from Dante Ryan.'"

"First of all, Uncle Looch didn't get to be his age by flapping his lips. Second, the other guy called first. He knew he had to wait till four o'clock so he'd already spoken to Looch when he pulled over."

"Just checking how paranoid I need to be."

"Right where you are is fine," Ryan said.

CHAPTER 44

As we followed the truck north on the New York State Thruway, I could see a jetty built out into the Buffalo River below us. There was a paved path along its spine where people were walking, jogging and cycling. They looked like they were walking on water. On the south side of the channel, overlooking the river, were grand mansions built in a Spanish colonial style.

"Look at these places," I said.

"Trust me," Ryan said. "You're seeing the best part first."

The truck turned onto the Scajaquada Expressway, as did we, and exited soon after the first toll booth onto Elmwood Avenue, past the rolling green spaces of the Olmsted parklands. A few turns later, we found ourselves on Lincoln Parkway, a wide boulevard with houses that wouldn't have been out of place in Forest Hill: Tudors, colonials, Georgians, all on spacious lots with well-maintained gardens.

The truck was slowing down.

Ryan had been keeping half a block back. At the first flash of the truck's brake lights, he pulled over immediately. Frank got out and walked down a driveway beside one of the larger colonial houses. Claudio pulled away from the curb and began backing down the drive, Frank guiding him. I noticed the truck didn't beep when in reverse. They'd probably disconnected the fuse that controlled it, a smart move given that the truck was generally put to nefarious use.

"Closer," I said.

We cruised slowly toward the house. The truck was backed up to a brick garage at the end of the driveway. A tall grey-haired man in his fifties was offloading cartons by hand. Claudio and Frank stayed on the sidelines as usual. There was no forklift or hand truck in sight.

"It's going to take that guy forever to unload if he has to do it himself," I said. "Let's park down the street."

Ryan drove to the end of the block, made a U-turn, and parked on the other side of the boulevard so we could watch the house. He turned off the engine and lowered the windows. He lit a cigarette and hung his arm out the window so the smoke wouldn't blow my way. The car felt quiet after the constant hum of the engine and the road.

"I wonder if there's a coffee shop in walking distance," I said. "I need a bathroom and a coffee, in that order."

His answer was, "What the fuck!"

The truck was coming back out the driveway.

"He couldn't have unloaded it all," I said.

"There's more than one drop-off," Ryan said. "Stay or follow?"

"Follow," I said. "The house isn't going anywhere."

Traffic was heavy as we tailed the truck south and west. Five o'clock on a hot afternoon, people were busting out of work, desperate to make it home to the yard, the porch, the air-conditioned den, anywhere they could peel off their work clothes and crack open something cold. American flags hung everywhere, limp in the heat. Some were probably out specifically for the Fourth of July, but many homes had permanent flagpoles fixed to their fronts, a lot more than you'd see in Canada. Some houses sported yellow ribbons and signs saying they were proud to be American. Lawn signs and bumper stickers, some in the form of furled ribbons, proclaimed support for soldiers in Iraq; some for the war itself. One car ahead of us, a big old Impala, had four bumper stickers: Proud to be a Vietnam Vet. Support Veterans of the Vietnam War. Support our Troops in Iraq. Insured by Smith & Wesson.

No, Geller, you are not in Toronto anymore, where most bumper stickers proclaim support for ecological and social causes and lawn signs warn government against privatizing health care and cutting school budgets.

"You want to see the real Buffalo? Check that out," Ryan said, pointing to a billboard that showed a smiling man in a blue uniform steam-cleaning a carpet. "Crime Scene Incorporated," the tagline read. "Cleaning and Restoring Buffalo Homes Since 1984."

"Ever seen one of those at home?" he asked.

"Never."

"I should apply for a franchise," he said. "I could present a hell of a business case, don't you think? I got experience, contacts and I'm motivated as hell to launch a new career."

The truck rumbled around a traffic circle and veered west onto Lafayette. The farther west we drove, the smaller the houses were. There were no public monuments, green spaces or architectural gems in this part of town. No colonials on generous lots. Just frame houses with stained siding and cars looking worse for the wear of Buffalo winters. Yards showed more brown grass than green, and were piled with old appliances, broken bicycles, discarded lumber and mud-spattered toys. Sidewalks were breaking where weeds pushed up from the ground. Windows were boarded up. Men sat against a fence outside a dirty bodega, drinking from big cans of malt liquor. At least half the businesses on the street had newspaper taped over the windows. Graffiti covered the sides of most buildings.

"Osama bin Laden lives," someone had written in white paint on a red-brick wall.

"Upstairs," someone had added in black.

A few minutes later, the truck pulled into the parking lot of a three-storey warehouse surrounded by a fence topped with rusting razor wire. Most of the windows at the rear were broken despite being shielded by metal grilles. We parked on a side street where we could see the back of the warehouse through the fence. Behind the building were tall cottonwood trees. Fluffy white clumps drifted down like large snowflakes only to be snagged by barbed wire or trapped by wind currents against the fence. Frank and Claudio perfected their idle routine while two hired hands unloaded the cases: first the loose ones, which they wheeled inside on a dolly, then the skids, which they removed using the same kind of forklift we'd seen at Silver's.

When the truck was empty, Claudio closed the back door and locked it, and all of them went inside. Half an hour later they were still there.

"If all they left at the house was a dozen or so cases, where do you think the rest is going?" Ryan asked.

"Once they're over the border, they can go anywhere: Rochester, Syracuse, Detroit, Cleveland."

Hundreds of thousands of vials, millions of pills, bound for hungry markets where aging boomers wanted—needed—to remain virile and healthy; where their parents were trying to cope with the onslaught of symptoms that storm the body in its eighth and ninth decades; where people of all ages with rare illnesses needed medications in amounts too small for the pharmaceutical industry to profit by unless the drugs were sold at exorbitant prices, which, of course, is what the industry did.

"Let's go back to the house," I said. "Try our luck on whoever is there."

"Are we down to banking on luck now?" he asked.

CHAPTER 45

P arking was suddenly at a premium near the house on Lincoln Parkway. Every available spot was taken for a full block in either direction. As we passed the house, an older man, extremely heavy and sweating through his shirt, was pushing an empty wheeled cart up the walk. He was at the bottom of the steps when the door opened and a man and a woman came out. The man was the one we'd seen unloading the van. He wore black jeans and a yellow T-shirt with a swirling portrait of Jerry Garcia in a cloud of smoke. The woman looked like a yachter in a Ralph Lauren ad. She carried a cardboard carton in her arms; the man had two. He had to use his backside to hold the door open for the older man as he backed up the stairs pulling his cart. They exchanged greetings as if well acquainted. I turned and watched through the rear window as the man and woman carried their cartons to a gold Infiniti sedan. He loaded the cases in for her, then kissed her on the cheek before trotting back to the house.

The nearest parking spot we could find was around the next corner, on Bedford Avenue. "Hope we don't need to make a fast exit," I said.

Ryan got out and opened the trunk of his car. He said, "First rule of a fast exit? Make sure there's no one left to chase you." He opened his metal gun case and slipped his Glock 20 into his waistband. He also took out a yellow hard hat and a clipboard.

He said, "I don't want to be seen walking with you, so I'll go first and walk down around the back. See if there's a way in." He put on the hard hat and held the clipboard smartly under his arm. "Anyone sees me, I'm Mr. City Inspector, looking at the wires and going *uh-huh* a lot."

"It would look better if you had a pen, Mr. C.I."

"I don't carry one. You saw what happens to guys who write shit down."

I gave him my pen.

He said, "See if you can get in the front. I'll hang out back. You need me in there, whistle sharp." He walked slowly toward the house, stopping occasionally to look up at telephone wires and make notations on his clipboard. I waited until he was out of sight down the driveway, then began walking toward the front entrance. As I approached the house, a dark-coloured SUV pulled up alongside me. My sphincter pursed momentarily, but the driver in no way resembled an assassin, unless they're hiring clean-cut young women who look like they're off to the library. I scanned the street. No other cars coming in either direction. No one on foot.

I was walking up the stairs, pondering entry strategies, when the front door opened and a sporty-looking fellow in his sixties emerged. He wore slacks and a blazer and a pressed golf shirt, with white hair swept back from his tanned face. He had a large canvas shopping bag in each hand, which he set down to pull the door shut behind him.

"Let me get that for you," I called and bounded up the last steps.

"Thanks," said the man. "Hope you're in no rush, though. They're quite a bit behind schedule today. I've never seen it this busy."

Great. A peanut gallery full of witnesses.

I stepped into the house and locked the door behind me. I was in a small foyer made smaller by a huge fern growing out of a brass umbrella stand. I brushed past it into a wider hallway that had a hardwood floor scuffed grey down the middle by years of traffic. On my right was a wide staircase going up to the second storey. On my left an empty den, lit only by a desk lamp. I could hear music and voices coming from the back half of the house, though. A lot of voices, men and women both, an ongoing din punctuated occasionally by laughter and friendly shouts.

Spare me, I thought. They're having a goddamn party.

"Hey," a man's voice called to me.

I braced myself and looked up to see a stocky fellow in his early fifties, his close-cropped dark hair and beard showing traces of white near the temples and around the mouth. He carried two cardboard cartons over which he could hardly see. A petite woman of about eighty walked beside him, gripping his arm tightly as she took small delicate steps.

"Mind getting the door?" he asked me.

"Not at all." I unlocked the front door and flattened myself against the wall so they could pass.

"Thanks, Ted," the woman said. "If you get me as far as the sidewalk, I'll be fine."

"You're still driving?" he asked.

"Don't be silly," she giggled. "I haven't driven since the first President Bush was in office. Amy was kind enough to call a taxi."

"You have someone on the other end to help you unload?"

"My grandson lives in the basement," she said. "He'll look after me."

I closed the door behind them, locked it and ventured farther down the hall. An archway on the left opened into a large living room with a marble fireplace and mantel. About a dozen people were standing by the fireplace or sitting on sofas that faced each other across a glass coffee table. A few looked me over and went back to their conversation.

A second, wider archway led from the living room to the dining room, where another fifteen or twenty people stood around a table that had wine, light beer, soda and other drinks. There were platters of fruit and cheese and a basket of bagels, surrounded by bowls of cream cheese and a plate of thinly sliced smoked salmon, garnished with onion, capers and lemon slices.

Most of the people ranged in age from late-forties to mid-sixties, the split between men and women about equal. Most were dressed casually yet expensively. The snatches of conversation I could hear revolved around the heat, plans for the long weekend, the exhibition of Chuck Close portraits at the Albright-Knox and the fickle nature of real estate.

I didn't see the long-haired guy who'd been unloading the truck. I was trying to figure out who Amy might be when a woman's voice said, "You're new."

I turned to see a trim fortyish woman in a mauve linen jacket and faded jeans. Long Navajo-style earrings dangled amid her feathered hair, a shade of red that wasn't her own but suited her blue eyes. As she held out her hand, a bracelet in the same style as her earrings slid down her forearm. "Cassandra Lawson. But everyone calls me Cass."

I took her hand. "Joel," I said. When lying about my name, I always choose something that sounds like my own.

"What's taking so long?" said the older man I had seen pushing his cart up the walk. He was reclining in a maroon leather Queen Anne knock-off. He was grossly overweight, his ankles puffy and purple above his socks. "It's nice they put out a spread and everything, but there's not a damn thing here I can eat."

"So have a drink, Harv," Cass said.

"The only thing I can drink is water, hon, and if I have one more glass I'll have to pee ten times tonight instead of the usual five. Did Barry say why everything's upside down today?

Normally I come when they tell me, I'm in, I'm out, goodbye, go home."

"The delivery was much bigger than usual," Cass said. "And it didn't come packed the way it normally does. It was just bulk cases. Amy has to open them up to fill the orders, unless you're willing to take a whole case of something."

"I already got a case of something!" Harv roared. "Why the hell else would I be here!"

"Can you tell me where Amy is?" I asked Cass. "Or Barry? I need to talk to them a minute."

"You're not from here," said Harv. "I can hear it in your voice. Canadian, *eh?*"

"I'm from Toronto," I said.

"Then why the hell are you buying medications here?" Harv asked. "The whole point is to get them cheaper from Canada."

"That would be illegal," I said, with all the innocence I could manage on short notice.

"Illegal! We can't have that, could we?" Harv laughed until the laugh turned into a rolling cough that ended with him clearing his throat and hawking something into a napkin. He took a couple of deep breaths and tucked the napkin into his jacket pocket. "Listen, kid," he wheezed, "I don't know what you're doing here. You look healthy enough to me. But I take ten medications a day—*ten*—between my heart condition and diabetes and cholesterol. Even with insurance, you know what the co-pay is?"

"Come on, Harv," a man cut in. He was dressed casually enough in jeans and a black silk shirt, but the watch on his wrist probably cost more than my Camry. He looked very fit for his age, which was early fifties. "I bet Medicare covers most of what you need."

"What do you know about Medicare, Marty? You got more money than the rest of us combined. I don't know why you even come here."

"I don't like paying full price for anything," Marty said.

"But you could if you had to. I can't. I went to a presentation on the Medicare guidelines last week, and I didn't understand half of what the guy was saying. And neither did he. Every question I asked him, he'd say, 'Well, I'll have to check that and get back to you.' I taught high school mathematics for thirty-two years, my friend, and the guidelines might as well have been in Greek."

"Hey, Harv," a voice called out behind me.

Harv's eyes widened and his face broke into a grin. I turned to see the grey-haired man in the Jerry Garcia shirt. He had a carton in his arms. He said, "Want me to take this straight out to the car for you?"

"Barry!" Harv said. "You're an angel."

"Just the one carton?"

"That was all the cash I could raise on short notice. If there's anything left on Monday, I'll see what I can do."

"I wouldn't count on it," Barry said. "Amy wants everything out of here as fast as possible." Then his eyes settled on me. Settled and narrowed to suspicious-looking slits. "I'm sorry," he said. "Do I know you?"

"He's new," Harv said.

"I can see that."

"My name is Joel," I said.

Barry set the box down and walked over to me. He was about my height and heavier. I hoped it wouldn't lead him to start something. Busting up his place—or him—wouldn't help any.

"If I don't know you," Barry said, "what are you doing in my house?"

"Can I speak to you privately?" I asked him.

"No."

"It will only take a few minutes," I said.

"What are you, a cop? A narc or something?" People were

stopping their conversations, looking our way, moving toward us. Marty in particular was glaring at me.

"I'm not a cop," I told Barry.

"Then get out, " he said. "This is a private party."

"As soon as we've had our conversation."

Marty walked over to Barry's side, about Barry's size but in better shape. "Why don't you get out like he asked?" he demanded. A man used to getting his way.

"If you're a police officer, you have to tell me, right?" Barry asked.

"I'm not a police officer, so I wouldn't know."

"FDA?"

"What?"

"Food and Drug Administration."

"No. I'm from Toronto."

He looked at me for a long moment, making up his mind. Maybe he was picturing the damage that might occur if his friend Marty and I got into it. "Okay," he said, nodding toward the back of the house. "In the kitchen." He asked Marty to help Harv out with his carton.

Marty looked disappointed, like he'd missed his chance to impress someone. Maybe himself. "You sure you don't want me to come with you?"

"I can handle it," Barry said and led me back to a large eat-in kitchen with a round oak table on ornate ball-and-claw legs. A woman sat at the table, surrounded by dozens of pill vials and boxes of all sizes. About a dozen cartons were stacked near the rear door behind her. I looked out the door; no sign of Ryan through its glass panes.

The woman, whom I presumed to be Amy, looked about fifty, with long grey hair pulled into a loose braid and striking grey-green eyes. She wore her clothes baggy and loose: wine-coloured harem pants and a billowing white linen blouse. If she was trying to hide her body, it wasn't working. Her curves were apparent and sweetly placed. "Who's your friend?" she asked Barry.

I took out my wallet and showed her my identification. The warmth in her eyes was replaced by a flinty glare. I let Barry look at it too. Amy's mouth tightened as she looked at her husband. "You walk an investigator right into our kitchen?"

"I'm strictly private," I assured her. "I'm not connected to the police or the FDA or any law enforcement agency in the U.S."

"Then what do you want?"

"Information."

"What kind?"

"This venture of yours has had ramifications you may not know about. At least I hope you don't."

"Go on," Amy said.

"A pharmacist was murdered in Toronto last month. He had been supplying Canadian medications to people here in Buffalo."

Their voices chimed in together: "What! Who?"

"Kenneth Page."

Neither showed any sign they knew the name.

"Now another has been targeted," I said. "A man named Jay Silver."

"Oh my God," Amy said.

She knew him. The possibility of his murder was clearly a personal horror, not abstract. Barry motioned her not to say anything but she cut him off with a downward slash of her hand.

"And it's not just him," I said. "His entire family will be killed. His wife and five-year-old son too. Jay, Laura and Lucas, all of them." *Listen to their names*, I thought. *Know them.*

"But all he's done is help people like us get prescriptions without going broke. Why would someone kill him?"

"Because he knows who murdered Kenneth Page and they can't trust him not to talk. And because the drugs in his store were worth millions. The truck that just left here—that entire load—was from his store. They basically looted it. They weren't afraid to, Amy, because they don't expect Silver or his family to live long enough to do anything about it."

"He's bullshitting us, Ames. Next he's going to tell us he should take the product off our hands. Get the fuck out of my house, man. I don't want to tell you again."

"You're going to get yourselves killed."

"Only if we talk," Amy cut in.

"Whether you talk or not."

"Why?" she demanded.

"Because the killing has started. Not just Kenneth Page, not just Silver and his family, but also a guy I worked with, another investigator. He was killed Monday. A witness—a retired old man—was beaten half to death on Wednesday. Someone has to stop them and it seems to have fallen to me. So help me. Please. Tell me who you work for."

The two of them stayed silent, looking at each other. Then Barry walked over to the table and put a hand on his wife's shoulder. She covered it with her own. "I'm sorry, Mr. Geller," Amy said. "I like Jay Silver. I hope nothing bad happens to his family, I really do. But it would be best if you left now."

I looked at her when I said, "You'll stand by while a family is killed?"

"He'll kill us if we talk."

"Who will?" I asked. "Ricky Messina?"

The fear in her eyes was palpable. "You *do* know him . . ."

"Yes," I said. "But I am not on his side. I can help take him off your backs."

"You and what army?" Barry scoffed. He drew himself up to his full height and stepped between me and Amy. "That's enough," he said. "Get out now."

"Barry—"

"We have to look out for ourselves. Now for the last fucking time, get out!"

I heard footsteps coming down the hall. A dozen men and women crowded into the doorway, Marty at the front of the pack. I moved toward the back door so none of them could get behind me.

"Everything okay?" Marty asked.

"Fine," Barry said. "He was just leaving."

I didn't move. The room became eerily quiet. Not a word was spoken; there was just the hiss of a candle in a cylindrical glass holder on the window sill.

"I can't go," I said.

"You heard Barry," Marty said. "Out of here, now."

He put a hand on my left shoulder, squeezed it and said, "I'll bounce you down the steps if you're not out by the time I count three."

Counting three. What did he think this was, a schoolyard? I drove my fist up into his armpit. There's a cluster of nerves in there that doesn't much like getting hit. It numbs the arm completely. Marty's grip loosened and he sank to the floor, his face as pale as marble. Then came the sound of breaking glass behind us. Amy's head snapped around. The kitchen door had nine glass panes in three rows of three. The pane closest to the doorknob had been shattered and a gloved hand was reaching in through the broken pane and turning the deadbolt.

Amy's eyes grew as wide as those of a horse in a barn fire. She stood up so fast the heavy oak table went up onto two legs, sending vials of pills of all colours rolling to the floor.

"Oh God," she gasped. "It's Ricky. Barry, it's Ricky. Don't let him in. Don't let him touch me. You promised, Barry. You swore."

Barry started toward the door but it banged open before he was halfway there and Dante Ryan stepped into the kitchen. His right hand was inside his jacket. Barry stopped where he was. Amy's breathing still came fast and shallow, but the fear in her eyes began to ebb. A strange, threatening man had just broken into her kitchen, but it wasn't Ricky. I wondered what he had done to get so far under her skin.

"It's okay," I said to Ryan. "One guy just got excited."

"Asshole," Marty rasped, his forehead beaded with sweat.

"You'll be all right," I told him. Then I went to Amy and said quietly, "I told you I wasn't with Ricky. This man and I are very much against him, in fact. I think he killed all the people I mentioned and tried to kill me. So talk to me. Help us get Ricky out of your life."

"How?" she whispered. She was trying hard to find some kind of centred calm, but the faint billowing of her blouse showed how shaky she was. "By reporting him to the police? Even if he got life in prison, he'd kill me the day he got out. Slowly, with his knife. He told me. He showed me." Her hands went to her belly and stayed there as if they were the only thing preventing her insides from spilling out onto the floor.

"Who said anything about prison?"

She looked into my eyes for a long moment. She was searching now to find what could live inside me that could take Ricky down.

"You think you can kill him?" she asked.

It wasn't a question I could answer out loud. I could only hold her gaze and hope she would see in Ryan the tacit but unspoken fact that it would be his professional *and* personal pleasure to clip Ricky Messina.

"Then do it," she said. "When he's dead I'll tell you every last thing. Until then I have nothing to say."

Ryan and I didn't want to be seen leaving the house together, so he stayed in a dark corner behind the garage. I told him I'd wait for him at the car.

I would have too if it weren't for the woman leaning against the passenger door of the Dadmobile, arms folded tightly across her chest. About forty in a light mauve suit, with

blue eyes and shoulder-length red hair that had been straightened. It looked as dry and stiff as an old paintbrush.

"Can I help you?" I asked.

She said, "That depends."

"On what?"

"How badly you want to stay out of jail."

CHAPTER 46

H er name was Christine Staples and she had the credentials to prove it, professionally presented in a genuine leather case. "I'm with the Food and Drug Administration's Office of Criminal Investigation. We're the investigative arm of the agency. The FBI of the FDA, if you will."

"A woman of letters," I said. She suppressed any sign of finding it funny. No Katherine Hollinger, this one. All business, down to her square-toed loafers.

She asked for ID and I showed her my licence. If it provided any credibility, she didn't show that either.

"I've been watching that house," she said. "Only today I've been watching you watching the house. What's your interest?"

"I'm house hunting," I said.

"From Ontario?"

"Society is tilting too far left there," I said.

Some people appreciate a little humour to help break the ice before intense discussions or negotiations. And some, like Christine Staples, look at you like they're fitting you for a dunce cap. "Do you know where our office is, Mr. Geller?"

"I'm looking for residential space, not commercial."

"We share a building downtown with the Buffalo field office of the FBI. Should we continue our discussion there?"

"You have powers of arrest?"

"No, the police and border enforcement folks do that for us. But I can have someone here real quick."

I could have told her to go to hell. But that would likely have meant exposing Ryan to the local feds, something he wouldn't care for in the least. I was about to ask Staples if we could talk somewhere else—give Ryan a chance to lose himself—when she surprised me by suggesting it first.

"Here's my best offer," she said. "We go to a Starbucks a few blocks from here and you tell me what you saw inside that house, or we go to the Federal Building and I lose your paperwork."

"The first one sounded better."

"Which is not to say the second won't follow if you don't come up with a better story than house hunting."

"I'll try."

"Are you armed?" she asked.

"No."

"Mind?"

"No."

She ran a hand around my waist. I lifted my pant legs so she could see there was no throwaway tucked in down there. "All right," she said. "We'll take my car."

It was a brown Crown Victoria with no markings on it. Not that a brown Crown needed any to scream government car.

At Starbucks we both ordered tall dark roasts. No foam, no flavours, no bullshit, each trying to show the other we were straight talkers.

"I'm going to start by giving you the benefit of the doubt," Staples said. "I'm going to concede that you are probably—*probably*—not involved in a criminal way with whatever is going on in that house. I won't say it in front of a lawyer, but that's what I think."

"Thank you. That's a good start."

She took out a small spiral notebook. "You're here in an investigative capacity?"

"Yes."

"On whose behalf?"

"My employer. Beacon Security of Toronto."

"More specific, please. Who hired Beacon to look into what?"

"That's two questions in one."

"So answer the first one first. Who hired you?"

"That's confidential."

"Not in New York State, it's not, because you're not licensed to operate here. You want to get home any time today?"

I looked at Christine Staples with her pale suit and eyes and helmet hair. "Without divulging the client's name," I said, "I can tell you what's been happening on the Canadian end. Then you tell me how it connects to Buffalo."

"No promises on what I tell you," she said. "And if I need your client's name down the road, for an affidavit or whatever, you can bet I'll get it."

Yeah, maybe if she battered me with her hair. "Okay. Someone hired us to investigate a local nursing home where a family member had died. They thought the staff might have been negligent in handling her medication. Our investigation led in two directions. One was a company called the Vista Mar Care Group, which owns a chain of nursing homes in Ontario, including the one where the death occurred. The other was a group of independent pharmacists who own large drugstores in Ontario. Nothing has been proven in court, you understand, but it seems these pharmacists were shipping medications illegally to the States, with the help of Vista Mar, which I believe is a front for a local Mob crew."

"As in *the* Mob? You're joking."

"I wish."

"Why would organized crime be interested in nursing homes?"

"It kept people from getting suspicious about the quantities of drugs being ordered by the pharmacists. They would supply far more to the nursing homes than they actually needed, and there are more than a dozen homes in the chain. At least two thousand residents. They could fake hundreds of prescriptions and ship the meds down here. The medical director at Vista Mar, a guy named Bader, signed all the prescriptions."

"And because he was director of the chain," Staples said, "the number of prescriptions he wrote never rang a bell with anyone."

"Right. And most of the pharmacists had wholesale licences, so they didn't ring one either."

"Have you actually met this Dr. Bader?"

"Yes."

"At Meadowvale?"

"Yes."

"Okay," Staples said. "Back to Buffalo. What's going on inside the Aiken house?"

"Aiken?"

"The owners," she said. "Barry Aiken. Fifty-five years of age, inherited the house from his father, Dr. Norman Aiken, a little over two years ago. Married to Amy Farber, aged fifty-four. Is that who you met inside?"

"Whom."

"What?"

"Whom I met inside."

She glared at me. Her eyes were so pale they couldn't muster much threat, but give the girl marks for trying. "I bought you a coffee. I'm trying to be nice. It's late and I want to get home too. So don't play games with me." She didn't raise her voice a decibel when she said it, but her tone sharpened to a fine glittering edge.

"Yes, that is whom I met inside," I said. "Barry and Amy."

"Who else?"

"There were a few people there. A little cocktail party. I didn't get any names." None I was going to give her, anyway.

"A cocktail party."

"Maybe more of a Tupperware thing."

"Only they're walking out with illegal prescription drugs."

"How would I know what's legal here?"

"I'm warning you, Geller. The coffee at the Fed is a lot worse than this."

"Can I tell you something, Agent Staples?"

"That would be a refreshing change."

"It's hardly the crime of the century going on in there. If you've been watching the house, you've seen who's going in and out. Ordinary people, a lot of them old and sick, trying to get medication they can't otherwise afford."

"Drug prices are not the purview of my office," she said. "It's our responsibility to ensure that any drugs coming into this country are safe, authentic and legally obtained. It's not the end users we're after. I'm not looking to fill jail cells with senior citizens. But we can't allow it to continue either. Now what about this Vista Mar group. What evidence do you have it's a front?"

"No hard evidence but I think a forensic audit would bear me out."

"And *whom* would it lead back to?"

"An Ontario crew with historic connections to the Magaddinos here. And that, Agent Staples, is all I know. So unless you have some information that you would like to share with me, I'd like to get back to my car."

"Give me the name of this crew."

Making the Di Pietra name part of the official record could do neither me nor Ryan any good. "Why?" I asked. "You have no jurisdiction in Ontario."

"I want to find out who they're working with on this end. We have a good working relationship with the feds. I told you, we're in the same building."

"On the advice of my physician, I decline to answer the question."

"You're in no position to make jokes. Cooperate with me and you can get on your way. Keep holding out and you're going to spend a lot more time in Buffalo than you planned. I'll have you charged for operating without a licence and anything else I can find. Did you bring a toothbrush? Change of clothes?"

Man, this woman was hard. Not hard enough to have made me float Marco's name if he'd still been alive. But he couldn't touch me anymore. Maybe giving up his name could get me some needed leverage.

"All right," I said. "You have me over a barrel. But there's something I want in return."

"In addition to being able to leave a free man?"

"What's going to happen to the Aikens?"

"What's it to you?"

It was a good question and not one I could readily answer. "They just don't strike me as people who should be jailed for what they're doing."

"What makes them different from other drug dealers?"

"Come on, Staples. The only reason they got into this was the pharmaceutical industry's gouge-fest."

"I will not debate the issue of affordable health care with a Canadian. You just charge it all to the taxpayers and run up debt every year. That is not the American way."

"No, you run up your debt on cluster bombs. Look, the only reason the Aikens are still in this, from what I saw, is coercion. They're afraid they'll be killed if they quit."

"By whom?"

"They wouldn't say. Not to me, anyway."

"All right. *If* they cooperate, but I mean really cooperate, I'll do my best to see they do no jail time. And I'll take care of any threats against them."

"And you and I say our goodbyes?"

"With no regrets," she said with a smile. The first she had shown all that time.

"You know your organized crime figures in Ontario?" I asked.

"I pick up things around the building."

"The name Di Pietra ring a bell?"

She sipped her coffee. "A father and two sons, if I recall."

"Three sons," I said. "But the father is more or less out of the picture now. He's old and had a stroke. I'm pretty sure the brothers own Vista Mar."

"Their names?"

"Vito, Marco and Stefano. The CEO of Vista Mar is a man named Steven Stone. I believe he and Stefano Di Pietra are the same man. His brothers have been providing the muscle."

"Okay," she said. "Let's visit the Aikens. Hear what they have to say in their own words."

We drove back in silence, past listless flags waiting for a breeze to lift them. Then something that had been bothering me before, something Staples said about Bader, fluttered into my consciousness, tapped me on the shoulder and whispered in my ear.

"Did you actually meet Dr. Bader?"

"Yes."

"At Meadowvale?"

"Yes."

Meadowvale. I hadn't mentioned the name. How had Staples known it?

CHAPTER 47

C hristine Staples was about to ring Barry Aiken's doorbell when I said, "Wait."

She turned impatiently, tightly gripping a brown leather briefcase she had retrieved from the trunk of her Crown Victoria. "What now?"

"Have you ever spoken to Dr. Bader?" I asked.

"Your Dr. Bader? Of course not."

"You knew he worked at Meadowvale."

"You told me that."

"I said he worked for Vista Mar but I never mentioned Meadowvale. Have you been there?"

"Don't cross-examine me, mister. I can have your can in a detention centre in one minute."

"So you keep saying."

"You don't think I'd do it?"

"I'm not sure you want to."

"Push me far enough, I'll do it, even if the paperwork takes all night."

"Have you ever been to Meadowvale?"

"No."

"Then how did you know the name?"

A man out washing his car in the driveway across the

street looked over at the sound of my raised voice. Staples's eyes moved from me to him and back to me, their colour more violet than blue. "All right, Geller. But I tell you this in strict confidence and you better respect it."

"Fine."

"I may be more familiar with the case than I allowed. We've been working with our Canadian counterparts for months."

"Why play dumb then?"

"I wanted to see if you were being frank with me."

"And?"

"I'm satisfied you are. Now can we please get on with it?"

I rang the doorbell. Silence. Rang again. More silence. I put my ear to the door. From within the house I heard a faint sound of music. "Around back," I said.

Staples and I went down the driveway to the rear of the house. The broken windowpane on the back door had been covered with a freshly cut piece of plywood. Through the other panes I could see Amy on a kitchen chair. She wasn't moving. Classical music was playing: a string quartet, a minor key, the first violin threading a mournful melody line high over the other instruments. For some reason, it evoked an image of the three dead men I had seen this morning. Of what the heat would have done to them if they hadn't yet been found.

Staples rapped on a glass pane and Amy jumped in her chair. When she saw me there she glared balefully at me. Then she saw Staples beside me with her identification pressed against the glass. She sighed deeply and opened the back door.

"You again," she said. "And look, you brought company. You sold us out, you shit."

"Take it easy, Ms. Farber," Staples said. "Mr. Geller has actually been advocating rather forcefully on your behalf."

"What?"

"That's right. Even though he might be in deep trouble himself, he's been quite insistent that we find a way to deal with this without you going to jail."

"Oh." Amy seemed slightly embarrassed by this. "Well."

"Shall we?" Staples asked.

Amy stood aside and let us in.

"Are we alone?" Staples asked.

"Yes. I sent Barry to the movies. That's what he likes to do when he—when there's trouble."

"Then let's see if we can't sort this out."

"Do I need a lawyer?" Amy asked.

"Only if you want to be treated as a suspect rather than a cooperating witness. Like I told Mr. Geller, I'm not interested in sending you or your customers to jail. I want to know who's behind it and stop it at the source."

Amy Farber looked at me with no warmth in her eyes. There was too much fear to leave room for anything else.

"If I tell you . . ." she said to Staples.

"Yes? Come on. Tell me what?"

Amy stood looking down at the floor, her arms crossed, one hand reaching up to knead the muscles near the base of her neck.

"If you're afraid you'll get in trouble, please consider that you are already in trouble," Staples said. "Very deep trouble. And I am your only way out." She sat down at the table, from which all pill boxes and vials had been cleared. Amy sat down across from her. I sat next to Amy. Staples snapped open her briefcase and took out her notebook and pen. She closed the briefcase and said, "From the top. Please."

Amy started her story with her diagnosis of rheumatoid arthritis in her late thirties. "I've needed anti-inflammatories and other medication for years. Plus I'm going through the . . . um, the change now. And Barry, God bless him, he's a delicate soul and he needs drugs for anxiety, for sleeping, for his back, you name it. But the prices are so high for everything, even with insurance. So a few years back, we all started using Canadian pharmacies that advertised on the Internet."

"'We all'?"

"People from the New Fifty."

"The what?" I asked.

"It's an association for people fifty or older who like staying active."

"How did you go from that to this distribution racket?" Staples asked.

"It's hardly a racket," Amy huffed. "I was vice-president of our New Fifty chapter and I knew so many people in the same boat. We got together so we could order in bulk and get better prices. We even organized bus trips to Toronto where you could fill your prescriptions and see a show. 'Pills and Pops,' we called it."

"Just stick to the story," Staples said.

"Everything was fine until they changed the law in Canada and pharmacies couldn't sell to us anymore. Luckily for us, Mr. Silver said he could keep sending us medications, only on the sly. We took a vote and decided to keep going. I would take people's orders and email them to Mr. Silver, and a week or so later a van would bring them down."

"How did Kevin Masilek become involved?"

"You know about—"

"Oh, yes. Keep going, please."

"Mr. Silver called one day to say we had to get our orders from Kevin. No more direct deliveries or trips to his store. We didn't like it. It cost more and we missed dealing with Mr. Silver. He was so much nicer. But he said we shouldn't contact him anymore and that was that."

"And what happened to Kevin?"

"He moved, I guess."

"Just up and moved?"

"We don't know. We can't get in touch with him."

"I'll bet you can't." Staples tapped her pencil absently against the knuckles of her other hand. "So how did you come to take over?"

"We were . . . we were asked to."

"By whom?"

Blood was draining from Amy's face as if she'd been fatally gored somewhere below the neck. "He didn't say. He just . . . just offered our medications free and we jumped at the chance, that's all."

Staples didn't look like she was buying that—not at market price anyway. "Did Mr. Silver ever mention partners?"

"No."

"No one else in Toronto?"

"No."

"Did he ever mention a Steven Stone?"

"No."

"A Stefano Di Pietra?"

"No."

"Any Di Pietra?"

"No."

"What about the men who made the delivery today?"

"The driver is Frank. The big one never talks."

"They ever mention anyone else in Buffalo?"

"No."

Staples made some notations in her book. "Where's the rest?"

"What?"

"Only part of today's delivery came here," Staples said. "Where's the rest?"

"I don't know," Amy said. "We just took what was ours and they went on their way."

"You'll have to do better than that if you want to stay out of jail."

Amy glared at her. "I have no idea. They could have gone to Mars for all I know."

I said, "Maybe I can help."

Staples looked at me expectantly.

"There's a warehouse on the west side," I said. "We followed them there and saw them unload the rest of the goods."

"We?"

Shit. Dumb mistake. "I did. I followed them."

"Then why did you say—"

I had to get her back on track. "They're probably still there as we speak."

"You should have told me this before," Staples snapped. "You might have cost us a chance to catch them in the act."

"I needed to know you were being frank with me," I said, throwing her own words back at her.

"Where exactly is this warehouse?"

"Everything square with Ms. Aiken?"

"Yes, yes," she said.

"And me?"

"The address, please?"

I gave her the address. She wrote it down, then opened her briefcase and stowed away the yellow pad and pen.

"What happens now?" Amy asked. "Am I going to be charged?"

"No," Staples said. "I can personally guarantee it."

She reached into her briefcase, pulled out a pistol with a silencer threaded onto the barrel and shot Amy twice in the chest.

CHAPTER 48

"I wish you could see the look on your face," Staples said. "It's priceless."

Amy Farber lay dead on her kitchen floor, the front of her white blouse soaked in blood. Her eyes stared lifelessly at the ceiling.

Staples sat in her chair, aiming the pistol at my chest. "You were right about one thing," she said. "You were never going to get within a mile of the Federal Building. Not where anyone could place us together."

"You knew you were going to kill me."

"Once I saw how much you knew, yes. Or did you think I invited you out for the pleasure of your company?"

"It's been known to happen."

"Not this time."

"Are you really an FDA agent? Or is the real Christine Staples lying dead somewhere too?"

"I'm the real Christine Staples," she said.

"The one nobody knows."

"You got that right," she said, nowhere near prim now, her smile ugly, almost lascivious. "Let's face it. A girl can only go so far on what the FDA pays. Steven was able to take me a whole lot farther."

"So you'd look the other way when the shipments came through."

"Which is what you should have done. You should have stayed in Canada. You're in the U.S. of A. now and we do things different here."

The gun looked like a 9-millimetre. Now—finally, Ryan might have said—I wanted a gun in my hand, my own Beretta Cougar with the slide racked and safety off. But as Ryan had predicted, I was caught empty-handed.

The silencer on the end of her gun was about three feet from my chest. I wondered if I could grab the end of it and twist before she fired.

"You going to shoot me here?" I asked.

"Yes. Then I'll wait until Hubby gets home from the movies and shoot him too."

How had this hellish piece of work passed any kind of employment screening?

"When the police find me here, it'll all blow open. Too many people in Toronto know what I'm working on."

"But they won't find you here," she said. "Frank and Claudio will collect you and dump you elsewhere. Nothing will connect you to the Aikens or their house."

"Except my blood, my fingerprints and the thirty people who saw me here tonight."

For a moment she looked less sure of herself. I made my move, lunging across the table to grab the gun barrel. But she pushed her chair back and jumped out of reach. She stood well back of the table, her thin lips stretched in a sick-looking smile. "Nice try, Geller. Quick and decisive. I like that in a man."

She levelled the gun at me, gripping it in both hands. She looked like she was ready to fire so I kept talking.

"It's quite an act you put on," I said.

"You bought it," she said. "So does everyone at the FDA.

I'm the wallflower who jumps if someone says boo. That's why no one will ever connect me to this."

"Don't be so sure. The Toronto Homicide Squad knows about Stone and Bader. How do you know they won't talk?"

"I know Steven won't."

"And Bader?"

"Not a problem."

"You're going to kill him too."

"Me personally? No. Someone else will handle it."

"Ricky Messina?"

"Oh, you *are* industrious," she said.

I felt a surge of pure hatred for this woman, this animal, who could talk about killing people like we were bugs who had made it through her screen door.

"That's quite a look," Staples said. "So angry. So vindictive. I think I liked your dumb look better."

She levelled the gun and I saw the knuckle around the trigger start to pull. I flinched as a sudden roar in my ears made them ring—a noise that came from behind, far too loud for a silenced pistol. Staples's chest exploded in a cloud of red and she stumbled backward against a butcher-block counter. Another shot and her throat burst open. She made a coarse strangled sound and slumped down to the floor, leaving a thick bloody smear on the cabinets behind her.

I turned around and saw Dante Ryan at the kitchen door, his Glock 20 in hand.

His first rule of a fast exit had been: *make sure there's no one left alive to chase you.*

He'd held up his end. I just had to get my ass out the door without kicking Christine Staples's dead face.

CHAPTER 49

We made it to the Peace Bridge in under ten minutes, melting into the long line of cars inching toward the border. It was getting dark, and not just because the sun was finally starting to set on a long June day. Thunderclouds were building in the northwest, gunmetal blue, stacked high like rearing horses. The heat wave was nearing its end.

Neither Ryan nor I had said a word since leaving the house. My lips and throat felt dry. My eyes were burning, my left ear ringing. I couldn't get the image of Amy Farber out of my mind. Her body on the floor, one leg draped over her fallen chair, the warmth and life gone out of her.

We cleared Canadian Customs without incident. Ryan's gun was back in the trunk of his car, locked in its metal case, and I had nothing to declare. Absolutely nothing.

The first raindrops fell as we sped along the flat stretch of land between Fort Erie and Niagara Falls. Ryan switched on the wipers. I lowered my window a few inches and felt splatters on my face and arm and breathed in the smell of ozone. "Thank you," I said to Ryan. "And don't make me say what for."

"Don't worry. We're pretty even."

"How so? I still don't know who ordered the hit on Silver. You might still have to carry it out for all we know."

"You gave it everything," he said. "So for that I owe you. Anything you ever need you can ask me, for the rest of your life. Or the rest of mine, anyway."

"How long were you outside?" I asked.

"I never left. When I came around front and saw you talking to that fed—"

"How'd you know she was a fed?"

"You kidding? That car? That suit? That hair? I knew something was up but where was I going to go? After you left, I went back to the garage and kept watch. When you got back, I moved up to the kitchen door to listen in. And did what I had to do."

"The husband's at the movies," I said. "That's the only reason he didn't get it too. He got the jitters and had to go sit in the dark until he calmed down."

"Lucky him."

"Some lucky. He's going to come home and find his wife lying dead with another dead woman he's never seen."

"At least he's alive."

"Because he wasn't man enough to stand by his wife when his nerves got bad."

"Didn't like him much?"

I pictured the warm, earthy woman who had let her hair go gray, confident enough in herself not to do anything about it. "I liked her more."

Rain was slanting through the beams of our headlights. The image of one dead body lying on the floor led to another. "I wonder if Marco and the others have been found yet," I said.

"This kind of heat, it can't take too long."

"Then what?"

"I don't know. I'm too tired to know. Tomorrow I'll make some calls and see what I can find out. Maybe Uncle Looch will give me the lay of the land."

"It would help if we knew who was pulling the strings in Buffalo. Ricky Messina doesn't strike me as management."

Ryan eased a cigarette out of his pack and lit up. I reached for the pack. He covered it with his right hand. "Don't," he said. "You'll hate yourself in the morning."

"I'm going to anyway."

He moved his hand and I took out a cigarette. I hadn't smoked one since Israel. I put it between my lips and lit up and blew a stream of smoke out my window. Some people think the first cigarette you smoke after you've quit a long time is the best. They're wrong. The second one is the best. The first you just have to get through without passing out or throwing up.

The rain started to fall harder, fat drops bouncing off the pavement in front of us. Ryan moved the wiper speed to double time. I took another drag off the cigarette and felt light-headed as nicotine rushed through my blood, tagging familiar receptors that whispered, *Where have you been all this time?*

I threw the fucking thing out the window and slept the rest of the way.

When I woke the car was at a full stop. I jerked upright in my seat, forgetting for a moment where I was. I peered out through the rain-streaked window—we were on Carlaw, north of Lakeshore—and remembered everything that had happened.

Forgetting had been better.

It was after eleven by Ryan's dashboard clock. The rain was still coming down hard. We drove north on Carlaw, past old warehouses that had been converted into film offices and workshops that created distressed pine neo-antiques. I told Ryan which street to take over to Broadview and we came to it just south of the high-rise I called home. As we neared the front of my building, Ryan asked where he could park without being seen. I pointed to the visitors' lot on the south side of the building.

"I need to get my guns out of the trunk," he said. "Since I know yours is probably in a shoebox in the attic."

"I don't have an attic."

"Yeah, you do. Only your steps don't go up all the way."

As we were pulling into the lot, I yelled, "Don't stop!"

A dark green SUV was idling in a parking spot just past the entrance, exhaust snaking around its rear tires. The window of the passenger side was all the way down in the rain.

"Turn around! Go! Go!"

A muzzle flashed on the passenger side and our front windshield shattered, showering us with glass. Ryan didn't need any further encouragement. He hit the gas and spun the wheel hard with the heel of his hand. The car fishtailed on the wet pavement. He spun the wheel the other way and floored it once we were pointed more or less at the street. We got out to Broadview with the SUV close on our tail.

"Right," I said.

He turned right and sped up the street. A northbound streetcar was stopped at the next corner, its rear doors open to let passengers off. Streetcars have the right of way in Toronto—when their doors are open, cars are supposed to come to a full stop, like it was a school bus. Ryan just hit his horn and kept going. A man about to step down from the rear exit jumped back up and yelled at us. The driver rang his bell as an admonition. Then the SUV sped through too, drawing another peal of protest.

Ryan gunned it north. "My guns!" he spat. "They're all in the fucking trunk!"

We blew through the red light at the next intersection. So did our pursuers. I remembered the manoeuvre I had pulled the other day in a similar situation, faking a turn left onto Pottery Road and then juking right through the streets of East York. The SUV didn't even give me the chance to suggest it. It pulled out into the southbound lane and roared up beside us on our left. We couldn't match his acceleration. When the SUV was alongside us, the passenger leaned out: Ricky the Clip, his round face wet and shiny with rain. Ryan's window exploded and he screamed and clutched his left eye. Blood streamed through his fingers and over his knuckles as the car began to drift toward a line of cars parked on our right. "I can't fucking see!" he cried.

I grabbed the wheel with my left hand and steered us back into our lane.

We were coming up to the Pottery Road intersection. I snapped off my seatbelt and got my left foot over the centre console and hit the brakes. The SUV driver, still accelerating, couldn't react fast enough and we slipped in behind him just in time to make a hard left turn down Pottery Road. The other driver hit his brakes, his lights flashing bright red in the darkness, reflecting on the wet road like two smears of blood. His wheelbase was too long to make a U-turn; he had to make a three-point turn instead, which gave us a lead. We swerved through one S curve after another down Pottery Road. I was trying to keep control with my left leg draped over Ryan's right, my foot jumping from gas to brake, and my left hand spinning the wheel back and forth like a helmsman on a wild sea. The road grew narrower as thick foliage reached out from both sides. The Dadmobile banged off the guardrail on our right. I overcorrected and we veered into the left lane, narrowly missing a northbound cab. Headlights appeared in our rear-view. The SUV was gaining. Bayview wasn't going to work. Pottery Road ended there. If we caught a red light, we'd have to come to a dead stop. Ducks waiting to be blasted.

An idea came to me. A way to better the odds. We were coming to the bike path where I'd rollerbladed the other day. If we could make them chase us on foot, they'd lose some of their advantage. I knew the path well. Ricky was from Buffalo; no way he'd be familiar with it. And the driver—Vito himself or one of his thugs—was equally unlikely to know it like I did. I hit the brakes and spun the wheel hard, and the car slid sideways into the fenced-off lot where the path

began. I undid the catch on Ryan's seatbelt, opened his door
and shoved him out. I popped the release on the trunk and
scrambled out my side.

Ryan's eye was a mess, but not from a bullet. He'd be dead
if he had taken a direct hit. Because the SUV stood so much
higher than the Volvo, the bullet had deflected downwards
when it hit the window, rather than penetrating it in a straight
line. But there had to be glass in his eye, the way blood and
tears were running out of it together.

I was reaching into the trunk for Ryan's gun case when the
SUV shrieked to a stop behind us. Two shots from the passenger side rang off the open trunk. We ducked. I grabbed Ryan's
hand. "This way," I said, and we slipped gunless through the
gap in the fence and ran down the road. I heard another shot
behind us and a bullet smacked into the trunk of a poplar. We
kept running, hunched down as far as we could while still making speed. To our left was the Don River, to the right the Don
Valley Parkway. We passed the first lifesaving station. Another
shot, another tree trunk pocked.

"Down the bank," I said.

Along the river were elms, cedars and oaks, their foliage
thick enough to provide cover. We slid down the bank and huddled behind a thick stand of hollyhock. My white shirt offered
too tempting a target. I ripped it open and shrugged out of it
and smeared cold black mud on my torso, arms and face. I got
Ryan to cup his hands and rinse his eye with river water.

"Can you see?"

"A little in my right."

"Ssh." I could hear footsteps on the road now. The beam
of a flashlight swept from side to side.

"Come out, come out, wherever you are," Ricky sang.

We started creeping silently along the muddy bank.

"Hey, Ryan!" Ricky called. "Dante Ryan? You know who
this is?" He paused as if Ryan were really dumb enough to

answer. "Ricky Messina. Remember? Out of Buffalo? We were introduced at the Ierullo funeral. They call me Ricky the Clip."

Even in his pain, Ryan mouthed the word *they* and shook his head.

"I've always admired your work, Ryan. You were like a future hall-of-famer in the trade. But this thing . . . taking up with detectives . . . turning down a fat fucking payday. Going against our thing? What the fuck were you thinking?"

I wished he'd shut up and let the other man speak, but Ricky wasn't through. "You'd never catch me consorting with outsiders like this. Telling tales. Leaking family news. Man, you fucked up. You and this Jew you're with. You there too, Jew?" he cackled. "Yoo-hoo! Jew-Jew! You're through, Jew. You and Ryan both, you're fucking done!"

His rant helped cover our sound as we crept upstream. Just as he stopped to take a breath, Ryan's foot slipped on a wet rock. The splash seemed as loud as a right whale breaching. Two shots came at us almost simultaneously. Two muzzle flashes. Two pocking sounds in the trees. So they both had guns. Two men with guns and a flashlight versus two unarmed men, one of them half blind. Our only chance lay a hundred yards away. I reached for Ryan's hand and we started moving again.

"Come on out, guys," Ricky called. "Come meet the new generation." His voice was almost lost amid the rushing sounds of the river and traffic. "I heard you're good with a knife, Ryan, that true? Say the word, I'll put down my gun and we'll go mano-a-mano, blade against blade, what do you say? You like to dance, Ryan? Not answering? That's okay. You'll make a fine trophy. I already know what I'm going to cut off the Jew, but you—I have to think about what part I'm going to take as a souvenir."

The other man still hadn't said a word. Maybe too dumb to think of anything to say. Or maybe the smart one.

"A little farther," I whispered to Ryan.

"What's there?"

"A lifesaver," I said.

I peered through the foliage at the road. Saw nothing but dark green leaves and the black sky beyond. We kept going. Branches scratched my arms and face. Ryan's hand felt wet and clammy in mine.

"There!" I hissed. A flash of orange in the trees. The lifesaving station with the long metal pole. Time to put the equipment to good use.

"Wait here," I told Ryan.

"For what?"

"You want Ricky?."

I crawled up the bank as quietly as I could. Judging by their flashlight beam, they were maybe twenty yards down the road. I picked up a rock and threw it as far as I could upstream. It hit some brush and landed in the water with a loud splash, drawing more gunfire.

"Up there," Ricky urged.

As they started up the road, I crept up to the lifesaving station and silently eased the pole off its hook. I waited in the shadows, hoping my pounding heart wasn't making as much noise outside my chest as it was inside. The men drew closer. The flashlight beam grew brighter. I could hear their shoes scraping the surface of the road. One man murmured something I couldn't hear.

"We'll get them," I heard Ricky say.

I kept the pole steady, careful not to snag any branches overhead. I breathed in and out, calming my body. The footsteps grew louder. The moon was hidden by clouds but tungsten lights on tall black stands lined the Parkway. I saw their cold light glint on gunmetal. Then I saw a hand holding the gun, then the arm.

Now!

As Ricky came into view I slipped the ring of the lifesaving pole over his head and yanked it as hard as I could. He gave a strangled cry and tumbled down the riverbank to where Ryan was waiting.

The other man yelled, "Ricky!"

The Clip's gun landed on the road a few feet in front of me. I was reaching for it when the other gun roared and a bullet smacked the pavement inches from my hand. I dove down the bank, rolling through brush. My right wrist hit a rock as I landed and went numb. I could hear Ryan and Ricky struggling in the water. There was the sound of a fist smacking something and one of them cried out. Which one?

A cedar had toppled over at the edge of the riverbank, its exposed root system creating a wall of dirt I could hide behind. I huddled there, wondering if I could make it across the river without getting shot in the back. A line of large stones made a natural walkway to the far side, and the water level was low at this time of year. The rocks looked either dry or just barely submerged. Up the opposite bank were railway tracks that led back to a crossing at Pottery Road, not far from Ryan's car and his case full of guns.

No. No way. I'd be in the open too long. If the man on the road was any kind of shot, he'd drop me before I made it halfway. I crouched beneath some brush and waited for him to make a move, listening to the splashing sounds where Ryan and the Clip were struggling. The numbness in my wrist started to give way to pain. I wondered if it was broken.

"Ricky!" the other man called. "Ricky, answer me."

I peered up through the leaves. I could see his arm and chest, his gun pointed at the water where Ryan and the Clip were entwined. No way he'd shoot; he'd be as likely to hit one as the other. As he watched them, I smeared more mud on my face and arms and started up the bank. My bad wrist made crawling awkward. I felt a gnarled root tear the skin of my belly as I dragged myself over it.

I reached the top and peered over the edge. Across the road metal glinted in the cold light. Something I could use as a weapon? No. A shopping cart miles from nowhere.

In the water behind me someone grunted loudly. There was a thrashing sound like a gator taking down its prey.

As I neared the top of the embankment, I could see the second gunman bracing himself against the trunk of an oak twice as thick as he was, pushing branches aside to get a better view of the water. I closed my left hand around a stone the size of a tennis ball and eased myself up onto the road. I stood looking at the gunman's profile. Like Roni Galil had said to me once in firearms training: you could be our King David, our *Melech David*, going up against Goliath with a slingshot. I wished I could get closer but the more I moved, the more noise I might make. I breathed in slowly, trying to blend in with the background and stay out of his peripheral vision. Just envision a catcher's mitt where his head is, I told myself, and whip it sidearm. An accurate shot would knock him out or kill him. And if it didn't kill him, I was fortunate to have on hand someone with the necessary skills, experience and tools to finish the job.

As I cocked my wrist to throw the stone, something rustled behind me in the bushes along the riverbank. The gunman turned to see it and swung his pistol my way, holding it in both hands, firing twice. I hit the road, scraping my hands and elbows. Eyes flashed in the darkness behind me as a red fox dashed across the road to the Parkway embankment and disappeared near the base of a willow.

The gunman looked at me, half-naked, smeared with mud, lying on the road. "Don't move," he said. "I'll shoot you, I swear."

I stayed where I was. I could see all of him now and he certainly wasn't Vito Di Pietra. He was all of five-five, slightly built and well dressed. Fine features. Delicate hands. It was the earnest young man I had seen at Meadowvale arguing with

Alice Stockwell. His eyes were wide and the hand holding the gun on me didn't look steady.

"So you're Geller," he said.

"And you're Stefano Di Pietra," I said. "Also known as Steven Stone."

"Make one move and I'll kill you."

"I believe you."

The thrashing in the river had stopped; there was just the sound of shallow water moving over rocks. The sound of traffic. The sound of Stefano's breathing and mine.

"Ricky!" he called. "Are you okay?"

The silence was comforting to a point. If the Clip was dead, Ryan might be able to take Stefano down before he shot me. But even if Ryan were still alive, he only had one good eye. In the land of the blind that might make him hot shit, but here and now I couldn't count on him. That left just three possible outcomes: rescue my own damn ass; pray to God to drop an anvil on Stefano's head; or take it like a man and hope that Katherine Hollinger would avenge me like a demented angel.

"Ricky?" he brayed. No answer. "Ricky!" Still nothing. "God help you if he's hurt," Stefano said.

I had to keep him looking at me, not down at the river where Ryan might be moving. If he was moving. I stood up. Stefano pointed the gun at me. I held my ground and kept my hands where he could see them. I said, "It's been you all along, hasn't it? The little brother. The one who wasn't supposed to be a player."

"Only because they never let me."

"Your brothers?"

"My father, too. Morons, all of them. They'd look at a truck full of medication and think, 'Hijack it.' I looked at the same truck and envisioned a fleet crossing the border."

"Your father should have put you in charge."

"Damn right. He named me for Don Magaddino, you know, because I was born the year he died. But I was small and sick a lot and mysteriously prone to being beaten up by my brothers. So my father made me the family bookkeeper, adding up numbers while my brothers ran the crews and made all the money. Got all the women. Played with the toys."

"You hooked up with Jay Silver when you did your MBA?"

"Taking that course was the smartest thing I ever did. I started to really see how things could work if they were run by a businessman instead of a thug. I truly understood how huge the market could be for good, clean Canadian pills."

"But when the law changed, you needed your brothers to keep the business going."

"My brothers? What do they have to do with this?"

"Isn't Vista Mar owned by all of you?"

"No. The Vista Mar Care Group is owned and operated by me."

"But what about Buffalo?"

"What about it?"

"Who was running the operation on that side?"

"You still don't get it, do you? When I say I run this show, I mean I conceived, coordinated and carried out the entire production."

Executed would have been a good word too. I was glad he didn't use it.

"My brothers never knew about it. Their confreres in Buffalo never knew about it."

"Then how did Ricky—"

"Ricky was with me, you idiot! Me. Not Marco, not Vito, not anyone in Buffalo."

"You could handle all the distribution with just one guy?"

"We didn't need a big infrastructure," Stefano said. "That was the beauty of it. It was already in place. This New Fifty club has chapters all over the Northeast. Full of people who'd go broke if they had to pay full fare for their meds."

Only then did I solve the mystery Dante Ryan had engaged me to investigate. Stefano had put the hit on the Silvers. Killing Page had not had the desired effect. It only pushed Jay Silver into committing the same rash act: telling Stefano he wanted out. Maybe Silver was counting on their school ties to shield him from harm. He had probably never seen Stefano as I saw him now; coldly murderous and without affect.

Now I just had to live long enough to tell Ryan the news.

"Why did you hire out Jay's killing?" I asked him. "Why pay fifty grand when Ricky could have done it free?"

"I wanted Silver and his family dead. I wanted the other pharmacists to know what would happen if they threatened me. And I wanted Dante Ryan kept busy while we took care of Marco. I was always afraid of Dante Ryan," he said. "He never hit me or did anything bad to me—he never even threatened me—but there was something about him. The way he looked at me."

"He looks at everyone that way."

Stefano's eyes darted toward the river and back at me. The silence was unnerving, but not to me. The longer it stayed quiet, the more sure I felt that Ryan had prevailed over Ricky. But where was he? Could he even see what was going on?

"Ricky killed Marco and his men?"

"I helped," Stefano smiled. "Ricky shot Tommy and Phil when we came in, but we both shot Marco. Ricky shot him in the chest and I shot him in the head."

"While he was asleep."

"Asleep or drunk, it was hard to tell."

"Good thing you were there to help,"

"Shut up! Every shitty thing he ever did to me—every time he beat me up or put me down or embarrassed me in front of friends because I was different—he's lucky all I did was shoot him in his sleep."

I heard a faint rumbling sound behind me and a light behind me cast my shadow along the road. Stefano looked over my shoulder and I turned too. A westbound train was coming around the bend, following the curve of the river. I looked back at Stefano and in the light cast by the train I saw a dark figure move up the riverbank behind him.

"Is Vito dead too?" I asked.

He nodded. "We took care of him just before we came to see you. Made it look like a robbery at a club he owns. Dad's going to be awfully upset when he hears about it, the old vegetable. I might have to water him extra to help him get over the shock."

I stood shivering in the rain, looking at this cold little bastard in his trim suit and polished shoes. The sound of the train grew louder. Then behind Stefano I saw Dante Ryan steal across the road, near the embankment that led up to the Parkway. What was he doing? Bailing on me?

The train blew a long loud whistle as it approached the level crossing. I heard bells ringing: the barrier lowering across Pottery Road. Ryan was behind the abandoned shopping cart, pushing it out of the weeds onto the road.

"Was Christine Staples in on it from the beginning?"

"Not quite," Stefano said. "She actually did her job at first, tried to stop us from bringing goods across. But she turned out to be a most impressive woman. She saw things the way I saw them. She understood what the future could hold."

Ryan was closing the gap between him and Stefano as the train drew closer, the sound of it getting louder, the light on Stefano's face growing brighter. When Ryan was ten or twelve feet behind Stefano, he broke into a run. Whatever noise the cart wheels made was drowned out by the sounds of the approaching train, the river and the Parkway. Stefano never heard it coming. The cart slammed into his back at full speed. The gun flew out of his hand. As his slight body lurched forward toward me, I stepped forward and kicked him hard in the chest. He staggered backward. I kicked him again and he sailed off the road and landed on his back in the river with a splash and a groan.

Ryan leaned on the cart. I asked if he was okay and he nodded.

"And the Clip?"

"Dead. Drowned. Busted his head with a rock and held him under."

"Saving my life is becoming a habit with you," I said. "Don't feel any need to kick it."

"We're not done," Ryan said. "We can't leave this one alive."

I swallowed hard. Killing someone in a fight was one thing. Doing it while he lay helpless was another.

Ryan picked up Stefano's gun.

"Just make it quick," I said.

"I'm not going to shoot him," Ryan said.

"No?"

"No," he said, extending the gun-butt to me. "You are."

CHAPTER 50

For the second time that day, I found myself questioning Ryan's sanity. The words *fucking* and *crazy* featured prominently in my remarks.

"I can't shoot an unarmed man," I hissed.

"But I can?"

"It's what you do."

"Nice, Geller. Real nice."

"I didn't mean it that way."

"The fuck you didn't."

"Come on."

"I should have let Staples shoot you. Or Stefano. Or Marco. How many times do I have to save your ass before you wake the fuck up?"

"But why?" I asked. "Why do I have to?"

"Because sooner or later, I'm going to have to face the old man, Vinnie Nickels. I'm going to have to look him in the eye and tell him I didn't do his boys, and it'd be easier if it was true. But the real reason is if I do it, you'll have witnessed three killings. Staples, Ricky and Stefano. You'll have that on me the rest of my life. I like you, Jonah, and I trust you, much as I do anyone. But how do I know what you'd say if the cops bring you in? How do I know you won't flip? You finish Stefano, at least we have something on each other."

"I would never say a word against you."

"You say it now and I believe you. Or at least I believe that you believe it. But it's different when the cops start sweating you, laying charges on you."

"So if I do it, I'm a co-conspirator. If I don't, I'm a witness. Is that it?"

"Yes."

"And you don't leave witnesses."

"Don't go there, Jonah. Please."

I looked down toward the river. I thought I could make out the dark shape of Ricky Messina's body in the water, partially obscured by fallen cedar boughs. Stefano Di Pietra was lying on the stepping stones that led from one side to the other. He wasn't moving. Maybe he was already dead and talk of killing him could stop. Then I heard him call out faintly for help. There would be no easy way out.

I looked at Dante Ryan. His left eye was horribly swollen. Blood was drying on his cheek. He had to tilt up his chin to look at me.

"I'm making my break," he said. "I'm going home to my wife and my son. I'm going to clean myself up and hope I don't lose my eye. I'm going to play with my boy, lie down with my wife and sleep for a week. Or until Vinnie Nickels calls me."

I said nothing.

Ryan laid the gun on the ground. "You do whatever you want with Stefano. Kill him or don't. If his life means that much to you, let him live. As long as you understand we'll both be dead in twenty-four hours."

Ryan started walking down the road toward the gate.

I picked up the gun and made my way down the riverbank, hoping Stefano would expire on his own or slip into an irreversible coma.

He was lying spread-eagled in the river, water lapping at

his sides. There were large granite rocks under him, one with a sharp edge, as if it had cleaved off a larger boulder. The edge was right under Stefano's neck. The tungsten lights brought out the pink of the granite. The water around him had a pink tinge too.

"I can't move," he said. "I can't feel anything."

I waded into the river and sat down on a rock beside him. The water level was halfway up his face, covering his ears. His eyes were glassy, unfocused. His hands bobbed in the water, palms up. Blood seeped out of a large gash in the back of his head, mixing in the water. Another pollutant fouling the Don.

"You should know Staples is dead."

He moved his eyes to where I was. Strained to bring me into focus. "No . . ."

"Ryan killed her. She was about to shoot me and he shot first. Once in the chest, once in the throat."

He groaned softly.

"I want you to know exactly how many people died because of you."

"I can't . . . feel my . . ."

"Can you feel this?" I tapped his chest with the barrel of his gun.

"Please . . ."

"Please what? Kill you or get you out of here?"

"Out?"

"You killed Kenneth Page."

"Ricky did—"

"You ordered it done, yes?"

His eyes moved to the gun against his chest and then back to mine. "Yes."

"And François Paradis."

"Yes."

"And Amy Farber."

"Who?"

"Barry's wife. Staples killed her before she took a shot at me."

"Not Barry?"

"No."

"She was supposed to get Barry too."

I stood up with the gun in my hand and looked down at Stefano. His injuries mirrored his worst qualities: a cold man shivering in cold river water; a twisted man whose limbs were broken and askew; an unfeeling man whose extremities were numb.

In all my time in the Israeli army, I rarely saw my enemies' faces. Stones would come flying out of a crowd. Masked men would open fire. Rockets would rain down from behind walls and orchards. Now I was looking an enemy in the face. The man responsible for so many deaths. Who would have killed me had he had the chance. Who'd still have me killed if I let him live.

The Book of Jonah says even your most intractable enemies are worthy of salvation. But what happens when you need saving more than they do?

I pointed the gun at Stefano Di Pietra. It felt much heavier than its one and three-quarter pounds. He closed his eyes.

I had to do it. The justice system couldn't help me. Even if there was enough evidence to convict Stefano, he could order my death from behind bars in a minute. He could kill us all. He'd be getting three meals a day while my body broke down in the ground somewhere, and my mother and Cara and Carlo Ryan and the Silvers' extended family mourned their losses.

I held the gun trained at his chest for what seemed like hours. Then my arm got tired and I lowered the gun. I used Stefano's shirttail to wipe it clean of prints, then dropped it in the water beside Stefano.

"Thank you," he said.

"Don't thank me yet."

I reached down into the water. The cold felt good on my right wrist. I took hold of the rock that was supporting Stefano's neck. Pulled. Pulled harder. Pulled till I eased it out from under him. His neck and head sank down under the water. Bubbles streamed from his nose and mouth. The rest of his body was still. His eyes stayed open the whole time.

After a while the bubbles stopped. I waded back through the water and found my shirt where I had left it in the brush. I washed as much mud as I could from my hands and face, then put on my shirt and climbed up the riverbank and went to find Dante Ryan.

"On my count of three," I said. "One . . . two . . ."

On three Jenn Raudsepp and I lifted the desk a few inches off the ground and scuttled sideways toward the one empty wall. We looked like a pair of crabs, if crabs could move an old teacher's desk the size of a Nimitz-class carrier.

We set it down. "That's it," I panted. "That's the last one." I flexed my wrist, which still ached from time to time, even though the cast had been off for two weeks.

We were in our new office space on Broadview south of Queen Street, on the third floor of a four-floor loft building. We had an anteroom with space for a receptionist—if ever business grew enough to warrant one—and an inner sanctum with room for three desks and a slew of filing cabinets, all bought at an auction of surplus equipment held by the Toronto District School Board.

It was the last week of August: sunny but dry, pleasant temperatures and a light breeze keeping us cool. A far cry from the heat wave that had ruled the end of June.

We were partners in a new agency, Jenn and I. My money from the sale of the house on Bain Avenue had finally come through and it had been more than enough to rent the space, buy the equipment we needed—the desks, cabinets, computers, cameras—and subscribe to half a dozen top databases and online search services. I had also bought a new car from Joe Avila. A two-year-old Accord, a nice anonymous ride the colour of wet cement.

When Jenn offered to come with me, I was thrilled. When she told me she was willing to invest $20,000 her parents had given her against the eventual sale of their farm, I was all over her like a Venus flytrap.

I didn't make the move because Clint fired me. He didn't, though he'd had every right to. I never told him the full story behind my disappearance during the investigation into Franny's murder, and he was still willing to give me another chance. I was touched by that but resigned all the same. I had learned something about myself that summer: if I was going to make it as an investigator, I had to be free to follow my instincts wherever they took me. I didn't think I could do that at Beacon. Most of all, I didn't want to have to lie to Clint anymore, or sneak around or steal time from one case to work another. I came to realize I valued him more as a friend and mentor than as a boss.

So a Jew and a lesbian open a detective agency . . . it sounded like the beginning of a bad joke. I hoped it wouldn't turn out that way.

Dante Ryan didn't lose his eye. The cornea was scratched but he was told it would heal with time and rest. He had to wear an eye patch for a while, which must have made him look more dangerous than ever. I don't know because I haven't seen him since the night Ricky and Stefano died. I keep saying they died, when they were killed, because I can't quite frame Stefano's death that way. Not yet.

I thought at first I'd hate Ryan. Forever. Then he called one night. He was back home living with Cara. We talked for a long time and I kept waiting for the hate to come. It just didn't. He told me he'd worked things out with Vinnie Nickels. Dante

Ryan was finally out of the game. I told him I was glad for him. He told me he was glad about my new agency. We wished each other well. We almost became good friends on our wild ride, but I doubt we'll see each other again.

Katherine Hollinger told me the killings of Kenneth Page and François Paradis had been attributed to the late Ricky Messina, whose gun matched slugs from their bodies. The killings of Ricky Messina, the Di Pietra brothers, Tommy "TV" Vetere and Phil "Philly Fits" Bernardi were chalked up to a Mob power struggle between "factions unknown." The irony was that the question of succession to Vinnie's throne became largely irrelevant, and not just because all the princes of his realm were dead. "Truth is," Hollinger said, "the Calabrian mob is on its way down. The other gangs smell blood and they're moving in on all fronts, and there isn't much Vinnie can do right now to stop them." She had even heard rumours that TFTOC—the Task Force on Traditional Organized Crime—might be disbanded, its resources folded into other intel squads that were tracking bikers, Asians, Russians, Jamaicans, Tamils and whatever other gangs were proliferating in and around Toronto.

I want to see Hollinger. Buy her a coffee and look into her eyes and see what's there now that the case is over. Maybe when things have died down a little more. When everything's farther behind us.

The killing of Amy Farber was attributed to Christine Staples, whose gun matched the slugs in Amy's chest. No arrests have been made to date in Staples's death. Given how dirty she had turned out to be, her passing was not widely mourned.

Ed Johnston, my neighbour, is still recovering from the beating he took. He gets headaches a lot. He needs dental work. He can't use his left hand much, because all the fingers on it were stomped. He's living with his daughter in Mississauga for now. I hope he comes back to our building. I owe him a lot but there's nothing I can do for him where he is. His daughter would probably call the police if I strayed over her suburban border.

I tried to avoid seeing my mother until my wrist healed and the scratches on my hands, face and neck where I had been whipped by branches had disappeared. No such luck. The week after the case ended, she invited me again for Shabbas dinner (inviting being a euphemism for insisting). Daniel was there with Marcy and their boys, Jason and Jeffrey. I told Mom I broke my wrist rollerblading and got the scratches when I'd tumbled off the path into the bushes. My standing with my nephews fell somewhat—I think the word *spaz* escaped their young lips—but Mom seemed to buy it.

My dreams have for the most part been disturbing, grotty little dramas that wake me in the early hours, my stomach as twisted as my sheets. But the other night I had one where Roni Galil and I were trapped in the usual alley as a torrential wave rushed through. I kept my feet but Roni was knocked over onto his back. I offered him my hand to pull him back up onto his feet, but he waved me off and stayed under water. He lit a joint and took a deep, long hit, but when he finally blew it out, no air bubbles rose past the surface: just a thin wisp of smoke. He didn't even offer to share it with me, the bugger, but I laughed it off. He took another toke, an even longer one this time, and gave me a big wink and a smile while he held his breath.

He looked very much at peace.

ACKNOWLEDGEMENTS

Valuable information and insight were provided by Manny Acacio and Trina Parcey, King Reed & Associates Investigation Services; Inspector Brian Raybold, Toronto Police Service, Homicide Squad; Superintendent Randall Monroe, TPS 51 Division; Greg Ujiye, Ontario College of Pharmacists; and Donna Monaco, Buffalo Field Office, U.S. Food and Drug Administration. Norm Bacal and Todd Robinson helped with fight techniques. Mark Pomerantz provided insight into pharmaceutical sales and production. Victor Malarek's reporting on the tobacco industry was inspiring, as was Adrian Humphreys's writing on organized crime in Ontario. Any errors or inventions regarding these matters are mine.

Special thanks to my agent, Helen Heller, who constantly challenged me to aim higher; to Anne Collins of Random House Canada, whose thoughtful edit helped bring the story home; to Marion Garner at Random House and freelance editors Barbara Czarnecki and Liba Berry; and to Jeffrey Harper for his incisive read of the first draft and more than a few thereafter.

Thanks to the Buffalo Pivers (Dr. M. Steven Piver, Susan Piver, Dr. Bobbie Piver Dukarm and Dr. Rob Dukarm) and Dr. Allan and Linda Gold of Toronto, for advice on geography, surgery and much more.

To Linwood Barclay, Peter Bernstein, Shawn Brant, Yael Brotman, Bev Caswell, Betty Clarke, Robin Cleland, Jeff Cohen, Chris Cook, Stephen Cooper, Jim Cuddy, Jack David, Fred Finkelberg, Didier Fiszel, Murray Kane, Harvey Kaplovitch, Mel Korn, Lee Kraemer, Colin MacAdam, Dennis Murphy, Jeff Oberman, Rena Polley, Peter Robinson, Allan Romano, Neil Seidman, Antanas Sileikas, Beth Sulman, David Talbot and Karl Thomson, all of whom provided support in one way or another. Special thanks to René Balcer for kind words then and now.

And finally, thanks to my mother and father, who remained eerily calm when I quit a government job to finish this book. And to Aaron and Jesse for understanding that Daddy had to write at weird hours and was sometimes too tired to play Twister. And most of all to Harriet.

Without her love, encouragement and support, this novel would still be in a drawer somewhere. Her instincts about the story and Jonah's character—and hearing her laugh in all the right places—helped keep the first draft flowing.